Staff of Life

Corrupted Coil Series: Book 2

Theo Mann

The Invisible Publishing Company

Corrupted Coil Series

Contents

Chapter 1

An explosion went off right next to Yann Dilnao's head. A spray of rock shards blasted him in the face and ear on that side.

He ducked under his arm, but he couldn't protect himself from flying debris and granite slabs hurtling at him from all directions.

A blast of seismic force ruptured to the soil to his left. It ejected tons of rock and dry mud into the air from somewhere underground.

A towering spire of jagged stone stabbed through the hole and kept rising into the air. Its size fractured more of the mudflats underfoot.

Yann dodged to the right to get away from the earthquake, but more tremors jolted the earth under him. He stumbled and almost fell.

His father lunged for him, seized Yann by his uniform jacket, and yanked him closer to the Black Watch. All the Watchmen ran for their lives across the mudflats as the landscape erupted in mayhem all around them.

The mountains ringing this valley erupted out of position, shot to massive heights, and then collapsed on themselves.

The rock didn't bounce and roll when it landed on the ground—not the way it should have. Blocks and boulders hit the ground once and levitated into the air. Gravity didn't work the same way.

The blocks smashed together, reformed into shapes of creatures, monsters, and animals, and shattered apart.

Other piles of rubble on the ground jointed together to form new mountains or gouged deep into the mudflats to carve fissures, riverbeds, and valleys that weren't there before.

The Watchmen swerved right and left trying to avoid these obstacles. Niyazi Trahan ran in front and sprang over a river getting wider by the second, but he got trapped on the other side when it spread too wide for the rest of the Watch to cross.

Yvan Dilnao, the Commander of the Watch, rushed down the bank and thrust out his hand. "Niyazi!" Yvan yelled, but it was too late.

A massive torrent of water rushed down the riverbed, but the flood didn't overflow the bank. It scored a deeper channel that plummeted into a gorge.

Niyazi's side of the river sprouted into a high plateau with him still on top. The Watchmen couldn't get him back.

At the same time, the mountains behind the Watch's position stretched too high, flattened themselves into a cliff wall, and the wall curved over on itself to loom over the mudflats.

The wall kept curling until it crashed down in a breaking wave of granite. All the slabs and boulders washed over the mudflats rumbling closer to the party.

The Barbarian Servant Anríq sprang between the wave and the Watchmen, unhooked his club, and planted himself there.

Yann shot out his arm to call his friend back. "Anríq—no!" Anríq wouldn't be able to stop that tide without his magic.

Yvan grabbed his son by the jacket again. "This way!" Yvan took off running down the river dragging Yann with him.

The wave of stone coming closer didn't cross the flats quickly enough. Anríq waited for the Watchmen to go first before he spun away and followed them.

Yvan ran down the river. In a few seconds, the massive expanse of water changed again. Grass sprouted out of it and then giant trees thrust their crowns through the surface.

"Now!" Yvan yelled and dodged into the trees.

Yann didn't know what to expect, but the river changed into a forest with a solid floor and leaf litter covering the ground.

Yvan hurdled fallen tree trunks, veered around rock outcroppings that sprang up in his path, and burst out the other side of the forest.

The landscape over here looked like the plateau where Niyazi got trapped. He ran along the top, and as soon as the Watchmen came out of the forest, a shriek of pelting wind hit the plateau from farther down the valley where the river had been flowing.

The wind scoured the plateau and started to erode it. Niyazi bent his head against the wind and ran straight into the hurricane. He ran down the slope just in time to meet up with the other Watchmen.

"This way!" Yvan called and kept running in that direction—away from where the river had been.

Yann didn't see anything over there that his father might be running toward, but that hardly mattered. Everywhere in this landscape would be equally unsafe.

The plateau shrank under the endless driving wind. The plateau retreated up the valley and left the flats clear.

The landscape kept rupturing all around the fleeing party. Parts of the terrain grew into new mountains while others imploded and vanished into bottomless pits.

Yann got lost in the mayhem. His father kept yelling at everyone to keep going.

Eliska wound up on the outside of the group. Another blast of exploding mud went off right next to her. She screamed when a million projectiles hit her in the face.

Yann grabbed her, pivoted her inward to the center of the Watchmen's cluster, and he rotated to the outside to keep her between himself and the other Watchmen.

They all closed the circle with her at the center....and then, somehow or other, Marine wound up in there, too.

Yann didn't see her running with the others, but she migrated farther forward as the landscape disintegrated. Neils Surette, Vidal Rom, and Omer Veco parted and slowed down. Then they closed their formation behind Marine to bring her into the center with Eliska.

Debris and falling missiles kept pelting down from the sky....and then all those bits of cracked mud and gravel turned to stinging rain.

It fell harder than it should have. Every droplet stabbed Yann's skin and burned his scalp. He yelled out in pain, but the rain only got stronger.

Eliska screamed again and so did Marine. Yann yanked his jacket off and threw it over his head for protection. Instinct made him move inward to cover Eliska with the jacket, too.

"Take off your cloak!" he yelled. "Spread it over you and Marine!"

He used his jacket to protect her while she tore off her cloak. All the Watchmen copied him, ripped their off jackets, and connected their corners together to make a tent over their heads.

"Keep moving!" Ivan roared. "This way."

He veered farther in the direction he had been going. Yann almost stopped running when he saw his father heading for mountains in the distance.

They kept detonating in more transformations. Rock jetted out of the skyline and morphed into towering Darklings that collapsed in on itself just as fast. Yann didn't want to go over there.

Long training kept the other Watchmen moving forward no matter what. Yvan didn't slow down or even check over his shoulder to make sure his men followed him.

That left them no choice but to keep up with him. He took off his jacket to protect him from the rain, but he didn't drop back to join the rest of the group.

Anríq ran behind everyone else. He took off his vest to cover his head, but it wasn't big enough to protect the rest of him.

He didn't try to join the rest of the group, either. He could have overtaken them in seconds, but he always stayed the same distance behind the others.

The mountains got closer—or maybe their constant growth made them look like they were getting closer. They crumbled at the center while the two outer ranges rose higher and higher without stopping.

Yvan just kept running straight into the heart of the worst mayhem. He headed for the gap between the two ranges, but that only brought him closer to the two sides exploding apart.

Avalanches of rock pounded down on the ground right in the group's path. Yann considered calling out to his father to stop.

None of the other Watchmen said a word, but they all slowed when they saw the danger. Giant boulders smashed down in the middle of the gap. No way could anyone survive going in there.

Yvan dove straight into it. "FATHER!!" Yann yelled out and started to draw back.

That was the moment when he saw a flash of something green on the other side. A beautiful landscape of grass, trees, and even tall buildings crowded with people spread beyond the gap.

Yvan vanished into the avalanche. The other Watchmen saw the other landscape at the same time, charged forward, ran into the mayhem to follow him.

They tightened their cluster. Their arms holding their jackets together formed a lattice over the two girls. Anríq ran closer behind and closed the space between him and the others.

Huge boulders smashed down on either side, in front of, and behind the party. By some miracle, those boulders never hit anyone in the group.

Yann didn't dare to check where he was. His father was on the other side of this mess.

Yann didn't ask himself how Yvan knew about this other landscape. That didn't matter. The party had to get through to safety.

Without warning, they ran under another torrent of falling granite and the whole mass of stone smashed into the gap behind the Watch.

Everyone stopped dead in their tracks as the rock fall closed the gap behind them. All the men of the Watch turned their eyes to the landscape in front of them.

Yvan stood there staring at everything. He didn't venture deeper into this new Island.

Grass, fields, trees, and tall buildings crowded with people did not spread out before him. Whatever he saw or Yvan saw from the other side of those mountains—it wasn't here anymore. Maybe it never had been here to begin with. Maybe it was all an illusion.

The group emerged in another massive expanse with not a single sign of human habitation anywhere.

Yann couldn't even see what kind of landscape it was. His feet crunched on a carpet of bones covering the ground.

A cold iron-grey ceiling of cloud cast the Island in shadow. A foul wind blew over everything. The bones shattered and resettled themselves every time one of the Watchmen took a step.

The bones stretched to the farthest horizon—which was as flat and barren as everything else in this place.

Chapter 2

E liska shivered and rubbed her arms together.

The air in this Island didn't chill her. The chill came from the inside. She couldn't stop jumping and glancing behind her every time one of the Watchmen stepped on the bones underfoot.

Every step they took in this wasteland startled her out of her skin. None of them could take a step without a bone snapping, crunching, or shifting in place.

Yvan led the way. Eliska no longer had a staff, but she wouldn't have been able to use it anyway. Her magic was all gone.

She cringed when she thought about how helpless she was. She didn't even have the magic to get out of this Island if she really needed to.

Marine jumped and screamed more than usual, too, which unsettled Eliska even more if that was possible.

The Watchmen didn't have the same problem. They didn't notice anything—apart from all these bones.

The lack of magic didn't affect them at all. They didn't miss what they never had.

Eliska hugged her arms more tightly around her. Yann took a step closer on that side. He'd been hovering over her ever since it happened.

She would have pushed him away before, but she couldn't do that now. Relief overwhelmed her when the Watchmen moved her to the inside of their circle to protect her.

How did they know? How did they automatically understand that she was helpless without her magic?

The memory of all the rude things she'd said to them made her sick to her stomach now. She would never be able to take those words back.

Yann and the other Watchmen put their jackets back on. That rain didn't seem to damage the fabric. The group had nothing else to do but walk and keep on walking.

The sky never lightened or darkened. No one could see the sun through the dense cloud cover. This place didn't seem to have any day or night.

Yvan didn't explain to anyone where he was going or why he was going there. He just kept on walking. He didn't check if everyone followed him.

He stepped on bones for more than two hours before he came to a river. The bones lay in mounds right up to the water's edge. The cloud and the desolate landscape made the water in the riverbed look black.

Rien Dugas stumbled forward gasping in relief, but Yvan stopped him. "It could be another Dark river." He turned to Eliska. "Can you tell if it's a Dark river or regular water?"

She turned her head away so she wouldn't have to look at him.

She shook her head. Everything hurt right now. "I can't tell....but there are Dark forces here. You saw the way the rock falls turned into Darklings. They're here, too."

Yvan glanced around, but before he could ask, Anríq stepped forward, went down on one knee at the water's edge, and scooped some of it into his mouth.

"It's safe to drink," he announced. "You should all drink some before we move on."

Yvan scowled at him. "You shouldn't have done that. It might have been dangerous."

"I wouldn't have done it if it was dangerous," Anríq replied.

Yvan clamped his mouth shut. He didn't stop glaring at Anríq while the Watchmen came forward and cupped the water into their mouths to drink it.

Yann touched Eliska's elbow. "Come on. You drink some, too."

Eliska didn't want to stop searching the countryside for.....what was she even looking for?

The horizon closed in on her even though it always stayed the same distance away. Her magic should have told her when something got close enough to threaten her. She didn't even have that anymore.

Yann wouldn't leave her alone until she went forward and drank some water, too. He kept watch over her every second, but she couldn't resent him for that.

Her skin crawled with some unnamed horror lurking just beneath the surface. She would fly apart into a million pieces any second now—and not from any Dark forces stalking her. She couldn't stand this.

Yvan drank last and then straightened up to narrow his eyes at the countryside down the river. God only knew what he saw down there. Eliska didn't care where the group went and no one else asked. The party was stuck here—probably forever.

Eliska really hoped none of these people asked her anything—like where they were or where they should go or what the hell they should do in this hellscape.

Yvan didn't turn around to ask her anything, which actually made her feel worse. She was useless to these people like this.

Everyone jumped when some of the bones resettled nearby. The Watch spun around only to see Yann rummaging in the mountains of bones lying everywhere.

He found a human skull, used his glaive to crack it in half, and scooped the skull into the river. He used the skull as a bowl to gather some water and took it over to Marine.

She retreated from him shrieking and snarling. "Leave her to die," Rien grumbled. "She's a fiend."

Everyone ignored him. Yann held out the skull bowl to her. "Do you want some water, Marine?"

She only screeched and bared her teeth. He finally left the skull bowl on the ground near her and went back to sit down next to Eliska.

Marine waited for him to leave and then scuttled to the bowl, picked it up, and guzzled the water.

Eliska turned her face away and gulped down the sting in her throat. She couldn't even take care of Marine. Someone else thought of that. Some friend Eliska turned out to be.

"I don't see any towns or anything," Yvan remarked. "We'll follow the river. At least we won't have to go looking for water. If anything is still alive in this place, it will come to the river to drink, so we'll be able to find it. Let's go."

The Watchmen stood up and formed a single-file line heading down the river. Eliska wound up near the back of the line with Yann and Vidal behind her.

The group had to clamber over thousands of bones to make any headway. A vast carpet of human, animal, and what looked like Darkling bones all jumbled up together underfoot.

Stepping on the uneven surface made everyone stumble, including Eliska. Yann came forward every time this happened. He held out his hands to her like he wanted to steady her and help her keep her balance, but he didn't usually have to.

His behavior both touched and infuriated her. He couldn't hide his caring nature, now that she really needed someone to care for and protect her. He didn't try to hide what he was doing and none of the other Watchmen treated his behavior as anything unusual.

The same actions enraged her. She hated herself for needing help and she hated him for being the one to give it. She shouldn't need help, especially from some imp Watchman.

He was the helpless one. He was the defenseless one. If he was that, she must be a complete waste of space.

Now she didn't even have the magic to vanish herself off the face of the earth. That's what she should have done to spare these Watchmen the burden of taking care of her.

She revolted even against the empty feeling in her hands. If she lost her staff in the Coil, she could have picked up any of these bones and used them instead. She could channel her magic through a twig, a piece of broken furniture, or even a rock.

Her skin crawled at the feeling that her magic was gone. She kept trying to look around and find it to make it come back.

She wouldn't be able to leave this Island, which meant she would never get her magic back. She would be an imp for the rest of her life. She couldn't imagine a worse fate.

Marine trailed the group at the end of the line. She kept her distance as usual.

The party traveled for two hours. The sky stayed the same color. It never lightened or darkened to show the time of day.

The river curved around a few corners. The group had to climb over mounds and down them to follow the river's contour.

The Watchmen stumbled along in a dazed trance. Eliska couldn't relax for anything. She would never be able to relax ever again.

The group topped another rise. Everyone stopped at the top when they heard bones rattling and the group saw movement ahead.

A cluster of ten waterbuck came down to the river to drink exactly the way Yvan predicted. No one moved or even breathed while the group watched in silence.

A large buck led a herd of three females, three tiny fawns, and two junior bucks. The two young bucks were fully grown but not as big as their stag leader.

Niyazi broke the silence by whispering, "I'll go. Stay here."

He raced away down the rise in the direction from which the Watch had come. He vanished behind another mound.

The waterbuck spotted the Watch and glanced up at the hilltop where everyone stood waiting in breathless silence.

The Watch must have been far enough away because the waterbuck didn't run. They kept a wary eye on the Watchmen, but the waterbuck continued to drink until they all got as much as they wanted.

The waterbuck raised their heads again, studied the people in the distance, and then left the river one by one.

The creatures started to pick their way over the bone piles heading away at a right angle to the riverbank.

They made it fifty feet before Niyazi sprang out from behind a different mound. He must have skirted the area, used the mounds as cover, and come out behind the herd.

The creatures startled, but not fast enough. He hurled his battle axe end over end through the air and struck down one of the junior bucks.

The others bolted into the landscape and left Niyazi there with his prize.

He waved up the hill to the rest of the Watch. Yvan started the long climb down the hill.

Niyazi wrenched his axe out of the fallen buck, hefted the creature onto his shoulder, and carried it back to the river to meet up with the Watch.

He squinted at the bone fields when he got back to Yvan. "Where do you want to do this?"

Yvan checked the sky. "It's impossible to tell when night will come and we've already been out here for hours. We might as well do it here." He kicked some of the bones away. "Some of you get to work gathering the larger rib bones. See if you can use them to construct some kind of shelter for us—and clear a flat place here by the water for Niyazi to work."

Yann passed Eliska to join his fellow Watchmen in following Yvan's order. Eliska hung back. She didn't want to get in the way and she had no idea how to help the Watchmen construct a shelter.

If this ever happened to her before, she would have just aimed her staff at the bones and magicked them into a shelter. She could have constructed an entire house in a few seconds.

She didn't even know where to begin to construct one without magic.

The situation got even worse when Niyazi dropped his buck on the ground next to the river, pulled out a knife, and started skinning and gutting the animal right there in front of her.

She didn't help construct the shelter and no one asked her to. She stood off to one side, completely useless.

That left her all the time in the world to watch Niyazi slice the hide away from the creature's legs and start skinning down the body.

He stripped off his uniform shirt and jacket and laid them aside to keep them clean while he gutted the animal. He cut open the belly and scooped out all the entrails onto the ground.

He got blood all over his chiseled arms and smudged it on his face when he wiped the sweat off his forehead.

Eliska tried to look away, but fascinated horror made her keep watching him. She never would have been able to do something like that.

She never would have been able to stick her bare arms all the way up inside a dead carcass, cut its esophagus and windpipe, and then gather the internal organs in her bare hands to pull them out.

She'd hunted for her survival almost every day of her life. She'd never gotten a speck of blood on her hands or her clothes.

The sight made her sick, but it also made her admire Niyazi in ways she never would have dreamed before.

He didn't shy away from any of it. He even got blood and muck in his hair.

He eventually had to move the buck onto the bone piles to keep it clean while he finished butchering it.

He noticed her watching and grinned at her, but he didn't say anything. He didn't joke around about how he could do this just as well with his hands and a knife as she could with her magic.

The process took a long time, but in the end, he wound up with exactly the same result.

He went down to the river and started washing his hands. In the end, he stripped off completely naked, dove in, and washed his whole body before he climbed out and put his clothes back on.

Eliska tried to look away from that, too, but she wound up watching him anyway. She couldn't get over the fascination of this whole process.

These Watchmen did know how to survive. They knew more about how to survive than she did.

Niyazi shook the water out of his hair while he pulled on his shirt. Now the party had something to eat tonight, thanks to him.

Chapter 3

Yvan walked over to Eliska. "Are you all right, young one?"

She jerked away so she wouldn't have to look at him or see him looking at her. "No!" she growled more harshly than she should have.

"Come over here and sit down." He raised his arm like he might want to put it around her, but he stopped himself. "We need to talk."

She didn't want to talk to him or go anywhere with him, but what choice did she have?

Her survival depended on these men. Their positions reversed in a matter of seconds. Now she was the one who wouldn't last a minute without these men protecting her.

He guided her to the river's edge and sat down on a stack of bones. He waved at the pile next to him. "Sit down."

She sat down and stared into the water for lack of anything else to look at. She sure as hell couldn't look at him.

Out of nowhere, he rested his hand on her shoulder and squeezed. "I know you aren't used to this," he murmured. "Just remember that you saved all of us many times before. We owe you our lives and that didn't change when you lost your magic."

"You wouldn't say that if you really knew how to survive in the Coil," she choked. "You can't afford to drag around a liability who will only jeopardize your men even more than they already are."

"You aren't jeopardizing us," Yvan murmured. "Something might happen where we would need you again. If Wesh is right about the Voyant coming after us—and if you're right about Dark forces inhabiting this landscape—then the Darklings will come after us here, too."

"And I won't be able to do anything!" Her voice spiked. "I'm as likely to get you all killed."

"No, young one," he breathed. "The Darklings would shatter this landscape and we would fall into the Layers the way we did before. Then we would need you as much as ever. This is all just a moment in time—a brief moment that will pass as quickly as it came."

She gulped down the lump in her throat. She hated him for trying to make her feel better—and at the same time, she wanted to bury herself in his care and protection.

Now she understood how Yann got to be the way he was. What would it be like—to be raised by someone like this?

He squeezed her shoulder again. She stiffened every time he did it. She always avoided touching anyone.

Now her heart and soul screamed for his touch—for any sign from him that he might care about her. She didn't want him to stop—and yet she just couldn't bring herself even to respond to it.

He took his hand down immediately. "You can do more than you think you can if you only try. Standing off to one side and letting the men do everything will only make you more afraid and helpless."

"But I don't know how to do anything—not without magic! Don't you see? I would never survive out here."

"Then it's time for you to start to learn. Try. That's what I'm telling you. If you start to try, you'll stop being afraid. It doesn't matter what you do. It doesn't even matter if you fail and make a mess of things, but you have to do something—not for us but for yourself. If you got stuck in this Island, you would need to learn, so you might as well start now. Come on. You can start by helping the men build the shelter."

He stood up and walked back to the rest of the Watchmen.

The men worked steadily to gather as many of the largest bones as they could find. Some of what looked like Darkling bones were massive.

Eliska stayed where she was staring into the water. She didn't want to break out of this stasis of fear and helplessness.

She definitely didn't want to fail and make a mess of things—not in front of the Watchmen. That would be worse than doing nothing.

Yvan's words drove her to her feet. He might by some miracle care about her as much as he pretended to.

If he did, she couldn't let him down. She had to do something if for no other reason than to prove herself worthy of his consideration.

She never thought she could be before—not without her magic. Her magic was the only thing making her worth the Watch's time. They wouldn't keep her with them for any other reason.

Wesh was the first person she'd ever met who ever acted like he wanted her to stick around. She told him and everyone else that he was the more powerful wizard, but they both knew it wasn't true.

He was the first older wizard she'd met with anything close to her power. Meeting him tempted her to hope he might be able to teach her a few things she hadn't been able to learn on her own.

The idea of actually learning from someone—of developing some kind of mentor relationship with him—it intoxicated her into investing too much feeling into him.

She started to care about him, too. Now he was gone along with any hope that he might be able to help her.

He wanted to. She knew that, now that he was dead and out of her reach. He really wanted to help her the way Yann and Yvan did.

Every instinct told her to push them away to protect herself. She couldn't let them see her needing help.

She couldn't push them away—not anymore. She needed them—all of them. She needed all these men—even Rien.

She needed Wesh, but he was dead. He would never be able to help her ever again.

She couldn't stand the pain of that, so she shook it off and turned away from the river. She started to climb over the bone mounds to where the men were busy rummaging through the piles.

Just then, Neils came walking back from somewhere. Eliska didn't notice before that he wasn't with the others. Even Anríq helped the Watchmen gather bones to make a shelter.

Neils pointed across the landscape in the direction the waterbuck herd ran. "There's almost an entire Darkling rib cage over there," he told Yvan. "The ribs are still attached to the backbone. We should use that as a shelter."

"Excellent." Yvan clapped him on the shoulder. "Let's go. Bring your buck, Niyazi. We're moving."

Niyazi hefted his skinned carcass back onto his shoulder. He carried the hide in one hand.

The Darkling skeleton lay on top of the bone fields a few hundred yards from where he killed the buck. He laid it nearby and left for some reason.

The rest of the party got to work stacking more bones around the rib cage to close in the walls.

Eliska hesitated watching them, but after a few minutes, she realized that they weren't doing anything too exceptional. They mainly gathered up the ribs from different skeletons lying around.

Vidal took over and directed everyone to stack the ribs around the Darkling skeleton to close in the gaps. Eliska could handle that. She didn't even have to decide where to put each bone. Vidal told her what to do.

The process took a long time, but Eliska kept working alongside the others until they finished. Even Yvan helped and obeyed Vidal's orders on where to put everything.

The walls started to rise off the ground. The party built the walls to head height before Marine came over. She scampered between the Watchmen, darted inside the skeleton shelter, and stayed there while the group finished working.

"Great," Rien muttered. "She'll keep us awake all night with her howling and muttering."

"Leave a gap at the top for air," Vidal ordered.

The group got close to finishing their shelter when Niyazi came back carrying an armload of dry brush.

He grinned at everyone when they made a big deal about it. "Where did you find that?" Neils asked.

Niyazi jerked his chin over his shoulder. "We need some way to cook this meat and I figured those bucks must be eating something, so I followed their tracks. It wasn't hard. They left a path of disturbed bones knocked out of place by their hooves. There's another branch of the river over there with vegetation. We should go over there tomorrow. It isn't much, but it's better than this river."

"Good idea," Yvan replied. "Well done."

Marine shrieked when Niyazi dumped his armload of brush inside the shelter. He left everyone there to finish work while he went back for a second and third load.

The group put the finishing touches on their house by the time he came back. Eliska glanced inside.

Marine huddled in a corner watching Niyazi squat in front of his pile of sticks. He snapped a bunch of them off, arranged them into a cone, and then used three others to construct some kind of bow.

"What are you doing?" Eliska asked.

"I'm lighting a fire." He shot her another grin. "I bet you never did it this way."

"How do you do it?"

"Watch." He extracted a twisty vine from the stack of brush, hooked it around his bow and another stick, used the bow to saw the stick into a different piece of wood. Smoke billowed out of it.

He blew on it and it ignited. "Whoa!" Eliska breathed.

He laughed at her. "You didn't think you were the only one, did you? You make a spit for the meat while I do this."

Eliska fumbled through the pile looking for sticks big enough to make a spit. Her first three efforts fell apart just in time for the other Watchmen to come in and see her making a fool of herself.

None of them even mentioned it. Rien sprawled on the floor to one side and threw his arm over his face. "Wake me up when we have something to eat."

"We should have brought water from the river," Vidal remarked. "None of us will want to walk all the way back there every time we get thirsty."

Yann stood up. "I'll go get it."

He left. Niyazi went outside and came back with one of the buck's legs quartered off the rest of the carcass. He boned it right there in front of everyone with his knife.

Eliska found herself marveling at the expert skill with which he did....well, everything. She never gave any of these men a chance to do anything before. She just did it with her magic first.

He put the meat on the spit and warmth filled the shelter.

Almost as if someone made it happen that way on purpose, the sky started to darken as soon as the group got under cover.

The sky turned black by the time Yann returned. He'd used his glaive to split open a much larger skull and turned it into a bowl to carry water.

He set it in the corner. "That should keep us going until morning if we all use it only for drinking."

"Well done, son," Yvan told him. "Good thinking—all of you."

"So what's the plan for tomorrow?" Omer asked.

"We have no way of knowing how long we'll be stuck in this Island," Yvan replied. "We could be here for years. We'll go over to this other river Niyazi mentioned and see what it's like. If it looks somewhat habitable, we'll set up over there and plan to stay as long as we have to. That will give us time to scout the terrain and see if we can find any other resources. If we can find a place with food, water, and shelter, I don't see any reason to go tramping across the countryside searching for anything else."

"If there are any people in this country, they'll be near food and water, too," Vidal pointed out. "Which could be a good thing or a bad thing."

"We'll just have to deal with them," Yvan replied. "We can't go without food and water, so we would have to go there anyway."

Niyazi took the first piece of meat off the spit. Neils unfolded his hog hide on the floor and Niyazi put the meat in front of him. Neils divided up the food while Niyazi got to work cooking the next haunch.

Neils went around the circle handing out meat to everyone. Yann left again while Neils worked.

Yann returned with another smaller skull fashioned into a bowl. Neils deposited Marine's portion into that.

Yann placed the bowl halfway between Marine and the rest of the Watch. Then everyone turned their backs on her so she could eat without them watching her.

The Watchmen talked while they ate. They kept it casual, discussed different options for directions they could go, and also related waterbuck habits that could lead the party to more plentiful hunting grounds.

Eliska listened in silence. She chewed her food to make it look like she couldn't interject.

The men knew a lot more about the outside world than she realized. Vidal, Omer, and Niyazi knew every detail of waterbuck behavior and activity.

The three men even discussed previous hunting trips they'd engaged in when they hunted waterbuck over multiple different types of terrain.

Eliska took in every word. These three men must have gone outside of Middleborough sometime or other. From the sound of it, they'd spent a lot of time outside Middleborough—maybe even years.

Their talk trailed off eventually and Niyazi turned around to put some more wood on the fire. "We should take turns staying up to keep this going," he suggested.

"You did all the work of bringing it here," Omer told him. "I'll go first."

Vidal shifted in his seat to move closer to Neils. Vidal glanced over his shoulder to where Marine sat hunched against the back wall.

For some reason, she didn't snarl and hiss and gnash her teeth and invisible enemies. She just sat there with her face turned toward the wall so she wouldn't see anyone.

"You could come over here and lie down," Vidal told her. "You would be warmer here."

She didn't respond.

Yvan did the same thing on his other side and moved closer to Barsali. "You lie down, too, Eliska. Lie down right here next to the fire. Take off your cloak and use it as a blanket."

She couldn't look at him. Yann scooted farther away on her other side. Both of them made a space there for her to curl up.

She distracted themselves from their attention by taking off her cloak and covering herself with it. She shut her eyes so she wouldn't see if the others were staring at her.

She must have been a lot more exhausted than she realized. She fell asleep the instant she shut her eyes, but not before she became aware of where she was and with whom.

All those men stopped talking stopped talking when she lay down. Only the faint crackling sound of the flames filled the little shelter.

The Watchmen's presence cast a protective halo over her. They were still there. Nothing could happen to her as long as they were still there.

Chapter 4

Y ann woke up and stiffened when he heard high-pitched, childish
laughter nearby. He frowned at the surroundings.

He lay on his side in the skeleton shelter he and the other Watchmen
built last night. The other Watchmen all lay asleep inside the shelter,
too. No one should be laughing in this hellhole.

He pushed himself up into a sitting position. Rien had been the
last man assigned to stay awake and keep the fire going, but he'd fallen
asleep on the job. Cold, black charcoal lay in the circle where the fire
should have been.

Eliska no longer occupied the place between Yann and Yvan where
she fell asleep last night. Marine wasn't inside anymore, either.

Right then, he heard Eliska talking to another woman outside. The
second woman had a high, musical voice and she said something that
made Eliska laugh.

Eliska had a softer, more reserved laugh. She tried to keep it to a
quiet chuckle. The first laugh Yann heard must have been someone
else's.

He left the shelter as carefully and quietly as he could to avoid
stepping on any of the other Watchmen. He walked outside.....and his
world stopped when he saw Eliska talking to Marine.

She'd cleaned herself up as well as she could under the circumstances. Her dress hung in dingy tatters the way it did yesterday, but she must have gone to the river to wash her face and hair.

She was still smiling at Eliska when Yann came outside. Marine's cheeks glowed with light. Her eyes twinkled and color washed over her face when she burst into a huge, mischievous grin.

Yann stared at her in stupid disbelief. This couldn't be the same person. That wasn't possible.

Her eyes darted to him and she blushed. Damn, she was beautiful!

Eliska turned around to see what Marine was looking at and Eliska saw Yann's reaction. "I told you she was beautiful, didn't I?"

Yann opened his mouth, but no sound came out.

Marine bit her lips to stop herself from smirking so much, but it didn't work. "Maybe he thinks I'm a changeling and I spirited the other Marine away to take her place."

Her voice rose and fell in a musical wave. She exaggerated the word, spirited, and raised her hands to simulate flying.

"Your dress gives it away," Eliska replied. "It's too bad you can't use your magic to fix it. That dress sure was beautiful."

"I suppose I can always get another one somewhere." Marine glanced at Eliska once and went back to returning Yann's stare. "Anyway, it's like the Watch Commander says. We might wind up back in some magical Layer soon enough."

"But then you'll go crazy again," Eliska pointed out. "Isn't there any way to protect yourself from the Dark?"

"I don't have to commune with the Dark," Marine replied. "I'm not communing with Darklings now. I do it when I want to and need to." She made a disgusted face and stuck out her tongue. "I wouldn't do it if I didn't have to. Pew!"

Eliska laughed again and Marine joined in.

Yann blinked at both of them. This….this was the real Marine—the Marine who had been hiding under all that dirt all this time? He didn't dare to believe it.

The two girls regarded him while he scrambled to come up with some reaction other than just slack-jawed shock.

Eliska snickered again, leaned close to Marine's ear, and murmured again, "I told you so."

Marine giggled like a little girl. Her dark eyes kept flicking upward to meet Yann's. Every glance from her made his stomach flip.

Eliska took a few steps away from her. She had to pass Yann to go back into the shelter. "Tell your father I'm going back to the river to get some more water for the men when they wake up. Tell him I'll be back in a little while."

She ducked into the shelter and took out the two skull bowls Yann made last night—the large water bowl and the small bowl Neils used to serve Marine her share of the food.

Yann stood rooted to the spot while Eliska passed him the second time, murmured, "Come on, Marine," and walked off toward the river.

Yann was still standing there with his jaw on the ground when the two girls walked away together and vanished behind the bone mounds.

Just then, his father came outside. "Where are the girls? I just heard them out here."

Yann pulled himself together as well as he could. "They went over to the river to get water for the men. Eliska said they would be back in a few minutes."

Yvan glanced around and frowned. "Where's Marine? Did she disappear on us again?"

"She went with Eliska. They went together."

Now Yvan frowned at Yann. "I don't understand. Did Marine follow her or something?"

"Marine regained her sanity sometime during the night," Yann explained. "She says she doesn't have to commune with Darklings all the time and I guess she doesn't have to do it now. She's back to normal—back to being funny and helpful and beautiful and friendly the way Eliska said she was in the other Layers. Remember?"

Yvan furrowed his brow at his son. "Are you sure? That shouldn't be possible."

"I just saw her. She's......" Words failed Yann. "You'll see when she gets back. She and Eliska were just out here talking and laughing and joking around like old friends."

Yvan wouldn't stop frowning. "Are you sure?"

"I saw them with my own eyes. I wouldn't have believed it if I didn't see it for myself. Just wait. They'll be back in a little while."

The rest of the men woke up while the girls were still away. Yann tried to explain the situation to them as best he could so they wouldn't be too shocked when Marine showed up looking like....well....like a princess.

He just flat didn't believe Eliska when she told the Watch that Marine was a princess.

Now he understood—now that he'd seen her himself.

She really was one. She had to be. He'd never seen any woman who matched his idea of a princess more than Marine. She only needed a beautiful, expensive gown to complete the picture.

The men went through a mixture of reactions when he told them. Omer only nodded, but Yann saw right away that even he didn't fully comprehend the profound change that came over Marine.

"I don't believe it," Rien countered. "I don't care what you say. I just don't believe it."

"I don't think I fully believe it, either, to tell you the truth," Yann replied.

"I'll believe it when I see it," Yvan added.

Neils brought the leftover buck meat outside. The men were in the middle of eating breakfast when the two girls came back.

The men heard Marine laughing before she got close enough to see her clearly. Her voice rang over the landscape and then Eliska's quieter laugh joined in.

The two young women talked non-stop from the minute they came over the farthest rise. They didn't stop talking until they returned to the skeleton shelter and rejoined the men.

"And then he skidded around a corner, crashed into the butler, and the cake flew up in the air," Marine blurted out in a breathless rush. "He was running so fast that the cake sailed across the passage and splatted into an oil painting of Great-Grandpa Leopold Heinrich Von Schtuben. The cake hit him right in the face!"

Both girls exploded in laughter....and then they noticed all the men staring at them.

Marine blushed. Eliska clamped her mouth shut and tried without success to get serious.

She squatted down, set the bowl of water in front of the men, and put the smaller skull bowl next to it. She kept coloring and lowering her eyes so she wouldn't look at anyone.

Marine stood off to one side and didn't come near the group, but her cheeks still glowed with life. Her eyes danced with laughter and her lips twitched up into little smirks when she saw the way the men were looking at her.

Yvan broke the uncomfortable silence by clearing his throat. "Ma rine....."

"Yes, Sir," Marine replied, threw back her shoulder, and shook her long, dark hair out of her eyes to face him.

He frowned when she called him that. He cleared his throat again. "Um....how long can we expect you to stay like this?"

"I'm sorry I can't tell you that, Sir. I'll probably have to commune with Darklings again while we're in this Island. I'm sorry I can't predict what will happen—and I can't predict whether I'll be one way or the other in any other Layer we wind up in."

"So.....there are Darklings in this Island? Is that what you're telling me?"

"Yes, Sir," she replied. "There are a lot of Dark forces in this Island. I'm surprised we haven't run into any yet."

"What have you been communing with them about if you can't convince them to leave us alone?" Rien demanded. "What's the point of communing with them at all? You might wind up attracting them to us."

His questions didn't offend her in the slightest. "I don't commune with them to make them leave us alone," she replied. "I don't think anyone can do that, especially not if the Voyant is the one sending them after you."

"Why do you commune with the Darklings?" Yvan asked. "Isn't that dangerous?"

"She does it to get information about the Voyant's plans and activities," Eliska cut in. "She's a member of the Guardian Templars. Her order dedicated themselves to stopping the Voyant and stabilizing the Coil. She's been traveling through the Dark Layers trying to find out why he's destabilizing it and what we might be able to do about it."

Yvan scowled at her. "I was asking this young lady here. I think she can answer for herself this time, don't you?"

Eliska cringed, turned bright red, and looked away. Fortunately for her, Neils held out a handful of the cooked buck meat just then and scooped the food into her hands.

She stared down at her food while she ate. She didn't look up or get involved in Yvan's conversation with Marine again.

Yvan turned back to Marine. Now it was her turn to clear her throat. "I commune with the Darklings to get information about the...."

"I heard her, Marine," Yvan interrupted. "Thank you very much."

"I also commune with the Darklings to find out what the Voyant wants from you and why he's coming after you to get it—if that helps," she blurted out. "I don't know if that helps or not, but....." She trailed off when she saw the expression on the Watch Commander's face.

"Have you found anything out?" Omer asked. "Do you know what it is he wants?"

"I'm sorry. No, I haven't. My whole order has been working on almost nothing else for the past few years."

Yvan searched the bone fields and muttered under his breath. "There must be some way to find out what it is."

"We've always assumed it was something magical," Marine went on. "Something that would increase his power."

"Then it can't be any of us or anything we have," Vidal pointed out. "None of us is magical. The only people here who have magic are Eliska, Anríq, and you—and we've already determined that the Voyant was sending Darklings after us before any of you joined us."

"I know!" Marine exclaimed. "It's a great mystery."

"If it's a mystery the Guardian Templars can't figure out, what chance do we have?" Yann asked.

"We don't—which is why we aren't going to try." Yvan stood up. "Pack up. We're heading for the other river Niyazi found yesterday." He turned to Marine and examined her a little more closely. He took in her torn dress and her shiny hair. "So.....there's no steps we can take to keep you like this?"

"I'm afraid not, Sir. If I thought it would help you at all for me to stay like this, I would do it."

"It would help us for you to stay like this. It would be so much more helpful to travel with a sane person than a wild thing that keeps shrieking and snarling and spitting at everyone."

Her jaw dropped. "Did I really do that?!"

"All the time," Barsali told her. "It gets really annoying after a while."

"But....wouldn't it be more helpful to find out what the Voyant is doing and why he's hunting you?" she asked.

Yvan grimaced and turned away. "I suppose so."

The other men stood up and got busy getting ready to leave. The process didn't take long at all because they had no baggage except their weapons.

Eliska put the small bowl into her shoulder bag and tucked the larger one under her arm to carry it that way. She looked up, made eye contact with Marine, and the two girls smiled at each other.

Yann and the others gathered their weapons. Neils wrapped what was left of the buck meat in his hog hide to take with them.

No one else had to do anything. Niyazi led the way farther inland. The group began another grey day of clambering over the bone fields.

Marine joined the line with Eliska. Yann took the same place behind Eliska, but the two young women spent most of the trip exchanging glances with each other. Neither of them paid any attention to Yann or any of the other Watchmen.

Yann spent most of the trip staring at Marine trying to understand how she could have just fallen from the sky like this. She walked straight upright like a normal person now.

She had a tall, willowy frame and stood at least five inches taller than Eliska. Marine carried herself with a regal bearing.

Her posture really did make her look like a princess. Her dress did absolutely nothing to dampen that impression.

The two girls posed such a stark contrast to each other. It staggered Yann's mind to think how different they were from each other—and yet they made friends.

Marine's warmth and outgoing personality would win anyone over —but it went further than that. These two young women understood each other at a deeper level.

They both had powerful magic. They both faced the same dangers and now they both carried out the same mission to find out the Voyant's plans and try to stop him.

Eliska brightened up so much around Marine. Yann had never seen Eliska so happy and unguarded, not even around him.

She smiled much more easily. Her eyes sparkled with a new kind of light. She actually looked excited about all of this instead of barricading herself behind granite walls and driving everyone off at the point of her staff.

The whole unfolding situation astounded Yann too much to feel jealous—of either of them. He could only marvel that Marine was here—that she really had replaced that crazy woman who followed the Watch from the Dark river.

Chapter 5

The group traveled for a mile of the vast bone fields. The same iron-grey clouds covered the whole sky. No sun shone through except a faint light for the travelers to see where they were going.

Yann felt himself slipping into a trance when a howl like strong wind snapped everyone to high alert.

The group turned to stare across the countryside at a funnel of fast-moving air spiraling down from the clouds.

It dipped out of the solid grey cloud cover, revolved into a cone, and then extended a long, curved finger toward the ground.

The tornado spiked into the bone fields a dozen miles away. For some reason, the wind didn't change around the party.

The wind definitely changed around the spiral. It kicked up bones from the ground and sent them spinning and wheeling in wild circles around the main funnel.

The spiral caught all those bones, whirled them together in the center, and they started to take shape.

More bones lifted off the ground—either from the wind or from something else. The bones came together in bizarre configurations. They formed into giant bodies towering over the landscape and then disintegrated.

All the bones fell apart and crashed down to lie where they were before.

The twister traveled across country heading away toward the first river.

More shapes of Darklings erupted in the twister's path. The funnel caught bones and put them together in the air before the shapes split apart and collapsed into piles where they'd been lying before.

The small hairs stood up on the back of Yann's neck when he saw Darklings in the storm.

"I told you they were here," Eliska murmured. "They just need the right combination of Dark power and a shifting landscape before they come out of the Layers to take this Island, too."

"How can we fight them without magic?" Marine asked.

"We'll just have to fight them hand to hand." Anríq stepped forward for the first time, unhooked his club and axe, and moved behind the party. He jerked his chin at Yvan. "Keep going on to the river. Take everyone with you."

Yann moved out of line. "I'm staying with you."

"I'll stay, too," Barsali offered.

"We can't all stay," Yvan pointed out. "Eliska, you and Marine move up to the front with Neils and Niyazi."

"Yes, Sir," Marine replied.

"The rest of you fall in line and keep moving," Yvan ordered. "Son, you and Barsali stay behind us with Anríq, but don't stop unless the Darklings attack. Understand? As long as they hold off, you keep moving and don't fall behind."

"I understand," Yann replied.

Anríq bowed and shut his eyes. "I will serve."

Yvan scowled at him once and then waved for the others to keep going.

Neils and Niyazi went in front with Niyazi leading the way. Yann didn't see any sign of the river ahead.

Did the landscape shift overnight? The river with all that vegetation and animal life might not be there anymore.

The Watch could wind up wandering around out here forever. They could be walking farther away from the one reliable source of water they knew already about.

Yann had his orders and so did everyone else. Eliska and Marine took their places behind Neils and Niyazi. Yvan, Rien, Omer, and Vidal filed after them.

Yann, Anríq, and Barsali stayed in the rear. Yann didn't want to turn his back on that twister in case it changed direction and rushed the party unawares.

He kept swiveling back to face the twister. He kept his glaive between it and himself—as if he could fight that twister with his glaive.

Anríq and Barsali reacted the same way. The three of them continually took turns walking backward. One of them would warn the others if the twister rushed them.

The twister migrated farther away toward the other river. The funnel kept shooting bones into the air and forming Darklings, but they never stayed Darklings for long.

The funnel made it as far as the river before it shrank back into the clouds. All the bones fell out of the vortex, hit the ground, and bounced back into place.

The twister left the landscape quiet and the bone fields as flat and empty as ever.

The minute the twister vanished into the clouds, another rumble shook the ground from the group's other side.

Yann and his two comrades spun around. Everyone ground to a halt again starting at more Darklings coming out of the ground a mile to the Watch's left.

These Darklings didn't need a twister to assemble their bones for them. Bones shifted on their stacks, snapped their ends together, and started to grow out of nothing.

They got taller....and taller....and built on top of each other to make bodies, heads, teeth, and every other body part they needed.

Their deep, booming roars echoed across the landscape. All the Watchmen closed in formation to meet the things, but they didn't come this way.

Anríq took a few steps out of line toward the Darklings. He still held his axe in one hand and his club in the other.

He wouldn't be able to do as much damage without setting off those magical explosions, but he would still be able to do a lot. He still had all his strength and fighting ability even without his magic.

The Darklings assembled themselves at a distance—and more kept locking together around the same area.

Five of them put themselves together within a few dozen yards of each other. They didn't seem to notice either each other or the travelers—not at first.

The Darklings lumbered around, smashed bones under their enormous feet, and kicked bones out of the way. The Darklings roared at the inconvenience....and then the inevitable happened when one of them noticed another.

The first Darkling rounded on its neighbor in a rage even though the second Darkling had just been standing there minding its own business.

The first one charged it and they clashed in another tempest of flying bones.

The Darklings didn't fall to pieces this time. The collision knocked their bones out of position, but they magically sailed back into place, stuck to all the other bones making up each Darkling, and they battled on as before.

They bellowed at each other, grappled with each other, and tried to throw each other to the ground. More bones whipped from the Darklings' sides, jointed together at their ends, and formed tentacles to slash and strike.

Long, curved, pointed bones jutted from the Darklings' mouths to gnash and chomp.

The noise and commotion attracted more Darklings. They assembled themselves out of the bone fields and charged inward from all sides to join the fight.

They clashed, exploded each other apart, reassembled, and did it all over again.

Yvan pulled everyone away. "Keep moving," he ordered. "We have to keep away from them."

The Watchmen backed off. Anríq backed away last. He stayed where he was with his weapons ready until the two girls and all the other Watchmen headed off across the countryside. Then Anríq took the very last place in line.

Yann fell back to join him. Yann didn't want any of these Darklings getting the jump on the group.

The Watch barely got moving before more Darklings started to assemble a few miles to the right. They grew out of the bone fields, fitted their joints together, and went through the same process of trundling around oblivious to each other.

Then the moment came when two of them tripped over each other and it was all on.

Two Darklings fighting seemed to magnetize more of them out of the ground—or maybe their Dark power acted on the surrounding bones.

The fights escalated in brutality. The noise boomed across the landscape. The tension built to the breaking point.

All that gathering power brought more bones together. The pressure crackled in the air and pulled the Darklings out of the ground.

They attacked each other on both sides. "Pick up the pace!" Anríq called from behind. "They're moving in!"

Yann glanced behind him to see what Anríq meant.

The two groups of Darklings kept getting bigger. They flanked the party's track. The Darklings of each battle didn't notice the other at first.

The two groups of Darklings kept swelling as more Darklings gathered by the minute. The outer edges of both battles crawled across the landscape closing on the travelers from either side.

Everyone set off walking faster, but not fast enough. The Darklings left only a few dozen yards between the two battles.

Neils and Niyazi burst into a run. The rest of the party followed, and at that moment, almost as if the Dark sensed the travelers running from it, the two Darkling battles rotated inward and rushed each other.

Anríq sprang backward and raised his club as Darklings closed on both sides. Yann tried to stand his ground, but he wouldn't be able to fight Darklings made out of bones—not with a single glaive.

Anríq swung his club and shattered a Darkling to smithereens. All the bones that made up its body flew apart—and then all those bones zoomed together into exactly the same shape. Anríq's blow accomplished absolutely nothing.

He turned from one direction to another striking thunderous blows with his club. He hacked his huge axe and snapped bones, but he couldn't make a dent in the Darklings.

Yann lunged for him and grabbed the back of his vest. "Come on! We gotta get out of here!"

Anríq stumbled away and finally turned and ran after the others. The Darklings were too busy fighting each other to come after the group.

That moment delayed Yann and Anríq and the two boys got caught in the confusion. Yann didn't see the rest of the Watch until he and Anríq staggered between a few more battling Darklings and broke through into the bone fields.

The Watchmen ran for fifteen minutes before Yann spotted trees ahead, but more Darklings erupted out of the ground and closed on the party from both sides.

The Darklings put themselves together almost instantaneously now. They shot out of the bone fields and charged inward to attack each other with the fleeing travelers trapped in the middle.

The travelers' route set off a domino effect in the landscape. The Darklings appeared on either side of the traveler's path. Yann didn't see Darklings shooting out of the ground anywhere else but right on either side of the Watch.

The emerging Darklings appeared faster and faster. The chain reaction swooped ahead of the travelers until Darklings ejected out of the mounds in front of the group.

Darklings crashing together and fighting each other blocked the party's way. Bone fragments and splintered shrapnel bombarded the fleeing Watchmen.

Eliska and Marine both screamed, threw their arms up to protect themselves, and would have stopped running.

Yvan rushed them from behind, grabbed Eliska, and pushed her forward. "Don't stop!" he yelled over the noise. "Keep going! Follow Niyazi—whatever you do!"

Omer caught up with Marine and got her moving with the rest. Yann and Anríq dropped back more than once to break apart Darklings that got too close from behind.

Vidal and Rien wound up defending the girls from the middle of the pack. Neils and Niyazi had to fight their way through battling Darklings just to keep the party going.

So many bones and broken shards pinwheeled through the air that Yann couldn't even see any Darklings anymore. A hurricane of bone fragments and random trash revolved in front of his eyes.

He and Anríq moved together, held onto each other to stay oriented, and pushed closer to the group from behind. Neils and Niyazi slowed trying to see where they were going. No trace remained of the trees ahead.

The Watch packed together into a tight cluster for protection. The men ringed the girls with every weapon pointed outward, but no more Darklings came after the party. They didn't have to. They submerged the Watch in a whirling mass of Darkness.

Niyazi bent his head, squinted at the terrain in front of him, and held his hand in front of his face, but he couldn't have seen anything over there, either.

Yann didn't understand when Niyazi yelled over his shoulder, "I see it! This way! We're almost there!"

Yann strained to see anything in the chaos. He and Anríq had to lean into the wind just to keep their balance. Yann didn't bother to raise his glaive now. There was nothing here to fight.

Without warning, Niyazi walked through some invisible barrier and vanished. Neils disappeared a second later and then the rest of the Watch evaporated one after another.

Yann and Anríq were holding onto each other and the other Watchmen too tightly to stop themselves before they fell through, too.

The wind died instantly. No more bone shards whistled through the air. In fact, Yann didn't feel any breeze at all.

He straightened up and blinked trying to get his brain to accept where he was. He and the other Watchmen looked all around them at a peaceful river valley winding through scrubby woods on either side.

No dark clouds blocked out the sun. It shone out of a clear blue sky. Not a single bone lay on the ground.

Yann and Anríq both looked behind them. They couldn't see the bone fields anymore. Rolling countryside and low bushes stretched out behind them.

Niyazi caught his breath. "This is it. This is the river I saw yesterday."

"You didn't say it was like this!" Vidal pointed out.

"No, it wasn't like this," Niyazi replied. "That barrier wasn't there. The bones came all the way down to the river....and there was less vegetation....and the dark clouds were still there. It wasn't sunny like this....or as beautiful."

Yvan frowned. "I don't like it. Something must have changed it."

"Does it matter?" Rien asked. "We're here now. This is where we wanted to go. You said we would stay here, so let's stay here."

"Spread out and see if we can find a good place to camp." Yvan pointed at everyone. "Niyazi, you take Omer, Vidal, and Barsali upriver going that way. The rest of you come with me. We'll go downstream."

Niyazi, Omer, Vidal, and Barsali walked away. The two girls joined Yann, Anríq, Rien, Neils, and Yvan heading in the opposite direction.

Chapter 6

The party hiked down the river, but Eliska didn't see any place better than any other for camping.

She couldn't figure out what Yvan was looking for. The spot where the Watch came through that barrier from the bone fields looked perfectly good to her—but she wasn't in charge.

She tried not to notice the Watchmen surrounding her and Marine, but she couldn't ignore it any longer.

Their behavior only drove home the point that she was defenseless in the Coil.

That battle between the bone Darklings wiped out whatever shred of confidence she got by following Yvan's instructions and helping the Watchmen build the skeleton shelter.

Now she jumped at the slightest noise again. She jumped when there was no noise.

A creeping sensation spread all over her skin and ate away at her insides. This all-consuming dread gnawed into her guts.

Marine reacted the same way. She kept jerking from right to left trying to see everything, but she didn't go insane the way she did before.

The Watchmen didn't ask Yvan what he was looking for, either. None of the men seemed too concerned about meeting any dangers. The men only acted concerned about protecting the two girls.

Yvan led the party a long way down the river. It kept winding left and right around corners, climbing over hills, and babbling over rocks.

The Watchmen studied the ground as much as anything else. Were they looking for animal tracks?

Eliska kicked herself for not learning how to track an animal before now. She always used magic to find her prey.

All at once, Yvan shot out his arm to stop everyone. "Shh!" he whispered. "Do you hear that?"

Everyone held their breath to listen.

"It sounds like voices," Neils remarked.

"It's more than voices," Yvan replied. "I hear armor."

The party climbed the next hill much more slowly. Yvan flattened himself on his stomach to look over the top.

The girls and the Watchmen did the same thing. They all stared down at another bend in the river.

A hundred men wearing armor milled around, saddled their horses in matching armor, and checked their weapons. A few flags with different heraldry embroidered on them fluttered around their camp.

These men must have been camping here. A few dying fires dotted the area. None of the knights were wearing their helms yet. They walked around the camp bareheaded.

Some of the knights were in the act of striking tents, dumping out kettles of water, or winding up lengths of rope.

Some of the knights turned to face the hilltop as they went about their business. They wore purple tunics over their armor with a large symbol embroidered on the chest in gold thread.

"What does that symbol mean?" Eliska whispered to Yvan.

"I've never seen it before," he whispered back. "It's too bad Wesh isn't here. He might be able to tell us."

"Can you tell if any of them have magic?" Yann asked.

Eliska shook her head. "I can't tell—but it doesn't look like any of them do. I don't see any of them using magic to do their work. This Island might block all magic—theirs as well as ours."

"It doesn't block the Dark, though, does it?" Marine pointed out.

"No, not that," Eliska agreed.

"The Dark might be blocking anything other than Dark magic," Anríq suggested. "The Dark might have constructed this Island so no one can use any other kind of magic here."

Eliska spun around and frowned at him. He'd been talking so much more than before. Why would he do that? He kept violating his vow of silence. What happened to that?

He saw her scowling at him and faced front. He didn't explain himself.

No one else acted like him talking meant anything—because none of the others knew about the Servant's path.

Marine knew about it, but she didn't seem to notice, either.

Eliska turned her attention to Marine instead. "Do you recognize that symbol? Do you know who these men are?"

She shook her head. "I don't know the symbol and I don't know them. I've never seen or heard of them before—but I never claimed to know everything."

Yvan pushed himself up. "We're going down there to find out. Let's go."

Eliska didn't want to go down there where a bunch of armed men were obviously getting ready to go out to some kind of battle.

The other Watchmen didn't hesitate. Anríq didn't hesitate, either. He, Yann, Neils, and Rien and stood up right away. They all took hold of their weapons and followed Yvan down the other side of the hill heading for the knights' camp.

Marine and Eliska scrambled to get to their feet a moment after the others. The two girls had to hustle to catch up with the men walking in front.

The men formed up in a shoulder-to-shoulder line this time. None of them tried to hide the fact that they were coming down the hill armed and ready for anything.

The only one of them who didn't hold his weapons in his hands was Anríq, but his size cast an intimidating figure enough already.

Yann gripped his glaive in both hands. Rien held his broken sword in his right hand. He didn't draw his second blade, but that somehow made him look more intimidating than if he had drawn it.

The girls wound up behind the men's line. Eliska didn't dare to walk side by side with them. She didn't have any weapon. She wouldn't even have been able to sneeze in the knights' direction.

The knights would have had to be blind not to see the Watchmen coming in. The knights stopped what they were doing. Then a dozen of them split off and gathered into a loose group to meet the Watchmen.

The two parties halted ten feet apart. "Can I help you?" a tall, dark-haired knight asked. He looked young and fresh-faced above the neck.

"We're members of the Black Watch as you can see." Yvan waved to those nearest him.

"*He* isn't." A scruffy, middle-aged knight curled his lip at Anríq. "He's a Barbarian."

"He's a Servant and he's our friend," Yann interrupted.

"A Servant!" the first knight exclaimed. "You should come with us. We could use your help."

"What's your business here?" Yvan asked. "How did you come here?" He jutted his chin at the knights' tunics. "What does that symbol mean? I've never seen it before. Our companion here is a member of the Guardian Templars and she's never seen it before, either."

"We belong to the Chivalric Order of Custodians," the first knight replied. "I am Amaury Marais, Captain of the Guard, and this is my lieutenant, Yves Sylvain." He waved to the scruffy man next to him. "Our mission is to hunt down the Voyant Mendicat and stop him from destroying everyone in the Coil."

Marine gasped, but Eliska grabbed her arm to stop her from saying anything. Yvan allowed himself to raise his eyebrows ever so slightly. "Do you know where the Voyant is? Do you know how to find him and how to defeat him?"

"That is our quest," Marais replied. "Our mission is to find out how to defeat him."

"Do you have magic?" Neils asked. "He's a powerful magic-user, you know."

"That's exactly why we have to defeat him. We can't allow him to use his magic to hold the rest of us in slavery."

"Is that what he's doing?" Anríq asked.

Marais and Sylvain both turned to confront him. "You're a Servant," Marais pointed out. "You should be with us. We could use your magic to heal wounds when we go into battle."

"I'm already serving that mission with these men of the Watch," Anríq replied. "Besides, I don't have any magic in this Island."

"Then you really are a Barbarian and you deserve to die." Sylvain took a threatening step forward and his hand flew to his sword hilt.

Yann sidestepped in front of Anríq and raised his glaive. "Lay a hand on him and you'll wind up fighting all of us," Yann snarled.

All the other Watchmen drew their weapons and closed around Yann and Anríq. Anríq didn't move, not even to touch his weapons.

Marais grabbed Sylvain's arm just as fast and pulled him back into place. "We have no quarrel with the Black Watch," Marais went on. "If you have no magic, then you wouldn't be any good to us anyway."

"I know," Anríq replied.

Marias's eyes darted from one Watchman to the other. "Stand down and put your weapons away. We're on the same side in this war. Fighting each other will accomplish nothing."

No one moved for a second until Yvan elbowed Rien. "Put your weapons down."

The Watchmen lowered their weapons and no longer pointed them outright at the knights, but none of the Watchmen slackened their guard even for a second.

Marais pulled Sylvain farther away and nodded at Yvan one more time. "Take your men aside until we leave. We didn't plan to stay in this river valley after this morning anyway. There's no reason for us to come to blows. We'll be on our way and you can go on yours."

Marais tugged Sylvain's sleeve one last time and then motioned all his men to back off. They turned to their horses and tents and left the Watch standing in the same place.

Yvan straightened his arm in front of Rien and the Watchmen backed up twenty feet before they turned away, too.

Marine and Eliska backed up behind the Watch. The party finally turned around to climb back up the hill they came from.

They discovered Niyazi, Omer, Barsali, and Vidal standing at the top watching the whole incident. All four men held their weapons ready.

The two groups rejoined on the hilltop. Yvan and the others turned around to look down at the knights' camp.

Yvan didn't flatten himself behind the hill this time nor did he suggest that any of his men do it. They all stayed where they were, armed in plain view, while they watched the knights finish packing up their camp.

The knights pretended not to see the Watchmen standing guard over the place. The knights got to work more energetically than before.

They finished folding up their gear, fitting out their horses, and the knights put on their helms before they mounted up.

They pulled the flags out of the ground and carried them in procession past the hill where the Watchmen stood.

Marais took the lead carrying a large red flag emblazoned with a roaring golden lion. He raised his flagstaff in salute to the Watchmen as the horses filed past.

None of the Watchmen answered that salute even with a wave. No one said a word until the horses vanished around another bend in the river farther upstream.

Chapter 7

Yvan sighed as soon as the knights of the Chivalric Order of Custodians left. "They'll probably all die before they get anywhere near the Voyant."

"I wonder if any of them has ever been out of this Island," Vidal remarked. "They don't seem to know anything about the Coil."

"There's another town over there." Niyazi pointed behind him—upriver where he and the others just scouted. "We should head for that."

Yvan only nodded and the whole party set off up the river. Walking along it sure was pleasant compared to walking over the bone fields.

The group didn't see any further sign of the Chivalric Order of Custodians. The countryside got steeper and the hills taller with deep channels and valleys between them.

Eliska checked at each hilltop. She never saw the knights again. They couldn't have traveled beyond this little pocket of serenity and stability, but they seemed to vanish into the landscape.

She tried to push them out of her mind. People had been disappearing out of her life for as long as she could remember. She accepted long ago that they probably died in the Coil.

She found it harder and harder to brush that off now. Some part of her finally woke up and revolted against all of this, including her own part in it.

The party topped another hill and Niyazi pointed out the town in the distance. It was much more than a town.

A cloud of those flying vehicles buzzed around tall buildings the way Marine and Eliska had seen them flying in that giant city in the illusion Layer. Was that city real after all?

Marine seemed to think cities like that existed throughout the Coil, so why not here?

What would it be like to go inside one of them and find out how everything worked? Eliska couldn't fathom that.

None of the Watchmen commented on how different the city looked from the other Islands they'd traveled through. Did any of the Watchmen even see the flying vehicles or the enormous, towering buildings made of glass?

The Watchmen all just kept walking as if Niyazi pointed out a quaint country town like Middleborough. They didn't even stop to study the city from a distance.

Niyazi led the way into a valley that joined up with a road leading to the city. The hills dropped away so the party could see the city getting bigger as they got nearer.

The sight of all that activity, prosperity, and magnificent advancement gave Eliska a feeling of impending doom. Maybe her instincts didn't go away when she lost her magic.

The travelers headed out into the open countryside to approach the city, but they only made it a few miles before storm clouds started to gather over the city's highest buildings.

"This looks bad," Omer muttered.

The clouds roiled and lightning crackled inside them even as they spread through a clear blue sky. The clouds obliterated the sunshine and the wind picked up.

The flying vehicles kept on with their business as if nothing was happening. None of the people in the streets or behind the windows seemed to realize anything was wrong.

The clouds covered the whole city, but they didn't spread beyond that. The lightning didn't leave the city, either.

Barsali stopped walking. "Are we really going in there? It looks dangerous."

Almost as if his words made it happen, at that moment a revolving funnel of fast-moving air snaked out of the clouds. Lightning twined around the spiral as it stretched downward toward the buildings.

It missed the buildings, stabbed between them, and hit the ground somewhere deep inside the city. The travelers couldn't see where it hit.

That one instant set off the disaster Eliska had been dreading. Darklings erupted out of the ground surrounding the city, ringed it exactly the way they ringed Middleborough, and attacked the buildings in fury.

The Darklings smashed the buildings to smithereens and sent a rain of debris and broken glass showering into the streets. People screamed and ran, but they couldn't run fast enough to get away from the Darklings.

These Darklings looked about the same size as the Darklings that destroyed Middleborough, too. They pulverized buildings, brought them down on fleeing citizens, and Darklings stormed through the city snatching up people left and right.

The Watch stopped at a distance. No one took another step toward that city. Everyone stared in sinking horror at the city crumbling before their eyes. So much for seeing how the city worked and discovering all its wonders.

The Darklings rising out of the earth cracked the soil from a Layer underneath. The ground rumbled when they emerged and those rumbles didn't stop. Fractures spread outward from the holes the Darklings broke through the surface.

The Darklings' stomping feet shook the terrain. The cracks and fissures kept spreading....

More Darklings blasted out of those cracks. Those closest to the city turned on the city. Those Darklings too far away turned on the only thing left—each other.

Omer wheeled away. "Run for it!"

Yvan grabbed the two girls. "Move!"

Eliska didn't dare to turn around to see how close the Darklings were getting. More forks and cracks split the soil under her feet. How soon would the Darklings come and devour the group, too?

The noise coming out of the city sent a wave of goosebumps over her skin. The screams of dying people mingled with crashes and booms of explosions mixed with the Darklings' feral roars.

The cracks and fissures overtook the party, but no Darklings broke through to pounce on the fugitives.

The fracturing landscape rushed past the group and swept forward in front of Omer and Niyazi who wound up in front.

The cracks swept the whole countryside. That wave of Dark wiped out the beautiful landscape—if it ever had been beautiful. Maybe that was all part of some illusion that turned the bone fields into something nicer.

Eliska would never know because she couldn't use her magic to find out.

The wave erased the sunshine, the blue sky, the trees, all the vegetation, and everything before it. Only the river remained, but it didn't look the way it looked before.

Lava bubbled down the channel. The wave of cracks shattered the illusion—or whatever it was. The Dark rewrote the landscape into a volcanic wasteland venting lava and sulfur from cones built out of solid rock.

Rivulets of lava trickled here and there, but the landscape showed a few signs of whatever it might have been before the Dark took it over. The crumbling remains of a few houses dotted the riverbank.

Churning red and orange vapors replaced the blue sky. Shadows of Darkness blocked out any sunlight. The lava gave the landscape a reddish glow of permanent night.

The Watchmen didn't stop running. Niyazi followed the river all the way back the way he came.

The group only made it a few hundred yards before it became obvious that they were still following the same river. It followed the same contour over the same hills and valleys.

The Watchmen had to divert around lava streams, leap from one section of solid rock to another, and then correct their course to keep going.

Marine staggered a few times. Yvan steadied her.

Eliska should have done that, but fear and horror wiped out every other thought beyond just staying alive.

Her terrified eyes darted around the landscape trying to see something—any trace of something that would help her to survive.

She'd never been in this kind of danger before—not ever. She'd always been able to do something to save her own life. Her magic always got her out of any dangerous situation.

Terror gripped her. It wiped out her mind and left her spinning in a nightmare of pure petrified fear and anguish.

Her brain no longer seemed capable of thinking anything—not even to come up with the most basic idea of how to help herself. Forget about helping anyone else.

Yvan stayed near the two girls. He was the one who helped them whenever they needed help. He guided them where they needed to go.

The group ran a long way before Omer and Niyazi finally slowed down and eventually stopped on top of one of the hills. Intense heat radiated off the lava river. It burned Eliska's skin, but her addled mind didn't even register enough to get her away from it.

She followed the Watchmen in a numb trance. She was going to die out here. She knew that now, but she couldn't even relax into the inevitable.

Fear froze her into a zombie hypnotic state. Every nerve stretched to the breaking point, but she couldn't even break into the hysterical panic lingering just beneath the surface. She really wished she could.

The other Watchmen pulled up on the hilltop. Rien doubled over propping his hands on his knees and gasping for breath. Neils buckled onto his seat panting hard.

Marine whimpered in terror looking all around her, wrung her hands in desperation, and her features screwed up in misery.

Yvan went from one person to the next checking on everyone. Then he stopped in front of the two girls.

He gave Eliska a hard look, but he softened when he made eye contact with her. Did he see just how close she was coming to losing it completely?

The others scanned the surroundings. "We won't be able to find food and water in this hellhole," Omer remarked.

"Then we'll just have to take the next best thing," Yvan replied. "Keep heading up the river—but walk. Find us one of these broken-down houses where we can shelter—at least for a little while. Something else is bound to happen to send us somewhere else."

Chapter 8

Y ann ducked under the low door frame and entered a charred
ruin barely standing upright in this volcanic wasteland.

The Watch had traveled for three hours before Neils spotted a
burned-out wreck of a building where the group could spend the
night—or whatever passed for night in this place.

The crumbling walls held up a broken roof with the swirling reddish sky showing through it. The Watchmen sat down on the floor in
a corner. No one spoke—except Yvan.

The Watch Commander steered Marine and Eliska into the corner,
too. "Sit down over here, young one," he told Eliska. "Sit down, Marine."

He pushed them down with the Watchmen. Eliska tugged her cloak
tighter around her shoulders. She hunched her head into her neck. Her
dark, haunted eyes skipped from one side to the other without seeing
anything.

Marine kept sobbing, whining, and knitting her fingers together in
terror. She didn't respond to anything Yvan said or did. He had to push
her down to make her sit on the floor.

He tugged off his jacket and wrapped it around her shoulders even
though it wasn't cold. Then he sat down in front of both of them,

pulled the jacket tighter around Marine, and shot both girls an evaluating look.

"You'll both be all right," he murmured under his breath. "You're afraid because you don't have your magic and you don't know how to cope with this, but you'll be all right. You'll see." He turned to Eliska, took hold of her cloak, and tugged it tighter around her, too. Then he squeezed and massaged both of her shoulders. "You'll be all right, young one. You'll see I'm right."

Her gaze shot to his face and her expression pinched in misery, but she definitely saw and recognized him.

Yann would have liked to be the one to go over there and take care of both girls. He would have liked to be the one to reassure them that everything would be all right, but he couldn't go over there while his father was already doing it.

Yann wasn't even sure he *could* do it. He wouldn't have wanted to make any promises to either girl that they would be all right.

Yvan didn't say that to any of the men. Yann didn't see how anything would be all right ever again under their circumstances.

None of the men said a word. They had no food or water and no way to get it. The Watch would be truly screwed if they got stuck in this lava world.

Yann didn't see how they would get out of it—except by some other Darkling attack or if the whole Island collapsed again.

He and Anríq sat down to one side. Yvan's voice gave the only sound in the deadly silence except for the occasional hiss of sulfur vents outside.

"You should both lie down and try to get some sleep," Yvan told the two girls. "We don't know how long we'll be here. We'll have to travel again soon, so you should rest while you can." He turned back to Marine.

Eliska made eye contact with him when he spoke to her, but she kept looking away. She huddled under her cloak. The outline of her hands kept twisting and gripping the fabric from underneath.

Marine didn't respond to anything Yvan said. She looked anywhere but at him.

He got her attention by clasping his hand around her knit fingers and pulling her hands down into her lap to stop her from wringing them so hard.

She resisted, but she eventually came out of her frenzy enough to realize what he was doing.

She grimaced in misery even worse when she finally worked up the courage to look at him.

"We aren't done yet, young one," he breathed in an even softer murmur. "We're still here—which means we can still find a way out of this. You'll be all right. You'll see. We'll wind up somewhere else soon and you'll get your magic back. You'll see. You both will."

She burst out in a broken howl. Her wild, petrified eyes raced around the room. "The Dark.....!" she blurted out. "Everything.....is so Dark....!"

Yvan compressed his lips. "I know, young one," he murmured. "Try to sleep. Everything will change soon. You'll see. Your magic is too strong to stay gone for long. It will come back and then you'll have all your old problems of communing with the Dark. Maybe you might even wish you were here in a land without magic so you could be sane for a little while."

Her face spasmed in some wretched combination of a smile and a sob. She looked up at him with eyes overflowing with pleading emotion before she nodded fast and cast her gaze down into her lap.

He never let go of her hands. He crushed them in his powerful fingers to stop her from hurting herself.

He held them for a long moment before he let them go. He gave both girls one last penetrating, evaluating look before he turned away.

He swiveled backward on his seat and came face to face with Yann and Anríq. The Watch Commander gave Yann an equally penetrating look. Yvan's eyes skimmed down Yann's uniform checking for any injuries.

When Yvan didn't see anything, he turned to Anríq and checked him, too.

Anríq sat bowed and silent leaning against the wall next to Yann. Anríq wasn't injured, either, but he didn't raise his eyes even to look at Yvan.

Yvan thrust out his hand and squeezed Anríq's shoulder. "You young ones did well. I'm proud of you both. You're both a credit to the Watch and I'm glad to have you with us."

He turned to the others. "All of you settle down and get some rest while you can. We'll use this house as a base while we venture out and see what we can find. You all need rest for that—and for whenever the landscape changes again."

No one said anything after that. No one laid down at first. Coal dust and scattered pieces of charcoal covered the floor, but that wouldn't have stopped Yann from lying down.

His tension took a long time before it faded enough for him to even think about sleep. The other Watchmen sat up for hours, too, before any of them curled up on the floor.

Anríq didn't, either, and Yvan didn't tell anyone to. He stayed where he was in front of the two girls and kept watch over them.

Eventually, Eliska lowered herself to the floor, hugged her cloak more tightly around her shoulders, and shut her eyes. Then Marine did the same thing.

Yvan arranged his jacket over her to act as a blanket. Then, for no particular reason, he passed his hand down the side of her hair in a petting motion before he left both girls alone.

The two girls lying down acted on the rest of the group. The men settled done one after another.

Yann's exhaustion became overwhelming, but he still found it difficult to shut his eyes or lower his guard even for a minute.

He didn't want to sleep. He wanted to stay awake in case something happened in the middle of the night. He would need to be ready to jump up and either fight or run away at a moment's notice.

Anríq stretched out first. He didn't take off his weapons when he curled up on his side. He only moved his club out of the way so he wouldn't lie on it. He kept his axe on his back as usual and pushed his bags behind him.

He folded his thick, muscular arm under his head and shut his eyes. He looked even more childlike in his sleep.

Yann experienced a rush of protective affection for him even though Anríq was so much bigger and stronger. His innocence made Yann feel older and more worldly by comparison even though he wasn't.

Yann's gaze darted to the two girls. He felt the same way about both of them, but his father sitting in front of them cast a different aura over the girls.

Yvan protected them, and by proxy, the two boys. How could Yann protect anyone when he was the one who needed his own father to protect him?

Yvan couldn't even protect himself, much less anyone else.

Anríq could protect himself better than any of them, but that didn't change the impression hanging over the whole group.

Yvan protected everyone—not by being the biggest and the strongest, but by being a father to them all.

Yann couldn't keep his eyes open a second longer, so he curled up next to Anríq.

The last thing Yann saw before he shut his eyes was his father still sitting there in the same place. He was the last man sitting up.

He gazed down at the two girls and cast occasional glances around the room at all the other sleeping Watchmen.

His presence—his eternal presence—gave Yann a matching sensation of being small, vulnerable, and weak—the way he was when he was a little boy.

His father was there. His father was always there—always older, smarter, stronger, better at everything.

Yann could finally let go of the need to protect himself because his father was there to protect him instead.

Chapter 9

Yann woke up in the middle of the night and stiffened. Something was wrong. He just didn't know what it was.

He pried his head off the floor and looked around. Anríq lay asleep right in front of him. Anríq had his eyes closed. He hadn't moved since he lay down on the floor of this ruined house.

The other Watchmen snored nearby. Even Yvan had finally dropped off.

Yann sat up and spotted Eliska huddled in a corner. She hugged her knees to her chest, trembled all over, and the outlines of her fists kept twisting and wrenching her cloak from underneath.

She went through an obsessive movement of trying to pull it tighter around her even though it wasn't cold. She couldn't tighten it more than it already was, but she kept doing it anyway.

Her eyes darted back and forth over the floor. She didn't look at Marine, Anríq, or the other Watchmen. She didn't look at anyone.

Yann stared at her for a second trying to understand what was wrong with her. She should have been asleep like the others. She definitely needed it.

Her agitation kept her awake.....and then he realized. She wasn't shaking with cold. She was shaking with fear.

Yann didn't dare to speak or even whisper. He didn't want to wake up the others. Drawing their attention to her distress would only make it worse.

He pushed himself to his feet, picked his way carefully across the room, and wedged himself into a tiny scrap of bare floor right next to her.

He rested his back against the wall, shifted over so he sat right against her side, and put his arms around her.

He really didn't give a crap if this was inappropriate or crossing a line or implying anything or any of that. She needed someone. He didn't really know what she needed, but he was the only person who could give it to her.

Her whole body quaked in his arms. She didn't respond at first, but she didn't shake him off, either.

He crossed a line in those tunnels with Anríq. He had to help her. None of the rest of it meant a thing.

He tightened his grip and pulled her against him. She toppled sideways and her weight fell on his chest. He clasped his arms around her trying to hold her tightly enough to stop her from trembling.

He no longer cared if this meant anything or led to anything or if she interpreted it as anything. He just wanted to help her—to give her some of his warmth and maybe make her feel better.

She huddled in his arms shaking uncontrollably. She didn't pull away.

Just because he felt like it, he raised his other hand, cupped the side of her head, kissed her hair, and then stroked his hand down her hair. He didn't think about or care what it meant or if it meant anything.

"The Dark...." she husked. "The Dark....it's out there...."

"I know," he whispered.

"It's all around us....." she choked. "I can't get away from it......and now I can't....do anything......"

He kissed the top of her head again. Then rested the back of his skull against the wall, shut his eyes, and settled into just being here.

He didn't have to make it okay. He couldn't anyway. He just held her and stroked her hair for what seemed like hours.

"The Darklings....." she rasped again. "They're coming after me......"

Yann's eyes snapped open. "Did you see that?" he whispered.

"I had a nightmare," she whispered back. "I always saw it in visions before. I used to see visions of Islands collapsing and Layers changing and Darklings coming out of the Layers. I saw it in a dream this time."

Yann stared into the darkness trying to think. She cowered in his arms still shaking like a leaf. She didn't try to sit up and he didn't let her go.

She had magic—or she did have magic before she came to this Layer. Her magic showed her what would happen before it happened. No wonder she always knew when something was about to happen to the group.

She didn't have magic now, but the same power must be operating through her dreams.

He shook that off and turned his head to kiss her hair again. "It doesn't mean anything," he whispered. "We already know the Darklings will come after us. They've been doing it all this time. It makes sense that you would see them coming again."

Her voice cracked from the strain. "What am I going to do?"

"You're going to keep traveling with us and we're going to keep helping each other in whatever way we can," he whispered. "You help us and we help you. Sometimes we go into a Layer where we can't take care of ourselves and you have to take care of us. Sometimes we go into a Layer where you can't take care of yourself and we have to take care of you. That's the way it works. It doesn't mean anything."

She did answer. She buried her face in his chest and hid there.

He held her tight and kissed her hair a few more times while he stroked her hair. Damn, she felt good!

He felt even better. Taking care of her felt better than anything he could ever remember. It meant everything.

He settled into it and prepared himself to sit here all night long if he had to. He even prepared himself for someone to wake up and find him with his arms around Eliska.

He didn't care about that anymore, either. He didn't have to ask about his father's past because Yann already knew who and what he was and what he was going to do.

Just then, he heard a whimpering noise coming from the other side of the room. Eliska heard it, too. She raised her head and sat up.

Yann unwrapped his arms from around her and they both looked around.

The noise came from Rien. He lay on the floor in the corner between Barsali and Vidal.

Rien jerked back and forth in his sleep. His eyebrows, cheeks, and mouth wrenched and twisted in between pathetic whimpering, but he didn't open his eyes.

"He must be having nightmares, too," Eliska whispered.

Yann leaned forward and gripped Rien's shoulder. "Rien! Wake up!" Yann whispered.

Rien jolted the other way and gasped in terror to get away from Yann's hand. Rien didn't wake up. He kept throwing himself from one side to the other to get away from whatever he saw in his nightmare.

Yann shook him a little harder and dared to raise his voice to a murmur. "Rien! Wake up! You're having a bad dream!"

Rien actually screamed out in terror, ripped himself away from Yann's touch, and threw himself into the corner. Rien slammed into the wall, plastered himself there, and his whole body convulsed.

He kept turning from right to left like he wanted to see everything at the same time, but he still didn't open his eyes.

His noise roused the other Watchmen. Yann couldn't wait any longer.

He grabbed Rien by both shoulders and shook him hard. Yann might even have slammed Rien against the wall without meaning to.

"Rien!" Yann yelled. "Wake up! You're all right! You're having a dream! Wake up!"

Rien's eyes snapped open, but he didn't see Yann. Rien's gaze kept skating back and forth and in all directions.

He gasped for breath, tensed every muscle, and held his hands in front of his body to protect himself from something that wasn't there.

"You're all right!" Yann repeated. "You had a bad dream. You're okay. You're with the Watch. See? Father and Vidal and Barsali are all here. See? You're okay."

The others sat up, looked around, and saw what was going on. Rien's terrified eyes flicked from face to face and then locked on Yann.

"It's okay," Yann breathed again. "You had a nightmare."

Rien's eyes darted away. "Darklings....." He glanced in the other direction toward Eliska. "Darklings.....they're everywhere....they're coming after me....."

"He might have had the same dream I just had," Eliska husked.

"That isn't possible," Yann replied over his shoulder. "Rien doesn't have any magic."

"How do you explain this, then?"

Yann turned back to Rien. Rien didn't lower his arms or relax at all. His eyes kept skimming around the room hardly seeing anything.

"There are no Darklings here, Rien," Yann breathed. "You can see that. There's just the Watch."

Yvan came over to them. "Is there any possibility he could have seen something real?"

Yann glanced at Eliska. He didn't want to tell his father what Eliska just said.

"I had a similar nightmare...." she blurted out. "But that could have been....you know.....just a nightmare."

Yvan scowled at Rien. "Hmmm. All right. Everyone settle down. It was just a nightmare. Nothing to see here."

The other Watchmen sat back listening to the conversation. Rien didn't settle down. He didn't seem to be aware of anyone around him.

His eyes flicked back and forth just as fast. "Darklings....." he whimpered. "Darklings.....they're coming....!"

"The Darklings aren't coming, Rien!" Yvan snapped. "We're all alone out here."

Just then, Anríq got to his feet and left the house without a word to anyone. His departure startled everyone—except Rien. Rien didn't notice.

A dangerous silence fell over the group after Anríq left—and then Rien screamed again. He spun to his left, jerked out of Yann's grip, and tried to throw himself farther back into the corner.

He raised his hands in front of his face, cringed, and cowered sobbing in terror.

"Rien!" Yann called.

"Darklings! Aaargh!" Rien shrieked. "Get them away from me!"

"Was it like this for you?" Yann asked Eliska over his shoulder.

She shook her head. "No, never."

Yann glanced in the other direction. He really wished Anríq was still here. Maybe Anríq knew a way to fix whatever was wrong with Rien.

Rien screeched again and huddled deeper into the corner. Niyazi pushed his way between the other Watchmen, stopped at Yann's side, and clamped his hands on either side of Rien's face.

Niyazi forced Rien to turn and look at him. "Rien—look at me! Look at me! The Darklings aren't here! You're seeing a vision!"

Rien yelped and tried to jerk away. He kept whipping right and left no matter what anyone did.

Yann backed off to let Niyazi take over. Yann had no idea how to help Rien.

Yann wound up scooting back to Eliska's side. Marine cowered in the opposite corner wringing her hands and grimacing in horror at the whole scene.

Niyazi got right in Rien's face and raised his voice over Rien's screams and whines. "We'll protect you from the Darklings, Rien! We'll protect you!"

Rien still didn't respond. The rest of the Watchmen sat back in silence.

Niyazi finally sank onto his ankles and stared at Rien in defeat. Yvan scooted forward to Niyazi's side. "Leave him alone. We'll just have to keep an eye on him until morning."

Yvan shot a sidelong glance at the two girls. He didn't say anything, but Yann read his father's expression loud and clear.

In any other Island, Yvan would have asked Eliska or Anríq to heal whatever was wrong with Rien—or at least to find out what was bothering him.

Yvan couldn't ask any of them that now.

How could a man completely devoid of magic see Darklings that weren't there—especially if this nightmare-vision matched what Eliska just described?

Niyazi stayed where he was for a minute and watched Rien jolting, jumping, and wheeling right and left. He gasped and sobbed in panic every time he did it. He kept cringing under his arms for protection.

Yann's heart went out to him. Whatever Rien saw terrified the life out of him, but no one could get rid of it.

The Watch could have fought the Darklings if real Darklings came after Rien. No one could fight Darklings they couldn't see.

"Could he be seeing invisible Darklings?" Yann murmured to Eliska.

She shrugged. "Anything is possible."

Yvan turned to Yann. "You said he had a nightmare."

Yann nodded. "I woke up in the middle of the night and I....." He broke off and decided not to tell his father about holding Eliska. "I heard him making noises in his sleep. I tried to wake him up, but he didn't respond. Then he started screaming and woke all of you up. That's when I shook him harder and he finally woke up—but then he didn't stop. He's been like this ever since."

"The nightmare I could understand—but not this." Yvan grimaced at Rien.

"What do you mean?" Eliska asked.

"Rien grew up in Middleborough. He was born there," Yvan replied. "He grew up watching the Dark encroach on the town and Darkling attacks that left the townspeople dead. He hates the Dark and the Layers outside the wall. That's why he joined the Watch."

She looked away. Maybe now she would understand why Rien hated her so much at the beginning.

Yann leaned back against the wall. He didn't return to his former place. He stayed next to Eliska.

No one else went back to sleep. They all stayed sitting up and keeping watch.

Niyazi rotated around and sat down next to Rien. Rien didn't respond to him or acknowledge Niyazi's presence.

No one said a word. One minute followed another and turned into hours. The men stayed sitting up and watchful for the rest of the night.

Chapter 10

Anríq returned, stuck his head into the charred, ruined house, and then ducked inside. He crossed the room to the corner where Rien huddled against the wall.

"He's exactly the same," Niyazi mumbled. "He never gets any better."

Anríq studied Rien for a minute and then looked away.

"You can't do anything, can you?" Niyazi croaked. "You can't help him without your magic."

Anríq shook his head down at the floor, turned away, and stood up.

Yann and Yvan both stood up at Anríq's arrival. "Did you see anything out there?" Yann asked. "Did you see anything from Rien's vision?"

"There's a front of wild magic moving this way," Anríq told them. "It's coming slowly. We won't have any problem keeping ahead of it—if we want to keep ahead of it."

"What other option is there?" Yvan asked.

"We could go straight into it and go somewhere else—somewhere Eliska, Marine, and I can get our magic back."

"We couldn't do that," Yvan countered. "We wouldn't survive traveling through the Layers."

"We could get you through the Layers if we got our magic back," Anríq explained.

"Why do you think we keep going through all these collapses and landscape shifts, but you still don't get your magic back?" Yann asked.

Anríq shrugged that away. "That's the problem, you see. The landscape might change with us still trapped in the same non-magical Layer—or we might be trapped in multiple non-magical Layers all collapsing on themselves, forming new Islands, and then fracturing again."

"What does that mean?" Yann asked.

"It means that, even if we went into the front and traveled out into the Layers, the three of us might not get our magic back. I can't guarantee that we *would* get our magic back—but I can guarantee that we *won't* get our magic back if we move away from this front and stay in this Island." Anríq turned back to the Watch Commander. "I can't make that decision for you."

Yvan scowled at him. "So you can't see anything beyond the front—like another landscape we might be able to get to if we went into it?"

"There is no landscape beyond the front," Anríq replied. "It's a chaos Layer breaking across this Island."

Yvan looked around. Niyazi still sat next to Rien. The rest of the party watched and listened to Anríq's report.

"We can't risk winding up in the Layers without your magic," Yvan finally decided. "We'll have to fall back to keep away from the front."

Those words got everyone moving. They all stood up—except for Rien. He jumped every few seconds and kept screaming, cringing, and yelling that the Darklings were trying to get him.

His behavior put everyone on edge. Eliska really wished he would shut the hell up, but she didn't say that.

She knew exactly how he felt. She didn't see Darklings around her right now, but she'd been suffering from the same mindless terror ever since the Watch fell into this Layer.

Now she couldn't even figure out which Layer the group was in or what to do about it.

Yvan and Anríq led the way outside. Omer, Neils, Vidal, and Barsali followed. Yann waited to escort Marine and Eliska outside.

Niyazi had to drag Rien to his feet and physically force him to leave the house. Rien screamed even louder, tried to fight his way out of Niyazi's grip, and fought back like Niyazi might be one of the Darklings haunting Rien.

Niyazi clamped his face shut in a granite wall of iron fury, tightened his grip on Rien's arm, and shoved him through the door.

The volcano landscape bubbled away the same as always. Nothing changed in this Island.

"Which direction is the front coming from?" Yvan asked.

Anríq pointed toward the lava river. "Over there."

"All right." Yvan ordered. "Let's move out."

The group fell into another loose formation heading in the opposite direction. Niyazi stayed in the very back this time. He never let go of Rien once.

Rien didn't notice anything except Niyazi holding onto him. Rien struggled every step of the way.

Eliska forced herself to face front. Rien's constant whimpering and yelping noises set her nerves on end. She would have given anything to make him be quiet—or at least face him in case he put the group in danger.

She didn't give herself the option to turn around. That would only agitate her more. She forced herself to keep walking no matter what.

Yann stayed behind the two girls in a guarding posture.

Yvan took the lead this time even though he couldn't possibly know where he was going. He set off through the lava fields, picked his way around rivers and rivulets, and sprang over sulfur beds to avoid the worst dangers.

Two lines of volcanic mountains rimmed the horizon going off in different directions. The mountain ranges converged in the center.

They looked like they might end in a staggered pattern with a pass between them, but Eliska couldn't be sure from this distance.

The lava fields had leveled most of the countryside. Only a few small hills rose out of a smooth, melted sheet of solidified rock.

The group had to climb one of these hills to continue on their way. Yvan stopped at the top and Anríq went over to him. They both turned around to check the terrain behind the party.

Eliska and the others stayed down on the flat ground. Thirst drove her out of her mind. These people wouldn't survive much longer without water.

They wouldn't find any water in this wasteland. The gap between the mountains looked miles away—maybe even hundreds of miles away—if there was a gap there at all.

Even if the group made it that far, no one could guarantee they would find water there—or anything other than more of this volcanic Island world.

Eliska never thought she'd live to see the day when she would wish the Darklings would attack and send her to another Layer.

She sure wished it now. If she had magic, she would have shattered this Layer long ago. Now she was stuck here—maybe forever.

Anríq's voice snapped her back to reality. "The front is moving faster than it was before," he told Yvan. "It will overtake us."

"Then we better keep moving." Yvan headed down the hill to rejoin the others. "If it can speed up, it might slow down and give us time to put some distance between us and it."

Anríq followed him back down to level ground. Yvan turned away to lead the party on their former route.

At that moment, Rien jerked out of Niyazi's hold. Eliska kept her back to them as much as possible. She didn't see if Niyazi relaxed his grip at all or if Rien just got the jump on him by leaping away so suddenly.

Rien sprang clear, landed ten feet away, and before anyone could move, he drew both his weapons.

He spun this way and that hacking at thin air. "Get away from me!" he screeched. "Get away from me, you fiends!"

Niyazi charged forward to intercept him. "RIEN!!"

Rien didn't hear or even see him. Rien spun the other way, chopped his broken sword at an invisible enemy, and stabbed with his left hand.

The other Watchmen moved in. Yvan stormed forward and stared at Rien from outside his weapons range.

The group watched him for a second before Yvan compressed his lips. "We'll have to restrain him. Anríq and Barsali, move in front of him and try to engage or disarm him. Vidal, you and Niyazi get behind Rien. As soon as they distract him, the three of us will tackle him and hold him down while the others take his weapons."

Everyone nodded. Eliska backed off. She didn't want to get involved in this.

Yann, Neils, and Omer moved forward to back up the rest of the Watch.

Anríq and Barsali drew their weapons and pivoted in front of Rien, but he kept swiveling back and forth. He didn't stay facing in any particular direction.

Yvan, Vidal, and Niyazi angled themselves behind Rien, but they wound up having the same problem. He occasionally faced them brandishing both weapons.

He kept slashing the air and yelling for the invisible Darklings to get away from him. No one could get an opening.

"That's it," Yvan growled after a few minutes. "The next time he turns away from us, we'll charge him."

Vidal and Niyazi both nodded and braced themselves to pounce.

Rien spun their way and immediately wheeled to hack his blade in the opposite direction.

Anríq darted forward at exactly that moment, hefted his club, and caught Rien's broken sword on the club's spikes.

Rien came to his senses for a split second when the two weapons met. His eyes cleared just enough to see Anríq standing in front of him with their weapons locked together.

The next instant, Yvan, Vidal, and Niyazi rushed in from behind.

They made it within two feet of Rien's back. He didn't disengage his weapon from Anríq's club in time to stop anyone from tackling him, taking him down, and maybe even tying him up.

At that moment, some unseen force struck Vidal across the side of the head. It hit him hard enough to knock him over.

It must have knocked him out cold because he toppled sideways. He didn't use his arms to break his fall before his whole body hit the ground in one stiff plank.

"VIDAL!!" Yann roared and sprinted forward.

He raised his glaive, spun around, and swiped the weapon in all directions trying to see what hit Vidal.

Neils and Omer saw the blow, too. They both rushed in to defend Vidal, but there was nothing there.

Yvan and Niyazi didn't realize what happened. They were both running too fast to grab Rien.

They got to him a second after it happened, yanked his arms away from Anríq's club, and tore the weapons out of Rien's hands.

He sprang away just as fast and went back to jerking here and there, gasping and whimpering in terror, and retreating from invisible Darklings.

Yvan glanced behind him in time to see Vidal on the ground with Yann, Neils, and Omer standing over him with their weapons drawn.

Yvan frowned at them.

Eliska rushed behind the men and bent over Vidal. A big purple welt covered the side of his face and ran up to his temple. The bruise kept swelling and a clear, dark slash marked the center of the bruise where something hit him.

"What the hell happened to him?!" Yvan snapped.

"Something hit him," Eliska explained.

"What was it?" Yvan demanded. "I didn't see anything."

Eliska opened her mouth to answer, but no sound came out. How could she explain any of this to the Watch Commander?

Omer saved her by speaking up in her place. "There was nothing there. It came out of nowhere. Whatever it was must have been invisible. It hit him without warning and he fell."

Yvan glared at everyone and then scowled down at Vidal. He didn't move.

Eliska touched his head before she remembered. She didn't have the magic to heal him. No one did, not even Anríq.

All the Watchmen exchanged glances and then searched the area. There was nothing here except Rien fighting invisible Darklings.

Could there really be something unseen here attacking not just him but Vidal, too?

Another wave of impending doom swept through Eliska's insides. She couldn't stay here.

Part of her wanted to run straight into the front of wild magic bearing down on the party.

She might get lucky and break through into another Layer where she would get her magic back. Anything would be better than this.

The Watchmen rotated in all directions aiming their weapons outward. They all searched the area for unseen enemies exactly the way Rien did.

He kept gasping, whining, and occasionally breaking out in yells. He no longer had his weapons, so he swatted the Darklings away with his bare hands.

"Get away from me!" he screeched. "Get off me, you bastards!"

Anríq walked over to him. Anríq walked steadily with no sign of slowing down.

The sight gave Eliska an inexpressible feeling of relief. Anríq would fix it. Anríq could heal anyone.....if he only had his magic back.

Before he got there, a blaze of light drew everyone's attention. It flared behind the party twenty feet in the direction the group had just come.

The same old man in the long white robe with the halo of brilliant light around him appeared standing there on the lava fields. He glared at the Watchmen just as menacingly.

The Watchmen rushed forward into a line and brandished their weapons at the Voyant, but at that moment, a curtain of shimmering sparks and lightning swept across the landscape.

It came from behind the Voyant, swept past him, and overtook the Watch before anyone could get away.

Eliska barely had time to stand up. The Voyant vanished behind the veil—and just as fast, Eliska's blood ran cold when she saw massive Darklings materialize right behind the sheet of flashing light and magical explosions.

These didn't look like any other Darklings the party encountered on their travels. These had a spikier look with some kind of plate armor covering their bodies.

Their tentacles looked like some kind of jointed mechanical appendages studded with razor blades and slashing sharp edges.

They functioned the same as tentacles, but the Darklings moved like some kind of machines instead of just monstrous shapes.

The Watchmen closed together with their weapons drawn, but at that moment, Rien screamed again. "They're here! They're here! That's them! They're the Darklings from my nightmare!"

He came out of whatever hallucination had been clouding his mind and rushed in to join the other Watchmen. He didn't have his weapons anymore after Niyazi took them away from him.

Niyazi didn't try to stop Rien from snatching both weapons back. He moved right into line with the others and aimed his weapons at the incoming Darklings.

None of the party got a chance to fight before the front of wild magic overtook them first.

A charge of energy crackled through the air as the front moved in. It raced across the landscape too fast for anyone to get away and bore down on the party in a wall of powerful, explosive energy.

The next instant, the front swept the group and the world blasted apart. A deep boom hit Eliska, tore her off her feet, and sent her spinning off somewhere.

Chapter 11

Yann slammed down hard on dry grass. He wasn't in the volcanic landscape anymore.

The next minute, Eliska, Marine, Anríq, and the other Watchmen slammed down on the ground near him.

He got onto his hands and knees to see if they were all right. As soon as he got into that position, his heart stopped when he saw the land caving in only a dozen yards away.

The soil crumbled and dropped off into a bottomless void of Darkness and vapor in some Layer somewhere.

The collapsing landscape inched closer right behind Eliska. She lay on the ground groaning and peeling herself out of the grass. The land fell away behind her where she couldn't see it coming closer to her feet.

"ELISKA!!" Yann yelled and dove for her, but not fast enough.

The instability dropped out from underneath her and she started to plummet. She screamed out, clawed at the grass, and tried to pull herself back up, but she fell too fast.

Before Yann could get there, Anríq dove for her. He happened to land just a few feet closer.

He seized her by the wrist and hauled her onto solid ground. They both scrambled to get out of the way in time.

The collapse didn't stop coming. Nothing could stop it.

It fell out from under Marine next. She went through the same process of screaming and trying to scuttle onto stable ground as the world dissolved underneath her.

Yann threw himself toward the edge to grab her, but everything solid evaporated the instant he got there.

He hurtled at her and caught her before they both plunged off into nothing. She screamed in his ear. "HOLD ON TO ME!!" he yelled back.

He didn't dare to look to see where they were or where they were going. They could be floating in the Layers forever if she didn't get her magic back.

He clamped his arms around her slender frame. She clung to him with all her might—and then they broke through some stretchy, rubbery barrier and hit the side of a hill.

They both crashed onto grass again—cool, green grass this time.

The rest of the Watch all tumbled down the same hill and sprawled on level ground at the bottom.

Yvan sat up rubbing his head. "I really gotta find a way to stop doing that."

Marine pushed herself off of Yann. He had to concentrate to make himself loosen his hold on her.

She pushed off his chest with one hand and propped herself on one elbow while she looked around. Then she looked straight down into his face from above.

Her hair hung around her cheeks and those deep, dark eyes caught him in an unimaginable tide.

She burst into the biggest, brightest, most angelic smile he'd ever seen. Her cheeks flushed and her skin glowed.

"Thank you, Yann!" she gasped.

He didn't know what to say. He just wanted to lie here on his back and look up at her forever, but another groan distracted both of them.

She sat up and so he did. The rest of the Watchmen picked themselves up. Anríq and Eliska sat next to each other fifteen feet away from Yann and Marine. Vidal leaned against the hillside holding his head.

"Are you okay?" Yvan asked him.

"No!" Vidal snarled. "My head is killing me."

"I'm not surprised after the way you got hit," Omer told him. "It's a miracle you're conscious at all."

"What happened?" Vidal demanded. "I never saw it coming."

"We don't know what happened," Neils told him. "None of us saw what hit you."

Vidal looked up. "You must have."

"There was nothing there," Neils replied. "You were running in to help Niyazi and the Watch Commander take care of Rien. The next minute, something hit you in the head and you fell over."

Vidal touched the bruise on the side of his face. "Damn! It hurts like hell."

"I'm telling you that was them!" Rien blurted out. His voice spiked to a shriek. "I'm telling you that was the Darklings I saw before! They were right there! They came after me! I'm telling the truth!"

Everyone turned around to stare at him.

He sat on the grass with the others, but he definitely recognized everyone now. He knew exactly where he was.

Yvan turned to Anríq. "Do you have your magic back? Can you heal him?"

"I don't have my magic back," Anríq murmured.

"Are you sure there's nothing else you can do for him?" Yvan persisted. "Anything at all?"

"There's nothing wrong with him," Anríq replied. "He's whole. He's just scared."

"How do you know he isn't seeing things?" Yvan asked. "He could be out of his mind. Without your magic...."

"He isn't seeing things," Marine interrupted in a tiny voice. "I've seen them, too."

Yvan spun around to stare at her, too. "You have?"

Rien dove for her, grabbed her arm, and pawed at her hand. "Oh, thank you!" he practically sobbed. "I thought I was going crazy. You've seen them? You know what they are? Tell me you've seen them."

"You aren't going crazy," she murmured. "I saw them in nightmares and then we all saw them in that sheet of magic that just took us."

"I saw them, too," Eliska murmured. "I had a nightmare about them that same night when Rien did."

"Are you sure they were the same kind?" Yann asked.

She nodded down at the grass. "They had the same armor and the same mechanical joints. I've never seen that kind of Darkling anywhere else."

"Neither have I," Marine replied. "I've never even heard of them."

"I thought they were only a nightmare," Eliska went on. "And then Vidal got hit....."

"This could be a completely new kind of Darkling," Marine suggested. "The instability could be morphing them into new, more dangerous Darklings that are more destructive. It could all be part of the same process."

"They aren't new." Omer's voice sent a chill through the group. "I've seen them before."

Everyone turned around the other way to face him.

He squinted away in another direction and didn't make eye contact with anyone. He barely spoke above a whisper, but his voice sent a prickle up Yann's scalp.

"You were too polite to ask me how I got to Middleborough," Omer murmured. "You were too happy to take any fighting man into the Watch. You wouldn't have been so quick to accept me if you knew where I came from."

No one made a sound. Yann didn't dare to breathe. Omer never talked about his past. He joined the Watch as a teenager when Yann was just a boy.

Omer grew up in the Watch and eventually took his oath when he got old enough. He never said a word about his family or his former life in all that time.

"I was born the only imp in a family of magic-users. I had to learn to fight to make up for not having magic. My family and their party fought the Darklings."

Omer shut his eyes, turned his head farther away, and his voice broke.

"I grew up from an early age watching the people I loved being torn apart and devoured. I couldn't take it anymore. I started to lose my mind. My family brought me to Middleborough and turned me over to the Watch so I could heal, but I will never forget those things I've seen." He heaved a shaky sigh, opened his eyes, and narrowed his eyes at the horizon. "Now it's all starting over again."

Yann wouldn't have broken that silence for any money, but Yvan did it instead.

He scrambled to his feet. "We can't stay here. Everybody get up. We have to keep moving."

Yann stood up automatically. His body responded instinctively to his father's order.

As soon as everyone stood up, they all saw that they were in another woodland. A few larger towns surrounded the area not too many miles away from where the Watch landed.

Yvan started walking, but the towns turned out to be farther away than anyone realized.

Everyone kept glancing around in agitation. Both Yann and Anríq stayed near the two girls. No one acted like this was anything out of the ordinary. The girls didn't, either.

The sun started to go down long before the group got near a town. Yann couldn't fathom what the Watch would do once they got there.

Chapter 12

Yvan turned off into a patch of woods, found a stream where they could all quench their thirst, and told everyone to make camp.

The Watchmen went through the old routine in silence. Vidal and Niyazi went hunting and came back with a biturong. It wasn't much, but it was better than nothing.

No one spoke around the fire. Rien kept grimacing, biting his lips, and rocking back and forth.

Neils cut up the cooked meat and handed it out as usual, but he did that in silence, too. A cloud hung over the group as they chewed their food.

Without any warning, Marine put her portion of the meat down, looked up at the faces glowing in the firelight, and started to sing.

Her clear, high voice drifted through the woods in a haunting melody.

"There once was a fair maid lived in Strawberry Lane
Loved by her master and her mistress the same.
But then a young sailor lad came sailing o'er the sea
And that was the beginning of her misery!"

Some of the Watchmen laughed. She grinned back at them before she launched into the rest of the song about how the sailor seduced the maid before he left her to return to sea.

Her voice sent another wave of goosebumps over Yann's skin. Her face radiated so much warmth and vitality. Her eyes sparkled with understanding and innocent fun when she made eye contact with each man one after another.

She shot an even kinder, more understanding smile at Rien, and when she saw him still anxious about his recent episode, she squeezed his hand.

"Where did you learn that song?" Barsali asked when she finished.

She laughed like his question was the funniest thing in the world. Her cheeks flushed and her eyelashes dipped so perfectly. She did everything perfectly. She really was a princess even when she was dirty.

"Would you believe it?!" she exclaimed. "There was a stable boy at the Temple where I trained. He fell in love with one of the kitchen girls and he used to sing that song to her to make her laugh. I got in so much trouble for spying on them and eavesdropping on their conversations."

"You're a rascal," Vidal told her. "You should have left them alone."

"Oh, they never found out I spied on them. I wouldn't do that to them. It was Master Octavi who busted me sneaking around watching them. He said such things were beneath me." She burst out in musical laughter again and then sighed. "The Templars should try it sometime. They would be so much happier."

"So did the stable boy seduce the kitchen maid and then run off to sea?" Neils asked. "Did he get her pregnant and leave her destitute?"

"Oh, no! They got married and he became the head groom and she became matron of the whole Temple. Everything worked out for them, but I guess that doesn't make for a very interesting story, does it?"

A few Watchmen laughed again. "Tell us another story from the Temple, Marine," Niyazi urged.

She giggled. "There was this other initiate when I was there. She was about my age and she became obsessed with one of the younger Brothers. She used to spend all her time in the dormitory planning how to catch him and bed him. She found books in the library on how to bewitch him into coming to her bed at night so no one found out what they were doing."

"But if you were in a dormitory, wouldn't *you* find out what they were doing?" Eliska asked.

Marine laughed even louder. "Of course! I would have been lying in the next bed watching everything—but fortunately for me, it never happened. She used to take these forbidden spell books into our study halls and put them inside the books we were supposed to be reading. She even muttered incantations when he was the Brother taking our classes."

"So what happened?" Niyazi asked.

"Master Octavi found her out. He took one of our classes and he had a habit of pacing around the room. He happened to pass her desk and realized she had another book inside the one she was supposed to be reading. He may also have seen her lips moving when they shouldn't have been. Anyway, he took the book and then, whoo! You can imagine the commotion when everyone realized what she was doing."

"What did they do to her?" Eliska asked.

"They threw her out. They sent her home and wrote a letter to her father saying she wasn't 'Templar' material." Marine made air quotes around her ears and snickered again. "She really wasn't. She thought of nothing all day long besides bedding some man. She was a hopeless scoundrel."

"What about you?" Omer interjected. "What were you thinking about while you were spying on the stable boy and the kitchen maid?

I'll bet you were as much of a scoundrel as she was—maybe even more."

Marine turned bright red and burst into childish giggles, but her eyes only twinkled at him. "I have no idea what you're talking about, Omer! I would never do something like that! How can you think that about me?!"

She made him laugh, too, which was a herculean feat.

"So which of the Brothers did you dream about bedding?" Niyazi asked. "Were any of them young enough for you?"

She wouldn't stop laughing. "Most of them were old enough to be living skeletons, but there were a few young enough to catch a girl's eye."

"A few!" Neils countered. "What would your father say?"

"He would never find out because I know how to keep those things to myself." She beamed around the circle. "I wouldn't dream of telling anyone if I was anywhere but here with all of you."

"That is truly a privilege, Marine," Niyazi replied. "Your secrets are safe with us."

She laughed again. Her behavior lightened the mood considerably, and when the conversation didn't restart, she started singing again.

She sang a softer, more melodious song this time. It was a much sadder love song, but her beautiful voice only eased the tension even more. It didn't make the men sad.

Yann found himself gazing at her across the fire. What a tragedy that she became insane by communing with the Dark forces. How much longer would the Watch be able to enjoy her company before she went back to that?

The idea of losing her became unbearable, but Yann himself wouldn't be able to prevent it. He just had to appreciate her while it lasted.

He became increasingly aware of Eliska's reaction as the song went on. She didn't look at Marine the way the men did.

Eliska turned her face away with a pained grimace. The two girls had been acting so friendly before. Yann didn't understand Eliska's distaste for what Marine was doing.

Marine didn't notice until she finished singing. Eliska sat next to her, so Marine looking all around the circle at the men distracted her from seeing Eliska's expression.

When Marine finished, she happened to glance down at Eliska sitting by her side. Eliska looked up at her at the same time and their eyes connected.

Marine saw Eliska's features twisted in misery, but Marine only smiled even more warmly if that was possible.

Marine shot out her hand and squeezed Eliska's wrist once before Marine went back to staring into the flames.

"Will you be able to sleep tonight, Rien?" Marine asked.

Rien stopped searching the dark woods on all sides. He dropped his eyes to the ground, but he didn't stop rocking and chewing his lips. "I don't know, young one. I really don't know. I wish I could."

"Do you still see Darklings everywhere?" she asked.

He nodded down at the earth between his boots. "All the time. They never go away."

"What does that mean?" Yann asked. "Does it mean those Darklings are here but invisible or does it mean something else?"

"Those Darklings came with the Voyant," Marine replied. "I would think they have something to do with him....."

"They don't," Omer interrupted.

Everyone turned to face him. "What do they mean, then?" Marine asked.

"They're just a different manifestation of the Dark—a deeper level of Dark," Omer replied. "That's what my father said. He said the Dark gets concentrated when the Coil degenerates. The Darklings become more dangerous and more sophisticated as the chaos increases."

"How could he know that if he didn't live through a destabilization cycle?" Eliska asked.

Yann thought of something else just then. "Do you know Costico Nastase? He belongs to a family of magic-users who fought Dark forces."

Omer only nodded at the flames. "He's my cousin."

"Does that help us?" Neils asked. "Does any of this help us deal with this situation?"

"It doesn't help us deal with the Voyant," Yvan replied. "If that was the Voyant we saw earlier."

"It was," Marine replied. "He appeared to Eliska and me when we got separated from you."

"Why is he appearing to us now?" Yann asked. "Is it because his Darklings keep failing to capture whatever it is he wants?"

"He doesn't use his magic against us," Eliska pointed out. "Maybe he doesn't actually want anything from us—except maybe to talk to us. Maybe that's why he's been following us."

"That's impossible," Yvan pointed out. "He wouldn't have sent Darklings after Middleborough for two whole years if he wanted to talk to us. He wouldn't have hired Barbarians to attack us if he only wanted to talk to us."

Eliska shrugged. "Okay. You're right—but that doesn't explain why he doesn't use his magic against us. He could have flattened us both times, but he didn't. He only showed himself to us."

"He used that magical curtain against us," Barsali pointed out. "That flattened us."

"It took us to another Layer, but it didn't kill us," she countered. "He could have. He could kill us anytime he wants."

"Why do you think he wants us, then?" Yann asked.

"I have no idea, but it can't be to kill us."

"He's killing plenty of other people," Marine pointed out. "Even if he doesn't want to kill us specifically, he's killing too many other people for us to just let him get away with it."

"From what I can tell, none of us has the power to stop him. You, me, and Anríq don't have the power to stop him even if we combined our magic together—and we don't even have any magic right now."

Marine opened her mouth to argue, but she stopped herself, cocked her head, and frowned when she finally realized what Eliska was saying.

"The question remains what we're going to do about all of this," Omer interjected. "If he's coming to us, then maybe the best policy is just to stand and wait for him to come. Maybe then we can at least find out what he wants. I don't know about the rest of you, but I'm tired of running."

"We have no choice but to move around if things continue to destabilize and every Island we come to collapses with us in it," Eliska pointed out. "We haven't run from him since the snow Island, but the Coil keeps sending us to different places. Deciding that we don't want to run from him might not make much difference in terms of what we actually do."

"Well, what do you think we should do?" Omer countered. "If we don't run and we can't fight him, what other option is there?"

Right then, something snapped out in the forest to one side.

Rien jumped out of his skin. His head shot up and he jolted to spin in that direction.

Everyone else looked, too. They all held their breath and listened. Something rustled out there. It traveled sideways, rummaged in the bushes, and eventually moved off.

Niyazi let his shoulders slump. "It's nothing. It's just a night animal."

That scare killed the conversation, but the men didn't fall back into the same gloomy depression.

Each man drifted into his own thoughts. No one made any effort to draw anyone else out, but the atmosphere stayed thoughtful instead of doomed.

Yvan finally stretched out on the ground, propped his head against a fallen stump, and shut his eyes. Barsali went to sleep next and the other men followed one after the other.

Eventually, even Rien curled up on the ground by the fire. He kept his eyes open and stared out into the forest for a long time, but in the end, he closed them and his breathing lengthened.

Yann stayed awake watching each person drift off. The two girls fell asleep near each other. He watched them for a while letting his own thoughts drift.

He marveled as much over how much he'd changed as how much both of them had changed.

No one in their party doubted any longer that Eliska was one of them. Whatever happened to her, she remained as staunchly committed to the Watch as any of the men.

Yann would probably never find out what made her change her mind. He didn't need to.

He admired her even more now because of that than he did when she had the magic to save them all. That moment in the charred ruin flipped a switch between her and the Watch as much as it did for Yann.

Whatever happened, it would happen to all of them. They were all in this now, for good or bad.

He still found it nearly impossible to believe how much Marine had changed. He never would have believed she could be like this—so warm and irresistibly attractive—and not because she was so beautiful.

She dedicated everything to stopping the Voyant, too. She went into the Dark to carry out her mission to help everyone in the Coil—and she would do it again. That was the hardest part to accept.

Everything great and wonderful about her would vanish in a breath of wind the next time the Coil turned.

A soft voice drifted out of the darkness to Yann's side. "You should sleep, too, Yann."

He glanced over to find Anríq sitting next to him. Yann couldn't look at his friend. "I should, but I don't want to."

"You must be tired," Anríq pointed out.

"I am. What about you? Are you going to sleep?"

"I will eventually."

Yann didn't say anything else. Anríq must have a lot on his mind, too. He might even be thinking all the same things Yann was thinking.

Yann didn't ask. He and Anríq stayed up sitting in silence for a long time watching over the others.

Everything Yann cared about in the world was right here. Wandering the Coil as a Servant was all very fine and noble.

It meant nothing compared to his dedication to these people right here. They deserved his service more than anyone else. Their mission was his mission—however they managed to carry it out—if they could even carry it out.

He didn't know what would happen to them tomorrow, but he would dedicate his best effort to them. He couldn't think of anything finer or nobler than that.

Chapter 13

Yann woke up earlier than he expected the next day. He thought he would sleep longer after staying up so late.

He raked his hair out of his eyes and stiffened when he saw Eliska standing off at a distance from all the sleeping Watchmen.

Yann got to his feet and went over to her. "Are you okay?" he murmured. "Did you have more nightmares?"

She waved her hand at nothing. "It's always like that. I've been having them for years. These are no different—except that the Darklings look different. These are the armored kind. I've never seen them before, so I don't know if the visions are coming from somewhere else or....." She shut her eyes and shook that thought out of her head. "I don't know what it means."

"Omer says the Dark is building in strength. Maybe that has something to do with it."

"I don't know." She looked away. "It sounds like he knows more about these Darklings than any of us."

"Just hold out a little longer. We'll eventually wind up in a Layer where you'll get your magic back. I mean.....everything keeps changing so fast. That has to change, too, doesn't it?"

She smiled up at him, but her features pinched. "Thanks. Thank you for everything you said the other night. I'm really grateful."

"I meant it. You're part of us now. We won't let anything happen to you."

Her lips trembled and her cheek spasmed. He really wanted to put his arms around her again, but just then, Marine stirred in her sleep.

She didn't wake up, but the movement drew Yann's and Eliska's attention back to the group.

"Did she do or say something to upset you yesterday?" Yann murmured. "Why did her stories bother you so much? I thought you liked her."

Eliska's voice rasped with buried emotion. "I do like her. I love her." She choked on the words and ran her hand across her face. "She's so.....so wonderful. I can't stand the thought of losing her. I've never met anyone like her....but I know I will lose her. She's the only friend I've ever had. She's so beautiful—inside and out. She's everything I wish I could be...."

"You're all those things, too," he insisted. "Don't you know how wonderful and beautiful you are?"

Him saying that only seemed to upset her even more. "She's special. She can at least make all of you feel better—if only for one night. She doesn't need magic to do it. She can do it with her voice and her eyes and her stories. I wish I could give you something like that...."

"You do," Yann breathed. "You care about us. Do you think we all don't see how much you care? None of us wants to lose you—and not because of your magic. You have something....something special....something special to all of us. You must know that by now."

She started to say, "I'm not like her....."

Right then, Rien woke up. He sat up, but he didn't look around. He bent over the coals and added a few twigs to make them smoke back into flames.

Yann and Eliska both returned to the circle without saying another word. They sat down in their old places across from each other.

Eliska proved everything Yann just said by turning to Rien. "How do you feel this morning?"

"I'm all right, I guess," he mumbled without looking up. "I don't know what happened to me."

"From what I saw, everything that happened to you happened to the rest of us," Yann interjected. "Something hit Vidal. Just because you were the only one who could see those Darklings doesn't mean they weren't there."

Rien's eyes shot up. "Do you think so?"

"How else can you explain what happened to Vidal?" Yann waved at the area around them. "Anything is possible in this chaos. I don't think any of us can doubt that anymore."

Their voices woke up everyone else. Yvan frowned when he saw Rien sitting there as quietly and calmly as anyone could hope.

"How are you feeling this morning, man?" Yvan asked.

Rien nodded. "I feel okay. I don't know what happened."

"Maybe it just passed—or maybe this Island made it better," Eliska suggested.

Their comments brought Rien farther out of his shell. He actually started to smile and his shoulders relaxed a little more.

The upturn only lasted a few minutes before the other men woke up. It became all too obvious all too soon that all was not right with the world.

Barsali left camp right away. He vanished into the trees, and when he came back, he paced back and forth apart from the camp. He didn't come back to rejoin everyone.

Vidal got to his feet, too, and started obsessively checking his weapons in between darting furtive glances into the forest.

Their behavior put Yvan and the others on edge. No one dared to go near those two.

Neils pretended not to see them. The group had finished off the biturong last night and no one ventured out to find anything else.

"We'll continue on to the town today. We shouldn't have any problem getting there this morning." Yvan went over to Vidal. "How's your head?"

"Fine," Vidal snapped and went back to what he was doing.

Yvan scowled at him. "Is there something I should know?"

"No," Vidal snapped. He kept adjusting the leather strap around his axe handle.

Yvan scrutinized him at close range. The bruise on the side of Vidal's head looked exactly the same.

He refused to meet the Watch Commander's gaze. That on its own meant something must be wrong.

Yvan left him there and went to check on Barsali. Barsali paced far enough away from camp that no one could hear their conversation.

Barsali didn't ignore the Watch Commander nor did Barsali give Yvan one-word answers. Yann and the others heard them talking at length, but Barsali still paced back and forth in front of Yvan. Barsali never stood still even for a second.

"I wonder if they had nightmares, too," Marine murmured.

"Did any of the rest of you have them?" Eliska asked.

"I always have them," Omer husked. "I've been having them all my life—but now I see the armored Darklings instead of the regular kind."

"It's the same for me," she told him. "What about the rest of you?"

"I've been having nightmares ever since we came to this Layer...if it is a Layer." Marine cast a desperate glance around the area. "I never had nightmares before—definitely not about the Dark or Darklings. I always felt comfortable there."

"Should we be worried that you're comfortable with Darklings?" Neils asked.

She burst into a grin, but just then, Yvan returned and squatted down with the others. "Barsali's all right. He had nightmares last night, but he's certain he'll be okay. He wants to travel, so we'll move out."

Everyone stood up. The air of tension followed the group out of the forest and back to the open countryside where they landed before.

The others set off, but Eliska stopped there just outside the tree line.

"What's wrong?" Yann asked.

"The town," she murmured. "It's the same distance away that it was yesterday. We don't get any closer."

"You're right!" Marine exclaimed. "I didn't notice before!"

"What does that mean?" Yann asked.

"This happened to us when Eliska and I were by ourselves. We tried to get to a city, but it always stayed the same distance away."

"And then we found out we were in an illusion Layer," Eliska finished.

The others gathered around to listen. "Are you saying this is all an illusion?"

"We may be in the land of nightmares," Anríq suggested. "We could be trapped in someone's nightmare—or in a bad memory."

Rien spun around to stare at him. "You can do that?!"

"Any landscape is possible in the Coil," Anríq replied. "We don't have the magic to find out where we are, but it would explain why all of you keep having nightmares."

The men scanned the landscape. Yann didn't see anything to threaten the party here, but maybe whatever threatened them was inside their own minds. That would be disastrous.

Yvan recovered first. "We'll have to test it. We'll walk toward the town and see if the same thing...."

He broke off and the whole group froze when the Voyant appeared before them again.

He didn't attack this time, either—not outright.

The instant he appeared, the landscape went haywire all around the party. The trees twisted out of position, stretched their limbs in all directions, changed into different shapes, and then erupted into Darklings.

These Darklings remained rooted in one place. They couldn't move. They thrashed and bellowed while they lashed their limbs everywhere, but the tree Darklings didn't attack the party, either.

The ground swelled and undulated all over the place. The road in the distance whipped from side to side. It no longer led in any particular direction.

The disruption caught the nearest town in the upheaval. Buildings blasted out of position and came alive only to collapse just as fast.

Bizarre creatures ejected from the soil only to get pulled back down by some unseen force beneath the surface.

A tempest broke out around the Voyant himself. Wind lashed in a whirling hurricane. The storm snatched up sticks, rocks, and debris from the ground.

All that crap revolved around him in a spiraling tornado, but none of it touched him. He stood at the center of his halo scowling as fiercely as ever. Not a hair on his head rustled in the wind.

Niyazi rushed forward raising his battle axe to attack the Voyant. Neils, Rien, and Omer stepped out of line to back up Niyazi.

Anríq dodged in front of them and held out his arm to stop them. "Don't touch him!"

"Are you out of your tree?!" Rien countered. "He's the one doing all of this! He destroyed Middleborough!"

"Attacking him outright always backfires on us," Anríq replied. "Remember what happened to Wesh? Don't attack him. Back off, Niyazi."

Niyazi obeyed him, but at that moment, a broken roar made everyone spin around fast. The Watchmen all raised their weapons to defend themselves.

Everyone froze a second time when Barsali lunged away from the group heading back toward the trees, but he didn't go into them.

He swung his battle axe and hacked the air. "Get away from me, you demons! Get away! Don't touch me!"

Rien's sword arm drooped to his side. "No!" he whimpered. "No, Barsali!"

Barsali didn't see or hear a thing. He kept hacking his axe at nothing, gasping in terror, and whirling somewhere else to defend himself against something that wasn't there.

The other Watchmen lowered their weapons one after another. Everyone stared at Barsali in defeat as the madness took him.

No one suggested tackling him to take his axe away from him. No one said a word.

He blundered close enough to the forest for one of the tree Darklings to hit him with its branch. It clipped the side of his shoulder.

He wheeled backward and chopped the limb with his axe. He severed it and the tree Darkling bellowed in pain and rage.

That roar sent a thunderclap through the surrounding countryside. The whole Island erupted in chaos at that moment. It didn't shatter or dissolve or fall apart. It just went completely insane in every possible way.

The short-clipped grass by the side of the road blasted out of the ground growing impossibly fast.

It tangled together in a solid wall of vegetation. Ever-lengthening stems twined around each other and knotted into ropes that thickened into pillars.

Pebbles lying peacefully by the roadside swelled and kept growing into boulders and eventually towering cliffs.

The buildings in the nearby town exploded in size, grew to gargantuan proportions, and morphed into monstrous shapes before they came alive, too.

The Voyant evaporated out of sight, and at some unseen signal, all those pillars of grass, massive cliffs, and towering grotesque buildings burst to life and turned into Darklings.

"Run!" Yvan yelled.

"Where?!" Neils hollered back.

Everyone in the party hesitated for a second while they considered where to go. They couldn't go back into the forest—not with all those whipping demonic trees thrashing their branches everywhere.

The group couldn't go out into the open—not with every single thing in the landscape turning into a Darkling.

The group got trapped there between the forest and everything else. The Darklings didn't come for the Watch this time—at least Yann didn't see them come for the Watch.

Darklings materialized out of all the stuff around the Watch—all the stuff that was already there before.

The Darklings didn't seem to attack each other, either. They just blundered around roaring and going crazy for no apparent reason.

They stumbled closer to the Watch by sheer accident. One of the Darklings would step on someone pretty soon.

Yvan hustled everyone sideways to follow the tree line. It was the only direction any of them could go.

"This way!" he ordered. "Keep moving!"

Yann turned away, but Eliska turned back. "Barsali!" she cried. "Barsali's in trouble!"

She took a few steps in Barsali's direction. Yann followed her and saw Barsali standing right at the edge of the trees.

A bunch of the tree Darklings' branches had caught him by his arms. More snaked around his chest and one wrapped around his thigh.

He struggled in panic, yelled, and screamed as he jerked from side to side trying to free himself. His axe lay on the ground next to him.

Eliska rushed the axe, used all her strength to heave it off the ground, and hacked away the branch around his right arm.

He broke free, but that only drew the tree Darklings' attention to Eliska.

They sent more lashing branches to capture her. She could barely lift Barsali's massive axe.

She tried to fight the branches off, and when that failed, she swung again and severed the branch on his left arm.

Freeing him seemed to bring him out of his insanity—at least a little bit. His vision cleared and his eyes locked on Eliska.

She charged him and held out his axe to give it back to him. He could free himself the rest of the way once he got his hands on it.

He held out his hand to take it from her, but at that moment, a catastrophic wave of destruction hit the landscape coming from beyond the town.

Yann didn't see it until a bunch of Darklings roared out there. He glanced in their direction just in time to see them plummet off the edge of the earth into nothing.

The town toppled out of sight and the wave chewed its way across the landscape swallowing every Darkling in its path.

Yann dove for Eliska to pull her away in time. He didn't have a clue where he would take her and he didn't plan to leave Barsali in danger, either, even though two more branches still held him in place.

Yann's brain didn't get as far as deciding how he would do that or even registering that he had to do it.

"ELISKA!!" he yelled and tried to grab her.

He turned his back on the wave for a split second and it yanked him away into a bottomless void.

Chapter 14

E liska blinked the stars out of her eyes and sat up trying to figure out where she was. The first thing she saw was Yann and Anríq both sitting near her.

Dry brown grass lay flattened underneath her. As soon as she sat up, she saw that the Watch had camped on the edge of a stream somewhere. Some scrubby trees lined the banks.

Yann smiled at her. "Do you feel better?"

"I didn't...." Her hand flew to her head. "I didn't think I felt bad. Where are we? What happened?"

"You got hurt in the last Layer collapse. Anríq has been healing you for two days. You should have your magic back now, too. Do you want to try it to make sure?"

Eliska glanced over at Anríq. He gazed back at her with his clear blue eyes.

Both he and Yann sat unnaturally close—but their presence felt good. She wouldn't have wanted anyone else here—or not as much.

She opened her palm and projected her Coil image. It revolved for a second before she shut her hand and made it disappear.

Yann burst out laughing. "Yay! You're back."

She found herself grinning at him and then at Anríq. "Thank you—both of you."

"We're both just glad to get you back. Here. I made this for you."

He pulled forward a short staff made out of a tree branch. He handed it to her.

She took it, examined it, and let her magic rush into it. Nothing ever felt so good. She never wanted to lose her magic again—ever.

"Just be careful where you point that thing," Yann teased. "We'll all be extra-special careful not to piss you off from now on."

She found herself laughing in relief. "I'll try to control my temper." She beamed at both of them and then glanced around. "Where is.....?"

She froze and all her relief and happiness drained away when she saw Marine crouching near a clump of trees on the other side of the river.

Her stringy, greasy dark hair hung over her face, but Eliska would never be able to mistake the sounds floating across the water from Marine.

She snarled, screeched, and bellowed. She turned her head far enough in Eliska's direction for Eliska to see Marine baring her teeth, biting at things that weren't there, and her wild eyes rolling in their sockets.

"Oh, no!" Eliska choked.

"She got her magic back, too, unfortunately," Yann murmured. "I guess she can commune with the Dark forces in this Island the way she did before."

Eliska gulped down the lump in her throat and looked away. A brick dropped into her stomach when she saw Barsali lying nearby. His eyes were closed.

Sick horror gripped her at the sight of him. She didn't even have to go near him to know what was wrong with him.

"The Dark took him," Anríq murmured. "It's poisoning him from the inside. I don't have the magic to heal him. He'll slip away tonight or tomorrow. I can't stop it."

She scooted over to sit next to Barsali. Once she got into that position, she saw his mother's ring dangling by its chain next to his neck. The chain had come loose from under his shirt.

The ring sealed something for Eliska. Barsali was the first Watchmen to connect with her during her first days with this group. Could she really sit back and watch him die?

She held out her hand a few inches above his chest and immediately pulled her hand back. The Darkness invading every part of him ate away at his organs—and something deeper inside his very being.

"You can't heal him," Anríq murmured. "Not without putting yourself in danger."

"I have to." Eliska heard the words coming out of her mouth.

"You could die," Anríq insisted. "You would be more useful to this group alive than he would be."

"How can you say that?! He's....." She broke off. She couldn't come up with the words to say what Barsali was.

She knew almost nothing about him, but what she did know was enough.

The ring hanging there told her everything she needed to know. It stared back at her challenging her to help Barsali.

Anríq read her mind. "If you do this, I won't be able to bring you back. The Dark is too big for me. If I tried, I would die along with you."

"You don't have to bring me back because I won't die. My magic is strong enough to take it."

"Your magic might be strong enough to keep you alive, but it won't be strong enough to save you from it. You know that."

She looked up at him. He stared down into her with eyes overflowing with inner pain and hopeless longing.

Everything he said was true. He knew too much to say something like that if it wasn't true.

She knew it from that first moment of putting her hand over Barsali's chest. Her magic was strong enough to take the Darkness out of him. She could save his life, but only by taking the Darkness on herself.

Her magic was strong enough to do that, too, but then she would have to live with all that Darkness in her. Could she really do that? Did she really want to live with that?

Another yowl from Marine caught her attention. She, Anríq, and Yann all glanced across the river at Marine lurking under the trees.

She was out there in the Dark Layers again. She communed with the Dark to wage this war against the Voyant.

Seeing Marine buried in madness made up Eliska's mind for her. Marine sacrificed everything to do something good for the rest of the Coil.

Now it was Eliska's turn. It was her turn to commune with Dark forces in ways only she knew how.

She turned to Yann and then to Anríq. She would have liked to touch both of them at least once, just to say goodbye and to thank them both for everything they'd done for her.

"Take care of the Watch for me—both of you," she choked. "Whatever happens—take care of the Watch."

"We will," Yann told her.

"You take care of the Watch, too, Eliska," Anríq murmured. "All of them—not just Barsali."

She tried to smile at him and failed. Looking at either him or Yann hurt too much. She cared about them too much. She would lose her nerve if she kept looking at them, so she swiveled the other way and faced Barsali.

Before she did anything else, she tucked the ring back under his shirt. She arranged it and pushed it into place so it stayed right there in the center of his chest where it belonged.

She took a deep breath to summon all her courage. Then she planted her hand on top of his jacket right above the ring buried underneath.

She made contact with him and a jolt of lightning went off between them. Her instincts told her to pull away and protect herself from all that Darkness, but she forced herself to press her hand down even harder.

She poured all her magic into him and clamped her eyes shut against the tide of Darkness overwhelming her.

She summoned all her power—more than she ever had to use to keep herself alive in the Coil. She never tapped this depth of power before.

A black torrent flooded into her and she rallied all her effort to draw the Dark into herself. It kept getting bigger and bigger....and stronger and stronger. Where would it end? How much Darkness could one imp hold?

He couldn't hold it. That was the problem. It was killing him.

She kept draining it off faster and faster, but it didn't slacken—not at all.

The ring under her hand started to radiate heat and light. It built to a blinding sun that torched its own secret magic into her soul, but not even that could drive the Darkness out of her.

Nothing would ever drive it out of her—not ever again. It was her Darkness now.

Her magic infiltrated the ring and the ring's own secret magic drove the Darkness out of Barsali. The ring drove the Darkness out of Barsali in the only direction it could drive it—into her.

She dove deeper inside him trying to find the source....and she dropped into an illusion Layer of Barsali's deepest consciousness.

She flashed into a rapidly changing landscape of Middleborough. The years raced past at lightning speed.

She ran into a crude house where a man and a woman worked around the one table in the one cramped main room. A bunch of kids ran around making noise, playing with toys, and two boys tried to help their father with his work.

Eliska found herself taking the role of one of the younger girls. She had to hold her hand above her head to open the doorknob to get inside the house.

One of the boys came over to her, took her hand, and led her to a trunk in the corner where they sat down side by side.

He pulled a fistful of nuts out of his pocket and scooped them into her hands. "Take these, Auriel. I've already eaten enough and Father says we won't get any more."

"You should keep them, Barsali," Eliska told him. "I don't want to take yours."

He smiled down at her with glowing affection. "We'll share them. I'll crack them for us."

Eliska glanced over at the fire. "Mother's too busy. She'll get mad if we do it here."

"Come with me. We'll do it outside."

He took the nuts back, dumped them into his pocket, and led her out onto the front step. They sat down together and he used his father's hatchet to crack the nuts. Barsali gave her some and ate others himself.

The scene sped up and a bunch of years passed. She reentered the same house as a much older girl, but the father wasn't there anymore.

The mother still worked over the fire. She'd aged considerably. She didn't look up when Eliska entered.

Barsali intercepted Eliska the minute she showed up. He looked like a much younger version of what he looked like now. He couldn't be more than sixteen.

He got in Eliska's face, lowered his voice to a whisper, and hissed in an undertone. "Where have you been, Auriel? I've been worried sick about you."

She opened her mouth to answer, but before she could move, he took hold of her arm, steered her outside, and shut the door behind him. The mother didn't look up even once.

"You've been out with Emilen Dugas again, haven't you?" Barsali demanded as soon as he shut the door. "I told you to stay away from him."

Eliska opened her mouth a second time, but no sound came out. She floundered in confusion trying to decide what to say to him.

His expression turned to granite. "Did he do something?" Barsali demanded. "Did he come for you after I told you not to go with him?"

"Barsali...." she stammered. "I tried to tell him...."

"Tell him what?" Barsali demanded. "You tried to tell him what?"

"That you and Mother....I told him I don't want to go with him, but he wouldn't listen....."

Barsali clamped his jaws shut. "What did he do, Auriel?" he snarled. "Tell me what he did."

She kept opening her mouth and shutting it like a stranded fish. Her throat constricted. "I.....I can't tell you, Barsali." Tears flooded her eyes. Her throat hurt too much to say another word.

He glared at her and then jerked away. He shoved the door open, seized her hand, dragged her into the house, and left her standing there on the threshold.

He stormed into a corner, ripped open a bundle of cloaks, took out his father's sword, threw the empty cloaks back into a corner, and stalked back to her.

"Stay in the house, Auriel," he growled. "Don't go outside, whatever you do. Stay here and help Mother. I'll be back in a little while."

He barged out of the house and slammed the door behind him. Dead silence fell over the room after he left.

She turned around to find her mother watching them—but it wasn't Eliska's mother. It was Barsali's mother.

Chapter 15

B arsali's memories kept flooding into Eliska's brain along with all the Darkness buried in his soul. The scene raced forward a bunch of years.

Eliska's connection with Barsali read every single day as it passed at super-speed. She was there. She lived the whole thing with him and felt every shade of emotion.

The flood of memories slowed down and Eliska's perspective shifted from Auriel to Barsali. He sat on a stool by the fire. His mother sat in her rocking chair next to him.

Tears streamed down her cheeks when she tugged off her wedding band and pressed it into his hand. "This is yours now, son. I don't have any more use for it. You take it."

He stared down at it. It burned a hole in his palm. "What should I do with it? I can't wear it."

"I don't know what you should do with it," his mother choked. "That will be for you to decide. Maybe you can keep it for the woman you marry someday. I know you'll make the right decision, but I can't wear it anymore. It hurts too much to see it there on my hand every day and know that I'm not married to your father anymore."

She broke down in wretched sobs. He pulled his stool close to her chair, put his arm around her, and held her while she cried.

He took that moment to stuff the ring into his pocket. He had no idea what he would do with it, but he had to do something with it just to get it away from her.

The years raced past and stopped again on Auriel's wedding day. Barsali stood with Auriel's husband as his groomsman.

An excruciating wave of painful love and pride overwhelmed her when the viewpoint switched to him watching her walk through town in her white dress. The townspeople threw flower petals at her and her new husband.

Her face radiated so much happiness. Tears came to Barsali's eyes when he saw the way she and her new husband looked at each other. He loved her so much. He loved her even more than Barsali did.

Then Barsali, his mother, his sisters, his brothers, and Auriel's husband's parents and family went back to Barsali's mother's house. She and her daughters laid out a massive spread and everyone sat down to eat together.

Auriel and her husband sat at the head of the table shining with more happiness than Barsali ever could have hoped for her.

The scene sped up again and slowed back down to its normal rate. It showed the same house—the same one room with all the same people in it—but they all looked another year older.

Auriel and her husband had two tiny baby children—a boy one year old and a newborn baby daughter.

Auriel held the baby in her arms. The boy lay asleep on the bed in the corner.

Auriel, her husband, Barsali's mother, and his other sister, his two brothers, and their wives gathered around Barsali.

He wore his black uniform emblazoned with the insignia of the Black Watch. His mother hugged him with tears in her eyes, but he only saw Auriel.

She beamed at him with just as much pride and painful love and longing as he remembered feeling for her on her wedding day.

She kissed him on the cheek. "I'm so proud of you. I love you so much."

He could barely speak above a whisper when he hugged her back and pressed his face into her hair for the last time. "I love you, too. You take care of your family. I'll be right across town standing guard over all of you."

He tore himself away, cast one last aching look at the people he loved most in the world, and walked out of the house.

He crossed Middleborough, entered the large white house near the wall, and met Yvan Dilnao there along with Omer Veco, Vidal Rom, and Niyazi Trahan.

They shook hands with Barsali and then hugged him and welcomed him as a brother. They even squeezed his neck and shoulders when he shed tears in front of them over the family he left behind just a few doors away.

The scene shifted, but it didn't speed past the years—not this time. It switched to a nighttime view of Barsali's bedroom on the top story of the Watch's house.

He stood at the window in his shirtsleeves while the rest of the Watchmen slept. He stared across town at a light glowing in the window of his mother's house. Auriel, her husband, and her children lived in that house now.

He saw them at a distance almost every day. He watched Auriel's children grow. He saw Auriel and their other sister get pregnant again.

They invited him over for meals once a week. They called him home when his mother got sick. He stayed as involved in their lives as much as ever. He just lived in another house and worked on the wall every day.

He lived his life through them......and then the scene sped up again. It flashed to a massive battle between the Watchmen and Darklings invading from out in the wild Layers.

Magic-users from the town helped the Watchmen drive the Darklings back—that time.

Eliska's connection with him sped through multiple battles, each one deadlier than the last—until the inevitable day when the Darklings breached the barricade.

They stormed through the streets and flattened a few houses. Auriel happened to be outside during the attack and a Darkling crushed her under its foot before the Watchmen and the local magic-users drove them back out of town.

The next scene showed Barsali bowed over Auriel's grave with her husband and her children sobbing nearby. He stared down at the grave, utterly broken.

He gave up any chance of having a family of his own so he could protect them—so he could protect her—but he couldn't. She died in the end because he failed.

His brother Watchmen surrounded him, crushed his shoulders in their powerful hands, and took him back to the Watch's house. They gave him what poor comfort they could while Auriel's husband, their children, and Barsali's mother went back to their own home.

Barsali threw himself into his duties ten times harder after that. He became single-mindedly obsessed with stopping the Darklings from invading again. He had to protect Auriel's children at all costs, but he couldn't stop the invasion.

The Darklings got bigger, stronger, and more ferocious with every passing day. They attacked harder with every incursion.

Barsali became frantic to do something—anything to make sure his nieces and nephews survived. He didn't even care if he died in their place as long as he kept them safe.....

And then came that fateful night. He, the Watch, Wesh, and Eliska sat around on that high rock shelf talking about why the Voyant was coming after them and what he wanted from them.

Barsali pulled out the ring he always wore on a chain around his neck. *I have this.*

The words burned a hole in his mind every hour of every day after that.

It reminds me of my family—my mother, my sisters, their husbands, and their children. They all lived in Middleborough. I joined the Watch to protect them...and now they're all gone.

The words would keep burning a hole in his mind every hour of every day for as long as he lived.

He forsook love and a normal life of his own so he could protect his family while they lived that life in his place.

Now they were all dead and he alone was left alive. He alone stayed behind to remember that they ever even existed.

The memories crushed him under an unbearable weight of grief, fury, and hatred. That Darkness ate away at him from the inside....and then all of it flooded into Eliska.

She dove into the bottommost recesses of his being and took every drop of that Darkness on herself. She took all the pain, all the loneliness, all the resentment to leave him pure, clean, and shining with the light radiating from the ring.

It flooded him with pure love and happiness. He fulfilled his oath. He protected them as well as anyone could. He would gladly have died in their place.

A cruel twist of fate made it work out differently, but not because he failed in his duty. He did his duty. If they died, they died knowing he was out there fighting for them.

The light cast that one beaming smile on Auriel's face as she kissed him goodbye. *I'm so proud of you. I love you so much.*

Barsali's heart contracted at those words. He suffered that tightening sensation a hundred times since the Watch got stranded in the Coil. He suffered it every time he remembered her saying it....and every time he remembered burying her.

Eliska clamped her eyes shut against that pain. No more Darkness remained anywhere in Barsali's being.

He was pure, clean, and healed now, but the pain didn't go away. It would never go away because nothing could bring Auriel back—or any of the rest of Barsali's family back. They were gone—probably forever.

Instead, all that Darkness rotted away in Eliska's insides now. It would never go away, either. Anríq couldn't take it away. Wesh wouldn't have been able to take it away. Wesh wasn't even alive anymore.

Eliska didn't know any other magic-user strong enough to take it away. She was stuck with it.

She swallowed hard and took her hand off Barsali's chest. He still lay there with his eyes closed, but he was only asleep now. He would rest for a day or two and then start to regain his strength.

She couldn't even be happy about that. She couldn't be happy about any of this. She would probably never feel happy about anything again—not with this poison chewing its way through her insides.

It corrupted her from the inside out. It disgusted her. Even the sight of Barsali lying there made her sick.

Marine's snarls and howls floating across the river made Eliska's skin crawl. She hated Marine just for being there. Marine didn't have magic strong enough to heal Eliska, either.

Eliska couldn't turn around. She couldn't stand the sight of Yann and Anríq looking at her.

She didn't have to guess how they would look at her. Their foreheads would crease with concern. They would wonder what they could do to make things better for her even if they didn't ask out loud.

They would hover around her or at least watch her from afar to see how she was handling all of this. She couldn't stand that.

Just the fact that they cared about her made her want to hurt someone. She wanted to hurt the whole world.

Fury, anguish, terror, and sick horror drove her to her feet. She couldn't stay here with these people. They cared about her too much. She didn't want to be around when Barsali woke up and acted all grateful to her for bringing him back.

She picked up the staff that Yann made for her and walked off up the river. She didn't look at the two boys—not even once.

She didn't want to use a staff that Yann made for her. She wanted to throw it away and make her own, but she couldn't even do that. She couldn't do that to him.

He would never forgive her and she would never forgive herself, so she just had to live with that insult on top of everything else.

Chapter 16

Yann turned a corner on the riverbank and hefted the skinned hog carcass higher on his shoulder. He caught Anríq grinning at him. "Do you want me to carry it for a while?" Anríq asked.

"I'm fine," Yann told him. "I don't need you to rescue me from hard work."

Anríq laughed, but they both stopped when they rounded the bend and the Watchmen's camp came in sight.

The group had been camping here for a week while they waited for Barsali to recover.

Eliska had been unconscious for the first two of those days. Now Barsali sat up by the fire. He still looked haggard and tired, but he would get stronger. He already looked better than when he first woke up.

Yann stiffened when he saw Eliska sitting at the edge of the clearing. Yvan, Niyazi, Rien, and Omer sat around the fire talking to Barsali. Neils squatted by the stream cleaning a knife.

Yann and Anríq had just parted from Vidal out in the trees. He was too busy hunting to come back to camp yet.

Eliska sat apart from everyone and made no move to join them. She sat sideways and faced the nearby hills. She didn't outright turn her back on everyone nor did she leave, but she didn't talk to anyone or even look at the Watchmen, not even Barsali.

She left for a full day after she healed Barsali. She used her magic to avoid anyone who went to look for her.

Anríq explained a thousand times about how she took on Barsali's Darkness to heal him, but the process still didn't make any sense to Yann.

Anríq couldn't exactly explain how Wesh healed Eliska after she took Anríq's Darkness to save his life, but Anríq couldn't take hers to bring her back from this.

She returned to camp surly, hostile, and aggressive when she bothered to talk to anyone at all. The Watchmen fell back on ignoring her whenever possible.

She didn't turn around when Yann and Anríq returned.

Neils quartered Yann's hog and put the meat on the spit. The Watchmen talked amongst themselves and didn't try to include Eliska in their conversation.

"Don't push yourself too hard," Yvan told Barsali. "We're safe here for now. We don't need to rush off before you get better."

"I'm all right," Barsali insisted. "I can handle walking across country."

"You might not be able to handle fighting Darklings," Niyazi pointed out. "Better for us to stay a few extra days and make sure you're back to full strength."

"I don't suppose it makes any difference where we go once we do move," Yvan remarked. "We might as well scout the countryside and see if we can find any towns. We have nothing better to do until something else happens."

He turned around and called over his shoulder.

"Do you have any ideas about where we should go, Eliska?" Yvan asked.

"I don't care," she muttered. "Go where you want."

"I detected an area of powerful magic to the south," Anríq chimed in.

"Is it another collapsing landscape?" Omer asked.

"No, it feels stable and healing to me. I think we should head for it." His eyes darted sideways toward Eliska. "They'll have powerful magic-users there. They might be powerful enough to help us."

"I suppose we have nothing to lose by trying." Yvan leaned forward to take his portion of meat from Neils. "Maybe they'll be powerful enough to keep their Island stable and stop it from collapsing."

Marine shrieked extra loudly just then and made everyone jump—everyone except Eliska. She kept her back to Marine all the time.

The Watchmen stared across the river. Marine didn't even see them.

Neils went back to carving up the meat. He served all the Watchmen and then dumped a portion into a bowl carved out of wood.

He carried it across the clearing and set it on the ground a few yards away from Eliska. She didn't turn around to acknowledge him.

He returned to the fire, prepared another bowl for Marine, crossed the stepping stones, and placed that bowl on the ground a little farther away from her.

He returned to the fire and got to work cutting up the rest of the haunch. He didn't see Eliska pick up her bowl and start eating without a word to anyone.

Yann, Anríq, and the other men on his side of the fire were the only ones who saw Eliska take the food. Every night followed the same routine. She acknowledged the Watchmen as little as possible.

Yann woke up every morning expecting her to be gone for good. He didn't understand why she stuck around if she hated everyone so much.

He had to continually remind himself that she got like this by saving Barsali's life. She sacrificed her whole connection with the group and especially her deeper connections with Yann, Anríq, Barsali, and Yvan. She did all that to bring Barsali back.

She must still care even though she did her best to act like she didn't. She would have left long ago if she didn't care.

Yann really wished he could get close to her. He would give anything to make it okay for her, but Anríq kept saying no one could. She would carry that Darkness for life now. Nothing would ever take it away.

Yann couldn't accept that. He had to find some way to bring her back. She deserved that much. She deserved a lot more. He just didn't know how to give it to her.

He lost the thread of the conversation while he watched her and tried to figure it out.

More noises from Marine brought him out of his thoughts. She emerged from the trees across the river, contorted her body into bizarre shapes, and the yowls and screeches coming from her got worse by the minute.

Rien stood up. "She's driving me crazy. We can't stay here. If we're going, let's go right now. Why wait? Waiting will only get on our nerves even more."

Yvan shrugged. "I don't suppose it matters very much." He turned to Anríq. "Do you have any objections to leaving right away?"

"I agree with Rien," Anríq replied. "Traveling to this magical place may offer some benefits for us that we can't find here."

Yvan nodded. "Let's go, then. Pack up the rest of the food, Neils. We'll wait for you to finish."

The process of breaking camp took longer, now that the Watchmen had more baggage. Neils divided the food into more than one hog hide package. Niyazi and Omer carried the other two.

Vidal came back while they worked. He only nodded when he heard the news.

The other Watchmen used the time to check, clean, and sharpen their weapons. Yann went over to Eliska, but he didn't do anything to get her attention. Would she follow the group or stay behind? No one knew.

He picked up the discarded wooden bowl Neils used to serve her meals. She jerked around to glare at Yann when he came up behind her.

"We're moving out soon," he told her. "You're coming with us, aren't you?"

She gave him a dirty look and turned the other way. "What difference does it make if I come with you? None of you wants me around anyway."

"Of course we do—and not because of the help you might give us with your magic. I keep telling you this and it's even more important now because you're hurting. You heard what Anríq said. These people where we're going might be able to heal you."

"No one can heal me," she snarled. "When are you going to realize that? I'm poison. I'll always be poison. I was poison even before this happened."

"I don't see it that way, but you....."

"That's because you're an idiot," she snapped. "You don't know anything about it. You don't know anything about anything."

"I know you took this Darkness on yourself to save Barsali. I know you're staying here with us right now because you still care about us and we still care about you. I know you probably don't want to, but I really hope you come with us. You'll be better off with us than by yourself. We might find another magic-user strong enough to heal you—or a bunch of magic-users strong enough to heal you. Wouldn't that be worth it?"

She didn't answer him at all nor did she turn around. She kept her head turned so he couldn't see her face.

Chapter 17

Yann walked away from Eliska and headed for the stream to clean the bowl.

He planned to go get the bowl Neils used to serve Marine and clean that, too. Then Yann would carry both bowls wherever it was the Watch traveled to next.

Yann got halfway to the stream when he spotted his father standing off to one side. Yann didn't see anything unusual about his father's behavior except that Yvan didn't get involved in the work of packing up the camp.

He usually went from man to man helping out or giving orders wherever the Watch needed him to. He never stood off alone like this—not ever.

He stood farther down the riverbank and he definitely did keep his back to the group. He didn't turn around or get involved when the men laughed, talked, joked, or even argued.

Yann went over to him and approached from behind the way he approached Eliska.

Yann realized long before he got there that something was very wrong with his father. Yvan kept jerking from side to side and letting out little gasps of strained breath each time he did it.

"Father?" Yann asked.

Yvan spun around fast. His crazed eyes barely registered his son standing right in front of him.

Yvan jolted away. His eyes darted the other way and he panted again. "They're here!" he whispered. "They followed us here!"

Yann's stomach dropped into his shoes. "Father....you can't be.....they aren't real. They aren't here. You're seeing things. It isn't real. Father—look at me!"

Yvan barely responded at all. He spun around to the other side. "They're coming for me! They're coming after me!"

Yann stared at his father in mounting horror. Watching this happen to Rien and then Barsali was bad enough.

The Watch couldn't lose Yvan. Everyone relied on his steady, unshakable leadership.

What would Yann do without his father? He couldn't even let himself think that.

He wasn't the only one to notice the Watch Commander's absence. Omer came over followed by Niyazi.

"We're ready to go," Omer began. "We can move out whenever you give the...."

He broke off when he saw the way Yvan was acting. Omer scowled.

"No!" Niyazi breathed. "No! Not him, too!"

Yann couldn't bring himself to speak to explain this. He didn't have to.

Omer stepped forward and tried to clap his hand on Yvan's shoulder. Yvan yanked away, but not because of Omer.

Yvan whirled in the opposite direction to face away from the three men, raised his hands in front of his face, and cringed from something that wasn't there.

Then he wheeled to the other side and gasped out loud when he reared away from some other invisible enemy coming at him from there.

"Now what are we supposed to do with him?" Niyazi asked.

"I'll tell you what we're going to do with him." Omer rushed the Watch Commander. Before Yvan realized what was happening, Omer pulled the Watch Commander's weapons from his belt.

Omer handed Niyazi the Watch Commander's swords, the long one and the short one. Yvan kept jumping, spinning, and letting out little pained gasps of fright while Omer caught him a second time and pulled the small dagger from Yvan's boot.

Omer stood back and slipped the dagger into his own boot. "It might not stop him from trying to fight them, but at least he won't put the rest of us in danger."

The others noticed something wrong and Vidal, Rien, and Barsali came over followed by Neils.

"What's wrong?" Rien asked and then saw Yvan. "Oh, no!"

"We just have to keep going and hope he comes out of it the way you did," Omer decided.

"But not the way Barsali did," Neils pointed out. "How do we even know the Watch Commander *will* come out of it? The Dark might take him the way it took Barsali and we wouldn't have....."

He broke off when he glanced in Eliska's direction. Yann didn't trust her to save a second Watchmen—not when saving Barsali cost her so much. She probably wouldn't survive a second dose of the same Darkness infecting her.

Omer straightened up to look over all the Watchmen's heads. Anríq squatted across the camp sharpening his axe.

"Go get him," Omer told Yann. "See if he can do anything about this."

Yann walked away gulping down miserable despair. Nothing better happen to his father. Yann couldn't live with that.

He walked over to Anríq. Anríq didn't look up. "Will you please come over here?" Yann asked.

Anríq kept passing his sharpening stone along his axe blade. "What's up?"

"My father....." Yann couldn't finish.

Anríq's hand froze on the blade. He went silent for a minute and then stood up.

He slipped his sharpening stone into one of his bags and slung his axe over his shoulder on the way back across the camp to rejoin the group.

All the Watchmen stood around staring at Yvan. They parted to let Anríq through and he frowned at the Watch Commander, too.

"Can you do anything?" Omer asked. "Can you bring him out of it?"

Anríq studied Yvan for a minute. Yvan didn't stop jumping away from Darklings only he could see.

"Hold onto him," Anríq replied. "Take his arms and hold him."

Niyazi and Barsali moved in on Yvan from both sides. Then they rushed him, grabbed his arms, and clamped him in a tight grip to stop him from getting away.

He jerked and struggled against their hold, but he didn't see or even seem to feel them. He completely lost awareness of where he was and what anyone else was doing.

Anríq placed his hand an inch above the Watch Commander's chest. Then Anríq did the same thing above Yvan's head. Yvan didn't notice that, either.

"The same thing is happening to him that happened to Rien," Anríq announced. "There's nothing wrong with him physically or even anything magical that I can heal. He's whole."

"Does that mean he's seeing something real?" Yann asked. "Does that mean the Darklings are real—and the rest of us just can't see them?"

"That isn't possible," Neils pointed out. "If they were real, they would affect all of us the same way."

"They are affecting all of us the same way," Niyazi pointed out. "They already affected Rien and Barsali. The Darklings are just affecting us one at a time. That should be obvious."

"Then how can they be real?" Neils asked. "If they're so real, their presence should affect us all at once."

Anríq stepped back. "I can't do anything for him. I'm sorry. Whatever is wrong with him just has to run its course."

"Why is this happening now and not in the other Islands?" Omer asked. "Why haven't these armored Darklings come for us before?"

"I can't answer that," Anríq replied. "I don't understand everything about the Coil. We may be in a Layer these armored Darklings inhabit—or we may be traveling through several Layers these Darklings inhabit. That may be why we keep traveling to different Islands but the same thing keeps happening."

"Could the Voyant be the one doing all of this?" Yann asked.

"I couldn't say for sure," Anríq replied. "As Omer says, I don't know why he would do it now instead of sending all his power against you from the beginning. You were weakest then—when you were in Middleborough. Wesh, Eliska, Marine, and I have been helping you since then—or perhaps he sees that we're helping you and thinks he needs to send more powerful forces against you. I can only guess. I'm sorry."

"What if we ask….*her?*" Neils shot his eyes toward Eliska again.

"No, leave her alone," Anríq replied. "She's done enough. Getting her involved in this will only hurt her more."

Omer sighed. "Let's move out. We'll head for this area of magic Anríq mentioned. We may find some resources there."

The men drifted away and went back to work. Yann stayed near his father. Yann didn't want to leave his father alone, but at the same time, Yann didn't want to be anywhere near Yvan when he was acting like this.

Omer didn't leave, either. "I'll take him in hand on the way," Omer murmured under his breath. "I'll make sure he stays with us and doesn't get lost."

Yann couldn't answer. He didn't want to look at his father going insane before his eyes, but Yann found it impossible to look at anything else.

"He'll come out of this," Omer murmured. "You'll see. He's strong. He'll find a way to come out of this."

Yann gulped. He wished he could believe that, but as Neils pointed out, Barsali wouldn't have come out of it without Eliska's intervention.

Omer bumped Yann's elbow. "Go back to work, young one. Leave him to me. We may find help soon. Go on."

Yann turned away feeling sick. He crossed the river and retrieved Marine's bowl.

Yann refused to look at his father. Yann squatted down by the stream to clean both bowls the way he originally planned to. He didn't look to see what Omer was doing with Yvan.

Yann should have been the one to take care of Yvan, but he couldn't do that. He couldn't cope with the sight of his father losing his mind. Yann couldn't even force himself to accept it.

He finished cleaning the bowls, shook them dry, and took them back up the bank. He planned to arrange some kind of carry bag like Anríq's to carry the bowls in.

He didn't get a chance to before Anríq came over to him. "Give them to me," Anríq told him. "I'll carry them."

Yann handed them over. He couldn't argue with anything right now. He didn't want to deal with any of this.

The other men stood around waiting. Omer told them to move out.

Anríq went in front to lead the way. He was the only person who knew where to go. Yann made himself go to the front, too. He walked right behind Anríq.

Their path led around hills and bends in the stream. Anríq followed the watercourse for a while heading upstream toward some mountains in the distance.

Yann tried not to be aware of anything going on behind him, but he wound up seeing anyway. The hills and riverbends gave Yann more of a view than he wanted of the party's formation.

Omer took hold of Yvan's shirt and half-pushed, half-dragged the Watch Commander after the rest of the group.

Yvan kept jolting every few seconds. He tried to jerk himself away from Omer, but Yvan still didn't see the man holding him.

Omer closed up his already stern face in a mask of stony determination, looked straight in front of him, and marched Yvan away whether he wanted to go or not.

Marine scuttled after the group still yowling, snarling, and biting at the air. She scampered over the countryside a lot faster than she usually did.

She didn't take so many pains to keep her distance from the group. Sometimes she ran fast enough to almost overtake Omer and Yvan.

Then she dropped back to spasm and contort in place for a while before she caught up again.

The group traveled for over an hour before Anríq led the way into a side valley heading inland. The Watch left the stream and started winding into the hills.

The two boys turned another corner and Yann happened to glimpse a lone figure silhouetted against the sky. The figure stood on a high hill at a distance from the party.

The wind caught long black hair and a black cloak. The wind blew both out to the side. The figure held a staff in one hand and used it as a walking stick.

Yann stopped to stare up at her. She followed them after all. Part of him always knew she would.

She didn't catch up. He only caught brief glimpses of her from a distance for the rest of the journey.

He couldn't even feel happy that she decided to stay with the group. He just wished like anything he could get her back—back to the way she was before this happened.

Chapter 18

Eliska climbed another hill and looked down at the line of black dots in the distance. The Watchmen snaked from one valley to another heading inland from the water course where they started.

She stood on the hilltop watching them for a while. She leaned on her staff while she decided if she should keep following them.

She shouldn't. She should leave right now if only to save them the trouble of dealing with her. No one in their right mind would want her poison around.

Some force she didn't understand kept her going. She climbed down the hill, passed through another valley, and climbed a second hill a little closer to the Watch.

She didn't understand her need to be near them even from a distance. She could protect them from the Dark by staying away from them.

She had nowhere else to go. That was the problem. No one and nowhere else in the Coil held any obligation, influence, or even any appeal for her. She didn't belong to anyone else or care about anyone else.

Her whole life seemed to be tied up with these people now even if she never became anything to them but a shadow on the distant horizon.

She followed them for a few more hours before they stopped in a valley full of trees. She couldn't tell from here what they were doing down there. She didn't want to know.

Marine got a lot closer to the group than Eliska did. Marine kept darting forward. She almost joined the Watch a few times before she scampered away and then came back.

Eliska couldn't tell what was going on with Marine and didn't really care. Marine was gone—the Marine Eliska considered a friend. That crazed wild animal down there wasn't Eliska's friend.

Eliska wouldn't have wanted Marine to see her like this anyway. Eliska couldn't have tolerated the real Marine getting all hurt and upset and worried about Eliska's Darkness.

Part of Eliska relaxed in relief that Marine didn't see her like this. Eliska would have been very happy for the men of the Watch never to see her like this, either. She hated herself like this.

She hated herself for snapping at Yann and turning her back to Neils's food and being rude to the Watch Commander.

She couldn't stop herself. The Dark ate away at her. She couldn't get rid of it. It turned everything to poison—everything about her.

Just being herself made her sick, but the Watch offered her one glimmer of hope. Yann was right. She still cared about them. The Dark couldn't poison that out of her.

She ached for one of them to do something—anything to take this burden away from her.

That would never happen. Anríq knew better than to try. She wouldn't want him to try. She would never wish for this curse to poison him the way it poisoned her.

She already was poisoned before she ever met these people. She could carry this curse. Anríq was too good and kind and innocent.

She had to carry it. She chose to carry it when she took it from Barsali. Now it was all hers.

She climbed onto a hill looking directly down on the Watch. Omer sat next to the Watch Commander and kept a firm grip on his jacket the entire time.

Yvan kept yanking from one side to the other trying to see invisible Darklings.

Eliska overheard the Watchmen's conversation about Yvan. She heard what Anríq said about Yvan being whole.

She also heard him suggest that this area of powerful magic might be able to heal her.

She would have taken Yvan's Darkness, too, if he had any. She would have taken it all to spare these people the fate she was going through right now.

She turned away gulping down the sting of bile in her throat. The sight of those people made her sick, but she just couldn't tear herself away. They were all she had even if she never spoke to any of them again.

That was the moment when she saw movement out of the corner of her eye. It came from behind where she'd just been standing. She wouldn't have seen it while she looked down at the Watch.

Now she saw a wave of shadow advancing across the countryside. It came from the north—from across the stream system where the Watch camped these last few days.

This shadow didn't look as black as the Darkness Eliska had been getting so used to lately. The wave didn't behave the same way.

It crawled across the landscape consuming everything in its path. She didn't need to see exactly what it was.

She fired a blast of light into the air to warn the Watchmen of the danger. She didn't go down there, though. She could protect the Watch better from up here.

The wave kept coming. It obliterated everything before it.

As it got nearer, she noticed plant shoots squirming, growing, and twining in a mass of other shoots. They knotted themselves together in a solid wall of thorns like the thorn landscape the Watch traveled through when they first left Middleborough.

The wave covered the horizon. The thorns swallowed forests, covered hills, and buried streams and rivers under the tangled carpet of twisted trunks. The thorns stabbed into other stalks and impaled them to form an impenetrable mass of wood.

The wave flowed over the landscape getting closer to the Watch. She couldn't wait any longer.

She took a running leap and launched herself off the hilltop. She fired her staff into the air and surrounded herself with a ball of magic to hover there above the landscape.

She looked down at the wave from above and fired her staff one more time. She erected a barrier to hold back the wave, but its Dark power overcame her in seconds.

The barrier shattered and the wave bore down on the Watch just as fast. Her magic did nothing to stop it.

Anríq sprang in front of the Watch and raised his club, but he wouldn't be able to hold back the wave, either. No one could.

Marine rushed up the channel trying to get to Anríq in time, but it was already too late. The Watchmen swiveled to face their doom. How puny and pathetic their weapons looked compared to the size of that wave.

Eliska released her spell and plummeted toward the ground at terminal velocity. She had to get there before the Dark overtook the Watch.

Anríq saw her coming and charged back to the Watchmen. Marine rushed into their group just as Eliska slammed into the ground full force. She drilled her staff into the soil at their feet and exploded the Island.

The Watchmen yelled out in alarm and fell through the crust just as the thorns raced over their heads and closed off the opening completely.

Everyone fell through multiple Layers and crashed down hard in another wasteland.

Eliska dragged herself off the ground and immediately felt something wrong—something more wrong than the Darkness inside her.

She looked down at the staff in her hands—the staff Yann made for her. It didn't vibrate with any kind of energy. It felt dead and cold.

She yanked her hand away and dropped it. It hit the ground and she rubbed her palm against her side to get that feeling off, but nothing would take it away. Her magic was gone again.

Marine stood a few feet away in her ruined dress. Eliska saw right away that Marine was back to full sanity. She stared around her, stunned, and then glanced down at her hands.

The Watchmen got to their feet. Yann's eyebrows shot up when he saw Eliska's staff lying on the ground. She squirmed under his questioning gaze. She couldn't tell him her magic was gone again. She couldn't go through that again, but it sure looked like she was about to.

Yvan distracted everyone by yelling out in a cracked undertone, "Get away from me! Get off me! Stop! Leave me alone!"

Omer must have let go of him when they fell through the Layers. Yvan scrambled to his feet, spasmed multiple times, slapped at different parts of his body, and batted his hands to fight off something attacking him.

He probably would have attacked the invisible Darklings with a weapon, but he didn't have any. He was too out of his mind to try to get one from the other Watchmen.

Eliska couldn't look at him. When she looked away, she saw the landscape in which the group landed this time.

Bones lay everywhere on a dry plateau, but the bones didn't lie in mounds covering the whole world. They scattered at a distance from each other with wide spaces between them.

A few scraggly trees struggled to raise their bare branches to an empty, white-blue sky. Eliska even spotted a few birds and other small animals moving around in the landscape.

Marine's eyes lifted to survey the landscape and her features crumbled in misery when she saw it. "No!" she sobbed. "No! It can't be!"

She buckled onto her knees and burst into bitter tears.

Yann took a step closer to her. "What's wrong?"

"NO!!" Her voice rose to a yell. Her swimming eyes stared at everything through her tears. "No!! It can't be! It can't!"

"What's wrong?" He squatted down next to her and tried to touch her shoulder. "What's the matter? Tell me!"

She shot away from him without seeing him, but she didn't lose her mind over invisible Darklings.

She took a few steps away, turned from one side to another, and searched the landscape. She raised her hand and pointed. "I.....This place.....it was beautiful....and green! It was overflowing with life....and there was a river......over there....."

She stumbled toward Yvan, but he didn't see her.

"How can you tell there was a river there?" Niyazi asked. "It's perfectly flat."

"Those hills….that valley over there…..They're the same…..but all the life is gone." She broke down in a pathetic sob again. "It can't be! It can't be!"

Yann glanced at Anríq. "Can you tell where we are?"

"Our magic is gone again," Anríq murmured low. "I won't be able to tell you anything about it, but this is the same landscape I saw before. Everything is in the same shape—this plateau, those mountains….it was all thriving and green before—and there was a river over there. Marine is right. The landscape must have changed."

The Watchmen exchanged glances. Yann turned back to Marine. "How do you know this place?"

She didn't hear him. She stumbled forward onto the plateau and kept going.

Chapter 19

M arine veered toward certain trees and startled the birds and animals into running away, but she always kept going in the same direction.

"Is she going toward where you said the magic was?" Yann asked Anríq.

Anríq nodded. "I can't detect anything anymore, but Marine must know this Island. Maybe she knows where we can find it."

The group fell into the same line except that Marine went in front this time. Her whimpering sobs drifted back through the line.

Eliska wound up included in their group. She should have stayed behind. She didn't want to be a part of this, but she supposed she had to be whether she wanted to be or not.

Omer collared Yvan again. He kept blurting out, "Get away from me! Don't touch me!" but he didn't say it to Omer.

Yvan kept swatting invisible Darklings and whimpering in terror. All those sounds set Eliska's teeth on edge. This was the absolute last thing in the world she needed right now.

Marine crossed the plateau to its farthest edge. The group passed a few wrecked buildings on the way, but fire didn't destroy this landscape.

Eliska couldn't tell what did destroy it. The buildings just seemed to crumble into ruins with stones fallen out of their walls and rooves caved in. None of the windows had glass in them anymore. They yawned into vacant rooms devoid of all life.

The few bones lying around didn't seem to lie any closer to the buildings than to anything else. Eliska didn't see any pattern to the destruction—not like the other destroyed towns and cities she'd seen.

Marine broke down sobbing her guts out every time the Watch passed any building. She folded onto her knees, buried her face in her hands, and her shoulders quaked in misery.

The Watchmen hung back and left her alone in her despair. Only Yann tried to comfort her.

He squatted down next to her each time this happened, put his arm around her shoulder, hugged her, and eventually encouraged her to stand up and keep going.

Eliska's stomach twisted in knots watching this. She should have been the one to comfort Marine. Marine obviously felt as bad about this as Eliska did about taking Barsali's Darkness.

Eliska couldn't go near Marine. Being near anyone right now made her skin crawl.

After the third building, Yann stayed by Marine's side even when she went in front of the rest of the Watch. He skipped the interval and put his arm around her whenever they even saw a building.

He kept her moving to the edge of the plateau. She stopped there and collapsed onto her knees again when she saw the countryside spread out below.

Eliska didn't see anything unusual about it. It looked exactly the same as the plateau with just as many bones, half-dead trees, and just as many ruined buildings. Some of them looked like houses.

Yann squatted down next to Marine. "Do you want to go down there?" he asked. "We don't have to. We can go somewhere else."

She didn't answer. She raised her streaming eyes to the valley floor spread out before her and her expression hardened.

She forced herself to her feet, marched sideways to the other edge of the plateau, and found a tiny footpath winding down the cliffs to level ground below. Eliska wouldn't have been able to find that footpath. Marine must have come to this Island before.

She made it to the bottom and set off across the flat countryside. Eliska didn't see anything Marine might be heading for. There was nothing here but more of the same.

Marine didn't stop at every building this time. She pressed forward without any encouragement from Yann.

She eventually stopped in front of a pile of rubble lying in a huge mound. She buried her face in her hands again and sobbed for a long time before she could bring herself to look at the wreckage.

"The Temple was here!" she wailed. "This was the Temple where I did my training! I spent years here! I knew everyone here!"

She started walking sideways to circle the wreck site. Only Yann went with her. He stayed close to her in ways no one else could.

Eliska, Anríq, and the Watchmen stood back watching. Eliska tried to look away. She didn't want to see Marine's devastation.

Eliska couldn't have coped with seeing everything she loved and cared about destroyed. Marine and the Watchmen were all so much stronger than she was.

Eliska thanked Heaven she lost everything before she remembered it. She never knew what she lost. That would have been too much.

Marine kept going in the same direction. She kept sobbing and going on about everyone who lived in the Temple and all the things they used to do together.

Those memories made her cry now. Would she ever be able to laugh about them again?

A different kind of sickness stabbed Eliska through the middle. She would gladly take all that pain away just to make Marine feel better.

Eliska would have gladly taken Barsali's pain away, too—and everyone else's. She already considered herself a wasted husk of a human being.

She would have carried it all to spare these people from the slightest discomfort—but she couldn't do that.

Marine made it twenty feet from the Watch before she saw something in the rubble mound. She screamed and charged the ruin.

She scrambled over slabs and boulders. Yann followed right behind her.

Eliska, Anríq, and the Watchmen raced over there and climbed up, too. Eliska dreaded what they would find.

By the time they got there, Yann stood alone on a boulder looking down at Marine. She'd lowered herself into a space between some giant slabs of wall that had fallen to either side.

They left a ten-foot gap of ornately tiled floor. An older man with a downward curving handlebar mustache lay on the tiles.

Blood stained his grey tunic with the gold cross embroidered on the chest. Dried blood saturated his pants and splattered his face. A pool of blood discolored the tiles underneath him.

Marine sobbed in loud gasps while she tried to pick him up.

"Don't...." he husked. "Don't.....my dear child.....please......don't touch me....."

"I have to!" Marine shrieked and burst into fresh sobs. "I have to....take you somewhere.....I have to.....heal you.....Brother Matherus! Answer me! Don't you dare die on me!"

She cast a desperate glance around, but when she saw Eliska and Anríq standing behind her with the rest of the Watch, Marine broke down even more.

She lowered Brother Matherus onto the floor, bent over him with her arms around him, and sobbed into his neck.

He shut his eyes and a blissful smile spread over his lips. "I can die contented," he whispered, "now that I've seen you one more time."

"You can't die!" she wailed. "I can't live without you! You're all I have left!"

"They're all gone, my sweet girl," he half-whispered. "The other Templars are all dead. You're the last one."

He pried his eyes open and forced himself to focus on her. Her tears only seemed to give him more peace.

"You have to listen to me, my love," he croaked. "You're the only one left who can carry out our mission."

"I can't!" she roared. "I can't do this without you!"

"You have to," he whispered. "The Voyant....he keeps getting stronger....and he'll keep getting stronger as long as people like us let him get away with it."

"I can't stop him alone!" she cried. "How am I supposed to do this by myself?"

Brother Matherus's eyes skimmed the group standing behind her. "You aren't alone. You will continue. I know you will."

He dragged his gaze back to her. Even moving his eyes took all his effort.

"You have to listen to me, my dear child. Listen to me very carefully. The Voyant is hunting for someone—someone who will kill him, take his power, and replace him as ruler of the Coil."

Marine choked a few more times, but those words definitely got through to her. Her sobs faded. "But that means...."

"He'll never stop until he finds and kills the person he believes threatens his rule. That's why he attacked the Temple. He sent instability to destroy the Temple, kill everyone inside, and strip us of our magic. He took all our power. He may have thought the person he seeks was in our Temple. I don't know. I only know it's up to you now. You have to find this person. I don't know who it is, but whoever it is must be a powerful magic-user if they can defeat the Voyant."

"But....how am I supposed to find the person?" Marine stammered. "I can't find out anything about the Voyant's plans. If the information about the person and how to defeat the Voyant wasn't in the Temple...." Her eyes shot up. "Was the Temple's knowledge lost with the Temple itself? Did the Voyant destroy all the Temple's knowledge, too?"

"We stored a bolus knowledge in the Layers," Brother Matherus rasped. "Our scrying visions showed us the instability moving on the Temple and we took measures to protect our knowledge. You need to find it and access the information. Then you have to find the person and protect them at all costs. If you have to, you can give the person your own magic to help them defeat the Voyant. It's the only way. Whoever this person is, they're the only person alive who can defeat the Voyant. The rest of us are just collateral."

"But how do I find the information?" Marine asked.

Brother Matherus opened his mouth to answer, but at that moment, a seizure gripped his body all over.

His face twisted in a horrible grimace before he collapsed, went limp, and stopped breathing.

"NO!!" Marine shrieked. She pounced on him, grabbed his tunic by the shoulders, and tried to lift him. "NO!!!"

She yanked at him a few times. When he didn't respond, she folded over him, threw herself down on top of him, and burst into loud, bitter sobs. Her whole body shook.

Eliska gulped down a lump in her throat.

Yann jumped down onto the floor next to Marine, squatted by the dead man, and rested his hand on her back while she poured out all her anguish and loss. He didn't try to stop her.

Neils turned away first. He shut his eyes, compressed his lips to stop them from trembling, and turned around to face the other way. Then Omer did the same thing.

The barren landscape offered no possibility of anything different. Every direction presented the same view of death, destruction, and hopeless waste. The Watch would find the same thing no matter where they went.

Without warning, Marine shot off the dead man's body and rocketed to her with an enraged roar.

She stood there flexing her fingers and bellowing down at him in hysterical fury. Then she spun around searching for something to attack.

Yann backed off. The noise drew Neils and Omer back to looking in her direction—and everyone saw the Voyant glowing with light.

He stood on another enormous boulder across the Temple ruin. He perched high above the party watching them from a distance.

Marine scrambled out of the gap much faster than she should have been able to in that dress. Yann climbed up to follow her.

She scaled the nearest slab, cast one frantic look around, and seized another rock from the crack between this slab and the next.

She hurled the rock at the Voyant and yelled at him, but the rock just vanished into his halo.

She wheeled away and lunged for the closest thing she could lay her hands on.

She ripped Yann's glaive out of his hands, raised it over her shoulder, and threw it headfirst at the Voyant.

She threw it with expert precision and it sailed straight and true with surprising force. It would have killed an ordinary man if she threw the weapon at him like that.

The glaive stabbed through the halo and the landscape exploded in a deafening boom.

The rubble and boulders that used to be the Guardian Temple erupted off the ground, revolved through the air, and then started to fall.

Chapter 20

Yann came to his senses lying on a cold, damp, stone slab. He struggled to sit up and shivered when he saw where he was. He lay on a shelf of rock sticking out over a vast, cold ocean tossed with pelting wind, stinging rain, and whitecaps churning on the coal-grey sea.

Wind and rain lashed his face, soaked his hair and uniform, and battered an ancient stone tower not far away.

It sat at the very farthest point of the shelf where the peninsula ended and the ocean began. The tower's far wall melded with the cliffs dropping to the waves below.

Yann struggled to get to his feet. His blood ran cold when he searched the area. He was completely alone. His father, Eliska, Marine, Anríq, and all the rest of the Watchmen—they were all gone.

At least he was on solid ground. This Island looked stable—for now.

It really did look like an island instead of just some Coil landscape lost in countless Layers of other landscapes.

The rock shelf met up with stony hills behind him. The others probably wouldn't be up there and he sure as hell didn't want to climb those mountains in the rain.

He started forward heading for the only place left—the tower.

Not a single light shone in its windows. He didn't hear any voices or any other sound coming from the place. It sounded hollow and deserted.

At least he would be able to get out of the rain there. He might even find something to eat or some other resources he could use. Anything was better than nothing.

He no longer had a weapon, either. He would have cursed Marine for that, but he couldn't do that considering how distraught she was over Brother Matherus's death.

Yann tried to put all of that out of his mind. Marine wasn't here. No one was here.

He headed for a small, cramped wooden door indented in the tower's outer wall. He didn't see any other entrance to the tower.

Heavy, wrought-iron bars and huge knobbed bolts held the door together. It looked sturdy enough—and it also looked locked. Yann would have to come up with another plan if it was.

He tried the handle and it opened for him easily. He stepped into a low, narrow hallway built of the same black stone.

The structure echoed when he shut the door behind him and shook the rain out of his hair. The still air inside felt warm compared to the cruel wind outside.

Rooms lined the hall on both sides. Dim light shone through windows in each room and cast out onto the hallway floor through the open doors.

He headed down the hall. Maybe he would be able to find a kitchen or maybe a fireplace with some wood near it, but he didn't hold out much hope for that. This tower didn't look like anyone had lived here for a long time.

Every room he passed contained the same roughly built wooden bedframe with no mattress or blankets or any other furnishings. He didn't see any other furniture in the place. This didn't look good.

He made it twenty feet down the passage when he heard his father call him from behind. "Over here, son!"

Yann spun around fast and spotted his father standing at the far end of the hall. Yvan stood up straight and his clear eyes made contact with Yann from that distance.

Yvan wore the same expression Yann remembered. His father didn't jump away or try to fight off Darklings who weren't there. He even smiled at Yann.

Yann turned around and strode down the hall to rejoin his father, but before Yann got there, Yvan sidestepped into a different passage where Yann couldn't see him.

Yann sped up, but when he made it to the spot where Yvan had been standing, Yann discovered a blank stone wall there instead of a side passage. Yvan couldn't have gone that way.

Yann looked around him in all directions. A side passage went off to his right—in the opposite direction Yvan just went.

Yann didn't see anything unusual about this side passage except that more light seemed to come from the far end of it.

He headed for it for lack of anything better to do. He made it halfway down that passage when he passed another side hallway leading somewhere else.

He didn't plan to go down there or even look down it. He drew level with it and stopped in his tracks when Anríq stepped out of one of the rooms down there.

"This way, Yann!" Anríq called.

Yann hesitated. Something weird was going on, but he went that way anyway. The temptation to meet up with someone he knew overruled everything else.

He headed for Anríq, but the same thing happened. He sidestepped into a different room and disappeared before Yann got near him.

When Yann found the room, it was completely empty. No other doors communicated with any other part of the tower.

Yann had the only doorway in sight the whole time. Anríq couldn't have gotten out any other way.

Now Yann knew something weird was going on. It must be something magical, but he didn't plan to play any more games.

He retraced his steps, followed the hallway with more light at the end, and came out in an interior courtyard.

His view of the tower from the outside didn't show that the structure was big enough to have an interior courtyard. One solid stone cylinder stood at the end of that peninsula. The whole tower looked fifty feet across at the most.

It only had one roof over the top of it—at the very top of the tower. This courtyard must have been an illusion, but it sure looked real.

The wind howled through multiple arched porticos on all four sides of the courtyard. Each arch led to another passageway leading to a different part of the structure.

The rain lashed down from the cold grey sky.

Yann stepped out into the courtyard and looked up at a high parapet wall surrounding four wings that formed this courtyard. The structure he'd seen outside definitely couldn't be the same one.

He ducked back into the same corridor to get out of the rain. He planned to go back outside by the same route he used to enter this place. He didn't want to get trapped in a magical maze. He might die of starvation before he found a way out.

He started on his way back and turned at the corner where he'd seen his father. The instant he got there, Omer appeared behind him near the courtyard entrance.

Omer called, "This way, boy!"

Yann spun around automatically, and as soon as he saw Omer, Omer took two steps to the side and vanished.

Yann stayed where he was. Every instinct told him to follow Omer, but Yann knew better now. This was all some kind of trick. He didn't know who was playing it, but he wouldn't fall for it.

Maybe someone cursed the tower to make it this impenetrable maze—or maybe the Coil's instability turned it into this.

He turned away again and headed down the last hall. Just a few more steps and he would make it back to the door through which he entered this hall. Then he would go back outside and.....do something else.

He would have to travel through the rain to get anywhere. He might just stay there right inside the door until the weather let up—if it ever let up.

Going out into the rain would probably be better than starving in this death trap.

Then again, if his father and the others were trapped in here, maybe he should stick around and try to find a way to get them out, too.

He didn't know how he would do that. He wouldn't be able to if this tower was a magical trap. He wouldn't be able to break the spell.

He made it ten feet before Eliska dove out of one of the side rooms. She rushed him so fast he startled back in alarm.

She grabbed his arm and held on. "Yann!" she gasped. "Thank goodness I found you!"

"Eliska! What are you doing here?" he asked.

"I've been wandering around in this maze for hours! We all have. The rest of the Watch is trapped in here, too. They keep appearing, telling me to go with them, and then vanishing."

"The same thing happened to me—but I just got here." He frowned at her. "What do you mean—you've been here for hours?"

Her eyes fell out of their sockets. "You just got here?! Like—just now?!"

"I just woke up on the rock shelf outside. I came in here to get out of the rain. I didn't know any of you were in here until I saw my father and Anríq and Omer just now."

She waved that away, but she wouldn't let go of his arm. "Never mind. This Island must be under a magical spell and I have my magic back. That's how I found you. We can find the others."

Yann didn't answer. This was the most she'd spoken to him in a week and definitely the most she'd acted like she cared if she got back with anyone from the Watch.

He didn't comment that nor did he tell her to let go of his arm. The feeling of her holding onto him so they wouldn't get separated—he liked that feeling. He didn't want to lose it when they left this place.

Did getting her magic back somehow erase the Darkness inside her—or was she just relieved to find someone she knew?

She pulled him away and they headed back down the hall toward the side passage leading to the courtyard.

"Let's go back to that side hallway," she suggested. "We can find someone there. They always appear there."

"How did you find me?" he asked.

"I laid a trap outside that bedroom and waited for someone to walk through it. From what I can tell, this building enchants people so they both wander the halls looking for people who aren't there at the same time that they appear to other people without being aware of it."

He frowned at her. "I don't understand. How can they do both?"

"That's the enchantment. Here. I'll show you."

They came to the intersection where Yann saw Anríq. Eliska stopped in the side hall. "Let's say I was walking along this hall from there to there."

She pointed at the intersection where Yann had seen his father. Then she pointed at the other end of the hall where it joined up with the courtyard.

"Let's say I passed this hall at the same time you passed the same hall down there." She pointed at the far end of the hall where Anríq disappeared. "I would see you and you would see me at the same time—the same way we would see each other in real life."

"Yeah?" he asked.

"So you would see me calling out to you to come this way and I would see you calling out to me to follow you, but neither of us would be aware that the other was seeing the other call out. See?"

"No, I don't. If that was the case, we would walk toward each other to meet up. Wouldn't we bump into each other? Then there would be no illusion because we would be together."

"That's the enchantment. Each person sees the other disappear before they get to meet up with the other."

"But wouldn't each of them notice if they magically wound up in a completely different part of the tower?"

"I don't exactly understand it myself." She turned away. "Let's go find the others. I don't want to stay in here any longer. Oh, by the way. Here. Take this."

She stuck her hand into the bag hanging by her side, pulled out what looked like a pebble, and held it out to him.

As soon as she opened her hand, the pebble expanded and turned back into his glaive.

He gasped when he saw it. "How did you get this?! I thought I lost it!"

"You would have, but the Layer shattered when Marine threw it at the Voyant. My magic came back immediately and the glaive fell through into the next Layer along with the rest of us. I magicked it so it wouldn't get lost. I've been carrying it around ever since so I could give it back to you if I ever met back up with you. Here. Take it."

She pushed it into his hands. He stared at it—and then his eyes snapped up to her face.

She really did care. He knew that now—as if he ever doubted it. He didn't doubt it. He just let her behavior make him doubt it.

She must have been thinking of essentially nothing else when Marine threw his glaive at the Voyant and the Layer shattered. Eliska must have been thinking of nothing but his safety.

She had the magic to find anyone in the group in this maze, but she came for him first.

He already knew she felt that way about him. He let his own doubts and insecurities confuse him.

Knowing how she felt about him didn't change the decision he had to make, but it did change something.

He had her back. Whatever happened between them and the rest of the Watch, he never had to doubt her again.

Chapter 21

"So how do we find the others?" Yann asked.

Eliska turned her head to look up at him. For a split second, he expected her to grin, but she stopped herself and looked away.

She looked down at a watery magical pool glimmering in her palm. It cleared to form a window showing different parts of the tower's interior corridors.

"Who should we start with first?" she asked. "I've seen almost all of them in here."

"What do you mean by *almost* all of them? Who's missing?"

"Barsali....and Omer. Everyone else is wandering around in here, including Marine."

"Marine and Anríq both must have their magic back, too," Yann pointed out. "They should be able to locate the others and start gathering everyone back together."

"I don't think so. Marine is crazy again. This tower might even be a Dark place—which explains why she's out in the Dark Layers again."

"What about Anríq? Why is he lost?"

"His magic doesn't work that way. He's a healer. He can't do this." She pointed to the window in her hand.

Now it was Yann's turn to look away. "That's what he said."

"He said what?"

"I asked him if he could create that Coil image that you use to find out where we are. He said he doesn't know how—but he used other methods to try to find out where the Watch was when we got separated from them."

Eliska shook that off. "Anyway, we can find them. Oh, look! There's your father."

Yann peered through the tiny window at his father wandering down a different corridor. He looked as sane as when Yann saw him at the intersection. Yvan didn't spin around and jump at unseen Darklings.

"How did he come back so quickly?" Yann asked.

"This place does some weird things to people's minds. It may be blocking his ability to see the Darklings—or for them to affect him—or whatever they're doing to him. Either way, the spell stops anyone from connecting to anything going inside the tower or outside it."

"Then how is Marine communing with the Dark?"

"I told you. This tower is Dark. The spell is a Dark spell. Dark forces are all over the place here. For all I know, she's using her connection to the Dark to try to find the others and get us all out of here, too."

"So how do we find my father?"

She opened her other hand and created a three-dimensional projection, but it wasn't an image of the Coil. It was a diagram of the tower itself.

Parts of it appeared as crisply distinct as Yann could hope. She rotated the image on her hand and studied the tower's layout from all sides.

Other parts of the tower blurred, morphed, and changed into different configurations before they reconnected to the rest of the tower.

"They don't reform in shapes that are even physically possible," Yann exclaimed. "Look at that one. If that was real, it would be sticking out into space."

"It's magic," she explained with long-suffering patience.

He made a face at her. "I know it's magic, thank you very much. You don't have to treat me like a toddler."

She actually did grin then. Her cheeks flushed, but she turned away to hide it and straightened her expression. "Let's go. The sooner we find everyone, the sooner we can get out of here."

She set off through the corridors. She used her diagram of the tower to find her way even when the tower shifted and changed to a completely different layout.

They wound through a labyrinth of passageways, climbed up a bunch of staircases and climbed down others, and walked through vaulted halls.

The pair entered a different hall that led into a bedroom that led into another courtyard a dozen stories off the ground.

The tower's interior kept adjusting every few minutes. Eliska had to keep her diagram open all the time and continually alter course to make sure she went in the right direction.

Yvan didn't make it easy to find him. He kept walking around trying to find his own way out.

Once, Yann and Eliska passed a different intersection where they spotted Vidal. He called out, "Yann! This way!"

Yann and Eliska spun around, but Vidal vanished as quickly as he appeared.

"Let's keep looking for your father," Eliska suggested. "We're already too close and the others will be more likely to join us if he's with us. We can go back for the others afterward."

They turned off into another passageway. The ceiling dropped lower than the others. Moss clung to walls dripping with water.

"This looks like it's underground," Yann remarked.

"It is. Look." Eliska showed it to him on her diagram.

"We were ten floors up a second ago."

"None of this makes sense." Eliska started to turn away from him to face front again.

She stopped dead in her tracks and stared at something behind him. "What's wrong?" Yann asked.

Her hand shook when she pointed a trembling finger past his shoulder. "Look, Yann!"

He turned around—and he froze when he saw what she was looking at.

Someone had drawn a bunch of childlike sketches on the tunnel wall. Actually someone must have painted them on with permanent ink. The water would have washed the drawings away long ago if the artist used anything else.

The very first image Yann laid eyes on showed a man in a long white robe with a golden aura radiating outward from his body.

Yann's blood chilled when he saw that characteristic murderous scowl. "The Voyant!"

"It can't be him," Eliska countered. "This man is young. The Voyant is an old man with white hair."

"He must have been young once—and these drawings must be old. Maybe whoever drew this did it when he was younger."

Her eyes swiveled away. She sidestepped down the tunnel and pointed at the wall farther away. "Look! This one is a woman!"

Yann followed her. Sure enough, pictures of the same glowing people covered the wall for twenty feet down the tunnel.

The glowing woman Eliska pointed to had long brown hair hanging loose to her waist. She also wore a beautiful smile that looked nothing like the Voyant.

"What do you think *that* is?" Yann stepped forward and pointed to a second light shining from the center of the woman's chest. The artist had painted it with a faint purple-pink hue.

"I don't recognize it." Eliska passed down the tunnel a few more paces. "Look. Here's a couple together."

Yann stopped at her side. They both looked at a picture of two people, a man and a woman.

Characteristic golden halos surrounded each of their bodies. Each of them also had the purple-pink glow in the center of their chests. The man and woman held hands through their halos.

"This one definitely can't be the Voyant," Yann remarked. "He looks like one of the Corsairs. His hair is black and his skin is darker—and he has dots tattooed on his face."

"We did think other people were doing it," Eliska replied.

Yann frowned at her. "What do you mean? Who thought who was doing what?"

She waved her hand in front of her face and shook her head. "Sorry. I got confused for a second. Marine and I had a conversation when we were alone together—about the Voyant. She said the Guardian Templars' records indicate the Voyant is responsible for all the instability cycles throughout history—not just this one. I asked if that meant other people were acting as the Voyant through the centuries. It wouldn't make sense that one guy has been alive all that time and that he's wreaking havoc on the Coil just for fun. If that was the case, he would also be responsible for the stability cycles, too—which means he isn't just doing this to gain power for himself."

"I still don't understand. So you're saying there's some kind of dynasty getting passed down from one person to another?"

"Brother Matherus did say the Voyant is trying to stop whoever will take his place. Maybe that's how it works. Maybe each Voyant has to kill the Voyant before him and take his power in order to rule."

"Then who's responsible for the stability cycles?" Yann asked. "Wesh seemed to think these stability cycles can last for centuries before the next wave of instability. Are you saying the Voyant just goes dormant and leaves everyone alone for hundreds of years? If he really does die, then how does the successor rise to take over?"

Her eyebrows came together in the center. "I don't know. It doesn't make sense."

They both turned back to the drawings. Both people in the couple pictures smiled broadly. They really looked happy together. The solo Voyants scowled.

Yann and Eliska inched down the tunnel. The mural showed dozens of people all surrounded by that golden aura. Some had the purple-pink glow in the center of their chests. Others didn't have it.

Some stood together as couples. Other pairs included two men together, also holding hands, or two women together, also holding hands.

"I don't get it," Eliska murmured. "What's the connection?"

"I don't understand it, either, but these are all definitely different people. They all look different from each other—and look. This is an old woman with a young man. They couldn't be a couple—not that kind—and these are two old men. I don't think this has anything to do with them being couples in the romantic sense."

"You're right," she murmured. "So why are they together? How are they sharing this power together?"

Right then, Yvan stepped out of a side room up ahead. "Yann!" he called. "Over here!"

Yann and Eliska both jumped. Yvan dodged into a side room. Yann and Eliska raced after him, but he vanished.

Chapter 22

Yann and Eliska raced up the tunnel trying to intercept Yvan. They got to the room where he disappeared, only to discover that the door had turned into another rock wall.

Yann slapped his hands against it. "Damn it!"

"Quick! We can't let him get away! Follow me." Eliska projected her diagram of the tower onto her hand. "He went this way."

She took off running, dodged into a few side passages, and burst out into another corridor.

High windows let light stream in from outside. She caught a glimpse of the turbulent ocean outside. She and Yann were on one of the tower's highest floors after they'd just been underground a few seconds ago.

Yann followed on her heels when she charged down the hall following her diagram. It showed how the tower morphed when Yvan stepped into that room.

She veered into a completely different room and saw him standing at the window. He looked down at the ocean, but he turned around when she and Yann entered.

His features started to harden. He didn't believe they were real—or maybe the tower's charm made him see them calling out to him and then vanishing.

She didn't hesitate an instant. The only place he could escape was out that window.

She no longer had a staff, so she raised her hands and bombarded him with bare magic. She blasted him as hard as she could and rushed the rest of the way to where he stood. "Yvan! It's me! It's Eliska! We found you!"

Yann crossed the room in a split second. "Father! Are you all right? We've been looking everywhere for you!"

He blinked at her and then up at him. "Son? Are you real?"

Yann burst out in relieved laughter. "Yeah! I saw you calling to me earlier and then you vanished. Eliska found me. She can use her magic to find the others."

He looked back and forth at both of them. His eyes softened when he looked down at Eliska—and his cheek twitched. "Thank you!" he choked. "I thought we would all be lost in here forever."

She burst into a grin. She couldn't hold it back. She never thought she'd be so happy to see anyone.

She grabbed his hand to pull him out of the room. "Come on. We have to stay together from now on so we don't get lost."

He pulled them out of the room and stopped in the corridor outside to check her diagram of the tower. "Vidal is closest to us."

"How are you doing this?" Yvan whispered.

"My magic came back when we landed in this Island. There's Vidal. Let's go."

The three friends traveled much faster through the corridors, and this time, Eliska pulled Yann and Yvan into a bedroom.

She lowered her voice to a confidential murmur. "We'll stay in here and ambush him. He'll pass in the hall outside and I'll hit him with my magic to break the spell."

"You'll what?!" Yvan countered.

"It's the same thing I did to both of you. Don't worry. I won't hurt him. He won't feel a thing until we get to him."

Yvan frowned. She couldn't take any more time to explain it to him. She heard Vidal's footsteps coming down the corridor.

Yann and Yvan backed off. Vidal passed the doorway and she slammed him with the same counter-spell she used on the other two.

He blinked in a daze when Eliska rushed up to him. "Vidal! It's me! We found you."

He glanced around at the other two Watchmen and frowned. "Are we....? What happened? Where have you all been? I've been wandering around in here for hours."

"Everyone is lost," Eliska explained. "We're going around freeing everyone. Oh, look! Anríq isn't too far away. Let's get him next. He can help us."

The party laid a trap for Anríq. Eliska monitored him as he passed through the tower.

He kept stopping, placing his hands near the walls, and scanning them with his magic. He must have been really confused by how the tower kept changing its configuration every few minutes.

He finally worked his way to a large gathering hall at the end of one of the corridors. Eliska pushed Yann, Yvan, and Vidal into a corner.

She wedged herself in with them where Anríq wouldn't see them when he first entered the hall.

The doors boomed open. He eased inside looking around at where the furnishings should have been.

She hit him with another burst of magic and then grabbed him. "Anríq! It's me! It's Eliska! We found you!"

He started to say, "Eliska....." and frowned.

She ran through the quickest explanation she could. "You have to stay with us. We don't want to lose anyone again."

He frowned even more when she used her diagram to locate Omer. "He's near the courtyard."

The party went through the tower from top to bottom more than once rounding up Rien, Neils, Omer, and finally Niyazi.

"Where's Barsali?" Vidal asked.

"I haven't seen him since I got here," Eliska told him. "I don't see him in the window, either. I don't know if he even is in this tower."

"He must be," Niyazi countered. "How can all the rest of us be here but not him? He's only one man. Even Marine is here. I've seen her."

"I know. I don't know why Barsali isn't here."

"Can you locate him?" Yvan asked.

Eliska searched her tower diagram. She was just about to suggest that the tower's magic might be concealing him somewhere. Then she remembered.

She shut her palm, made the tower diagram disappear, and projected her Coil image instead.

She studied the Layers until she found the tower, but she couldn't see individual people inside it.

She glanced around at nothing. Marine wasn't here. Then she had an idea. "Anríq....."

He looked up at her.

"I need to touch you. Okay?" she told him. "It's....it's in service to humanity."

He nodded and she took his hand. It felt big and strong and rough in hers. Calluses covered the ridge of skin along his fingers and thumb where he held his club and battle axe.

She placed his hand under hers with his palm facing up toward her knuckles. "Add your magic to mine."

She projected the Coil image and he sent a flow of magic into her hand. The image expanded and showed a bunch of golden lines tracing through the image.

All the lines went to one Layer—except for one line that went to the next Layer down from this one. "That has to be Barsali," Yann murmured.

"It is. Look—he's an imp." She pointed at the image and then closed it before she looked around at the others. "So he's in another Layer. We'll get Marine and travel there to find him."

"But....that was a chaos Layer," Niyazi pointed out. "He isn't in an Island. The place was full of Darklings."

"All the more reason we should get out of here so we can help him."

"How will we convince Marine to go with us?" Yvan asked. "She was out of her mind when I saw her."

Eliska glanced around again and held out her hand to Yann. "Give me your glaive."

He handed it over immediately. "What are you going to do with it?"

"As soon as we locate Marine, I'll shatter this Island and we'll fall down into the chaos Layer where Barsali is. Get your weapons ready so we can fight the Darklings as soon as we get there."

"Take this." Anríq took out his machete and handed it to her. "You'll need something to fight with when you get there."

She found herself smiling at him, but the rest of the men taking out their weapons distracted her.

She hefted the blade a few times trying to get the feel of it. She'd never used a weapon as a channel for her magic before. This would be a whole new experience.

She checked her diagram and found Marine in the courtyard. The group had to travel through multiple different tower transformations to get back there.

Eliska paused inside the doorway out of the rain and took a deep breath. "Okay. Here's what we're going to do. I'm going to hit her with my magic to break the spell. I'll do that from in here so she doesn't use her own magic to get away from us. As soon as I hit her, we'll run out there and I'll use Yann's glaive to shatter the Island."

"How will I get my glaive back once we fall through?" Yann asked.

"Stay near me. Keep your hand on the shaft with me. As soon as I hit the floor, I'll let go of your glaive and you can take it back."

He nodded. "Okay."

She faced the courtyard. "Here we go."

She raised her hand and pointed Anríq's blade at Marine. Marine cowered in a corner snarling at empty space.

Eliska sent a shivering crackle of magic down the blade and it jetted across the courtyard.

The Watchmen burst into the open even before the blast hit her. They charged her.

Her eyes widened when she saw them coming at her with their weapons drawn.

Yann and Eliska both gripped the glaive staff as they sprinted across the courtyard. They skidded to a halt next to Marine and Eliska slammed the staff down into the floor.

It exploded in a deafening smash and everyone pitched through into the Layer below.

Chapter 23

Yann felt the moment when Eliska released her grip on his glaive. He pulled it back toward himself while he fell through the Layer into a world of chaos and danger.

Gargantuan Darklings towered over an empty landscape. From what Yann could tell, the Darklings were the only things in this Layer.

These Darklings grew to a colossal size. They wouldn't have fit in any other Layer without shattering it.

They stood on some kind of plain, flat, featureless floor with no mountains, hills, rivers, or any other landscape features.

They might have been in an enormous room with bare walls—except that Yann couldn't see any walls at all. He couldn't see anything confining these Darklings here.

Light shone from all sides and cast everything in an orange tint. The Darklings bellowed in fury, gaped their massive jaws with huge teeth, and dozens of giant tentacles slashed from each Darkling.

Magic rippled and sparked on their skin, shimmered down their tentacles, and the Darklings let off blasts of magic from the end of every tentacle.

One man stood alone in the center of all that madness. Barsali looked tiny down there on the floor with the Darklings towering over him.

Five of them surrounded him, lashed their tentacles at him, fired magical explosions at him, and smashed their enormous feet on the floor all around him. Only a miracle kept him alive this long.

All the Darklings reared away bellowing in rage when the stone from the tower floor fell on their heads. The Watch fell through, too, and dropped right in front of all those Darklings' faces.

Yann twisted away to turn his glaive at the Darklings' eyes. He stabbed into one of them and his glaive stuck.

He used the shaft to propel himself up onto the Darkling's head where the creature couldn't bite him.

He yanked his glaive free, but standing up here didn't stop the Darkling from slashing its tentacles at him.

Two of them whistled past his head and made him duck for cover. These tentacles must have been two feet thick. They could crush him in seconds, but the magic forking off them put him in more danger.

The tentacles looped around, aimed their ends at him, and fired from a distance. He couldn't defend himself against them.

He dove and rolled away from the first assault, but that only took him farther away from the Darkling's head. He wouldn't be able to kill the thing from here.

He wouldn't be able to kill a monster this big anyway—not without magic. He looked around for Anríq and Eliska.

Anríq fell past a different Darkling. His magic buoyed him in front of its face for a split second—just long enough for it to open its mouth and lunge in to chomp him in half.

He wound back his club and dealt it a brutal smash across the face. An explosion went off from his club and the Darkling staggered.

He hurtled at it and brought down his battle axe into the creature's forehead. Another ear-splitting boom echoed from the strike and the Darkling buckled to the floor.

Anríq vaulted on top of the creature's head just as one of its tentacles whipped around to plaster him. He jumped free, grabbed the tentacle, and let it carry him back up to the breach in the ceiling.

He let go at the highest point of his arc, somersaulted, dropped onto another Darkling's head, brought his club down on the creature's skull, and rode the body to the floor.

Eliska stretched Anríq's blade in front of her, narrowed her eyes to slits, and plunged for a different Darkling. She tucked her chin against her chest, braced her whole body, and used all her momentum to drive the blade into the Darkling's neck.

That stab wound on its own wouldn't have killed the creature, but at the point of impact, she drove the blade in to the hilt and fired her magic through the blade.

A brilliant spray of light ejected from the blade and drove the two sides of the wound farther apart. Eliska's weight fell against the handle and her magic followed the slice all the way down the creature's neck.

She landed on the floor where all the Watchmen surrounded Barsali. She charged over to them.

Eliska called over her shoulder and then yelled up at Yann and Anríq. "Get ready to break through to another Layer! Come on! We got Barsali! We're getting out of here!"

Yann tried to see a way to get down from on top of this Darkling. He didn't kill it with his last attack. Its body lay on the floor, but it kept sending its tentacles around to swipe at him and shoot magical blasts at him.

Anríq's club kept thumping in the distance. Yann didn't have time to see what Anríq was doing over there, but it sounded serious.

Yann took a page out of Eliska's book. The next time one of those tentacles came after him, he launched himself into space, flew toward the tentacle about to shoot him, and nailed his glaive blade into it full force.

He jammed the blade in, but he didn't try to take it out or cut the tentacle. He just held on for dear life while the tentacle cracked away at high speed and took him with it.

The tentacle pitched him into the air and across the Layer. He yanked his glaive loose and sailed free over the head of the first Darkling Anríq killed.

Yann landed on top of the Darkling and ran down its back to the floor. Then he had to run around the body to rejoin the rest of the Watch.

The Watchmen surrounded Barsali, but they all had to fight their hardest to hold all the tentacles at bay. More Darklings moved in to take the place of those the party neutralized in its first surprise attack.

Yann dashed into the group and wheeled backward between Vidal and Rien. Yann aimed his glaive outward at the Darklings stalking closer.

Tentacles snaked and crackled all around his head. He stabbed any of them that came too close, but the Darklings figured out all too soon that they didn't have to come any closer.

They fired their magical bursts from farther out of range where the Watchmen couldn't hit them.

Anríq kept vaulting from Darkling to Darkling pulverizing them with his club. He brought them to the ground, but not fast enough to save the Watchmen from more Darklings closing from all sides.

Eliska skidded around a Darkling thirty yards across the floor. Yann was too busy keeping himself and his fellow Watchmen alive to see what she was doing until she got closer.

She ran down the Darkling's side and slashed her blade across its flank. Magic erupted from the weapon and carved a line down its skin.

An explosion went off and she somersaulted away from that Darkling before she burst into a dead run for the Watchmen. Yann really hoped she planned to shatter this Layer as soon as she got here.

Her eyes narrowed as she got nearer, but at that moment, an almighty explosion went off behind Yann's back.

One of the Darklings must have hit the Watch with its magic. The concussion hurled Yann off his feet and sent him flying away.

He landed hard near a different Darkling's foot. He scrambled to get out of the way before it stepped on him and then Anríq brought the creature to the ground with brutal force.

The impact quaked the floor. Yann ran for it to get clear before the creature's body crushed him. Anríq was already jumping to the next Darkling in line.

Without warning, a tentacle zinged out of nowhere and nailed Yann across the back. It sent him sprawling across the floor and stars exploded in his eyes.

He rolled onto his stomach and pushed himself up in time to see Omer, Barsali, Neils, and Niyazi still standing in the same place. They formed a circle with their weapons pointed outward.

Rien and Vidal lay unconscious where they fell. Yann didn't see his father anywhere.

Darklings surrounded the party. The four Watchmen had to fight with everything they had, but more Darklings gathered from all over. One more blast would finish them all.

Yann burst into a run only to get flattened by another tentacle. He landed hard on his stomach trying to catch his breath.

In that moment, Eliska plummeted from somewhere high above. She landed right in the center of the group of Watchmen and raised her machete on high. Her whole body braced to drive it into the floor to break them through to another Layer.

The next instant, a different tentacle whipped out of nowhere and slammed her hard from the side. The blow sent her cartwheeling through the air and she crashed full force into a completely different Darkling.

She pitched across the floor, but not even that blow could knock her out. She started to pick herself up.

Right then, another discharge erupted from one of the many tentacles slashing around. The shot forked across the Layer and hit Barsali in the head.

Eliska launched herself to her feet, roaring, "NO!!" but it was too late.

The shot sailed past Barsali and hit Omer in the back. It took him down instantly, and at the same moment, the Darkling nearest to Eliska bellowed, reared upright, and stomped down on top of her with all its might.

Yann froze staring at the whole horrible scene. This couldn't be happening right in front of him.

Before he could think to move, before any of the Watch even fully realized what just happened, Anríq slammed down on the floor from way up there.

His weight thumped through the floor and he smashed his club down with all his enormous strength. The Layer collapsed and everyone fell through.

Chapter 24

Eliska opened her eyes and saw Yann and Anríq both sitting next to her. She also saw Yvan, Niyazi, and Rien sitting nearby.

She blinked, remembered, and her throat tightened.

Anríq barely glanced at her before he looked away. Yann's eyes said it all.

"No!" she choked. "No!"

"I'm so sorry," Yann husked. "You tried everything…"

"NO!!" She heard her voice rising. "He can't be gone! He can't be!"

Yann lowered his eyes. It was true. Barsali was dead.

Eliska couldn't stand the pain. The Dark poison inside her made it a thousand times worse. The Dark immediately turned that pain against her. It was her fault. Barsali would be alive right now if she only shattered that Layer sooner.

She couldn't hold back tears. She twisted onto her side facing away from Yann so he wouldn't see.

As soon as she moved, she felt the lingering pain of injuries she sustained when the Darkling stepped on her. Anríq must have healed her of multiple broken bones and damaged organs. She still couldn't move very well.

She broke down in tears. She tried her best to do it silently, but they tore her apart anyway. She was the one who got Barsali killed—and

Omer. She didn't have to open her eyes to realize the truth. Omer wasn't here, either.

Yann rested his hand on her shoulder from behind. "It wasn't your fault....."

She lashed out at him, threw her elbow at him to knock his hand away, and shrieked her loudest before she thought to stop herself. "Leave me alone!" she screeched.

He took his hand away, but he didn't leave.

Her own reaction made her curl up in a ball of shame. She couldn't even accept the comfort of the people who mattered to her most.

She should leave right now to protect all of them from herself, but she couldn't even do that—not while she was injured.

She shouldn't be crying right now. She hardly knew Barsali—or Omer—and yet she shared something with both of them, especially Barsali. He was the one who first connected with her—apart from Yann.

She shared Barsali's memories. She knew the deep connection between him and his brother Watchmen. They lost more than she did when he and Omer died.

None of them sat over there crying over their lost comrades. They lost a lot more in Middleborough, but they just kept going. They kept doing their jobs no matter what else happened. Even Barsali did that.

She couldn't hold back the anguish, though. These tears—they came from somewhere deeper than losing Barsali. She just kept caring about these people more and more every day, but she couldn't save any of them.

Every ounce of care and energy she put into them just wound up getting thrown back in her face. Losing Barsali hurt worse than any other insult yet. Why did she have to meet him and start to care about him—only to lose him?

He didn't leave the Watch when Auriel died. He doubled down and committed himself even more than before.

Eliska should do the same thing. She knew that, but this poison inside her twisted everything the wrong way. God, she hated herself! Everything about herself revolted her.

Shame and disgust burned her from the inside when she thought about all her many colossal failures.

She should have made sure Barsali stayed with the group when they fell into that tower maze. He and Omer would be alive right now if she only did the right thing by all of them.

She should have shattered the chaos Layer immediately instead of screwing around killing Darklings. She let her excitement run away with her. The thought of killing Darklings took over and distracted her from protecting the Watchmen.

She would never be able to wash away the stain of their deaths. Wesh's death was her fault, too. She should have protected him from the Voyant or at least stopped Wesh from attacking him.

All these people....lost.....

She broke down sobbing again. No one tried to stop her this time. Even that made her simmer with resentment that no one cared enough to stop her—the heartless bastards.

They left her there for what seemed like a long time. She eventually couldn't cry anymore.

The pain of Barsali's loss added its poison to the growing pocket of sludge inside her.

She would carry that for life—along with all the other insults and brutalities of her miserable existence.

What was the point of her taking Barsali's poison only for him to wind up dead? She shouldn't have bothered to save him at all.

Now she was stuck with it. She was the one who had to live with it—for nothing. She would never get rid of it.

She lay on her side and tried not to listen to the men talking. She didn't know or even care where the Watch landed or what they were doing or what they planned to do. What the hell did she care?

Just then, another hand came to rest on her shoulder. It wasn't Yann. It couldn't be. It felt too heavy.

She stiffened, and before she could move, the hand shifted down to her back—to some of the bones the Darkling broke when it stepped on her.

Magic flooded her and surrounded her spine. Anríq. She shut her eyes and tried to block out the feeling of him touching her.

He pressed his palm into her back between her shoulder blades and then crawled his hand up to the back of her neck.

His powerful fingers clamped around her neck and the base of her skull. His magic invaded her in a torrent of warmth.

Her instincts told her to fight him off, but his magic gripped her. She went limp in his grasp.

That feeling of being totally helpless in his hands—and at the same time totally safe with him—it made her start crying again—not for Barsali but for herself.

God, what she wouldn't give for someone to heal her from this Darkness! The Guardian Templars of Marine's order might have healed her if the Voyant hadn't wiped out their Temple before she got there.

Anríq wouldn't take the Darkness away from her and she didn't want him to. She didn't want to risk him.

He kept his hand around her neck from behind and his other hand closed on her forehead. His magic flooded every part of her and knit all her bones back together.

The pain started to subside—the physical pain did. Nothing could ever heal the other pain because nothing could bring Barsali back.

She should have grieved over Omer as much as she grieved over Barsali. Wasn't Omer's life just as valuable as Barsali's? She knew it was. Omer probably killed more Darklings in his life than Eliska ever killed.

Anríq worked on her head and neck for a while and then shifted in front of her. He didn't go away just because she hated herself.

His eyes overflowed with sympathy and understanding when he gazed down at her. He placed his big hand on her chest and his magic flooded her heart.

Tears sprang back to her eyes, but they meant something different now.

He didn't hide from them. He kept gazing into her face the whole time he worked on her.

His magic did something to her heart. It didn't heal her, but it somehow made the poison more tolerable. She couldn't hate herself.

She would gladly have died in Barsali's place. She spent all her effort and attention in that chaos Layer trying to get near enough to shatter the Layer to take the Watchmen to safety.

She'd been about to do it when she got hit—and then he got hit while she was down. It really wasn't her fault.

Thinking that tore her guts out. She would much rather believe that it was her fault. Then at least she would know who to hate.

Hating herself and blaming herself made it all so much easier. Then she didn't have to live with the sheer senseless finality that those two fine, upright, courageous men were really dead.

Anríq pushed her over onto her back. She lacked the strength to resist, but she didn't want to resist him. She couldn't resist someone as kind and caring as Anríq.

He started working on her stomach to repair her internal organs. That position brought her face to face with Yann. He didn't leave her alone when she screamed at him.

He would never leave her alone. She knew that now. He would always stay with her no matter what. Her getting poisoned by the Dark would never be enough to make him leave her.

He gazed down at her with just as much painful care and heartfelt understanding as Anríq. Looking at Yann while Anríq radiated his magic into her—it stabbed her in the heart.

Yann made it a thousand times worse by taking her hand and clasping it between both of his. He did it in front of Anríq, Yvan, and all the other men. Yann didn't even try to hide what he was doing.

Tears streaked down both sides of her face. She turned her head so she wouldn't have to look at Yann, but she couldn't take her hand back. His touch felt so damn good—as good as Anríq's.

She couldn't lose this. She couldn't lose this one small handful of people who actually cared about her. These men—each of them was more priceless than pure gold. She would give her life for any of them, even Rien.

Her eyes kept migrating back to Yann. He held her hand the whole time Anríq worked on her.

He moved down to her pelvis, gripped her hip bones on both sides, and sent another rush of heat into her from both sides.

She felt in that flow of magic that she must have shattered her pelvis along with probably every other bone in her body.

She should be grateful to him for healing her—and she was grateful. She just couldn't be happy about anything anymore. This poison inside her turned the whole world Dark. It even turned these two young men Dark.

Chapter 25

A nríq worked on Eliska for a long time. He finished with her pelvis, worked his way down her legs, and then told her to turn onto her stomach.

She obeyed him without a word and Yann finally let go of her hand.

Anríq started working on her spine again starting at her tailbone. She pretended not to notice how intimately he was touching her. It didn't mean anything—and yet it meant everything.

His magic tried to soften all the armored tension that kept her locked up inside herself all these years. He made her relax a little bit, but he couldn't tear down the barriers.

When he finished, he sat back, folded his arms on his knees, buried his face in his arms, and fell asleep.

Yann's hand came to rest on Eliska's back. "Try to sit up and eat something. You need to build up your strength."

She peeled herself off the floor and sat up. When she did, she noticed for the first time where she was. She'd been so busy feeling sorry for herself that she didn't notice before.

The group sat in the hayloft of a barn somewhere. Daylight streamed through gaps in the roof boards and through a wide bay at the end of the loft.

The men had laid a large piece of sheet metal on the floorboards and built their fire on top of that to protect the floor.

A massive hay rick full of hay covered half the loft. The men built their fire closer to the open bay so they didn't put the hay in danger.

Neils, Niyazi, Rien, Vidal, and Yvan sat crosslegged around the fire the same way they sat around the fire out in the wild Layers.

Yann handed Eliska her old wooden bowl full of meat shaved off the carcass of some animal roasting on the spit.

The men had constructed the spit out of pieces of metal this time. Where did they get it? She was too grateful to ask.

A pad of folded blankets made a bed under Eliska where she'd been lying just a few minutes ago.

She mumbled, "Thank you," to anyone and everyone who might have had something to do with giving her this food—and to anyone and everyone who might have had anything to do with saving her life.

Anríq didn't hear her—or maybe he did. He kept his head down and didn't rejoin the group.

She bent over her bowl, picked up a piece of the juicy meat, and put it in her mouth. She chewed it while she looked around the loft one more time.

She froze when she saw Marine lying to one side with her eyes closed. A dirty woolen blanket covered her from the neck down.

Yann read Eliska's mind. "She's going to be okay. She got hurt by the Darklings, too. Anríq has been working on her in between working on you. She's been asleep for a few days, but he says she'll recover the same way you will."

Eliska swallowed the food in her mouth. "I didn't see her during the fight."

"None of us did," Niyazi replied. "No one realized she got hurt until we landed in this Island."

"Where are we? How did we get here?"

"We don't know where we are because none of us can use your Coil projection," Yann told her. "We just landed here—about three miles from here. We carried both of you overland until we found this barn."

"Are we.....?"

Eliska faltered when she realized what he just said. The Watch carried her and Marine three miles overland trying to find somewhere safe for them to recover.

Did Anríq carry Eliska...or one of the others? She didn't dare to ask.

"Are we near a town or anything?" She glanced around the loft. "Are we on some farmer's land? Is that why we're here?"

"This is the only building we've seen in this Island," Yvan told her. "The *only* building. We were lucky to find this."

Yann broke the silence by getting to his feet. He picked up a second bowl—the one the men used to serve Marine.

Neils deposited a portion of the food into it. Yann carried it around Eliska's bed and laid his hand on Anríq's shoulder. "Eat something," Yann told him. "You need it."

Anríq dragged his head up with an effort. He struggled to open his eyes, but he took the bowl, bowed over it, and started eating.

"At least we know a few more things about the Voyant now," Vidal remarked. "We know he's looking for a person."

"He's looking for someone magical," Rien added. "Someone with the power to defeat him—so it can't be any of us."

"It could be Eliska," Neils pointed out.

"Then why send the Darklings to attack Middleborough?" Yvan countered. "That's the whole reason we discounted Eliska in the first place. Wesh said the Guardian Templars detected the Voyant coming after Middleborough two years before Eliska ever went there."

"If I'm the one, maybe I should leave," Eliska suggested. "I don't want to put you in more danger....."

"No!" Yvan snapped. "You aren't going anywhere."

"You have to stay, Eliska," Neils insisted. "At least with us you would have some protection. You can't go out there and face him alone."

"You saved Barsali's life once already—and all the rest of us," Yvan went on. "We would have died that very first day without you. Every day we've been alive out here we owe to you."

She didn't want to listen to all of them talk about how great she was, so she changed the subject. "Who else would the Voyant want? Anríq is the only other magic-user here and we know the Voyant isn't after him."

"It doesn't matter who or what the Voyant is after," Yvan interjected. "You're staying with us and that's final."

No one said anything for a minute. Eliska didn't feel like eating all of a sudden. The thought of eating anything made her want to puke.

"We also know that these Voyant Mendicats come in pairs," Yann finally added. "Or that they can come in pairs."

"Maybe the thing he wants is that purple glowing thing you mentioned," Vidal suggested.

"How can it be when we don't have it?" Rien pointed out. "We would know if we had something like that."

"There is one other possible explanation for what we saw in that tunnel," Eliska blurted out.

Everyone turned around to look at her. "What explanation is that?" Yann asked.

"There might be a lot of these Voyants running around. There might be dozens of them. Maybe those pictures we saw weren't Voyants past, but they're actually portraits of Voyants who are currently still alive. They might have a whole order like the Guardian Templars or the Chivalric Order of Custodians. They might all be working together to combine their magic to control the Coil for their own ends. We might only know about one because we've only seen one."

"Then why did Brother Matherus think the Voyant was hunting someone to stop them from taking his place?" Yvan asked.

"Marine told me that Wesh's order was behind on current events and that they got a lot of things wrong. They didn't even believe the Voyant was real or that he had the power to control the Coil. Wesh only found that out for certain after he joined us. It's possible Marine's order got a few things wrong, too. Maybe the Voyant isn't looking for the person to kill them to stop them from replacing him. Maybe he's trying to recruit the person to join their order."

"Then whoever he recruited would have to be an extremely powerful magic-user," Niyazi pointed out. "Who do we know who's more powerful than you?"

Eliska tried her best to shrug that away. "Maybe the person doesn't have to be a magic-user at all. Maybe that purple glowing thing gives the person the power—or maybe the order has another way to bestow that golden halo on the person and then they become as powerful as all the other Voyants."

"Are you seriously suggesting that an imp could become a magic-user?!" Neils countered. "That's impossible!"

"I would have thought so, too, but how else do you explain it? The Voyant went after Middleborough when I wasn't there—which means whatever he wanted was in Middleborough. Then Darklings destroyed the town and only imps survived—and yet the Voyant is still coming after you. Therefore, he must be after you even though you're imps. I don't see any other explanation."

All the Watchmen looked at each other. "But....if any of us could become a magic-user powerful enough to defeat the Voyant....."

"He wouldn't give you the power so you could defeat him," Eliska corrected. "He would give you the power so you could join him. You would become the Voyant—which is exactly what Brother Matherus said he would do."

Neils's hand flew to his head. "My God! Do you mean any of us could become a magic-user—even Rien here?!"

"Shut the hell up!" Rien fired back. "The Voyant doesn't want me. That's stupid."

Some of the others laughed.

Eliska bent over her bowl thinking everything over. She really, really didn't want to be the one the Voyant wanted....but wasn't she just thinking a few short minutes ago that she would make any sacrifice to help these men?

Why not this, too? Why not turn herself over to the Voyant if it made him leave the Watch alone?

The men of the Watch would never let her do that. She didn't even have to ask.

That was their real strength. Each of them would die to protect her, too—a worthless, filthy, wretched Coil rat. Even Rien who hated everything related to the Coil would die to protect her. She already knew that.

Chapter 26

Yann glanced down at Eliska walking next to him. She glanced up at him at the same moment and they both smiled. Her cheeks flushed and he felt his burning.

They both carried bundles of firewood on their way back to the barn. The crisp chill of autumn in the air made their breath come out in clouds of steam.

Eliska glowed with pleasure and happiness, especially when she smiled up at Yann. He couldn't remember her looking this happy since she took Barsali's Darkness.

It still came out in subtle ways—and in not so subtle ways. She still occasionally snapped at people or pushed people away or said she didn't care what the group did.

She slowly worked her way back into the group, but the Darkness never went away completely. It never would. Yann knew that now. He didn't have to ask. It would haunt her for the rest of her life.

He just wanted to give her days like today—days where she could enjoy herself and smile a little bit.

She let herself get closer to the other Watchmen, too. Barsali's loss brought her closer to all of them. She really was one of them now.

They took extra care around her now. They all understood and accepted her Darkness. They knew why she acted the way she did and they treated her gently when she lost control of it.

Yann's eyes darted up from her face to Anríq walking on Eliska's other side. Anríq carried a bigger bundle of firewood than Yann's and Eliska's combined.

Anríq faced front and pretended not to notice Yann and Eliska smiling and blushing at each other. Anríq did that a lot.

Yann pretended not to notice all the little smiles, blushes, and intimacies between Eliska and Anríq, too. All three of them went out of their way to pretend that none of that was happening between any of them.

None of them took any steps to further the situation—in any direction. Neither of the boys advanced things with her—not that Anríq ever did in the first place.

Yann holding Eliska's hand while Anríq healed her didn't mean anything more than him taking care of her. No one treated it as more.

She never mentioned taking it further with either of them and she never acted on it. She smiled, blushed, and showed all her little affections to both of them equally. Anyone looking from the outside would see her treating both of them platonically as just two more of her brother Watchmen.

Yann could live with that. He liked things the way they were now. He didn't need anything else.

The three travelers made it back to the barn. Anríq transferred his load to his left arm while he hauled open the sliding door at the end of the barn.

He slid it shut behind them and dumped his load on the floor before he climbed up to the hayloft.

He lowered a rope on a pulley and waited while Yann tied a bundle of wood into the noose. Then Anríq hoisted it up to the loft, unloaded it, and did the same thing again.

The three friends worked to ferry the wood upstairs and then Yann and Eliska climbed up. Yann kept an eye on Eliska as usual to make sure she made it all right.

She had regained her strength in the three days since she woke up. She was back to normal.

Yann didn't really need to keep an eye on her anymore, but he did it anyway. It had become a habit for him to look after her, sit near her, to make sure she ate and slept enough, and he went everywhere with her.

Anríq did all those things, too, except that he didn't talk to Eliska while he did it. Yann, Eliska, and Anríq had developed a habit of going everywhere together, sitting together around the fire, and they slept next to each other every night.

No one questioned this, not even the three of them. It just happened naturally.

The minute Yann got up to the loft, he saw Marine sitting up. This was the first time she'd woken up since Barsali's and Omer's deaths. She'd been unconscious ever since.

Anríq and Eliska spent hours every day performing healing magic on Marine, but they always insisted that there was nothing wrong with her physically. She'd gone so far out into the Dark that they didn't dare to bring her back.

Anríq and Eliska went straight over to her, but she scuttled away from them yowling and shrieking. She huddled in a corner and glared at them from under her long dark hair.

Eliska stopped in her tracks and stared after her. "I suppose we should be happy about her getting back to normal."

"She's still in there," Yann told her. "You know she is. The real Marine isn't gone."

"I know." Eliska sighed. "I just wish I could see her again—just once."

"You will. We all will."

"But for how long? Whenever we see her, it will be temporary. We'll never get her back for good."

Yann shrugged. "You're right. I guess we just have to enjoy her company while we can."

Eliska stayed there studying Marine even after Anríq turned away. He squatted down by the fire to add some of the new wood to it.

Neils sat there and Rien squatted while he skinned a waterbuck he'd killed. Eliska joined them.

"Would you like me to do that for you?" she asked.

"I can do it," Rien asked. "Thank you for offering, but I'm almost done."

She sat down on Anríq's other side. "Let me know if you want any help."

"Thank you. I will."

Yann turned to Anríq. "Is Marine back to normal?"

Anríq nodded. "She's whole again."

Yann let it go and looked around the loft. The Watchmen had closed off the big open bay to keep the warm air in, now that winter was on the way.

The Watch had boarded up the bay on the other end of the barn, too, but only halfway. That left a good-sized window to let in light and air.

That was the moment when Yann saw his father and Niyazi standing off to one side. They talked in low tones so no one could overhear.

Yann picked up something wrong right away. "What's wrong with Niyazi?"

"We don't know," Neils murmured. "He won't talk to any of us and the Watch Commander won't tell us anything."

Yann knew better than to go over there to find out, but just then, Yvan left Niyazi standing there, strode over to the fire, and looked down at the three young people.

"Would you two mind coming over here for a minute?" he asked. "I need to talk to you."

Anríq and Eliska stood up and followed Yvan back to where Niyazi waited for them.

Yvan didn't specifically invite Yann to join their conference, but Yann went anyway. He couldn't even explain why, but whatever this was concerned him as much as the others.

Eliska looked back and forth between Yvan and Niyazi. "What's going on?"

"Niyazi has been having nightmares," Yvan began.

"And day-mares....or whatever the hell you call them," Niyazi muttered. He stood with his shoulders slumped and his eyes cast down to the floor.

"Are you seeing those armored Darklings again?" Eliska asked.

"No, not them. These are the old kind—the normal kind, I guess you could call them—the same kind that destroyed Middleborough."

"And you see them in the daytime, too?" she asked.

Niyazi nodded without looking up. Yann couldn't remember him ever acting so defeated and deflated.

"Is this the first time it's happened?" Eliska asked. "You seemed fine right up until now. Did it just start—like last night or something?"

Niyazi's gaze darted to Yvan. They exchanged glances.

Yvan took a deep breath. "Niyazi is an orphan," Yvan began. "His family died in a plague in another city and the Black Watch adopted him. He grew up in the Watch and eventually took the oath himself. When he was just a boy younger than Yann is now, he was on watch with his brother Watchmen on the wall when that city came under a Darkling assault. He got pulled into the Dark Layers before some of his brother Watchmen pulled him out." Yvan shot Niyazi one more sidelong glance. "He's suffered from nightmares ever since. He never told anyone except for me."

"So this is the same nightmare you've been having all along?" Eliska asked and glanced at Yvan. "I don't understand why you're asking us to intervene if this is normal for you."

"It never happened during the day before." Niyazi glanced up. His eyes darted from one face to the next before he looked back down at the floor. "I'm losing my mind."

"Not necessarily," she replied. "We still don't know what these things are. They might be real."

Anríq stepped forward and passed his hand up and down in front of Niyazi's head. A ripple of magic passed over Niyazi's face before Anríq stepped back.

"He's normal, isn't he?" Eliska asked. "He's as normal as Rien, Barsali, and the Watch Commander were when they started having these nightmares."

Anríq nodded.

"You see?" Eliska went on. "Whatever is happening to all of you isn't affecting you physically, mentally, or magically."

"What does that mean?" Niyazi asked.

"It's the closest evidence I think we're ever going to get that these invisible Darklings really are real. I don't see how neither Anríq nor I could detect anything wrong with any of you if the Darklings weren't real. It's the only logical explanation as far as I can tell."

"That doesn't explain why Niyazi is seeing regular Darklings instead of the armored ones," Yann interjected.

"We're in a different Layer," Eliska suggested. "Those armored Darklings might have been confined to that Layer."

"It's too bad we can't ask Omer which Layer they were in when he saw them," Yvan suggested.

Eliska turned back to Niyazi. "I don't know what to tell you except that it will hopefully pass. Rien and the Watch Commander are both back to normal. I'm sorry, but you just have to go through it."

He groaned and passed his hand across his eyes. "Can't you just put me in a coma for four days until it's over? I can't live like this."

She smiled up at him. "I really wish I could."

The barn door banged open and then slid shut downstairs. Vidal must have returned from hunting.

That sound did something to everyone involved in this conversation. They ended their discussion and turned away to return to the fire.

At that moment, a hissing sound swept toward the barn from the opposite side. It sounded like a sheet of heavy rain covering the landscape as clouds moved in.

Everyone glanced toward the open bay window as the curtain of water covered the countryside.

Yann barely had time to turn around. He saw in one split second that it wasn't rain or water. It was a solid curtain of pure, wild magic.

The next instant, it enveloped the barn and completely wiped it off the face of the earth.

Chapter 27

Magical rain pattered sparks all over Yann's skin, but it wasn't rain. It fizzed and prickled in a sheet moving over his arms, shoulders, face, and head.

The sheet traveled from one side of his body to the other before it swept away across the countryside.

The Watchmen looked around. They stood on the ground. The barn was gone.

Vidal stood there with them. He must have been downstairs in the barn when it vanished.

At least everyone in the Watch still had their weapons, but Rien's waterbuck also disappeared along with the Watchmen's blankets and all the other goods they'd been using while they stayed here.

Marine stood nearby looking all around her and down at her hands and dress. Then her eyes lifted and she made eye contact with Yann. She was back—but for how long?

Eliska looked down at her hands, too. "Our magic is gone again." She sighed. "I really wish it wouldn't do that."

"Any idea where we are this time?" Yvan asked.

"It looks like we're in the same Island." Eliska squinted at the horizon. "Or a different version of it."

The group surveyed the area. The same combination of ditches, hills, and the contour of the horizon all looked the same.

Different species of trees and bushes grew in different places than before. This Island wasn't as lush—and it wasn't a crisp autumn day anymore.

This country was hotter, more arid, and the vegetation had to struggle harder to survive.

Tough scrub grass grew in clumps where fresh green fields used to carpet the terrain. No one would build a barn full of hay here.

"I guess we might as well move on," Yvan decided. "There's nothing here."

No one said a word. He headed off toward the west. It was as good a direction as any.

The group getting smaller sobered everyone and made them all more serious. Marine didn't joke around to try to cheer everyone up.

Yann, Anríq, and Eliska walked together the way they usually did. Marine joined them for some reason.

Yann found himself adjusting his position so she could walk next to Eliska. Eliska usually walked between the two boys.

Now he made room for Marine there, too. The two boys walked on the outside with the two girls inside. It just made sense for them to arrange themselves that way.

Yvan and Niyazi went in front. Niyazi took Omer's place as Yvan's senior Watchmen. Neils followed them and Yann heard Neils talking to them on the way.

Vidal brought up the rear with Rien behind the three in front. That was the whole Watch—five men.

The group's size chilled Yann to the bone. Omer's and Barsali's loss confirmed something Yann kept hidden from himself all this time. Everyone here was going to die.

He somehow tricked himself into thinking everyone in the group would make it out of this alive. He fooled himself into thinking the Watch would keep dodging bullets until some opportunity gave them the chance to escape from this disaster.

Not even Wesh's death brought home the simple inevitable fact. They wouldn't make it out—because there was no way out.

Yann would have to watch each of these people die—probably in horrific ways. Nothing would save them because they couldn't be saved.

The Coil would continue to collapse on itself. The instability would get worse.

He would have to let these people go one after the other. Then he would never see them again. Could he really do that?

He didn't know where his father was going—and it didn't even really matter anymore. Nowhere would be any safer than any other.

Another sheet of wild magic could overtake the group and restore Anríq's and Eliska's magic—and rob Marine of her sanity again. Was that really worth it? Was any of this really worth it?

Yann had spent the days of Eliska's recovery fashioning another staff for her. She kept it with her this time instead of throwing it away when she lost her magic.

Yvan headed across the countryside toward some hills in the distance. The trip took hours.

When they got there, they spotted a good-sized town on the horizon. "It looks bigger than Middleborough," Neils remarked.

"Maybe we shouldn't go there," Niyazi suggested. "Maybe we should hold off. I don't want to put those people in danger the next time the Voyant comes after us."

Yvan looked around at the bleak countryside. "The alternative is staying out here."

"We've lived in the open before," Rien pointed out.

"We don't know if we'd be putting them in danger or not," Neils added. "They might need the Watch. We might be able to do them some good."

"They don't need a bunch of Watchmen who are being hunting by the Voyant," Yvan decided. "I'm with Niyazi. Let's find a place to camp."

"I saw a thicker cluster of trees over there." Neils pointed behind him to the south. "We might find water there."

"Let's go check it out." Yvan waved everyone to head off in that direction.

The minute everyone turned away from the town, the landscape in front of them started to morph and change.

It didn't implode or collapse nor did any Darklings come out to attack the party or each other.

The trees in the distance grew, shrank, and twisted in bizarre shapes. Hills undulated out of position.

Spikes of rock sprouted from flat fields, contorted into rubbery, surreal pictures of different creatures, and then sank back into the soil.

None of these changes put the Watch in danger. The ground didn't quake or fracture.

The grass around the Watchmen's feet came alive, slithered over Yann's ankles, and then fell away.

Fragments of grass stems ejected out of the mat of vegetation underfoot, soared around in flocks, changed into what might have been insects or maybe tiny buzzing machines, and then dove back into the grass where they came from.

The Watchmen looked all around them trying to understand what was happening. The instability kept spreading. The clouds of stuff flying around got thicker, but still none of it put the travelers in danger.

Yann looked everywhere trying to see something coming to attack the party, but nothing did come. None of these strange shapes or objects ever formed into Darklings. Why not?

Just then, the Voyant appeared out of nowhere. He wasn't there before.

His golden halo burst out of thin air and blazed to life a hundred yards away to the south.

The instability followed him in a wave coming from the north and moving west.

Yvan's arm shot out and he pointed. "He's going for the town! The town is in danger! Come on!"

He took off sprinting across the countryside. Everyone followed him. The instability definitely got worse with every yard of terrain the Voyant covered.

The instability escalated getting closer to the town. Yann couldn't stop to see if the instability faded after the Voyant passed by.

The Watchmen dove in front of the Voyant and everyone pivoted backward to confront him. Yann raised his glaive.

He didn't know what he would do with it against such a powerful wizard. Marine already tried that.

The Voyant's expression didn't change when the Watchmen blocked his path. Did he even see the men standing in front of him?

The radiant golden beams shooting out of his halo merged with all the debris and flying particles around him.

His presence tore up the landscape more than ever. A vortex of chaos surrounded his halo. Yann couldn't even really see anything solid around the Voyant's halo. He blurred reality close to him.

Sections of the landscape erupted out of position outside that rim of chaos. Rock, vegetation, weird creatures, the shapes of Darklings and other monsters, and even people's faces appeared in a sea of random stuff all growing, morphing, twisting, writhing, and dropping away to nothing.

None of that stuff attacked the Watch—but the Voyant didn't stop, either.

He migrated ever closer to the town taking his wave of chaos with him.

Rien charged him first, swung his broken sword in a downward chop, and hacked straight into the Voyant's halo.

The Voyant didn't even look at Rien. The strike blasted Rien away and he hurtled backward.

Niyazi, Anríq, Yvan, and Vidal all rushed the Voyant at the same time. Anríq hacked his axe down into the halo at the same time Vidal and Niyazi attacked with their own axes.

The landscape itself reacted, but it still didn't counterattack—not really.

A sudden upheaval in the bedrock right next to the Voyant hurled Vidal and Anríq out of place. It pitched them into a sea of living grass that tumbled both men outside of weapons range.

Another cloud of grass stems blasted out of the scrub at the Watchmen's feet, took wing, and changed into some kind of tiny whizzing insects.

They surrounded Yvan and Niyazi. Millions of the things snatched the two Watchmen by their uniforms and sent them cartwheeling out of the way.

The Voyant kept floating toward the town in the distance. The mayhem and destruction around him kept building. When would the landscape explode and take the Watchmen with it?

Yann lunged forward to join the fight and defend his fellow Watchmen, but Eliska grabbed him and held him back. "Don't!" she yelled over the noise. "You can't defeat him that way!"

Anríq must have been thinking the same thing. He got to his feet, but he didn't attack the Voyant again.

The other Watchmen didn't get the message. Rien, Yvan, Niyazi, Neils, and Vidal all closed on the Voyant at the same time.

He never even looked at them when they raised their weapons. Now Yann knew the Voyant didn't see them. He only saw the town in the distance.

The Watchmen all struck at the same instant and an explosion went off. It hurled the Watchmen away, but the same blast caught the four young people in the same tempest.

An almighty force slapped Yann backward and he rolled across the ground.

He somersaulted onto his stomach and immediately pushed himself onto all fours. He scrambled to grab his glaive while he checked to see where he was.

The blast threw him farther than he realized. He found himself only a dozen yards in front of the town's outer wall.

The other Watchmen picked themselves up, too, but none of them was in any danger anymore.

Yann didn't see the Voyant anymore, but the wave of instability still hovered there the same distance from the town. The wave didn't move.

The landscape, vegetation, grass, and everything else kept seething in rippling patterns of living things, morphing into the shapes of Darklings, and then changing into something else a few seconds later.

"Why doesn't it come any closer?" Rien husked.

Eliska clambered to her feet and the others all got up. Yann didn't want to take his eyes off the wall of chaos in the distance. It wasn't nearly distant enough.

The Watchmen closed together watching it. Yann waited, but it always stayed over there the same distance away.

The worst chaos drifted a little farther sideways to the east and then back toward the west where it had been before. It swept across the countryside and even receded a little before it returned to the same position.

"I don't like this at all," Niyazi muttered. "It could overtake us anytime. We wouldn't be able to stop it."

"We can't stop him, either," Eliska pointed out.

"Why doesn't he just take what he wants if he's so powerful?" Rien asked. "What is he waiting for?"

Just then, a deep, booming voice rumbled across the area from behind the party. "Don't come any closer! Take another step and we'll open fire!"

Chapter 28

The Watchmen turned around extra slowly. Yann stiffened when he saw how close he and his fellow travelers stood to the town's walls. Giant metal gates led into the town, but those gates remained firmly locked to keep out any unwanted visitors.

Armed men lined the top of the wall—and they all aimed their weapons at the Watch.

These people didn't use the kind of weapons Yann knew about. The townsfolk had set up some kind of iron turrets all along the wall with long barrels pointing down at the travelers.

The townsfolk had also constructed projectile launchers with missiles thicker than Yann's arm aimed outward the countryside.

"Put your weapons down," Yvan murmured. "Show them we aren't here to threaten them."

He lowered his sword to the ground at his feet and slowly raised his hands. Yann had to summon all his willpower to put down his glaive, but townspeople would have been able to obliterate the Watch considering the weapons these people had.

"We aren't here to threaten you!" Yvan called out. "We belong to the Black Watch! We were trying to protect you from that wizard who was about to attack your town! If you don't want us here, we'll back away and leave the area—but if he came here to attack you once, he'll do it again." Yvan pointed to the instability in the distance.

A bunch of the men up there glanced in that direction, but they didn't take their weapons off the Watchmen.

The other Watchmen threw or put down their weapons one after the other. Eliska kept hold of her staff. It didn't act as a weapon without her magic.

Anríq hung his club on his belt and slung his axe back across his back. He didn't put either weapon down nor did he raise his hands in surrender.

A tall man with dark hair stepped up on something behind the wall so he could see better. "Who are you?!" he demanded. "Where do you come from?"

"My name is Yvan Dilnao, Commander of the Watch from a town called Middleborough. We suffered a Darkling attack and the town was lost to the Layers. We've been traveling the Coil ever since." Yvan pointed behind him. "That glowing halo you saw is a Dark wizard causing all this instability. We've been trying to find a way to defeat him."

"Why are you traveling with a Barbarian?" the man demanded. "We don't allow his kind here."

"He's a Servant-healer," Yvan called back. "He defends the defenseless and heals the sick. He's here to defeat the Voyant, too. If you take us, he can help you. He's a good man and a powerful warrior."

The men on the wall held a hasty murmured conversation. "Are you sure we should stay here?" Niyazi asked Yvan in an undertone. "Didn't we just decide our presence would put the town in danger?"

"It looks to me like the town is already in danger if the Voyant is going after it," Neils pointed out. "We can at least try to help defend them."

The tall man jumped down behind the wall, and a second later, the big entrance gates opened.

The tall man and a dozen other men came out all armed with some very different weapons. These looked like long metal tubes with wooden handles.

The men kept the wooden ends jammed into their shoulders and aimed the tubes at the Watchmen. These must have been some other kind of projectile weapon like a smaller version of those missile launchers up there.

The men of this town all wore plain canvas pants, boots with pointed toes, and fabric vests over long-sleeved shirts despite the heat.

The townspeople surrounded the Watchmen and aimed their weapons inward to threaten the travelers. Yvan stayed where he was with his hands up.

The tall guy scrutinized Yvan and then the guy's gaze dipped to Yvan's insignia. "We haven't seen the Black Watch in decades. We thought they were all wiped out."

"Not completely," Yvan replied. "We've been trying to find a town that needed the Watch. If you don't want to let us in, we'll stay in the area and do what we can to defend you from out here."

"No one can defend us," the guy returned. "We've been fending off Darkling attacks for years and now the landscape is going crazy."

Yvan sighed and nodded. "It's the same everywhere we go. The Voyant Mendicat is the one causing all of this." He jerked his thumb toward Marine. "Our friends have been trying to find a way to defeat him, but we haven't figured it out yet."

The townspeople inspected the party for another second before the guy nodded. "You better come inside. We need the Black Watch." He waved to his people. "Put your guns down."

The townmen lowered their weapons. Yann resisted the urge to bombard these people with questions about what kind of weapons they were using.

None of the townspeople tried to stop Yvan from picking up his sword. Niyazi and Vidal both picked up their axes. Yann dared to pick up his glaive.

The tall man waved Yvan forward and led the way through the gate.

The Watchmen froze on the threshold. None of them noticed the townspeople shutting the gates with the Watchmen inside.

Yann stared in stunned amazement at the town hidden behind the wall. Motorized vehicles rumbled through paved streets. Machines he didn't understand chugged and puffed all over the place.

Lighted screens flickered behind the windows of houses all around him. Pictures, faces, and scenes flashed across those screens along with lettering and even music.

The houses looked nothing like anything he'd ever seen in his life. They dwarfed any house in Middleborough. All these machines, screens, and vehicles made his head swim.

The people inside the town wore a curious combination of clothing, too. Some more of the men much fancier versions of the same pants, boots, and vests.

Others wore cylindrical top hats, brocade jackets, and carried decorative walking sticks.

The women wore elaborate, ruffled dresses that bunched up behind their waists. All the women visible from the street carried tiny umbrellas that could only have been decorative, too, because it wasn't raining.

The women all wore hats, but these were tiny, frilly, ridiculous affairs perched high on towers of curls. Yann didn't understand their aesthetic appeal at all. Their clothes and appearance made them look incapable of doing anything.

Their skirts fell all the way to the ground and hid the women's feet entirely. The women took extra pains not to show their feet and legs even when they walked.

Their long skirts gave the appearance that they weren't walking at all. They seemed to float along the ground like something from another reality.

Some of them whispered to each other about the travelers. Yann could just imagine what these people were thinking about Eliska and Marine.

The tall man distracted everyone by stepping forward. He held out his hand to Yvan. "Welcome to Tenby. My name is Atian Niccao. It's an honor to meet anyone from the Black Watch."

Yvan shook his hand. "This is quite the town you have. I'm interested to learn all about how you do things. This is Niyazi Trahan, Neils Surette, Rien Dugas, and Vidal Rom. This is my son, Yann, and this is Anríq. He's a friend. You can trust him with your town's safety."

Marine interrupted by stepping forward. "Um.....would you have a computer I can use? I want to do some research into the Voyant's activities and contact some of the cities that might be monitoring him."

Atian frowned at her. "A...what? A....computer? I don't know that word."

Her shoulders slumped and she looked away. "Oh. Sorry. I thought you did."

"This is Marine," Yvan explained. "She belongs to the Guardian Templars. They've taken it as their mission to learn as much about the Voyant's activities so they can defeat him."

Atian narrowed his eyes at her and curled his lip at her hair and dress. "She doesn't look like much, does she?"

Yvan saved the day by interrupting. "Are you in charge of this town? Do you have a Watch Commander—or something equivalent?"

"We don't have any structure like that," Atian replied. "We organize our defense amongst ourselves. We've been stranded out here for years with no contact with the rest of the Coil."

"How is that possible when you have all this technology?" Marine asked. "Where do you get your broadcasts from—and your fuel?"

Yvan raised his hand. "I'm sure that's none of our business. If you show us where to go, we'll be happy to take our posts on the wall."

"What about *them?*" Atian cast another critical glance at Eliska and Marine. He tried not to include Anríq in that glance, but he wound up doing it anyway.

Before Yvan could reply, a different man hustled out of the surrounding neighborhoods somewhere. Yann didn't see where the guy came from.

He was a much older man. He couldn't have been younger than sixty. He wore his grey hair cut in a bowl shape around his ears and he wore a long robe-like jacket down to his knees.

It had a banded collar like the Watchmen's uniforms, but his jacket had a deep, midnight-blue color with no insignia.

He rushed up to the group and went man to man shaking hands with all the Watchmen.

"The Black Watch!" the man exclaimed. "I haven't seen a Watchmen in years! Welcome, welcome!"

The guy came to Anríq, held out his hand....and froze when he realized what he was looking at.

The guy shuddered, shook his hand, faltered, and then hustled away to shake Yann's hand instead.

"It's wonderful that you're here!" the old man exclaimed. "We thought we might be the last living people in the Coil."

"You aren't," Niyazi told him.

The guy only smiled at him and practically pumped Niyazi's arm off his shoulder. "Welcome, welcome! It's always a blessing to see any man of the Watch."

"Thank you," Yvan replied.

"This is O'akim Mossant," Atian interjected. "He's our town mendicant."

"Mendicant!" Rien snapped. "Do you work for the Voyant?"

O'akim frowned at him. "What's a voyant?"

"He's a healer," Anríq cut in.

O'akim glanced at him, tried to smile, and failed. He distracted himself by turning back to the Watchmen. His eyes misted over when he gazed at them. "I haven't seen a member of the Black Watch since I was young. Seeing all of you gives me hope that this town might survive after all."

"O'akim has an extensive library of information from all over the Coil," Atian added. "If you want to do research, he's your man."

Marine rushed in. "Really?! Would you mind if I take a look? I'm a member of the Guardian Templars."

O'akim's eyes shot open. "Are you, really?! This is wonderful! I always hoped I would meet one of the Templars! This is truly a lucky day! Come with me, my dear. I'll show you everything!"

He took her hand and led her off down the street. They turned into a side avenue and vanished.

"We'll probably never see her again," Rien muttered.

"O'akim will take good care of her," Atian replied. "He has a heart of gold, but he gets lonely without someone to talk to about everything that interests him." He waved behind him. "Follow me and I'll show you where to go."

Yvan and the other Watchmen followed him. Yann moved closer to Eliska with Anríq on her other side.

"So...these people have no magic?" Yann whispered. "That mendicant or whatever he was—he's not magical, is he?"

Eliska shook her head. "If Anríq and I don't have magic in this town, no one else will have it, either." She shot a sidelong glance at some of the nearby house windows. Screens flickered behind every single one of them. "It doesn't look like they need it."

The group got to the wall just then. Atian led Yvan to a metal stairway rising to a scaffold of walkways and platforms built into the wall from behind.

The men worked up there to man their defenses. Others sat behind the wall cleaning, checking, and working on the smaller tube weapons—guns, Atian called them.

Yvan followed Atian up the ladder onto the scaffold where they could see over the top. Atian pointed across the countryside toward the wave of instability in the distance.

It rose off the ground to form a curtain. No one could see the terrain behind it.

Niyazi, Rien, and Vidal followed him. Neils got halfway up there before he wound up talking to some of the other men nearest him.

Yvan turned around and waved for Yann to join him. "Here we go," Yann breathed and set off for the wall with Anríq right behind him.

Chapter 29

E liska stood back and watched Yann and Anríq climb the scaffold to join Atian on the wall.

The local Tenby town defenders had a mixture of reactions to Anríq's arrival. Some shook his hand and even kissed it. Others reared away from him in horror. Some even pulled their weapons on him until Atian told them not to.

He took it all in his usual stride and didn't react to any of it, good or bad. Eventually, he and Yann worked their way up to the top of the wall to join the rest of the Watch.

Atian kept pointing out different features of the landscape and explaining things to the group. Eliska couldn't hear them from here and she didn't want to.

Now what was she supposed to do? Everyone else had something to do. She couldn't help defend this town without her magic.

She didn't know where Marine was, but Eliska didn't belong in any dusty library. She didn't even know how to read. Marine and O'akim would laugh her out of the room.

She glanced around the local streets and cringed when she saw all the ladies in their finery and frilly dresses. Even the young girls wore them.

They all gave Eliska strange looks like these women had to think real hard to figure out if Eliska was even human. She couldn't stay here.

She took off walking through Tenby and tried not to look at anyone of either sex, but she couldn't unsee all the machines, screens, vehicles, street paving, and the extravagant construction of all the buildings.

Tenby didn't have any vehicles actually flying through the air and it didn't have any computers. Other than that, Eliska didn't see much difference between this town and the giant cities she visited with Marine.

After a while, the hustle and bustle—not to mention the citizens' constant staring—got the better of Eliska. She turned off into a random alley and cut through to a different street.

The houses and buildings looked exactly the same here. Everything looked exactly the same here, but everyone seemed to be too busy to notice her. The defenders on the wall going out to bring in the travelers under guard attracted too much attention.

She couldn't figure out what anybody in this town was doing with themselves. She didn't understand all the machines they worked on or contraptions they used for their everyday life.

If she ever felt marginally tempted to go near one of the buildings, the dozens of screens everywhere changed her mind real quick. She didn't want to see them or find out what might be on them.

She dodged from one street to the next just trying to make sure no one noticed her. Her clothes always allowed her to blend in anywhere she went in the Coil. Now they made her stick out for all the world to see. She was the only female in the entire town wearing pants.

She worked her way to the opposite end of town only to run into the other side of the wall. Men stood their posts here, too.

She would have liked to climb up there to see what was going on with the landscape, but she couldn't do that with the men there.

She turned back. The thought of going back through the entire town to find someone she knew sounded like her idea of Hell.

She needed to find somewhere dark and quiet where she could just sit by herself and be alone.

She needed anywhere she could go where these people wouldn't see her and stare at her. She couldn't tolerate seeing all the questions racing through their minds.

She looked around in panic, but right then, a little boy walked up to her. He barely came up to her chest.

He wore the same pants and shoes as the men but in a smaller size, obviously. He also wore a different style of cap. It hugged the top of his head with a brim that curved down on either side of his eyebrows.

He cocked his head and frowned up at her. "Who are you?"

"Eliska," she replied. "Who are you?"

"Hani," the boy replied and frowned a little deeper. "Who are you? You don't live in Tenby."

"No, I'm just visiting."

His eyes flew wide open. "Ah—of course! The visitors!"

"If you know about the visitors, how do you not know about me?" Eliska tried not to look at him too closely. She didn't want to get on friendly terms with these people, especially not anyone who wanted to talk to her.

"The visitors are all over on the wall by the gate with Atian," Hani pointed across town. "All except for that lady talking to O'akim in his library." The boy frowned at her again. "What are you doing over here? Are you standing on the wall?"

"You can see that I'm not. I don't stand on the wall."

"What do you do?"

She looked away. "Nothing. I don't do anything. I was just walking around town looking at everything."

"That lady in the library was really nice."

Eliska looked up. "You talked to her?"

Hani nodded. "I run errands for O'akim sometimes. She talked to me about stuff."

Eliska made a command decision not to ask what stuff Marine talked to this boy about.

Eliska also made a command decision not to ask Hani to point her in the direction of somewhere dark and quiet where she could sit by herself and be alone.

The whole point of being alone was for no one to know where she was. He would know if she asked him.

He might feel tempted at some point to tell someone where she was. He might even tell Yann—or Yvan. That would be disastrous.

"Do you know that lady?" Hani asked.

"Who—Marine? Yes, I know her. She's my friend."

He brightened up again. "I could show you where she is. Were you looking for her? I can go to O'akim's library whenever I want to. He told me I could. He even told me I could read any of his books if I wanted to."

Eliska looked away again. "That was nice of him."

"Come with me and I'll show you where it is. Then you could read the books, too."

She didn't dare to tell him that he knew how to read better than she did. She also didn't dare to tell him why she didn't want to see Marine and O'akim.

Anything was better than wandering around town with nothing to do and nowhere to go, so she followed the boy.

He led the way back through town, up and down a few different streets, and entered some random building.

The ground floor looked exactly like the ground floor of every other building in this town that wasn't someone's house.

Hani climbed the stairs to the second floor and passed through a different area that had to be some kind of hospital.

Patients lay on beds with women in white uniforms working over them. Men in white coats went back and forth from bed to bed. Eliska couldn't figure out what they were doing.

She'd never seen people treating the sick without magic—or maybe these people were injured. She would never know.

Hani went to another stairwell that rose to the building's fifth floor, passed down an enormous corridor lined with rooms all teeming with people, and entered an extremely luxurious office lined on opposite walls with towering bookshelves.

Marine sat at a high table in the center of the room flipping the pages of a massive book almost as big as the tabletop itself.

She'd cleaned herself up in the short time since she left the Watch by the gate. She'd changed into a fresh, clean dress and she even looked like she'd taken a bath.

Eliska didn't see how Marine could have done any of that without magic, but Marine was back to looking like a princess.

She bent over the pages and didn't look up when Hani and Eliska walked in. "This says the Crippling Voruta is poisonous to the sementilated Xuinerth."

"Yes, of course it is," O'akim replied without turning around.

He worked across the room over one of the town's many machines. Eliska didn't try to figure out what it was.

"How can it be when the Xuinerth lives in the Jeweled Enclave?" Marine asked. "The crippling voruta is one of the few available food sources the Xuinerth uses to stay alive. The Xuinerth would have gone extinct without the voruta for food."

Eliska went over to Marine's desk. "Are you finding out anything about the Voyant?"

"These people don't have any information about the Voyant, but this is just as interesting." Marine turned another page. "I've been trying to find out about these plants for years."

Their conversation drew O'akim's attention. "Oh, good. Hani's back. I need you to take a message to Atian, Hani." O'akim handed the boy a folded piece of paper. "Run along, now."

The boy left. Marine went back to poring over her book.

"This says the crippling voruta has a scaly purple seed pod. That's wrong," she announced. "It has a scaly purple seed pod in its first year, but after that, the pod turns grey."

O'akim looked up and smiled at her. "Of course you're right, my dear. You should go through all my books and correct any other errors you find."

She shot him a smirk and went back to reading. "That's just your way of trying to get me to stay."

"Can you blame me? No one else in this town wants to talk about the crippling voruta or the sementilated Xuinerth."

Marine stood up, closed the book, climbed a ladder, and slid the book back into place. She took down a different book, took it back to her desk, and started reading it.

"This one actually lists histories of civilizations in different Layers of the Coil," she remarked. "I thought you said you didn't have any information about anything that happened outside of Tenby."

O'akim looked up. "It does? It's news to me if it does."

Eliska drifted a little closer to the door. She didn't know or want to know half of what these two were talking about.

Hani wasn't here. Marine and O'akim wouldn't notice if Eliska disappeared, too.

Just as she got to the threshold, Marine called out, "Listen to this! This book tells the story of the knights who founded the Guardian Templars! I didn't think anyone outside the Temple knew about this."

"A different Templar came through here when I was just a boy," O'akim replied over his shoulder. "He was an old man and he suffered a stroke while he was here. He died and left that book behind. That's the only reason it's here. I haven't met anyone from the order since then."

Eliska slipped out of the room and took off walking fast down the corridor in the direction Hani led her to come here.

Eliska beat it back out to the street. Now she was alone again. She needed to get out of sight before someone else came to find her.

She wandered around for a little longer, but she didn't see anything promising until she passed down another alley.

It cut between two enormous houses. They would have been castles if they existed anywhere else in the Coil.

The alley walls overlooked giant gardens, each bigger than the whole town of Middleborough.

Eliska hopped over the wall into one of the gardens. Stands of trees separated the garden's outer areas from the massive house just a dozen yards away. No one could see her here.

She wandered through the trees and came out on a flagstone walkway leading between some tall hedges. This was perfect.

A long glass solarium jutted out from one end of the house. The solarium had a solid back wall to trap heat on that side.

She sat down behind that wall. She was completely invisible to the rest of the world. Now she could finally relax. No one would ever find her.

Chapter 30

"The attacks usually come from over there when they do come." Atian pointed to the country east of Tenby.

"You said earlier that it's usually Darklings who attack you," Yann suggested.

Atian nodded. "Almost always." He squinted at the instability in the distance. "I don't know why they aren't coming out now. It doesn't make any sense."

"The instability is moving away," Vidal pointed out.

"It never goes away," Atian replied.

"Have you suffered any landscape collapses?" Yvan asked. "I mean total collapses?"

"Nothing like that. It happened to some neighboring towns. We don't know why it hasn't happened to us. We're all just counting down the days and trying to enjoy the time we have left."

Yvan frowned to himself. "I wonder why not. Maybe it has something to do with the Voyant coming after this town."

"Why would he?" Yann asked. "These people aren't magical. At least we had magic-users in Middleborough."

"If Eliska is right, then the Voyant doesn't care if someone is a magic-user." Yvan looked around. "Where is she?"

"Who?" Atian asked.

"Eliska—the girl who came in with us." Yvan turned to Yann. "Did you see where she went?"

"She was standing down there when we came up here. Maybe she went to see what Marine is doing."

"She should be here," Yvan decided. "She knows more about the Coil than any of us. See? Look up there."

He pointed at the instability in the distance. The ever-shifting combinations of vegetation, soil eruptions, and landscape changes heaved into the air before sinking back into the earth.

The transformations affected the air itself and rose higher into the sky. They changed the colors of the sky to vapor and merged with other Layers collapsing from above.

They compressed on top of each other, burst apart, reformed, and collapsed again. Different landscapes revolved through the Layers.

Some only gave brief glimpses into other worlds, other towns and cities, or landscapes morphing and transforming before they vanished into vapor Layers or disintegrated in chaos.

"What could Eliska tell us about that?" Neils asked. "It isn't anything we haven't already seen."

"She might recognize some of those Layers," Yvan replied. "She might be able to tell us where we are. We won't lose anything by getting her opinion."

Just then, Niyazi got Yvan's attention.

Niyazi had been talking to one of the Tenby defenders and getting the man to explain his weapon to him.

"Be careful where you point that," Atian told him. "Don't point it at anything until you're ready to shoot."

"How does it work?" Yvan asked. "I've never seen a weapon like it before."

Atian's eyes fell out of their sockets. "You haven't?! You're serious?!"

"No, never. None of us have. What is it?"

Atian shut his mouth with difficulty and took the weapon from Niyazi. "This one is a rifle. You load it with ammunition here—into this magazine. You pull the trigger here and it fires a projectile out through the barrel—here. These rockets work the same way."

Yvan raised his eyebrows. "That's so complicated."

"It works. You should try it sometime." Atian gave the weapon back to its owner. "You can hit them before they actually get onto the wall."

"What happens after they get onto the wall?" Yann asked. "Do you have any special weapons for fighting them hand to hand?"

Atian made a face. "No, after that, it's all down to blades, axes, and brute strength. Guns don't help at all when that happens—but it's better than nothing, I guess." He narrowed his eyes at Anríq. "You look like you know how to handle a few Darklings."

"I was better when I had magic," Anríq replied. "Now it's down to brute strength like you said."

"Anríq is a good man to have with or without magic," Yvan chimed in. "He won't let you down."

"Well, we'll be glad to have you," Atian replied. "Any friend of the Black Watch is a friend of ours."

"I'm going to find Eliska," Yvan announced. "You men stay here and man your posts. I'll be back in a little while."

"What can she tell us that we don't already know?" Atian asked. "We already know Tenby will fall as soon as the instability overtakes us."

"She spent decades surviving in the Coil. She's forgotten more about the Coil than any of us will ever know. We'll all be better off with her here than anywhere else."

Yvan climbed down the scaffold and set off walking through town. Atian waved to the Watchmen. "Follow me and I'll assign you to your posts."

He walked down the wall assigning each man to a different spot. He assigned Rien, Niyazi, Neils, and Vidal in turn.

Atian waited until the last to assign Yann and Anríq to a watchtower on the eastern side of town. The tower faced the instability.

Three Tenby men occupied the tower. One of them stood at the tower's eastern window. He studied the instability through a pair of field glasses.

The other two men stood at the two adjoining windows looking north and south. Both men held their weapons, but they didn't pay as much attention to the surroundings as they should have.

Atian gave them orders that Yann and Anríq would be joining them and for these men to show the boys the ropes. Then Atian left the five of them alone.

The man at the north window turned around and nodded at the boys. "Good to meet you."

"Good to meet you, too," Yann replied. "I'm Yann Dilnao. This is Anríq."

"I'm Americ Lanou. That's Valer Alain and Rosh Orei." Americ indicated the man across from him and lastly the man with the field glasses.

Rosh didn't turn around. He kept staring through the glasses at the instability in the distance. "It never comes any closer."

Yann looked over the man's shoulder. "It actually looks like it's moving farther away."

Rosh didn't take his glasses down. "It doesn't mean anything. It could sweep back on us any minute now."

"Why don't the Darklings show themselves?" Valer asked. "They always came for us before."

"Atian says they've gotten as far as the walls before," Yann repeated.

Americ nodded. "We would have gotten eaten if not for our rockets. Our supplies will run out eventually and that will be it."

"Where do you get your supplies?" Yann asked. "How do you run this town if you're so cut off from everything?"

Americ opened his mouth to answer, but Valer interrupted. "If Atian didn't tell you that, then we shouldn't, either."

Yann shrugged it away. "Don't tell me, then. It's none of my business. We'll defend you, either way."

Valer narrowed his eyes at Yann and then shot a glare at Anríq. "Why doesn't he talk?"

"He's a Servant. He's taken a vow of silence unless it's strategically necessary for him to say something."

"Strategically necessary!" Valer snorted. "By then, it will be too late."

"It isn't too late now, is it?" Yann pointed out. "He doesn't need to tell you anything because I'm telling you."

Valer scowled at Anríq. "I don't like having a Barbarian inside the walls."

"You'll like it when the Darklings come." Yann studied each man one after the other. Rosh still didn't turn around. "Have you men lived here all your lives?"

"Born and raised," Americ asked. "Where did you come from?"

"Middleborough," Yann replied. "It was a town in another Layer, but the Layer collapsed and wiped out the town. I don't know where Anríq is from."

"You mean it wasn't strategically important?" Valer shot back and burst into loud, braying laughter.

Yann only smiled at him. Anríq's eyes twinkled watching Valer slap his thighs and wipe tears of laughter out of his eyes.

"Good one," Yann replied. "Would you know where it was if he told you the name?"

"Probably not," Valer replied. "In fact, I'm sure I wouldn't. I don't know one Layer from the other." He slammed his hand on Anríq's shoulder. "Come over here and sit down, boys. We aren't on watch for a few minutes yet."

Yann didn't know what he meant, but right at that moment, Rosh put down his glasses, turned around, handed them to Americ, and Americ took his place at the east window to keep watch on the instability.

Rosh and Valer threw themselves down in two chairs sitting in the corner. The watchtower consisted of a room eight feet square with walls as high as a man's waist.

The top half of each wall stood open to the air so the men could see out in all directions.

"Shouldn't we be keeping watch?" Yann asked.

"We are keeping watch. Americ will tell us if anything comes. Here. Take this." Valer pulled open a wooden chest in the corner and took out a flat square slab of something wrapped in paper. He slapped the slab into Yann's hand.

"What is it?" Yann asked.

"It's chocolate," Valer told him. "You eat it."

Yann frowned. "I've never heard of it. What does it taste like?"

The defenders' eyes fell out of their sockets. Americ actually took his field glasses down and turned around to gape at Yann. "You've never heard of chocolate?!"

"No. Should I have?" Yann glanced at Anríq. "Have you ever heard of it?"

Anríq shook his head.

Americ clucked his tongue and turned back to surveying the landscape. "Now I've heard everything."

"Well, allow me to deflower your youth, my young friend." Valer leaned forward, took the bar out of Yann's hand, tore the paper wrapper off, and handed it back. "Eat it. Give some to your friend here, too. You need to seriously catch up on your education."

Yann turned the bar over in his hand and wrinkled his nose at it. "It looks disgusting. It looks like compressed manure."

The men exploded in laughter. Valer slapped his thighs again. "If you don't eat it, I'll know you're both cowards. Eat it or I'll have to tell Atian to assign you both to the laundry."

Yann and Anríq exchanged glances. Yann could just imagine how revolting this brown, rubbery mass would taste when he put it in his mouth.

This must be some kind of initiation test the Tenby defenders inflicted on newcomers to make sure they had the backbone to really stand a post on the wall.

The bar had been stamped with indented lines in the shape of a grid to form smaller squares. Yann snapped off two squares and handed one to Anríq.

They exchanged one last glance. This chocolate stuff could be poison. These men might be trying to eliminate the outsiders to protect the town from something or other.

Yann took a deep breath, put the square in his mouth, and bit down. A rush of delicious sweetness flooded his mouth and spread to his whole head.

He actually froze with a mouthful of the chocolate as it started to melt. He swallowed. He'd never tasted anything so delicious.

The Tenby defenders laughed themselves silly watching Yann and Anríq eat it.

"What did I tell you?!" Valer crowed. "Maybe you'll listen to me from now on."

"Thank you," Yann mumbled around his mouthful. He tried to chew and swallow at the same time.

The men wiped their eyes and settled back into their chairs. They took out some metal cans of some kind of beverage.

The drink inside fizzed and snapped when the men tore the tops off the cans. Then both men settled back with their drinks.

Valer raised his can to the two boys. "Congratulations. Consider your cherries popped."

"What does that mean?" Yann asked.

The men burst out laughing again, but they didn't explain what they meant.

Yann broke the bar in half and gave Anríq his share. The boys ate it, and by the time they finished, Yvan returned.

"What did Eliska say about the Layers?" Yann asked.

"I can't find her. She vanished."

Yann shot to his feet. "She couldn't have. She must be somewhere. Let me go look for her."

"No, you and Anríq come with me." Yvan shot a hard look at the Tenby men sitting there sipping their drinks. Yvan would never allow that kind of thing on his Watch.

He turned away with a disgusted grimace and waved both boys out of the tower. "Atian is showing us a house where we can stay. Follow me and I'll take you there."

Yvan led the way back down to the ground. Yann didn't feel right about leaving the wall so soon, but Yvan and Atian must have come to some agreement about the Watchmen's duties.

Yvan showed the two boys to a modest house farther down the wall from the entrance gate. "Atian says no one is using this house, so we can stay here. The bedrooms are upstairs. We'll have to pair up, so you two can share a room with each other."

Yann looked around at the main downstairs room. A bunch of machines he didn't understand stood along one section of the wall with a counter between them and the seats and couches in the main living area.

"What are we supposed to do while we're here?" Yann asked.

"I don't know," Yvan told him. "Try to relax and get some sleep. Maybe take a bath and clean your clothes. I don't know. You're old enough to figure it out." He turned to leave.

"Are you sure you don't want me to go look for Eliska?" Yann asked. "If something happened to her...."

"Nothing happened to her, son. She's hiding from us—or maybe she's hiding from the townspeople."

Yann shut his mouth. Of course. He should have paid more attention when the Watch entered this town. Everyone had somewhere to go and something to do, but she didn't.

Yvan headed for the door. "Stay here. Don't make me have to go looking for you, too."

Chapter 31

Eliska picked up a twig and used it to scratch geometric designs in the dust at her feet. The sun was starting to go down.

She would have to leave the shelter of this garden eventually. The alternative would be to sleep here behind the solarium.

She'd slept in worse places. Anything would be better than going out there and dealing with the townspeople.

She didn't know where Marine, Anríq, and the Watchmen were or what they were doing. O'akim would probably give Marine a place to stay. It would probably be a very nice place, too.

Atian would take care of the Watchmen. He might take them to some kind of barracks or wherever the Tenby defenders stayed.

Then again, the Tenby defenders weren't members of the Black Watch. All those men probably had homes and families they stayed with when the men went off duty.

That left Eliska out in the cold by herself as usual. What the hell was she even doing in this town?

She should walk out that gate right now, walk into the chaos, and get herself sent back to some magical Layer. She knew exactly what to do there. She belonged there. No one had to tell her and she didn't have to hide from anyone.

She stiffened just then when she heard a thump followed by footsteps. Someone strode through the garden behind her.

The person didn't make any effort to hide what they were doing. They snapped twigs underfoot and then bootheels struck the flagstones on the other side of the solarium.

She held her breath waiting for the person to leave. None of the garden's walkways passed behind the solarium. The person had no reason to come back here.

Her heart stopped when Yvan stepped out from behind the solarium and saw her siting there.

"There you are," he exclaimed. "I've been looking everywhere for you."

She forced herself to look away. "You found me. Now I have to find somewhere else."

"You don't have to find somewhere else. I want you to come to the wall with us. We need you."

"You don't need me for anything," she mumbled. "I would be no good to you on the wall."

"I don't mean we need you to defend us with your magic. I mean I need you to check the situation with the Layers and tell me if you can see anything up there that might indicate where we are or what's coming."

She turned her head even farther away. "I can't tell you that. No one can tell you that."

"You don't know because you haven't looked. I need you to come up to the wall."

"Leave me alone," she growled. "I don't want to look at those people and they sure as hell don't want to look at me."

She kept her head turned so she wouldn't see his reaction. She really wished he'd leave. Life was so much simpler and easier without all these people around.

He stood there staring down at her in silence for a minute. Maybe now he would realize that leaving her here would be simpler and easier for everyone else involved, too.

She counted down the seconds before he walked away. Then she could go back to being blissfully alone in the silence.

She would have to find another hiding place, though. He found her.

She probably wouldn't be able to find another place in Tenby to hide. All the more reason to leave here and go on her way.

Just then, he surprised her by sitting down next to her. Her instincts told her to leap away from him or at least move aside to put more space between them.

He sat way too close—almost close enough for their shoulders to touch.

She didn't leap away even though she wanted to. She sat rooted to the spot. What was he going to do to her? Was he going to reprimand her for letting him and the Watch down?

She winced when she thought that. She was letting him down. She threw her fate in with these men. She was the one violating that by running away like this.

He didn't say anything for a long time. He just sat there in silence.

He stayed where he was for so long that she had no choice but to relax and start breathing again.

What the hell did he want from her? Why did he constantly thrust himself into her awareness like this when she made it so abundantly clear that she didn't want him to?

He was as bad as Yann that way. Neither of them would leave her the hell alone.

The silence did something to her—something other than what it did before. It didn't give her the same peace—and yet it did.

That silence didn't call out to her to fill it with words. Yvan didn't fill it with words. He just let it sit there. How long would he let it sit there? He acted like he could wait forever.

Could it possibly be that he liked to sit alone in the silence, too—somewhere far away from everyone who wanted anything from him?

What had his life been like all these years as Commander of the Watch in Middleborough? He must not have gotten a minute to himself in all that time.

Maybe he really wanted to run away and hide, too. Maybe he really wanted to run away and hide all the time, but he couldn't because everyone always needed him to stay on duty.

He would have been on duty around the clock, even when he and the other Watchmen slept. He would have been on call every hour of every day in case anything threatened the town.

He finally spoke up, but he did it softly in a low murmur. "We have a house where the Watchmen are staying. There's a room there where you can stay with Marine. You should come back and stay with us. Don't stay out here."

She gulped and looked away. The words stung. He didn't ask her to do anything except to come back and stay with the Watch.

Her heart ached to go back to them. She invested so much in them these last few days—and not just by putting herself in danger to help them survive.

She just wanted to be one of them. They all kept saying she *was* one of them. She just wished she could believe that.

She didn't dare to say that out loud—or to voice this stabbing pain in her middle that kept telling her she never would be one of them.

"Come back to the house, young one," Yvan murmured. "No one cares if you have magic or if you can see anything in the Layers. Just come. You can't stay out here. You belong with us."

She clamped her eyes shut to block out that word. Belong. She didn't belong with them. She didn't belong with anyone.

The burning ache to belong with someone and to someone—it became unbearable. His presence at her side tormented her worse than all the Darkness in her soul.

She lost Barsali for these people. She lost Wesh for these people. Now she couldn't even be one of them the way she so desperately wanted to be.

Out of nowhere, Yvan put his arm around her shoulders and squeezed.

He felt different than Yann. She tried to stiffen and pull away, but she couldn't even do that.

Yvan should have been the one to pull away from her. He would have if he knew about the poison boiling away inside her.

Or maybe he already knew and stayed near her anyway. Yann and Anríq did it. Why not Yvan, too?

She wanted to pull away as much to protect him as to protect herself, but she found herself softening to him instead.

Being near him didn't carry the same weight it did with Yann. Yann putting his arms around her meant something.

Yvan putting his arm around her meant something, too, but it meant something different—something she could actually accept if she really stretched.

Yvan would never expect anything more from an embrace like that. He did it out of genuine protective affection. It could never be anything else.

It meant something so much more because of that. It meant something so much purer precisely because he never could or would ask or expect anything else. He only did it because he cared about her—and not the way Yann did.

She floundered in a confused turmoil of emotions, but she couldn't pull away. She wanted to, but she also didn't want to.

She just wanted to feel this. Someone actually cared. They all did. That was the most excruciating thing about all of this.

All of the Watchmen cared about her like that now. Yann. Anríq. Yvan. Niyazi. Neils. Vidal. Even Rien cared about her like that now.

She clamped her eyes shut against a fresh torrent of crushing despair when she thought about Barsali. He and Omer both cared about her the same way.

She couldn't betray Barsali's memory by leaving the Watch. Even spending the night out here behind this solarium somehow betrayed some trust between her and the others.

Yvan took his arm down, stood up, and waited for her to do the same thing. They climbed over the garden wall together and headed back toward the entrance gate.

Chapter 32

Y ann bent his head low and studied one of the machines in the Watchmen's house. "What do you think this one does?"

"It's used for cooking," Anríq told him from the other side of the room. "It creates a fire. If you look in the cupboards near your knees, you'll find pots and pans to cook things on the fire."

Yann frowned at the machine and then at Anríq. "How do you know that?"

"I saw some of the housewives doing it when I looked through the windows of other houses. They put the pans on that grate there, turn those knobs, and the fire comes out of those holes underneath the pan."

Yann frowned at the contraption again and then raised his eyes and shook his head. "This is all too complicated for me."

"It isn't complicated." Anríq crossed the room to his side, took hold of one of the knobs, and turned it. Tiny blue flames shot out of the holes and created a small ring under the grate. "See? It's simple. It's just different from the way we're used to doing it."

"You can do the cooking, then. You can become the Watch's new housewife."

Anríq laughed. "You'll have to learn to cook for yourself if we stay in this Island for very long—unless you find a girl and marry her. Then she can cook for you."

Yann glared at him. Anríq only laughed at him and went back to what he had been doing before, which was walking around the living room. He studied all the furnishings with great interest.

Yann turned away from the fire machine—or whatever it was. He went through the room trying to figure out what all the other machines were for.

He didn't want to ask Anríq. Yann didn't want to admit that Anríq noticed more and learned more about Tenby in a few short hours than Yann did.

He came to a different machine that looked like a large wardrobe. He opened one of the doors and a rush of cold air hit him in the face.

"Hey!" he called over his shoulder. "This one is full of food!"

"Enjoy yourself," Anríq replied over his shoulder.

Yann hesitated. "I don't recognize any of it."

Anríq finally came over to him and shouldered Yann out of the way. "You really need a wife to cook for you. Stand aside. I'll do it."

Yann stepped out of the way. Anríq started taking things out of the wardrobe, laying them on the counter, and then he pulled out a whole bunch of other utensils, pots, pans, and a few small kitchen knives.

"What are you doing?" Yann asked.

"I'm cooking. I'm hungry."

Yann stood back and watched him cut up vegetables and meat. Anríq also dug up some potatoes from somewhere.

He turned the knob to make flames come out of the fire machine. He also switched on a device that looked like a water pump. It poured water into one of his pots and he put it over the flames.

"How do you know so much about these machines?" Yann asked.

"I told you. I watched the housewives doing it. Didn't you take your turn cooking for the Watch in Middleborough?"

"Yes, but that was different. We didn't have all this."

"We didn't have all this when we camped in the open, either, but you didn't forget how you did things in Middleborough." Anríq dumped a bunch of cut potatoes into his pot of boiling water.

He went back to cutting up the vegetables when Yvan came in with Eliska. Both of them frowned when they saw what Anríq was doing.

"What are you doing?" she asked.

"Eating." Anríq went over to the wardrobe, opened it, pulled out a block of chocolate wrapped in paper, and stuck it into her hand. "Eat this."

She turned it over in her hand and studied it from all sides. "What is it? I'm not eating anything if I don't know what it is."

"You young ones stay here," Yvan told them. "I'm going back out to the wall to check in with Atian and the other Watchmen. I don't know what duty rotation he wants us to follow. The men might be coming in later."

"I'll make enough for everyone," Anríq told him.

Yvan left. Eliska put the bar of chocolate down on the counter without taking the wrapper off. Yann made a mental note to introduce Eliska to chocolate later.

She watched Anríq cutting up meat and vegetables and putting them into a pan to fry them. "How did you learn to do all this?"

"He watched the housewives through their windows," Yann explained.

"It isn't hard," Anríq replied. "It's the same as cooking over an open fire."

"Not quite the same," Eliska pointed out.

Yann turned to her. "What did you see out on the wall? Father said he was going to get your opinion on the Layers collapsing."

She looked away. "He didn't take me to the wall. He brought me straight here."

Just then, Marine burst in glowing with life. She'd cleaned herself up, changed her dress, and she radiated with beautiful vivacious energy.

"You won't believe the books O'akim has in his library!" she gushed. "I could spend the rest of my life reading them and never get bored. Oh, Anríq! You're the greatest! I'm starving!" She kissed him on the cheek and made him blush.

Yann stared at her in stunned shock. He had only ever let himself imagine what she looked like all cleaned up with her hair combed and her clothes neat.

He never dared to dream she could look like this. Eliska said Marine was a princess and that she looked and acted like one.

She acted like one before, but now she really looked like one. She shone like some kind of star fallen to Earth.

She wore one of the frilly dresses all the other women in town wore, but without the elaborate extra skirts underneath that made them stick out in the back.

This one surrounded her in lemon-beige ruffles. They billowed from her shoulders, ran down her chest, and came together in a tight, flat cone that surrounded her hips before they flared down to her skirts.

Her glistening black hair tumbled over her shoulders and her eyes sparkled with high energy.

She only belatedly noticed what Anríq was doing. "How do you know how to do all this?"

"That's what I want to know," Yann interjected.

"I already told you how I know," Anríq replied.

"Are you going to become a cook?" Marine teased.

He only smiled at her. "I'm a Servant. I serve where I'm needed."

"What does it take to become a Servant?" Marine asked. "Do you have to go through some kind if ritual where the other Servants decide if you can join?"

"Nothing like that. You just decide you want to be one and then you go off and do it. Ask Yann. He already is one."

Yann froze when both girls spun around to stare at him. "You are?" Marine gasped.

"I am?" Yann asked.

"Aren't you?" Anríq asked. "Isn't that what happened when we freed Amala and the others from the Dark Layers? You became a Servant, didn't you?"

Yann shrugged that away, but he still found himself smiling. "I guess I am."

"How is he a Servant and we aren't?" Eliska asked.

Anríq looked up from his work. *"Are* you a Servant?"

She squirmed, but right then, Marine changed the subject as though they never had been talking about Servants at all. "You should all see the books O'akim has! He has histories of all the civilizations in the Coil going back thousands of years."

"Does he have anything about the Voyant?" Yann asked.

Marine's face fell, but not even that could make her look less radiant or excited. "Unfortunately not. I don't think this Island has any history of magic at all. Anyway, I might be able to find out something in the histories. I mean, if Eliska is right about there being more than one Voyant, then they would have to come from somewhere, right? These Voyants must be bringing in people from the regular population....."

"Unless they're recruiting their own children," Eliska pointed out. "Then the new recruits wouldn't show up on any history."

"Aha!" Marine pointed at her and burst into one of her mischievous smirks. "But we know they aren't recruiting their own children or the Voyant wouldn't be after a bunch of imp Watchmen from Middleborough. If he is trying to find someone to replace him—or to stop someone from replacing him—then that person must come from the regular population."

Eliska shrugged. "You're right."

"Ooo! Chocolate!" Marine pounced on the bar, tore it open, and started munching.

"What I don't understand is why no one is keeping a history on the Voyants," Marine went on. "If they really control the Coil, then someone must have been keeping track of who they are and where they came from. I mean, every kingdom in the Hallowed Vales keeps detailed records of all the kings, their families, marriages, births, and deaths, and every detail of the kings' reign. We have historians who do nothing else but keep track of what everyone in all the royal families is doing every day. You would think it would be even more important to do the same thing with the people who control the entire Coil. Wouldn't you?"

"Maybe the Voyants keep that information secret between themselves," Yann pointed out.

She burst out in high-pitched, childish giggles. "Should we send someone in undercover to find out?" She exploded in giggles. "We would send someone in to stop someone from going in!"

Yann found himself laughing, not so much because what she said was so funny.

Her laughter infected him with the need to laugh. He laughed just because she found everything so engaging and exciting.

Anríq interrupted their conversation. "Maybe you should be looking for the bolus of knowledge Brother Matherus and the other Templars hid in the Layers."

She spun around, gasped out loud, and shot out her hand to grab his arm. "Anríq! You're a genius! Of course! Why didn't I think of that?! You're so much smarter than I am! I can't believe I didn't think of that!"

She dove in and kissed him on the cheek again before she raced away.

"I have to go back to the library!" she exclaimed. "I have to find out how to locate the bolus in the Layers."

"Hey!" Yann yelled after her. "Don't you want to eat something first?"

"Later!" she yelled and the door slammed behind her.

Yann and Eliska exchanged glances. Then they turned around to find Anríq serving the food onto plates.

He'd somehow combined the potatoes, meat, and vegetables into a creamy goulash swimming in bright yellow sauce. The smell wafting off the food made Yann's head explode.

"Aargh!" Yann groaned. "That smells incredible."

Anríq handed each of them a bowl. "I hope you like it."

Yann lifted the dish to his nose and his knees trembled when he took a deep breath of the smell. "Where did you learn to do all this?"

Anríq shrugged. "You learn a lot of things wandering around in the Coil."

He took the last plate for himself, forked a bite into his mouth, and then set the dish aside. He went to work making another batch of exactly the same food for the other Watchmen.

Yann and Eliska stood there in stunned amazement while Anríq went back and forth between all the machines in the house.

Now that Yann saw someone doing all of this at close range, he seemed to recall catching fleeting glimpses of the Tenby housewives working like this through the windows outside.

Anríq kept working and made an absolute ton of food as mind-blowingly delicious as the dish he served Yann and Eliska.

They eventually sat down at the table and ate it while he finished. Yann didn't know what to think, but as usual, he did come to one conclusion above all others.

Anríq would always be better at everything. He could do anything and women gravitated to him. He was basically the perfect man.

Chapter 33

Eliska woke up hearing a strange noise in the middle of the night. She stared at the ceiling trying to figure out what it was.

She sat up in bed. Marine lay sound asleep in the bed next to her.

The two girls shared a bedroom on the upper story of the house the Tenby townsfolk gave to the Black Watch.

The other Watchmen paired off into the other bedrooms with Yann and Anríq together next door.

The sound didn't come from there. It came from farther away.

At first she thought it sounded like some kind of animal, but that couldn't be right.

She hadn't seen a single animal anywhere in Tenby, not even pets or livestock. Now that she thought about it, she couldn't even remember seeing any birds in the sky or insects buzzing through the air.

She eased out of bed and tiptoed across the room so she wouldn't wake up Marine. A beam of faint light streamed through the window and gave Marine an angelic glow. Marine always had an angelic glow.

Anyone looking at her might think nothing bad could ever happen to her. No one would ever believe she spent so much time communing with the Dark.

Eliska let herself out of the room and eased the door shut. The sound definitely got louder out here.

She followed it to a different bedroom down the hall. It was the room Neils shared with Niyazi.

The door stood ajar, but just a crack. The sound came from inside.

She nudged the door open just a little farther. Neils and Niyazi sat side by side on one of the beds.

Neils clutched his head in both hands. The sound came from him.

Niyazi rested his hand on Neils's shoulder and murmured low in his ear. "It's all right. It will pass. Don't worry. Everything will be all right. You'll see."

"Make it go away!" Neils moaned. "I can't stand it!"

Niyazi noticed the door swinging inward if only a little bit. He looked up and saw Eliska standing out in the hall.

She couldn't exactly run away, so she stepped into the room and approached the bed. "Did you have nightmares?"

"They're everywhere!" Neils whimpered. "They're right here in this room right now!"

"The same thing happened to me," Niyazi murmured. "It will pass."

"You didn't say it passed!" Neils countered. "You never said it went away!"

Niyazi lowered his eyes to the floor. "No, I never said that."

"So you still see them?" Eliska asked.

Niyazi nodded at the carpet. "I just pretend they aren't there, but they are."

"Do you still see them in this room—right now?"

Niyazi tried to shrug and looked away. "They're always there."

"You see?!" Neils blurted out. His eyes darted around the room. "So it won't pass! It will never go away! I might as well end it right now."

"Don't say that," Eliska murmured. "Rien came around and so did the Watch Commander. They're both okay now—and Barsali was okay before the Dark took him."

"You don't know that!" Neils's voice started rising. He would wake up the whole house pretty soon. "Maybe they just learned to live with it the way Niyazi says."

Eliska opened her mouth to say something. She really didn't know what to say to either of these men. She couldn't do anything without her magic.

She might not have been able to do anything even with her magic. Anríq hadn't been able to heal any of these men even during the times when he got his magic back.

He always said the men were whole. No one would be able to heal them if these invisible Darklings really were real.

She didn't get a chance to say anything before Yvan barged in. "What's going on?" he demanded.

"Neils is having nightmares," Eliska explained.

"Oh." Yvan frowned at Neils and Niyazi. "That's not good."

"What are we supposed to do?" Niyazi asked. "We can't function like this."

"You functioned just fine yesterday," Eliska pointed out.

She considered asking Yvan if he still saw Darklings everywhere, but she decided not to.

He saw her studying him and his eyes locked on hers. The connection between them kept growing and getting deeper.

"You can't do anything about this, can you?" he asked. "None of you can."

"Do you still see them?" she asked. "Do you still see these Darklings even when you're awake?"

He squirmed in his uniform. "That doesn't matter. Someone has to defend this town. I'll keep standing the watch until something kills me. I don't care if I'm seeing things."

"Don't you see, though?" she countered. "If you're seeing them....and Neils and Niyazi are seeing them....and Rien is seeing them....then that means you're almost a majority of the Watch that sees these Darklings. What happens when Yann, Vidal, and the rest of us start seeing them?"

"I don't understand what you're telling me," he replied. "What will happen?"

"Then none of us will be able to claim anymore that the Darklings are invisible because they won't be invisible. We'll all be able to see them the same way we can see every other kind of Darkling."

"Then how do you explain the fact that only some of us can see them now?" Niyazi asked. "How can some of us see something that's there and some of us not see it?"

"I can't explain it, but if I'm right and these Darklings really are real, then pretty soon we'll all be able to see them and we'll all have to deal with them."

"But these Darklings haven't attacked us," Yvan pointed out. "They're just there. They just hang around not doing anything."

"They attacked Vidal," Eliska pointed out. "Maybe they have to reach some kind of threshold before they attack in force."

"So what are we supposed to do about that?" Neils asked. "We can't do anything because none of you has any magic."

"I don't know what we can do, but we should probably do something before they get too strong for us to defeat them at all."

"What do you suggest?" Yvan asked.

Eliska turned back to Neils. "Have you ever seen these Darklings before? Have you....?" She broke off when she glanced over at Niyazi.

"Neils is an orphan, too," Yvan told her, "but he was born in the Coil. His parents were magic-users and they got killed in the Coil. Some travelers found him and turned him over to the Watch. If he was remembering something that happened when he was little, don't you think he would have remembered it before now?"

Eliska opened her mouth a second time. She was about to suggest that the group go back out into the magical Layers. At least Eliska and Anríq would be able to fight the Darklings there.

Yann walked in just then. He squinted at the four people sitting up awake. "What's going on?"

"Nothing," Yvan replied. "The sun will be coming up soon. All of you get ready to go out on watch. You come with us, Eliska. I want you to take a look at the instability and see if you can tell us anything about it."

The group split up. Yvan left first followed by Yann. He studied Eliska and then Neils and Niyazi. Of course Yann could see that something was going on regardless of what his father said.

Yann didn't ask. He probably already knew.

Eliska stayed in the room with Neils and Niyazi, but when neither of them said anything else, so she left, too.

She heard both men talking as soon as she left. She really would have liked to do something for Neils—and all the rest of them.

The commotion roused the rest of the house. Rien, Marine, Vidal, and Anríq all woke up from the noise. Yvan gave orders for all of them to get ready for the day.

Eliska returned to the room she shared with Marine. Marine woke up as chipper as usual. Eliska didn't have the heart to ruin Marine's mood along with everyone else's.

Eliska finished getting dressed and headed for the stairs to go down to the kitchen. She already heard pots and pans banging around down there. Was Anríq cooking again or one of the Watchmen?

Before she got to the stairs, she heard Yvan talking in a room nearby. It was the room he shared with Rien, but Rien wasn't in there. Yann was.

"I don't like to put this on you, son," Yvan was saying. "I don't know what else to do about it."

"What can I do about it?" Yann asked. "What can any of us do about it?"

Eliska inched closer to the door. It stood all the way open, so she wasn't exactly eavesdropping.

Yvan paced around the room running his fingers through his hair. He didn't see her.

Yann stood with his back to the door watching his father stride back and forth in obvious agitation.

As soon as Eliska spotted them, Yvan pulled up short and got in his son's face. "You're the only man of the Watch who hasn't had nightmares."

"What about Vidal?" Yann asked.

Yvan waved that away. Was Vidal having nightmares that no one knew about?

Yvan lowered his voice to an undertone. "The time may come when you have to take command of the Watch, son. I know you're young, but I trust you to make the right call for all of us."

"If you can't do anything and Eliska and Anríq can't do anything, I won't be able to, either," Yann pointed out. "Whatever is happening to all of you will happen to me, too."

"Whether you can do anything isn't as important as just taking charge. If all of us go down to this thing, we'll need one person who can still think straight. You're holding up the best of the whole Watch. If that happens, don't hesitate to step in—even if it means taking one of us off duty. Do you understand, son? That includes me."

Yann dipped his chin once. "I understand. I won't let you down."

"I know you won't." Yvan gripped Yann's shoulders with both hands. "I'm proud of you, son. You're a Watchmen any Watch Commander would be proud of."

Yvan pulled Yann into a quick, rough hug and Eliska hurried away. She didn't want them to catch her listening to their conversation.

Chapter 34

E liska went downstairs and ate breakfast with the others. Anríq left the house first. Then Marine went off to O'akim's library.

Eliska took her staff with her to the wall when the Watchmen reported for duty. God only knew why she kept carrying this staff around with her.

She remembered when she saw the situation beyond the wall.

The instability kept wavering back and forth across the countryside out there. "It goes back and forth getting closer and then migrating farther away," Atian reported.

Yvan pointed up at the sky. "The Layers are getting more chaotic. More of them are visible and they're collapsing and reforming faster than they were even yesterday." He turned to Eliska. "Can you tell anything from here?"

She stared up at multiple Layers towering into the atmosphere as far as the eye could see. "I've seen this part of the Coil before. I know where we are, but it doesn't help us. I can't predict what will happen, what will come after us, or where we'll wind up when it does. I'm sorry I can't tell you more than that."

"I've seen this before, too," Yann chimed in.

Yvan spun around. "You have? Where?"

"Anríq and I saw it when we got separated from you. The Layers became visible, but they were spiraling around in a vortex—like a funnel."

Yvan sliced his finger at the other Watchmen. "You men come with me and I'll show you where you're posted. We'll need to keep an eye on things as the situation escalates. It's bound to overtake the town sooner or later."

He set off down the wall with Atian and the other Watchmen. Neither of them remembered to give Eliska an assignment. They left her standing there with nothing to do again.

The Tenby defenders standing nearest gave her strange looks, especially her clothes and staff.

She couldn't exactly blame them. She looked nothing like any other woman in town. Even Marine looked so much more feminine than Eliska did.

She pretended she really did have somewhere to go and something to do. She planned to go back to one of the other gardens she'd seen in that alley—not the same one. She didn't want Yvan coming to find her again.

Yvan wouldn't come to find her because she already told him everything she didn't know about the Layers moving in. He didn't need her anymore.

She didn't plan to lock herself away in that house around the clock. She would rather sit in a garden by herself.

She passed down a few different streets not looking at anything in particular. She let her thoughts drift.

She still didn't see these invisible Darklings. From what she could gather from the Watchmen, the Darklings weren't as invisible as they seemed.

Were the Watchmen in distress because they thought they were seeing something that wasn't there—or did the Dark make them crazy?

She turned off toward the alley leading toward the gardens, but she stopped dead in her tracks when she saw a structure she didn't notice yesterday.

A large pavilion stood on the other side of the street. Four pillars held up a broad roof. The pavilion had no walls, but it did have tables, benches, and what looked like another outdoor kitchen counter underneath it.

All the same machines occupied all the same positions they occupied in the Black Watch's house, but that wasn't the most amazing part of the scene.

Anríq stood under the roof working over the fire. Fifteen children crowded around him all talking at once, including Hani.

Anríq pulled out pots and pans, heated them on the stove, and cut up meat, vegetables, and other stuff before adding everything to his many pans.

The noise of children's voices floated out of the pavilion. Then Eliska heard Anríq's deeper voice talking back to them and even laughing.

She took a few steps closer to watch. The children tried to help him and wound up getting in his way.

One little boy actually crawled into a cupboard by Anríq's knees and pulled out a pot too big for the boy to carry. He tried to lift it and dropped it on the floor with a bang.

Anríq picked up the pan, set it on the counter, and then picked up the boy with both hands. "Sit up here where you can watch. You'll need to learn for when you become a famous chef."

The boy laughed. "I don't want to be a chef. I want to be a doctor."

"Then you'll need to learn your knife skills for cutting people open."

A bunch of the kids laughed. Another little boy crossed the kitchen just then and stopped next to Anríq's cutting board where the boy could watch. Anríq placed his beefy hand behind the boy's back to steer him toward one of the tables before Anríq went back to work.

"Are you going to make rice, Anríq?" an older girl asked.

"Where is it?" he asked over his shoulder. "Get it out for me and measure it so I can put it in the pot."

"Can I help, too, Anríq?" the first boy asked from his seat on the counter.

"Here. You can peel the potatoes."

Anríq handed the boy the peeler and moved a basket of potatoes next to him on the counter.

Just then, a tiny little girl toddled over to Anríq. She couldn't have been more than two.

She tugged the leg of his pants and raised both arms to him. She opened her closed her fingers in a grasping motion. "Ta-ta!" she called.

He stopped what he was doing, picked her up, and sat her on his hip where he supported her behind her back with one muscular arm.

"Hello, precious little princess," he told her. "Yes, you can come and watch, too."

She started playing with the shells and beads tied in his hair. He lifted one of the strings and bounced it up and down in front of her eyes. It made a jingling noise and she laughed.

He grinned back at her and placed it in her hands so she could play with it while he worked.

The older girl came over with a container of rice just then. She set the rice next to Anríq's elbow.

"Thank you, sweetheart," he told her. "Would you please cut up that fruit and cheese and serve it to these little ones? You can use this knife here."

He set her up with a cutting board and a knife of her own. He had to do everything one-handed while he held the little girl in his other arm.

"What are you doing?" Eliska blurted out.

Anríq didn't look up from stirring his pots. "I'm cooking as you can see."

"Who are you?" the first little boy asked.

"This is Eliska," Anríq replied. "She's a friend of ours who came in with us yesterday. She's here to help defend the town."

"Why don't you wear dresses?" another younger girl asked.

"I've never worn a dress in my life," Eliska countered. She tried not to sound too hostile about it, but it came out that way anyway. She turned back to Anríq. "What are you doing here? Aren't you supposed to be standing on the wall with the Watchmen?"

"I serve all humanity. These children's parents are all stricken with the same disease. All the healthy adults are helping the patients, so I'm taking care of the children."

"Shouldn't you be working to heal their parents, then?"

"Tenby has its own healers and non-magical ways of healing. My service is needed here."

"Could I become a Servant, too, Anríq?" the first boy asked.

"You couldn't be a Servant," the older girl told him. "Servants are magic-users."

"You can become a Servant if you want to," Anríq told the boy. "Wait until you get older to make sure it's what you really want to do. If you become a doctor, you might not have to become a Servant. You can stay here with your family and do the same job."

"That's what I'm going to do," the boy announced. "I don't want to leave Tenby."

The little girl squirmed out of Anríq's arms and he lowered her to the ground before she toddled off somewhere else.

"The potatoes are ready, Anríq," the first boy told him.

"Thank you, young one." He took the cutting board and scraped the potatoes into a different pot. Then he went back to cutting up hunks of meat.

Hani noticed Eliska standing there. "What are *you* doing today?"

"I'm not doing anything," she told him. "There's nothing I can do."

"If you want something to do, you can help me," Anríq told her.

She hesitated. She'd never been comfortable around children.

Just then, another tiny boy charged through Anríq's work area. Eliska didn't see what this kid was doing or where he was going.

He missed his direction, collided with Anríq's leg, bounced off, and sprawled flat on his back. He burst into loud sobs.

Anríq stopped everything, picked up the little one, dusted him off, and then held him in the crook of his arm while Anríq pretended to check all the kid's non-existent injuries.

"Is it here? Is this the broken bone?" Anríq squeezed up the boy's arm even though there was nothing wrong with it. "What about here?"

He wriggled his fingers into the boy's neck and tickled him. The boy's sobs faded, but only slightly. He looked around in confusion trying to figure out where he actually was hurt.

"Did you get internal organ damage—here?" Anríq poked the kid in the stomach and the boy burst out in one guffaw of laughter before he remembered to start crying again.

"I have an idea," Anríq announced. "You must have a curse inside you. I'll turn you over and shake you so it falls out through your mouth. Then you'll be all back to normal. Okay?"

The boy blinked at nothing trying to decide if this was a good idea.

Anríq didn't wait for him to come to a decision. He turned the boy over, took hold of the kid's ankles in both powerful hands, and swung the kid back and forth and up and down in big, gentle swoops.

The boy exploded in shrieks of laughter. He waved his arms around trying to figure out what was happening.

"Is it out yet?" Anríq yelled over the noise. "Do you feel better yet?"

The boy was laughing too hard to hear him. The other kids sitting around laughed, too.

The boy's shirt fell down to his neck and left his midsection exposed. Anríq hefted the boy higher and blew a loud raspberry into the kid's stomach.

The boy screeched with laughter. Anríq turned the boy over, sat him on his elbow again, and straightened his clothes while the boy caught his breath.

"I think you're okay now," Anríq decided. "I'll do another examination later to make sure the curse doesn't come back. Okay?"

He kissed the boy on the side of the neck, set him down, and steered him back to the tables where the older girl was just setting out a bunch of food for the children to snack on.

Another younger girl rushed over to Anríq right away and raised her arms. "Swing me around like that, Anríq!"

"Just a minute," he told her. He went from pot to pot checking, stirring, and covering a few things.

When he finished, he picked up the girl, but he didn't do the same upside-down, shaking-out-the-curse routine.

He took her out of the pavilion—right out into the street.

He swiveled her around, grabbed hold of one arm and one leg, and spun around faster and faster flying her through the air at high speed.

She squealed with excitement and all the children flooded out of the pavilion for their turns. Only the older girl stayed behind.

She beamed at all the children crowding around Anríq. Some of them climbed up his clothes and perched on his back and shoulders while he gave others rides.

Eliska watched for a minute before she realized. None of them was around anymore. He wasn't preparing the food—and she wasn't helping him. She wasn't helping anyone.

She would never have been able to play with children so uninhibitedly. Anríq never acted like this around the Watchmen—or anyone else. She never imagined he could be so affectionate and outgoing with anyone.

She tore herself away with an effort, checked a few of his pots, and took out a stack of plates to set the table.

He kept playing with the children. He didn't notice when she took his food off the fire, turned off the machine, and served the food onto all the plates for the children to eat.

The girl kept working, too. "Sit down and eat something," Eliska told her. "I'll take care of this."

The girl obeyed her. Eliska found herself falling into a comfortable rhythm of setting the table, serving the food for any children who came over to eat it, and then washing the dishes afterward.

She didn't think she would find any job to do in this town. Everyone else had something to do.

Doing something useful that actually helped people felt good. It eased the feeling that she didn't belong here at all.

Anríq finally must have gotten tired of playing—or maybe the children got tired first.

He came back to the pavilion with them hanging off every limb. Two sat on his feet and held onto his legs while he walked. One little boy sat on his shoulders while another rode piggyback.

He held two tiny ones in his arms and lowered them onto the benches in front of the food Eliska had served.

"Sit down and eat your food," he told them. "Once you finish, I'll take you back to the creche. You can play there."

He went around the table making sure everyone sat in the right places. He had to pay extra attention to some of the children and straighten them out.

He made it all the way around the other side of the table before the little toddler girl from earlier came back.

She raised her arms to him and said, "Ta-ta!" again. He picked her up, sat down on the nearest bench, set her on his lap, and pulled a plate forward so she could eat out of it.

She ate with her hands. He used a towel to clean up the drips. He didn't try to make her eat more neatly.

He kept glancing down at her to make sure she got more of the food into her mouth than on her clothes.

Eliska found herself smiling over her shoulder at him and the children while she finished the dishes. Helping him felt good. Helping anyone felt good—better than she'd felt in a long time.

She was just drying some of the empty pots and putting them away when Yann showed up.

"Father asked me to come and get you," he told Eliska.

"Is the instability moving in?"

"We don't know. I think that's what he wants to ask you. He can't tell."

Eliska glanced over at Anríq. He watched and listened to their conversation, but he didn't get up or put the little girl down.

He stayed where he was when Eliska got her staff and followed Yann back to the wall.

Chapter 35

Yann climbed up the scaffold to where Yvan, Atian, Vidal, Neils, Niyazi, and Rien stood looking out over the countryside.

Yann hardly needed to climb the scaffold to see what was going on out there. The chaos covered the whole sky now—or it would have if a curtain of invisible magic didn't hold it off.

The magical front kept sweeping toward Tenby and then moving off. The wall of chaos behind that front blocked out any view of the countryside beyond.

Countless Layers revolved out there. They formed a vortex, but the invisible barrier held the whole spiraling mass of destruction at a distance from the town.

The men on the wall could snatch glimpses of landscapes in the confusion, but none lasted more than a few seconds before they evaporated.

Eliska climbed up and took her place with the men. "Jesus!" she breathed. "It's so much worse now than it was just a few hours ago!"

"Why do you think it's holding off?" Atian asked.

"If whatever the Voyant wants is in this town, that could explain why he doesn't just level it outright," Rien suggested.

"That didn't stop him from leveling Middleborough," Yvan pointed out. "He never hesitated to attack us before."

"At least no Darklings are coming for us this time," Atian remarked. "That would be the worst."

Yann checked the Tenby men standing around. None of them seemed to hear Rien mention the Voyant wanting something.

How long would it take the Tenby locals to figure out that the Voyant Mendicat was after the Black Watch for something he needed? Yann could well imagine how that would go.

Before anyone could say or decide anything, Vidal exploded out of position and lunged for the wall.

"Get away from them!" he roared. "Leave them alone! Get back, you bastards! I'll kill you!"

He crashed into Neils and Niyazi standing on the other side of the group. Vidal would have barreled straight through them.

Yann had half a second to realize Vidal was heading straight for the edge of the wall—the edge facing out into the countryside.

If he jumped over that wall, nothing would stop him from running.....anywhere.

Vidal plunged through the group before anyone realized what was happening. Neils and Niyazi both stumbled out of his path as he blasted between them...and then they realized where he was going.

Both men dove in from either side and grabbed him at the last second before he leapt over the wall. "No, Vidal!" Neils yelled.

Vidal didn't hear him. "GET AWAY FROM THEM!! LEAVE THEM ALONE!! YOU BASTARDS!!"

Yann, his father, and Rien all dove in to help restrain Vidal—and then everyone saw what he was raving about.

A single-file line of figures snaked through the chaos beyond the veil. Four of them looked bigger than the others.

Those four fired magical blasts from what looked like staffs. They bombarded armored Darklings thundering out of the Layers to surround the party.

Those four magic-users crowded the rest of their party toward the center. Everyone else in the group looked much smaller. Some were less than half the size.

"My God!" Yvan husked. "They're children!"

"Let me go!!" Vidal roared. "Let me go! I have to help them!"

Neils and Niyazi grappled him away from the edge with an almighty effort. "You are NOT going out there!" Niyazi yelled in Vidal's ear. "You'll die out there!"

"Let me go!" Vidal raised his voice and bellowed into the hurricane. "You bastards! Leave them alone!"

Yvan sprang forward, grabbed Vidal by the collar, and hauled him away from the edge. "Quiet down! You aren't going anywhere."

Vidal exploded the other way, tore out of Neils's and Niyazi's grip, and spun around in a circle. He drew his battle axe before anyone could get near him.

He swiped it at thin air, stumbled, and fell off the scaffold. He crashed down onto the pavement below, scrambled to his feet, and went back to attacking Darklings that weren't there.

"Restrain him and get him back to the house!" Yvan snapped. "Surround him and disarm him. You help us, Eliska."

Yvan herded everyone down the stairs to the ground. Yann became aware of the men on the wall watching Vidal lose his mind right here in public.

Neils, Niyazi, Rien, Yvan, Yann, and Eliska all descended and formed a ring around Vidal. He kept chopping his axe in circles to drive them away, but he didn't see them. He didn't see anything.

He gasped from the effort of fighting the invisible Darklings off. He swung his axe with such force that he nearly knocked himself off his feet.

Yann took his place behind Vidal. Niyazi drew his axe and Yvan drew his sword.

Yann planned to rush Vidal as soon as the others engaged him and occupied his weapon. Then Yann could grab Vidal and tackle him to the ground the way Yann tackled that old woman in her house.

He pivoted into position and caught his father's eye. Yvan nodded and everyone braced themselves for the fight.

Yann spotted Anríq striding through town toward them. He would be able to subdue Vidal if no one else could.

Right then, Vidal gave another vicious chop with his axe and really did knock himself over. His legs twisted around each other and he toppled sideways.

Yann rushed him. The rest of the Watch pounced, pinned him down, and Niyazi stomped on Vidal's axe to slam it down on the ground.

Eliska dove into the mix, and quick as lightning, she lashed a length of rope around his wrists and ankles. She trussed him up like a pig so he couldn't move.

He burst into another insane fit of furious raving, but he didn't yell any words this time. He blurted out a string of nonsense syllables.

The Watchmen peeled themselves off him just as Anríq pulled up to join them. Vidal lay on his side on the ground with his arms behind his back and his feet pulled behind him.

He craned his head and shoulders off the ground ejecting a steady stream of gibberish. His eyes darted from face to face with a pleading expression like he really needed to convince them all of something important.

The Watchmen stood back and stared down at him while they caught their breath. "Is he speaking another language?" Yann asked.

"It's no language I've ever heard." Eliska turned to Anríq. "Have you ever heard it before? Do you know what he's saying?"

Anríq shook his head.

Yvan cast a flinty look around and noticed all the Tenby defenders staring. None of them seemed to be looking out at the landscape.

"Get him back to the house," Yvan ordered. "We'll deal with him there."

Anríq moved in to help Rien, Neils, and Niyazi carry Vidal back to the house. Anríq took one of his arms. The others carrying Vidal by his other limbs.

He didn't make it easy for them. He kept trying to twist around and bombard them with whatever he was trying to tell them. He didn't stop all the way to the house.

Yvan, Yann, and Eliska followed.

The men set Vidal down on the living floor and left him there.

Yvan shut the door to muffle the noise. "Now what the hell are we supposed to do with him?" Rien demanded. "We can't stand a post and babysit him all day and night."

"I'll keep an eye on him," Eliska offered. "I'm not doing anything else."

Yvan passed his hand across his eyes and heaved a shaky sigh. "This is the last thing we need right now."

"Did you hear him out there?" Neils half-whispered. "He was yelling for the Darklings to get away from *them*. All the rest of you said for the Darklings to get away from *you*. He's the first one to tell them to get away from someone else."

"He didn't yell at invisible Darklings, either," Niyazi pointed out. "We all saw those Darklings attacking the...."

He broke off as the reality sank in again. That group out there in the Coil....The four magic-users had been trying to defend a bunch of children.

Yvan pointed at Neils. "Go back out to the wall and see if they're still out there."

Neils vanished. That left everyone to stand around in silence listening to Vidal raving.

He kept trying to twist himself in circles so he could see everyone in the circle. He appealed to each person one after another, including Anríq and Eliska. Vidal didn't pay any one person any more attention than the others.

Neils came back before anyone worked up the nerve to say anything. "They're gone—or at least we can't see them anymore. The Layers are thicker closer to the ground, so we wouldn't be able to see those people or any Darklings if they were there."

Yvan sighed. "The rest of you get back out to your posts. We're already one man down." He turned to Eliska. "You don't mind staying?"

"Not at all. I'll do what I can for him."

Yvan only nodded.

"I could stay, too, Father," Yann offered.

"No, we need you on the wall. We're already shorthanded enough." Yvan looked around and saw Anríq standing there. "You come, too, young one. We need your axe up there."

The group filed out of the house one after the other. Eliska stayed behind.

"Are you gonna be okay?" Yann asked on his way out.

She nodded up at him...and then she smiled. A light came on in her eyes—a light he hadn't seen there before. He couldn't remember seeing it even before she took Barsali's Darkness.

Anríq waited for Yann to catch up. He didn't want to leave her alone with Vidal. Yann couldn't make up his mind which of them he was more worried about.

Chapter 36

Yann stepped out of the room he shared with Anríq and turned
off toward the bathroom. Yann froze in his tracks when he saw
Neils standing in the hall.

Neils didn't see him. Neils kept jerking from one side to another,
darting away from threats that weren't there, and gasping in fright
every time he did it.

Yann stared down the hall while he decided what to do. He didn't
go near Neils. Yann had seen this too many times before.

How long would this last? How long would it take Neils to come
out of it—if he ever came out of it?

Yann was still standing there when Rien came out of the room he
shared with Yvan. Rien's expression turned to a wall of ice when he
saw Neils.

"I think you better come in here, boy," Rien muttered.

Yann didn't know what Rien wanted to talk to him about, but Yann
found out when he entered his father's bedroom.

Yvan sat on the edge of the bed crushing his knees in both hands.
His eyes darted around the room and in all directions. "They're here!"
he husked. "They're right here in this room!"

Yann sighed. "How long has he been like this?"

"He was like this when I woke up this morning," Rien replied.

"We can't take him out to the wall like this," Yann remarked. "Either of them."

"What do you want to do?" Rien asked.

Yann's head shot up. "Me?! You're the senior Watchman now. Niyazi is behind you and I'm junior to all of you."

Rien skewered him with a hard look, and without a word, Rien unsheathed both his blades and held them out to Yann. "You better take these."

Yann gaped at Rien in horror when he realized what Rien meant. It was happening exactly the way Yvan predicted. The whole Watch was going down with only Yann left standing.

He gulped hard and took Rien's weapons. Rien bent over Yvan and took his weapons, too. Rien handed them all over to Yann.

He gathered them in his arms, left his father there, and went back out into the hall. Neils stood in exactly the same place jumping and shrinking from invisible enemies.

He didn't see Yann walk up to him and take his weapons, too. Now Yvan, Rien, and Neils were all unarmed. This truly was the greatest disaster Yann could imagine.

Rien followed him downstairs and they stashed all those weapons in a broom closet. Heaven only knew what these men would use to defend the wall if anything attacked Tenby.

Yann found Eliska in the living room. She'd untied Vidal.

He sat on the floor with his knees propped up and his elbows resting on them.

"Why did you untie him?" Yann demanded. "He's supposed to be restrained."

"He's back to normal," she told him. "He doesn't remember anything."

Yann turned to Vidal. Vidal looked up at Yann with clear eyes. "How are you feeling this morning?" Yann asked.

Vidal nodded. "I feel okay. Eliska was just telling me about the party we saw out in the Coil."

"So you don't remember them? You don't remember yelling at all of us in another language?"

Vidal frowned. "I did?"

"You sounded very insistent on whatever you were trying to tell us. You don't remember fighting Neils and Niyazi so you could jump over the wall and run out into the Coil?"

Vidal's eyes popped. "I would have remembered that."

"Well, you did. Give me one reason why I should let you walk out of the house today."

Vidal's features hardened. "You? You don't let me do anything. You aren't even a fully instated Watchman. I'm your senior. If anyone orders me to stay inside, it will be the Watch Commander."

"I'm the Watch Commander as of now," Yann countered. "My father told me to take over if all of you went down—and it looks to me like you're well and truly down. Tell me I'm wrong."

Right then, Yvan came downstairs. He walked straight upright and glanced around at everyone exactly the way he always did. "Does anyone know what happened to my weapons? I had them right next to my bed last night. Now they're gone."

Yann and Rien exchanged glances, and a second later, Niyazi came downstairs with Neils, Anríq, and Marine.

They all started talking normally. Neils stayed quieter than usual and kept glancing around the room.

Other than that, Yann didn't see anything out of the ordinary in Yvan's behavior. He didn't seem to remember the episode from his bedroom. He didn't remember Rien disarming him.

Yvan pulled Vidal to his feet, asked him how he was feeling, and they both went on with their morning routine as usual.

Vidal didn't tell Yvan about Yann trying to take over as Watch Commander. Did Vidal even remember that?

Yann would have started to doubt his own sanity if he didn't keep exchanging glances with Rien. Rien's expression told Yann loud and clear that he didn't just imagine this.

The group got through breakfast somehow or another. Cold dread crept into Yann's guts as the time got closer for the Watchmen to go out to the wall. He could just imagine the disaster if one of them lost his head out there.

What was Yann thinking? They already were losing their heads. Every single man here teetered on the brink of insanity. So why didn't Yann? Why did he of all people escape whatever was wrong with them?

Eliska and Anríq didn't suffer from it, either. Eliska and Marine already dangled over the Dark, so why not Anríq? What protected him and Yann from the same fate?

Yann had to go through the same process in reverse of taking all the weapons out of the broom closet and returning them to the men he took them from.

"I don't want them," Rien muttered.

"You better take them," Yvan told him. "You won't be any good to us on the wall without them."

Rien took them. He refused to look at anyone when he buckled his swords back on. Yann cringed when he gave Vidal back his axe and Yvan his swords.

Yann planned to hang back and ask Rien what to do about this. The irony really bit that Yann was about to ask Rien what to do when Rien was the one who just as Yann what to do.

This would definitely be the first time in history that Yann or Rien ever doubted Yvan's judgment. What should Yann do—lock up his own father?

Yann was really starting to consider the option, but he didn't get a chance to ask Rien anything before Yvan ordered everyone out to the wall. Eliska and Anríq came with them. Only Marine went off somewhere else.

Vidal walked out of the house at the front of the group. He talked to Yvan the whole time about which men Atian posted in different spots on the scaffold. Vidal seemed to have learned more about the Tenby defenders than anyone else in the Watch.

Niyazi stayed near Neils when they left the house. Niyazi hovered extra close to Neils, either to protect him or to step in if anything went wrong.

Yann and Rien stayed close to each other. Yann saw Anríq and Eliska trying to assume their previous formation with Eliska between the two boys.

Yann wanted to stay near Rien today. Yann wanted to stay near anyone who realized just how explosive this situation had become.

No one besides Rien seemed to realize because only Rien had been in that room with Yann this morning. Only Rien knew that none of these people should be armed—and yet all of them were armed.

Yann would have liked to get as far away from all of them as possible, but he couldn't. He had to go outside, climb up the stairs, and take his place on the scaffold with the others while they assessed the landscape surrounding Tenby.

Chapter 37

The margin of chaos and disintegration kept sweeping across the countryside toward Tenby and then pulling back.

The curtain sizzled and crackled with magic sparking and jetting over the landscape. The veil rippled with Layers swelling and exploding behind it, but it still didn't break through.

"How much longer before it gets here?" Yvan asked one of Atian's men.

"There's no way to say. It's been coming and going all night."

The minute the Watch got up on the scaffold, Neils broke away from the group. He jerked sideways and sprang away from something on his other side. "Get away!" he shrieked. "Get your hands off me! Don't touch me!"

Niyazi gasped. "Neils—!"

Niyazi took a step forward to intervene, but Anríq shot out an arm and blocked Niyazi from going anywhere near Neils.

Neils's voice spiked to the danger zone. "You bastards! Get your hands off me! Leave me alone!"

He whirled farther away down the catwalk, tripped, and pitched off it. He slammed down on the pavement below, sprang up, and immediately went back to spinning here and there, jolting away from invisible attackers, and gasping, whimpering, and even screaming every time he saw something coming after him.

The Watch wheeled backward to head for the stairs to get down there and deal with the situation.

The instant everyone turned their back on him, Vidal broke out of line, let out another feral bellow in some other language, and dove behind the group.

No one got to him fast enough before he plunged over the wall, fell down on his knees in the dirt outside Tenby, staggered upright, and took off running for the margin a few miles away.

"VIDAL!!" everyone bellowed, but he was already too far away.

Eliska grabbed Yvan's arm. "I can go after him! I can find him in the storm and bring him back!"

She shoved him aside, hefted her staff, and took a few steps toward the wall.

Yvan yanked her back too hard. "No, Eliska! You aren't going out there!"

"I have to! I'll get my magic back as soon as I cross the curtain. He'll die out there if I don't go!"

She tried to fight him off, but Yvan lunged for her just as she made it to the wall, strapped his arms around her torso, and wrestled her back by force.

"I SAID NO, ELISKA!!" he roared. "We need you here too much! DO YOU HEAR ME?! WE NEED YOU!!"

She kicked and struggled, but in a few minutes, Vidal vanished behind the curtain. No one could see him anymore.

Yvan fought Eliska back from the edge, yanked her around, and jammed her feet down on the scaffold.

He bent low and yelled right in her face. "No one cares if you have magic or not, young one! We need you here! You are NOT going to throw your life away out there! Do you understand?! We need you here!"

Something he said must have gotten through to her, but she didn't like it. She glared at him and whirled away to turn her back on him, but she only wound up looking out over the countryside. Vidal was long gone.

"What happened?" Niyazi choked. "Why did he go out there? The children aren't even there anymore."

"GET YOUR HANDS OFF ME!!" Neils shrieked. "DON'T TOUCH ME, YOU FIENDS!!"

Everyone turned around to stare at Neils in the street below.

He held his blades in his hands now and hacked at the air. He kept whirling in mindless circles to fight off invisible Darklings.

Yvan sighed again. "Now we have to deal with him. Let's go."

Everyone descended to the ground. Yvan glared at Eliska and made her go first so she didn't run off into the mayhem, too.

The curtain of magic kept fizzing and crackling across the landscape. It made a hissing, sparking sound like rain every time it came close to overrunning Tenby or moving away.

Yann glanced over his shoulder to make sure it was still far enough away.

He turned back to follow the other Watchmen down to the ground. Yann didn't look forward to this any more than he looked forward to subduing Vidal.

"Get behind him, son," Yvan ordered. "You and Eliska get ready to tie him up as soon as....."

A brutal, animal roar interrupted him. Neils lunged for the Watch before they got into position.

He hacked his sword at Niyazi, but Anríq got there in time and thrust his axe between them.

He caught Neils's sword on the axe blade and the two weapons clanged together.

All the other Watchmen charged in to surround Neils, but he went ballistic and spun away too fast.

Before Yann realized what was happening, Neils charged him and raised his blade to chop Yann in half.

Yann raised his glaive to protect himself, but not fast enough. The blade came down heading straight for Yann's skull.

Eliska struck out with her staff and slammed the end into Neils's jaw. Bone cracked and his head whipped aside from the impact, but that didn't slow him down one bit.

The other Watchmen closed from all sides to restrain him, but just as they moved in, he whirled the other way and swung again.

His sword blade connected full force with the side of Niyazi's head and the blade stuck there. Neils couldn't get it out no matter how hard he tugged it.

Niyazi buckled on the spot and all the Watchmen smashed Neils between them. Anríq grabbed him the way Yvan grabbed Eliska just a few minutes ago.

Anríq clamped his thick arms around Neils from behind, squashed his arms against his sides, and hauled him spitting, kicking, and cursing back to the house.

Neils's enraged bellows fell silent when the door slammed with him and Anríq inside. That left Yvan, Rien, Yann, and Eliska standing there staring down at Niyazi's body. Neils's sword still stuck out of the side of Niyazi's head.

Yvan yanked the sword out, let it fall onto the pavement, and he sank down on his ankles next to the body. He buried his head in his hands fighting to breathe.

Yann gulped down a lump in his throat. He told himself a hundred times to look away, but some unstoppable power kept his eyes glued to Niyazi's ruined face.

The Watch couldn't stand to lose anyone right now, especially not a good, strong, steady man who always did his duty to his brother Watchmen and his oath. Niyazi was one of the very few still keeping his sanity right now.

His loss would have been a cruel blow even if he had been losing his mind. Niyazi always held the line—always. He got along with everyone. He always fought his hardest and gave his best to everyone no matter what.

Yann couldn't remember a single time, since his earliest memories, when Yvan or any of the other Watchmen ever doubted Niyazi. Yann couldn't remember his father ever reprimanding Niyazi or even saying anything to correct Niyazi's behavior.

Niyazi always conducted himself with the utmost tact. He always did the right thing. He and Omer were the two Watchmen Yann most admired after his father.

Yann held them up as models of what every Watchman should be—and now they were both gone.

His stomach turned when he thought about how Neils would react when he finally came out of this insanity and realized that he was the one who killed Niyazi.

How could Neils come back from that? How could anyone?

Yann didn't want to look around him. Four people. The Watch had four people left plus Anríq. Yann couldn't even count on his father or even Rien anymore.

At least Yann still had Eliska—and Anríq. Was that it? Is that what Yann had to look forward to—the last of the Watchmen losing their minds and either killing themselves, killing each other, or getting killed by Darklings?

Did he have to look forward to the day when he only had Eliska and Anríq left of the whole party—and maybe not even them?

He would become Commander of a one-man Watch. What a joke.

Just then, just when things couldn't get any worse, Atian climbed down the stairs from the scaffold. His footsteps rang extra loudly in the silence.

Those clanging footsteps announced to the whole world that the Tenby men had been watching from the wall when Neils killed Niyazi. They all saw. The Watch couldn't deny anymore just how bad the situation had gotten.

Atian halted there next to Yvan—right next to Niyazi's body.

For some reason Yann couldn't figure out, Atian wound up addressing Yann instead of Rien or Yvan.

"Um.....I'm really sorry about this...." Atian stammered, "but I think it's best for everyone if you take your people and go your own way. I didn't want to say anything before, but it's obvious now that you men are too unstable to stay here. You can't help us defend this place any better than we can defend it on our own. You can bury your friend in our cemetery and then I'd be really grateful if you just leave. I'm sorry, but that's just the way it has to be."

Yvan stayed there squatting next to Niyazi's body. Rien didn't say anything, so Yann just said, "Of course we understand and we'll respect your wishes. I'm very sorry if our presence disturbed your town or put your people in danger. We'll leave as soon as possible like you say. We're all deeply grateful for the hospitality you've shown us. We're forever in your debt."

Atian nodded once and walked away. The ominous silence didn't lift. No one spoke up on the scaffold. The peaceful hum of Tenby didn't revive to fill the air.

Yann considered how to tell his father to stand up and help decide what to do with Niyazi's body. Yann didn't even know where the Tenby town cemetery was.

Fortunately, Anríq came back just then. He didn't ask Yvan to move. Anríq took hold of Niyazi's wrist and hoisted the body onto his shoulder. Anríq looked around.

"The cemetery is over there," Eliska murmured and pointed behind her. "I'll show you where it is."

Chapter 38

E liska led Anríq through the Tenby streets. The funereal silence hung heavy over the whole town. No one moved or breathed as Anríq carried Niyazi's body through the streets. It wasn't the nicest funeral, but it was more than Barsali and Omer got.

She led Anríq, Yann, and Rien to the cemetery. It occupied the same block with all those garden homes. Trees, lawns, flower beds, and fountains surrounded the rows of graves.

She showed Anríq where to put Niyazi under a tree. She didn't know if the townspeople wanted the Watch to bury Niyazi here, but anything was better than nothing.

Yvan showed up a few minutes later. He followed the group to the cemetery.

Eliska got a shovel out of the garden shed. Anríq, Rien, Yann, and Yvan all got tools, too, and they started digging the grave in silence.

Eliska could have used her magic to dig this grave, but this seemed somehow more appropriate.

Niyazi's body lay on the grass nearby. He had his eyes closed. He looked like he was asleep.

She didn't break down over his death the way she broke down over Barsali's death. Niyazi's death meant something different.

She worked steadily and committed her effort to Yann and the others. They all needed to honor Niyazi before they walked away from him forever.

Then they would all have to deal with Neils. Traveling across country with a crazy man would be nearly impossible.

She made up her mind to suggest to Yvan—or whoever the hell happened to take charge—that the group reenter the chaos Layers where she and Anríq could get their magic back. She really didn't see any other option.

The group didn't finish digging the grave until late afternoon. Anríq laid Niyazi in it and arranged his body in as comfortable a position as possible.

"He was one of the finest Watchmen I've ever known," Yvan quavered when they all stood around the open grave. "He dedicated his life to the Watch and he died trying to help a brother Watchman. I can't give him any higher praise than that."

"He treated every Watchman as a brother," Rien rasped. "The world is poorer without him."

No one else said anything. Eliska should have said something, but the words wouldn't come. No words seemed good enough to describe what Niyazi was.

He would never be any of that again.

The group got busy shoveling the dirt over him, tamping it down, and then everyone dragged their sorry backsides back to the house.

They found Neils tied up so tight he couldn't move any part of his body except for his head.

He kept gasping and jerking from right to left trying to see his enemies coming for him. Yann left immediately, went upstairs, and locked himself in the bedroom for the rest of the evening.

The other Watchmen separated. Rien sat down in the living room to keep an eye on Neils. Anríq left the house and Yvan went upstairs, too.

Eliska went into the kitchen. She'd seen enough of Anríq's work under the pavilion. Someone had to feed this group tonight and no one else looked like they were going to do it.

She worked steadily for over an hour before Anríq came back. He sat down on the other side of the counter from her, but he didn't talk to her. He unwrapped and rewrapped the leather strap around his axe handle while she worked.

Marine returned a little while later. She bounced into the house as bubbly and excited as ever. "I still haven't found any trace of the bolus of knowledge, but I'm working on it! I'll find it one of these days. Then I'll be able to learn everything the Templars knew before the....."

She broke off when she noticed the subdued atmosphere.

"What's wrong?" she asked.

Eliska glanced over at Rien sitting in the chair right next to Neils. "Ask me later."

Marine opened her mouth, closed it, and blinked. She glanced at Anríq, but he didn't explain, either. Eliska dreaded telling Marine the truth.

"Whatever you want to do in O'akim's library, I suggest you do it now," Eliska told her. "We'll be leaving Tenby in the morning."

Marine gasped in horror. "What?! No! Why?! Everything was going so well...."

"Not so well," Eliska murmured.

"I don't understand! This is the best Island we've found so far! Why do we have to leave?! Don't tell me it's because you two are so hot to get your magic back! That can't be the reason...."

"It isn't," Eliska replied.

"Then why?! I don't want to leave! I'm just getting started...."

"Then you better go back to O'akim's library and catch up on whatever it is you want to know. We're leaving tomorrow."

Marine opened her mouth one more time, but she stopped herself when she saw Anríq gazing back at her.

She lowered her voice to a half-whisper. "Something happened, didn't it?"

"Ask me later," Eliska repeated. "Now, if you aren't going back to the library, would you please go upstairs and call Yann and Yvan down for dinner?"

Marine opened her mouth a third time—and her mind clicked. Her expression transformed in horror. Then her hand flew to her mouth and she stifled a sob.

She bolted up the stairs, and a second later, the door slammed on the bedroom she shared with Eliska.

Eliska glanced over at Anríq at the same moment he glanced at her. She read her own thoughts written all over his face.

Neither of them would have done anything to get the group thrown out of this Island—not even for the chance to get their magic back.

Now they were going back out there. That curtain of upheaval out there threatened Tenby too closely.

The group would go back out there and she and Anríq would get their magic back whether they wanted it or not. Maybe it was for the best, but they no longer had a choice about it.

She would have liked to talk to Anríq about what would happen once the group left this Island, but what was there to say?

She set the table with two fewer places tonight. Marine must have locked herself in her room, too. She didn't send Yann and Yvan downstairs.

In the end, Eliska had to go up there herself and call all three of them down to dinner.

Rien and Anríq came first. Rien didn't suggest untying Neils or even feeding him.

Yann, Yvan, and Marine showed up a minute later. The six friends sat down and Eliska served them her food. It wasn't as extravagant a meal as Anríq could make, but no one complained.

"Does anyone have any brilliant ideas about where we should go after this?" Rien asked after a long silence.

"Somewhere magical," Eliska blurted out right away. "Traveling without our magic is idiotic."

"I agree," Anríq added.

"So do I," Yann chimed in.

"That means we'll lose Marine," Yvan pointed out.

"I'm no good to you the way I am anyway." Marine sighed. "I don't see that it makes much difference either way—and Anríq and Eliska can help all of you more than I can if they get their magic back."

"Right now, I can't even tell where we are or where we should go," Eliska went on. "At least with my magic we'll be able to find any stable Islands that are left."

"Would you be able to use your Coil projection to see where the Voyant is and whether he's coming after us?" Yann asked.

"I might. I would have a better chance if Anríq and I join our magic together. I haven't explored that as well as I could have, but I can't do any of that here."

Yvan nodded. "That sounds like the vote is carried."

"Vote?" Yann countered. "Since when do we vote on anything?"

Yvan pushed his food back and forth on his plate. "I don't know much about anything anymore. Everything seems to be falling apart."

"That's kind of the point, isn't it?" Marine pointed out. "The Coil is disintegrating and everything we know to be true is disintegrating along with it."

"Did you get any information at all about the Templars' bolus of knowledge?" Eliska asked.

Marine squirmed in her seat. "I wish I could say I did. It's probably better if we leave this Island. I won't be able to find out anything magical here—or use magic to find it."

"Would you be able to find it if you're communing with Darklings?" Yann asked. "Are you sure you won't be too out of your mind to remember that you're supposed to find it?"

She shot him another huge, glowing grin and then remembered that she shouldn't be that happy. "I'll try to remember—but I would be more likely to find it out there than here. I mean, I would be more likely to find it when I'm communing with Darklings. Brother Matherus said the Templars hid the bolus in the Layers. I assume he meant the Dark Layers."

Eliska gasped. "Why would they hide it there? The Voyant or the Darklings or anyone could find it there. They could have destroyed the bolus before you ever find it."

"I don't think so," Marine breezed. "The Templars wouldn't have hidden it anywhere anyone could find it. Wherever it is, it's going to take an act of God to find it—and it would be much better hidden in the Dark Layers than anywhere else."

Eliska made a face. "I don't like where this is going."

Marine started to laugh and cut that off, too. "You don't have to go. I'll go."

"You realize what this means, don't you?" Eliska countered.

Marine frowned. "What does it mean?"

"You've already been communing with Darklings for who knows how long and you haven't found the bolus yet. There's a chance you won't be able to find it at all."

"I didn't find it because I wasn't looking for it."

"Who do you think you're talking to, Marine?" Eliska asked. "You might have to combine your magic with mine—or maybe even all three of us combining our magic together to find the bolus. Then all three of us would have to travel to the Dark Layers."

"Well, what would be wrong with that? At least we would find it and use the Templars' information to defeat the Voyant."

Yann interrupted. "You don't know that the bolus contains the information about how to defeat the Voyant."

"Of course it does!" Marine exclaimed. "It has to. Why else would Brother Matherus tell me about it?"

"Because you asked him whether the Voyant destroyed all the Templars' knowledge," Eliska pointed out. "That's why Brother Matherus told you about the bolus. He never said it contained the information to defeat the Voyant."

Marine opened her mouth, blinked, and shut it again. Eliska glanced over at Anríq again. Would he be willing to travel to the Dark Layers to retrieve the Templars' bolus of knowledge?

She'd never actually asked him if he would be willing to do all that—or if he would join his magic with hers and Marine's to make it happen.

She really didn't know anything about him. Eliska realized that under the pavilion.

Marine was right. The person he was behind this veil of silence must be something vastly different than what anyone could see from the outside.

Chapter 39

Yann woke up the next morning, put his feet on the floor, and heaved a deep sigh. Niyazi was dead and now the group would leave Tenby behind.

It was bound to happen sooner or later. Yann just didn't think it would happen like this.

Anríq already sat on the edge of his bed looking straight back at Yann. Yann read his own thoughts going through Anríq's mind.

The group would head off into the magical chaos with three unstable Watchmen. Yann couldn't count on any of them to stay sane for very long.

Marine would lose her mind the instant the group crossed the barrier. Then Yann wouldn't be able to rely on her, either.

At least he wouldn't have to worry about her swinging a weapon around trying to kill everyone in sight.

Anríq pulled his vest over his big shoulders, hung his bags across his chest, and strapped on his weapons. He took them everywhere even in the middle of Tenby.

Yann got his glaive and the two boys went downstairs. Eliska was already there making breakfast. She sure took this cooking business seriously now.

Neils and Rien sat at the table eating the food she put in front of them. Neils acted perfectly normal.

He didn't act distraught about killing Niyazi. Did he even know? Yvan and Marine came downstairs and Neils didn't ask where Niyazi was. Rien must have told Neils the truth while everyone else was out of the room.

Eliska served everyone else. The party ate in silence and left the house in silence.

The minute they got outside, they spotted Atian standing at the gate waiting to let the travelers out. He didn't waste any time. He couldn't wait to get rid of the Watch—what was left of it.

The curtain of wild magic crackled and flashed just a mile away from Tenby. The curtain undulated and hissed all the way up to the sky with Dark Layers towering over the town.

"I could pull that margin back," Eliska blurted out.

Everyone turned around to stare at her. "What?" Yvan asked.

"I could pull it back—if I went out there. I could go behind the veil and pull it away from the town."

Yvan looked away. "You would get lost in the storm. We would never see you again."

"But the town would be safe," she pointed out. "What's one person compared to all these people's lives? Besides, it isn't like I would die. I would just go back into the Coil and all of you would stay here."

"Forget it," Yvan snarled. "We're going together the way we planned."

She didn't argue. The group advanced toward the gate.

They made it twenty feet before O'akim charged out of somewhere, rushed Marine, threw his arms around her, and burst into tears.

"I can't believe you have to go!" he wailed. "I only just found you and now you're leaving! What am I going to do?"

"You'll keep taking care of the people of this town the way you always have," Marine murmured. "You don't need me distracting you from that."

"I don't want you to go!" he sobbed. "Isn't there some way we can work out a compromise?"

"I'm afraid not. I have my own mission to fulfill and I can't do that here. I'm so grateful for your help and all your kindness. I hope we meet again someday."

He burst into a fresh flood of tears. He wouldn't stop hugging her. She had to use an extra little bit of force to push him off. "Stay here, O'akim," she told him. "Don't make a fuss. Your people need you and mine need me. We'll always be together in that."

She turned her back on him and the rest of the group surrounded her on their way to the gate.

Atian had to work hard to make eye contact with everyone. "Thank you for doing this."

"Thank you for everything," Yvan told him. "I only wish we could have done more for you."

"Travel safely." Atian unlocked the gate and swung it open.

The travelers marched out of Tenby and faced the huge, towering curtain of magic right in front of them.

It touched down a mile away, but its sheer size made it seem much closer and much more dangerous.

Landscapes formed, collapsed, exploded, and contorted behind the veil. They collided, merged, tumbled over each other, and blasted apart into new mountain ranges.

Oceans ejected from the fissures of earthquakes and inundated everything before another Layer wiped out the oceans.

The group paused there right outside the gate to take in the magnitude of the void in front of them.

"Ready?" Yvan asked.

Eliska raised her staff. "Ready."

Anríq unhooked his club. The other Watchmen drew their weapons to be ready for anything they encountered as soon as they entered the Layers.

Yann took hold of his glaive and squared his shoulders to walk into that sea of mayhem. He'd always run from it before. Now he was going there headfirst and in full knowledge of the risks.

Yvan said, "Let's go," and the group started forward shoulder to shoulder. No one backed down. Neils showed no sign of losing his mind again.

The group made it a hundred yards away from the walls before the Voyant floated through the veil right in front of them. No one saw even the smallest trace of light in there before he showed up.

He emerged from the mayhem in the blink of an eye, broke the curtain, and floated in front of the group glowing as brightly as ever.

The minute he crossed that barrier, the invisible boundary evaporated and all that chaos exploded across the countryside heading straight for Tenby.

Yann dug his legs into the ground to brace himself against the torrential wind. He raised his glaive.

Anríq held out his arm again. "Don't attack him! Stand your ground!"

Screams and roars drew Yann's attention to the wall behind him. The Tenby defenders stood up there ready to defend the town—except that they didn't defend the town.

Yann hardly dared to tear his eyes off the Voyant even for a second, but when he did, he almost forgot to keep the Voyant in sight after all.

Men fought each other on the wall, clawed at their own eyes, and a few men stood on top of the wall shooting their rifles at enemies who weren't there. Some turned their weapons on themselves or other townsfolk.

Whirling tornados of debris and rubble pinwheeled through the air. The hurricane swallowed Tenby in seconds, but the Voyant still didn't move in. He always stayed the same distance from the wall.

"Back up!" Yvan bellowed. "Defend the town!"

"How can we if he doesn't attack?!" Rien hollered back.

No one answered, but everyone backed up. Anríq pulled his axe forward and faced the Voyant with both weapons. Yann searched the surrounding terrain for anything coming after the town.

He didn't see anything except the Voyant and a whole lot of chaos. Splinters and rock shards pelted through the air and stung Yann's face.

Random creatures he didn't recognize cartwheeled past his head. They squealed and shrieked in terror, but not even they couldn't save themselves.

"I don't see any Darklings!" Rien yelled.

"Stand fast!" Yvan told him.

Another brutal scream echoed from behind followed by gunshots. Yann didn't dare to turn around to see how bad things were getting on the wall.

The tempest raging across the countryside escalated to a catastrophic whirlwind. Yann couldn't tell anymore where the veil had been just a few minutes ago. He could barely see at all.

"We still don't have our magic!" Eliska called over the noise. "The Voyant must be holding it back!"

"How can he when this front *is* magic?" Yann asked.

Eliska yelled something back at him. He couldn't hear her over the noise, and right at that moment, a deafening explosion went off behind the party. A massive fireball hit the gate from behind and blasted it off its hinges.

It burst open from the inside and left the town wide open and exposed to anyone or anything that wanted to come in.

Almost as if someone planned it that way, twenty massive Darklings erupted out of the mayhem at that exact moment. Their enormous booming feet shook the ground with every step and they charged Tenby.

"Everybody to the wall!!" Yvan ordered. "Everybody get up on the wall to defend the town!"

The whole group spun away to run back onto the wall. Eliska and Marine went, too, even though neither of them had any magic.

The party sprinted through the open gate and up the stairs to the scaffold.

Townspeople battled each other all over town. More armed men fired their rifles into thin air. Others used their rifles as clubs to drive away Darklings no one could see. These people kept screaming at the Darklings to leave them alone.

Other townspeople ran through the streets in hysterical panic. Yann couldn't tell from here if they were losing their minds or just terrified of the impending disaster.

He couldn't pay attention to that right now. He leapt up the stairs and pushed a few mindless townspeople out of the way to clamber up onto the wall.

Anríq, the two girls, and the last four Watchmen made it there at the same time. The party looked out over the countryside with the Darklings closing fast.

Seven people. That was the whole Watch now. Marine was totally unarmed and Eliska only had her staff. No way could seven people fight twenty Darklings, especially not Darklings as big as this.

Yann dove aside and pulled Eliska out of line. "Get to the rocket launcher! Quick! It's our only chance!"

"What?!" she shrieked. "I don't even know how to use it!"

"Figure it out!" he roared. "Go now, Eliska! We'll never beat them any other way!"

She stared at him in abject horror as the truth sank in. He couldn't explain it to her any better than that.

She clamped her mouth shut, dropped her staff, and took off running down the wall. Yann couldn't look to see if she made it or if the rocket launcher even worked anymore.

He turned outward to face the Darklings. This was it. This battle would decide the fate of Tenby, but it was already over. Those Darklings could flatten the town with their massive stomping feet.

The Darklings closed around the town from all sides. The Watch spread out to confront as many Darklings as possible, but seven people could never be enough.

A giant dark-brown Darkling stopped in front of Yann. Its tentacles whipped and snaked all around him. Magic crackled down each one. He didn't stand a chance against this thing.

One tentacle hissed just a little too close. He slashed his glaive at it and severed it from the main trunk.

The Darkling roared and that sound set off all the others. They closed for the kill, and at that moment, a rocket released from somewhere to Yann's left.

A vapor trail corkscrewed across the landscape and the rocket detonated in one of the Darklings' faces—the Darkling standing in front of Anríq.

That explosion set off a matching reaction in the Watchmen. Anríq took a flying leap off the wall, landed on the ground outside, and charged the Darklings.

He raced from one to another hacking his axe into their feet and ankles to bring them to the ground. They bellowed in pain and rage, turned away from the wall, and tried to stomp on him instead.

All the Watchmen dove in to attack. Yann jumped, but he never hit the ground before a tentacle caught him, crushed the air out of his body, and tossed him high into the air.

Chapter 40

Yann looked down on the battle descending into chaos. Eliska sat behind her rocket launcher unloading one missile after another on the Darklings.

Americ crouched on the wall next to her cramming rockets into the tubes as fast as he possibly could work. He barely got them loaded before she fired again.

Marine took off running the other way down the wall heading for a different rocket launcher. Heaven only knew how she would be able to get it working.

Yann curved in the air at the top of his arc and started to fall, but he knew what he had to do now. He pivoted toward the nearest Darkling.

Another tentacle hit him, but that only broke his fall, sent him tumbling toward another Darkling, and miraculously positioned him right where he could impale his glaive into its side.

The monster reared away bellowing in fury and carried him with it. It flung him toward a different Darkling only for him to get nearly squashed when Eliska hit that one in the head with one of her rockets.

Yann lost track of all the explosions going off everywhere. He saw his father, Anríq, Rien, and Neils all fighting in the confusion.

Yann dodged away from one dead Darkling toppling to crush him only to run into another tentacle whistling through the air.

A discharge of magic smashed Yann in the chest and he hurtled backward to land hard on the ground.

He blinked the stars out of his eyes. He might have passed out for a minute because no one stood in the same places on the battlefield—except for the two girls.

Americ wasn't there anymore resupplying Eliska. Yann didn't see Eliska or his father anywhere, either. Were they both dead?

Anríq stood in front of the wall wielding his axe in one hand and his club in the other. Rien occupied a position far down the wall almost too far away for Yann to see him.

Yann looked around for Neils. Yann took a second before he spotted Neils on top of the wall.

Neils sprinted toward Eliska's rocket launcher. Yann didn't see what Neils would be able to do there. Yann didn't see what anyone would be able to do about any of this.

One remaining Darkling stomped away from Yann to go after Neils. Eliska and Marine must have killed a lot more Darklings than Yann realized. He only saw five now.

Two faced Anríq, but they left him to go after Neils, too. Yann didn't see why.

Tentacles whipped over the wall. Neils hurdled them, teetered on the very top of the wall, and kept running at full speed. He wouldn't be able to load and fire the rocket launcher fast enough. He didn't even know how to use it.

Three Darklings surrounded him right on that part of the wall. Anríq charged over there and hacked the Darklings' legs and feet with his axe, but he couldn't distract them.

Two more Darklings from Rien's part of the battlefield noticed their surviving friends getting interested in something important.

Both of them turned away from Rien, but they didn't make their move in time.

More tentacles surrounded Neils. He barely escaped the first one. The second one flattened him and he pitched onto his face on top of the wall.

The Darklings roared and loomed over him baring all their fangs. He looked up. He couldn't fail to see the truth. He was as good as dead already.

One of them reared and brought its tentacle down with all its strength to crush him.

He dove out of the way, rolled across the wall, and in his last act, he snatched up the crate of rockets from the pedestal next to the launcher.

He didn't have time to do anything other than wrap his arms around the crate before a third tentacle lashed around his body, yanked him into the air, and whisked him out over the battlefield.

Yann opened his mouth to yell—and then he saw something else. Neils hovered a hundred feet above the ground holding a crate containing twenty rockets. He'd also grabbed one of the Tenby defenders' smaller handguns in his other hand.

Yann shot to his feet in a heartbeat and took off running for the open gate. "ANRÍQ!!" Yann bellowed. "GET INSIDE!!"

Anríq hesitated for a split second before the Darkling dropped Neils, the crate, and the gun into its yawning mouth.

Yann couldn't look. He bent his head and ran for it. Anríq followed a dozen yards behind Yann. Would it be enough?

Another Darkling roared and then a bone-crushing boom went off behind Yann's back. The impact smacked him off his feet and sent him somersaulting through the gate onto the paved streets.

Anríq tumbled to a halt next to him and both boys sprawled there.

Yann hardly dared to look up. Were the Darklings coming into town right now?

He didn't feel any wind or debris flying around. In fact, he didn't hear anything at all.

He pried his head off the ground and he and Anríq looked at each other.

"Are you okay?" Yann croaked.

Anríq nodded and his blue eyes darted toward the gate. "Are we the only ones left?"

"I saw Rien earlier. He was far enough away."

Yann peeled himself off the pavement, pushed himself to his feet, and picked up Anríq. Both boys dusted themselves off.

Dead bodies lay all over the street. Yann spotted Atian tangled up in a pile of seven men lying together near one of the houses.

Yann glanced through the gate. The magical curtain shimmered and crackled at a distance from the town. It had returned to its former position.

"Let me guess," Yann murmured. "You don't have your magic back, do you?"

"No," Anríq replied. "I agree with Eliska. The Voyant must have done something to stop it."

Yann looked around. "Let's spread out and see if we can find the others—or anyone else alive around here."

The boys separated. Yann went back outside the gate and met up with Rien coming from the left.

"Did you see that?" Rien breathed. "Neils killed the Darklings!"

"I didn't see. I was running too hard to get away from the explosion."

"They surrounded him—all except the two who were too far away. Three of them went after him, and when that one swallowed him, he blew up all three of them."

"Then what happened?" Yann asked.

"The explosion made the Voyant disappear. He flew back into the confusion and the curtain went back to where it was before."

"Do you know if anyone else is alive?"

"I think the Watch Commander is over there."

Rien pointed to the right—farther down the wall. Yann wouldn't have been able to see over there during the battle.

He and Rien crossed the fields and found Yvan lying on the ground with a broken leg. Yann and Rien picked him up and helped him back inside.

They passed through the gate and met up with Anríq coming back with Eliska and Americ.

"He saved my life," Eliska exclaimed. "The Darklings came after the rocket launcher. They would have killed me, but Americ tackled me behind the wall just in time."

"Where's Marine?" Yann asked.

"I don't know. I haven't seen her."

Yann turned around to tell Rien to help him take his father to the hospital, but just then Marine and O'akim rushed over from somewhere. "Follow me!" O'akim told Yann. "I'll show you where to take him."

The group all went together to take Yvan to the hospital. Yann and Rien lowered him onto a bed with wheels on it. The doctors and nurses took Yvan away and left the others with nothing to do but look at each other.

They left the building, but once the group got outside, the bleak surroundings didn't offer any clarity on what to do next.

"I guess we'll just go back to the same house," Yann suggested. "We have nowhere else to go."

"Atian told us to leave town," Eliska pointed out. "It's safer now. We could still do it—and then we would get somewhere magical."

"I agree with Eliska," Marine added. "I don't want to stay somewhere we aren't welcome."

"Atian is dead," Yann told them. "I wonder if...."

He broke off when Rosh, Valer, and Americ came up to the Watch. The three men came side by side. Yann would have to be blind not to see they had something on their minds.

"We want to say....thank you for everything you just did for us," Americ began.

"Thank you for saving Eliska," Yann replied. "We won't forget it—and we haven't forgotten that you asked us to leave. We were just on our way...."

"We would really appreciate it if you stayed," Americ blurted out. "That's what we came to tell you. Not everyone agreed with Atian's decision after your friend died—and now your other friend gave his life to defeat those Darklings. We would really appreciate it if you stayed. We need all the fighters we can get now and you've all proven yourselves. Don't leave. Please. We need you too much."

The friends exchanged glances. How could Yann say no to that?

O'akim dove in and seized Marine's hand. "Yes! This is fantastic! Now we can continue our studies as if none of this ever happened."

"Not exactly," Eliska pointed out.

Yann turned to Rien. "What about you? You're the last man besides Father who has been having nightmares. We can expect them to continue if we stay."

Rien twisted his shoulders inside his uniform and looked away. "I guess I never walked away from my duty just for my own convenience. If you all stay, I'll stay, too."

"Your father put you in Command of the Watch if he and the others went down," Eliska added. "It looks pretty straightforward to me."

Yann didn't ask how she knew that.

"We've never been well organized," Valer interjected. "You men at least have some training and leadership skills. Atian was the only leader we ever had. None of us is qualified to take his place."

"I doubt that," Yann replied. "He told us no one around here was more in charge than anyone else. You would be just as qualified to take his place as anyone."

"Not more qualified than you."

"Me!" Yann countered. "I'm just a kid! I haven't even taken my oath yet."

"You might as well have," Anríq cut in.

"Your father put you in command," Rien pointed out. "What more do you need to know?"

"What about you?" Yann fired back. "You're more than fifteen years older than I am. You have way more experience than I do—and Father will be back on his feet one of these days."

"But until that happens, you're the best man for the job," Rien pointed out. "As you just said, I could start having nightmares again. It has to be you."

Yann shut his mouth. He could think of a whole boatload of reasons why a seventeen-year-old boy shouldn't be made Commander of the Watch.

Hadn't Yann told Eliska just a few short days ago that the party wasn't the Black Watch anymore? That day seemed like ten years ago now.

They weren't the Black Watch anymore. They had three men left. Why did Yann even think of them as the Black Watch when they weren't?

Americ and the others read his decision in his eyes. "We have to bury our dead. You should return to your house. You can come out to organize the defense tomorrow."

Yann nodded. "You might want to get someone working on repairing the gate, too. We can't leave it standing open like that."

Chapter 41

E liska came downstairs and found Yvan sitting at the kitchen counter. He'd spread a piece of scrap fabric over the surface, disassembled one of the Tenby defenders' rifles, and laid out all the pieces in front of him.

He worked through the rifle cleaning all the parts and putting the weapon back together. He'd been doing little else since he got out of the hospital.

The Tenby doctors had some way of fixing broken bones—a way that didn't involve magic. Eliska didn't try to understand it. She was just glad to get Yvan back in one piece.

"How is it coming along?" she asked.

He smiled at her. "I can do it with my eyes closed now."

She laughed at him. "That should come in handy when you're in battle against the Darklings."

"As long as we're here, we might as well learn how to use the available weapons. Considering how well those rockets worked last time, we should start with those instead of our usual weapons."

Eliska got serious. "Has anyone told you how many rockets the townspeople have left in their supplies?"

"No one will tell me anything about supplies—of anything. No one will talk about where they get all this stuff, how they fuel it, or anything else. I'm starting to get a little suspicious if you really want to know the truth."

"Just a little?"

He made a face. "Are you going out to the wall? I'll go with you."

He put down his half-assembled rifle and left it there while the two of them walked out of the house.

She checked to make sure he could walk okay, but he didn't limp anymore the way he did when he first got out of the hospital.

He seemed fine and went about his duties as usual. He didn't act tired.

He also didn't hesitate to take over as soon as he found out about the Tenby defenders asking Yann to become Commander of the Watch.

Yvan never mentioned it. He just asserted his authority. Yann accepted everything in silence. Of course he didn't try to pull rank on his father.

Yann went straight back to acting like Rien's subordinate, too, but something switched for everyone else in the party—and everyone on the Tenby side, too.

If anything went wrong—anything at all—Yann would step in. Everyone pretended not to, but they all watched Rien and Yvan like hawks for the slightest hint that they were becoming unstable again.

Yvan and Eliska climbed the stairs to the wall where Yann, Anríq, and Rien stood talking to Americ, Rosh, and Valer.

Those three acted as lieutenants for the Tenby defenders. The three men relayed orders from whoever happened to be in charge to all the men guarding the wall.

Eliska noticed a definite spike in tension when Yvan showed up. Yann might have been telling the defenders what to do in his father's absence instead of telling them to ask Yvan.

"What's the situation?" Yvan asked the group at large.

"The chaos beyond the veil is picking up again and the curtain is moving closer," Yann replied. "This is the same build-up we saw before the last attack."

"It's interesting that it hasn't affected us this time," Rien pointed out. "The nightmares and day terrors escalated at the same time before. That isn't happening now."

"Maybe you're immune," Americ suggested.

"What does that mean?" Yann asked. "I don't know that word."

"It means you got a disease and now your body is able to fight it. You won't get the same disease again."

"I can definitely get it again," Rien countered. "It keeps coming back."

Americ waved that away. "I guess magical ailments don't work the same way."

"This isn't an ailment," Yann replied. "The Voyant is attacking us the same way he....."

"Look!" Eliska lunged forward and pointed across the countryside. "The children are back!"

Everyone strained their eyes to see the same group of tiny figures dwarfed by the chaos. Two of the adults had vanished. Two remained to guard the children. The group of children looked smaller, too.

"Don't tell me they've been trapped out there all this time!" Rien growled.

Eliska turned away "I'm going out there to help them. I can pull the margin back while I'm out there."

Yvan stopped her. "We've already gone over this before, Eliska. You can't go out there."

"I can and I'm going to. We won't survive another attack—and if we do, we won't survive the next one. We can't keep defending this town the way we are—not without falling back on some kind of magical defense. Besides, I'm not leaving children out in that storm unprotected. They've already lost two adult magic-users. If the other two go down, the children won't stand a chance."

"I'll go with you," Anríq chimed in. "Two of us will be better than one."

"You have to stay here to defend the town and Marine would lose her mind again if she went out there. I'm going."

She didn't tear herself out of Yvan's grip this time. The two of them had covered too much ground together for her to throw his concern back in his face.

She waited until he took his hand away willingly. He scowled at her and then pursed his lips. "Just be careful—and come back. Don't you get lost out there, too."

"I'll be fine—and I'll see you soon."

She swung her leg over the wall and hopped down. She didn't wait for someone to open the gate for her. She walked off toward the magical curtain in the distance.

She knew exactly what she was doing now. Determination gave her a strange kind of peace. She didn't have to cower behind walls waiting for the Voyant to strike.

The crackling energy built up as she got closer to the veil. She tightened her grip on her staff. She would have to be ready to use it as soon as she crossed that line.

She had fallen out of practice in Tenby. She never had to use magic to do anything.

Now she was back and ready to burst out of her shell.

Her resolve hardened when she saw the children struggling through the storm. She saw them more clearly now. They looked like the children from Tenby. None of them could have been older than ten.

The two remaining magic-users fired countless blasts into the storm, but they couldn't protect the children from everything.

Explosions went off all over the place, hit the children, knocked them down, and made them tumble backward in the punishing wind.

Eliska didn't see any Darklings attacking. This storm was just a chaos Layer butting right up against the margin from its other side.

She strode straight through the veil and a rush of exhilaration coursed through her veins when her magic returned.

Then the hurricane hit her side on. Now was not the time to celebrate.

She bent her head, squinted her eyes against one assault after another, and fired her staff into the wind.

A curved field ejected from the end of her staff. It protected her from the worst assault, but it couldn't protect her from everything.

Sheets of wild magic whipped across her face. Some felt like fire. Others like freezing water soaked through her clothes. Some stabbed her with a million needles.

She scrambled to see the children in the mayhem, but she lost sight of them. She fired her staff behind her and magicked herself to transport to their location, but when she got there, she didn't find them.

She couldn't see anything, so she magicked back to where she started. Maybe she would see them where she originally spotted them.

She didn't see the children or their magic-user escorts. She did see Tenby.

The town shivered just beyond the veil. The curtain must have swept closer to the town just since she entered this chaos Layer.

She fought her way to the margin to pull it back, but at that moment, something very fast and very hard shrieked out of the confusion from her right.

She didn't see it before it struck her hard and knocked her over.

She sprawled on some solid surface, but when she looked down, she didn't see anything underneath her. She was no longer in the Tenby Island.

A vast bottomless void full of vapors and swirling Dark fell away underneath her.

Before she could even pick herself up, she heard the same shrieking noise coming closer.

She flipped onto her back and fired her staff upward even though she couldn't see anything.

Whatever had been about to hit her smashed into that blast of magic and deflected off. Something out there was trying to attack her.

She scrambled to her feet, took hold of her staff in one hand, and opened her palm window in the other.

The watery pool showed her a fast-moving jet of fire aiming for her from far across the Layer.

The jet came in a straight line. It didn't know yet that she could see it coming.

She counted down the seconds, sprang clear just in time, and fired another burst at it.

She hit the streak and it pelted away, but her attack only shattered it into ten different identical streaks.

They all came whizzing back at her from every direction. She wouldn't be able to hit them all.

The margin swept a little closer to Tenby. She could see Yann, Anríq, Americ, Yvan, Rien, and all the other Tenby defenders right there through the veil.

At the same time, the Dark vapors crossing the veil started to gather into Darkling shapes. She couldn't let them form.

She dove for the Layer's outer margin and locked her staff under her arm with one end pointing forward and the other end pointing behind her.

She channeled all her power into her staff and fired from both ends.

A magical shield erupted behind her just as those ten streaks smashed into it from all sides. They pounded and hammered trying to break through and bombard her.

She ejected a huge net of fibers from the front end of her staff and anchored all those fibers to the Layer's forward margin. Could the defenders see her as well as she could see them?

She locked her fibers into the margin, and one painstaking inch at a time, she dragged it backward.

The streaks escalated their assault. Their shrieking noise built to a deafening screech in her ears.

She clamped her eyes shut and willed herself to take one torturous step backward after another.

The effort took every ounce of her strength, but she didn't stop until she pulled it back to where it was. Now she just had to hold it there.

How long could she last? She still had to go look for those children.

She didn't dare to turn around with those streaks nailing her from all sides. They kept ricocheting off her field, scattering, multiplying, and coming back to bombard her again and again. This couldn't go on.

She had to come up with something better—some way to hold the margin at a distance from Tenby for a long time—possibly forever.

If she could come up with a way to get rid of these streaks at the same time, so much the better.

She wouldn't be able to do any of that by shooting at them, so she threw caution to the wind, braced herself, and turned around.

She dropped her field in an instant and all the streaks converged coming way too fast. She summoned all her power, raised her staff, and nailed it backward into the margin's outer edge.

At the same time, she ejected another burst from the other end of the staff, but this one didn't shoot outward.

It caught the streaks in an undertow and used their own speed against them. The staff sucked their power into itself and fired all of it at the margin behind her.

A brutal smash exploded through the margin, hit Eliska, and shot her across the landscape at bone-crushing speed.

The force ripped her and the margin away, hurtled them across the countryside, and sent her wheeling through multiple Layers to somewhere deep in the forgotten recesses of the Coil.

Chapter 42

Eliska rolled over and picked herself up. She found herself still in the same vapor Layer with an invisible floor. Chaos and Dark swirled under her and all around her.

She studied her surroundings, but she didn't see any way out of here. She didn't even know where she was.

She opened her hand to study her Coil projection. At least she had her magic back.

She found where she was, but she couldn't locate the Tenby Island. If Anríq had been here, she could have combined their magic and found her way back to the Island.

She also couldn't find the children. They might already be dead.

Anríq wasn't here. She was alone—exactly the way she'd always been before she went to Middleborough.

She located another Island a few Layers below her, so she shattered the surface beneath her feet, tumbled through multiple Layers of chaos and vapor, fought her way through a bunch of Darklings, and eventually landed in a field outside a rustic country town.

How strange everything looked here compared to Tenby. All the machines, vehicles, and conveniences of Tenby didn't exist here. None of these people even knew what chocolate was.

She wandered into town just to take a look. To think she'd been living like this for her entire life and never known anything else.

That amazing city she saw with Marine—those people must think Tenby was a rustic country town living in the dirt.

No one looked at Eliska strangely here. Hardly anyone looked at her at all.

She made her way to the town's central market and looked around for someone who might want to buy her skills in exchange for supplies. She wouldn't find any wardrobe full of chilled food waiting for her to cook it.

She stood back out of the way watching all the old familiar scenes of village life. Mangy dogs trotted around looking for scraps to steal. Rats scurried along the foundations of houses.

Dirty children played in the water troughs while their mothers yelled at them not to.

She found herself smiling at them...and then she spotted two other children who weren't playing in the water trough.

A little boy and an even younger girl sat on a doorstep across the market from Eliska's position.

The boy held up a bowl to passersby and begged them to give him anything so he and his sister could buy food.

While Eliska stood there watching, a man in a white apron came out the door behind the two beggar children. He yelled curses at them and used his broom to beat the two children off the doorstep.

He sent them running for it and they vanished into the alleys surrounding the market. Eliska didn't see the two children again.

She would have turned a blind eye to a scene like that in the past. She turned a blind eye to countless scenes like that in the past.

She couldn't remember ever even considering helping someone like that—or anyone in need—ever.

She found herself looking around for Anríq. What would he have done if he was here right now? Would he have tracked those children down, bought them some food, or just talked to them to make them feel better?

Did it really matter what Anríq would have done? He would have done something even if he had to trade his skills to buy the food to give to them.

He wasn't here to do it—and neither were the children. They were gone.

Eliska walked away and headed out into the open country. She walked all day through the Island without seeing a single living human being.

She sat down under a tree to spend the night and pulled her cloak tight around her to keep warm.

How many nights had she spent just like this? She couldn't even begin to count them.

She used to love spending the night like this—all alone in the middle of nowhere. She used to think spending the night alone was the definition of Heaven. No one bothered her. She didn't have to worry about anyone attacking her.

She could just observe the night, listen to the noises, think her own thoughts, and drift off whenever she wanted to. She didn't have to worry about when she woke up or where she would go tomorrow.

The cold ate into her bones now. Her mind inevitably drifted back to the Watch.

She fired her staff into a pile of leaves and ignited them into a fire. She never would have done that before.

The flames flared up and she added twigs to them. The fire warmed her, but it also chilled her. It reminded her of all the faces sitting around that fire—faces she would never see again.

Wesh. Barsali. Omer. Neils. Niyazi.

She might not see Rien, Yvan, Yann, Anríq, or Marine sitting around that fire ever again, either. She didn't know where they were or how to get back to them.

The world sure felt bleak and empty without them.

She wrapped her arms around herself, but that only reminded her of Yann. Who else in the world would have held her like that when she trembled with fear because she lost her magic?

Who would have kissed her on the head and told her it would be all right?

Who would have told her that sometimes they traveled to places where the men couldn't take care of themselves so she did it for them—and sometimes they traveled to places where she couldn't take care of herself so the men did it for her? Who would do something like that if not him?

Yvan would do it. Anríq would do it. Even Rien would do it. She no longer doubted him.

Marine would do it, too. She would do it differently, but she cared about Eliska in the same way. Eliska didn't have to doubt that.

What was this world worth without those people in it? What would her life be worth if she wandered the Coil forever and never found them?

She looked down the long, cold, dark barrel of years—maybe even decades—of nothing. She might never find the Watch. She probably never would. She had no way to find them.

Was life even worth living without them? She couldn't live like this.

Her whole life changed when she got involved in their journey. She couldn't go back to the way she was before.

She couldn't stand to be alone anymore—not like that—and yet she was alone right now. She could look forward to being alone from now on—unless she changed something.

She barely slept that night. She woke up in darkness, kicked out what was left of the fire, and started walking even before the sun came up.

She made it to another town, went straight to the market, and settled down to observe people. She'd never made this much effort to be around people before.

She wasn't exactly sure what she should be looking for, but she was definitely looking for something—something that would show her where to go.

She watched the vendors for a while. Then she watched the beggars, but they weren't the answer, either.

She observed mothers with their children. The mothers acted so much like Anríq—all except for the part where he swung the children around and made them laugh.

She did see fathers doing that. She saw fathers tossing their children into the air, catching them, diving into their children's necks, and pretending to gnaw at them while the fathers growled like animals devouring their prey.

The children shrieked with laughter—and when it was all over, the fathers held their children on their arms exactly the way Anríq did.

The children rested their heads on their father's shoulders while the fathers went about their business. Some of the children even fell asleep like that.

Eliska watched until midday, but she still didn't find what she was looking for.

She got to her feet and picked up her staff to leave town. Maybe she would find something at the next town.

Just then, an old, grey-haired woman came up to her. "Magic-user?" the woman asked.

"Yes," Eliska replied. "Can I help you?"

"My daughter....she's very sick. Would you heal her? I'll pay. I have money. Just please....come to my home and heal her."

Eliska opened her mouth to say she was just about to leave town. Then she noticed the old woman in front of her.

The woman walked with a pronounced stoop. She wore filthy rags with another filthy rag tied around her sparse hair. This old woman needed healing more than anyone.

Eliska highly doubted this woman had two pennies to rub together—much less as much as most magic-users charged for healing someone's sick relative.

The woman saw Eliska hesitate, grabbed Eliska's hand, and pulled Eliska forward.

Eliska had seen too many Servants in the Coil. She'd seen the way people went out to find them, grabbed their hands, and begged them to come with them to heal someone—or a lot of someones.

Eliska dragged her heels, but eventually, the woman tugged her into a dingy hovel buried among countless other hovels just like it.

The woman lying on the bed in the corner looked almost as old as the elderly mother.

Eliska didn't even have to look at the patient to know what was wrong with her.

Eliska tossed back the blanket. A deep gash in the patient's leg had turned septic and leeched its poison into the woman's blood. It would kill her in a day or two.

Eliska raised her staff. The patient screamed when Eliska planted the staff on the woman's thigh.

The mother stood back wringing her hands and whimpering in desperation.

Eliska fired her magic through the staff and into the woman's leg. Eliska's eyes snapped shut.

She had to fight her own Darkness to drive out the Darkness of the infection. The Dark she took from Barsali didn't want her to heal anyone.

The Dark wanted her to pour her Darkness into others and make it multiply.

She fought it down and forced her magic into the woman's blood. Eliska gathered all that Dark and sucked it out of the woman.

The woman's infection didn't even make a drop in the ocean of the Darkness already infecting Eliska's soul.

She didn't feel the Darkness until now. She could ignore it in Tenby.

Losing Neils and Niyazi.....and fighting the Darklings.....and pulling the margin away from the town....

Even wandering alone these last two days—they all played a part in the Darkness that was her own true self. She'd been living with it all her life.

Barsali's Darkness only drove it deeper and made it more entrenched. Now it all came back to life with a vengeance. She was Dark. She would always be Dark. Nothing would ever change that.

She opened her eyes and stood back to study the patient. The woman passed out in an exhausted slumber.

"She's whole now," Eliska murmured. "She'll wake up hungry, so give her something to eat and keep her warm."

The old woman burst into tears, seized Eliska's hand, and kissed her knuckles. How many times had Eliska seen people doing that to the Servants?

"Oh, bless you!" the old woman sobbed. "Bless you! Please—take this."

She crossed the room, opened a rough wooden box, and took out a plain gold wedding band. It was way too thick to belong to a woman.

Eliska had a flashback to Barsali wearing his mother's wedding ring on a chain around his neck. How long had this woman been going without food and basic necessities so she could keep her husband's wedding band?

"I don't want payment." Eliska sidestepped around the woman to leave the house. "I'm glad she's better. You use the gold to buy food. You need it more than I do."

Chapter 43

E liska walked out of the house so the old woman wouldn't have time to protest. Eliska set off walking fast through the town. She needed to get out of here.

She didn't understand what the hell she just did. She shouldn't have turned down payment for her services, but the whole experience came together in a moment of startling clarity.

She got something priceless when she met up with the Watch. She found people she would never be able to replace.

She might not get them back, but she could get back something of what she lost.

She got something when she helped Anríq feed those children—and when she cooked for the Watchmen—and when she helped take care of them—or tried to take care of them.

Those few scattered moments gave her the only reprieve from the Darkness eating away at her.

Life wasn't worth living without those people, but she still had those moments—moments when something mattered—something other than just her next meal.

She turned a corner planning to go back out into the countryside. She needed to be alone to think about what just happened to her.

What if....?

What if she spent her life wandering from place to place....but instead of just trying to survive.....what if people came out of their towns to find her?

What if they asked her to come back with them to heal their sick and injured?

What if they thanked her with tears in their eyes for doing what no one else could do? Wouldn't that be a life worth living?

She wasn't a Servant—not like Anríq. She would never be that, but maybe life without the Watch wasn't a complete waste of time.

She plunged so deep into her thoughts that she didn't look where she was going. She practically collided with a horse coming the other way.

The animal reared back, squealed in alarm, and before she knew what was happening, the big man in the saddle rotated a long staff down from his hand and slammed the tip into Eliska's chest to force her back.

"Magic-user!" he snapped. "What are you doing in my town?!"

She took a second to figure out what he was saying. A quadruple chin hung over his collar. He had thick, short black hair and heavy black eyebrows and he wore extremely fancy clothes. She wouldn't have thought such a stuff-shirt would ride his own horse.

"*Your* town?" She glanced around. "Do you own this town?"

"I am the healer in this town—not you!" he boomed. "I saw you enter that woman's house and heal her sick daughter!"

"So what if I did?" Eliska asked. "I didn't see you doing it."

"This is *my* town! The people of this town come to *me* for healing—not some worthless Coil rat! How dare you trespass here and steal my business?!"

Eliska felt her temper rising. She tightened her grip on her staff.... .and then she realized.

She let her shoulders relax, straightened up, and shook her loose hair out of her eyes. "I'm a Servant," she told him. "I didn't take payment from that woman. I'm leaving town now, so you don't have to worry. You can have the town all to yourself."

The man furrowed his thick, dark eyebrows and cast his gaze up and down her clothes. "You don't look like a Servant. You aren't a Barbarian."

"Well, I am a Servant just the same. I just came into town and that woman asked for my help—so I gave it to her. Now I'm leaving."

"I don't believe you are a Servant!" the man snapped. "Show me your Servant's mark."

Eliska thought fast. "I don't have it yet. I just became a Servant.....a short time ago. I haven't gotten the mark yet."

The guy gritted his teeth. "If I find out you accepted payment for healing that woman...."

"I didn't—but I can see that you're sincerely concerned about healing the sick and injured in this town—so I'll move on and leave you to tend to your flock. Have a nice day."

She strode around the horse to walk away. She didn't have time for this nonsense. She didn't even know this joker's name and didn't care to know it.

"Magic-user!" the guy called after her. "Stop where you are or I'll have you arrested!"

She stopped in her tracks, but she had to wrestle her temper under control before she let herself turn around to face him.

"What do you want now?" she demanded.

He clamped his mouth shut, puffed out his cheeks, and pretended to shrug before he looked away. "This town....has a lot of sick people in it. I....could hire you out.....in exchange for a share of the takings....."

She took that in as quickly as possible. Whoever this idiot was, he liked the finer things in life.

He probably planned to send her out to do the actually healing while he raked in the profits and paid her a pittance for her trouble.

She sized him up in an instant and jutted her chin at him. "That sounds like a really good offer.

"It is!" he exclaimed. "It's an excellent offer. You won't get a better offer from anyone else."

She took a few steps forward and stopped next to his horse. He had to restrain the animal not to shy away.

She looked straight up into his black eyes. "Hold out your hand."

"What for?" he demanded.

"To seal the deal."

He shifted the reins to his other hand and opened his palm for her to take.

She stuck out her hand, but she didn't shake his. She placed her own hand over his with her palm pointing upward in the same direction.

"Send your magic into my hand," she told him.

He frowned. "What for? You said it would seal the deal."

"It will. Just do it."

He gasped in exasperation and sent a stream of magic into her hand. She created her Coil projection.

His magic added to hers and the projection blew up to triple its usual size. Whoever this guy was, he certainly had powerful magic.

She took a split second to locate the golden lines of the Watch leading to Tenby. A silvery thread showed her which Layers the lost children and their two escorts traveled to.

She shut her hand and the projection vanished. She smiled up at the man in genuine gratitude. "Thanks."

"What the....Hey! Where the hell do you think you're going?!"

"I have things to do," she replied over her shoulder. "Thank you again for the offer."

"You said you would seal the deal!" he bellowed.

"But I didn't—therefore, there is no deal."

She walked off without another word. She knew where she needed to go and what she needed to do. Everything else was incidental.

She left town by the shortest possible route and hustled up the road to a patch of woods around the next bend.

She strode under the trees and checked to make sure no one was around.

She didn't want to shatter this Island. It wasn't a bad Island as Islands went—and it was quite stable. Destroying it would be a waste—not to mention being deadly for all the people who lived here.

She fired her staff into the tree roots at her feet, but she kept the hole small. The roots twined around each other and snaked apart to let her sink through to the next Layer.

She plunged through a chaos Layer full of Darklings, but they were all too busy fighting each other even to see her.

She smashed through what felt like a cold stone floor, plummeted through a starry sky, and crashed into another chaos Layer.

She emerged high in the vapors whipping her from all sides. Wisps of Dark energy sliced through her and made her scream.

Cruel wind and hurtling ice shards peppered her all over and gravity yanked her down on a death plunge to a massive chaos landscape far below.

She fired her staff to slow herself down, but the scene on the ground only looked more dangerous with every passing second.

The landscape heaved out of position, fractured in granite slabs that erupted into mountains, and the mountains changed into giants rampaging everywhere.

They raised their knees high, smashed their enormous feet down on the ground, and pulverized more mountains before they could turn into giants, too.

The giants punched their massive fists down and quaked the whole Layer with vicious blows.

Other giants stalked back and forth across their Layer raising massive hammers and bringing them down with unbelievable force. How did they keep doing this without shattering the Layer?

Eliska spotted the children right away. Two magic-users, a man and a woman, worked overtime trying to defend the children from the giants—and from the landscape upheaval going on all around their party.

The adults' magic couldn't keep up with all the hazards flying around. One of the adults fired a magical blast at a giant about to pound his fist right down on top of the children.

The shot hit his hand and made him yank it back just in time, but that only infuriated him more.

He roared to the skies and raised his hammer to pulverize the group. The two adults dove inward to surround the children, circled the whole cluster with their arms, and magicked the children out of the way just in time.

They wound up transporting the children right into the path of a bunch of rock falling from a fresh eruption ejecting out of the ground.

The woman saw it in time, wheeled in that direction, and fired. Both adults channeled their magic through staffs the way Eliska did. A jet of magic shot from the end of the woman's staff and created a protective field over the children, but the two adults stood too far apart.

The woman's field didn't extend far enough to protect the man. He got caught outside and rock pounded down on top of him.

Eliska slowed herself as she passed the giants' heads. She fired her staff at the giants and exploded them back into rock, but so much rubble, boulders, and even huge slabs put the children in danger just as much as the giants.

She fired again and again both to destroy the giants and to set up fields of protection over the children.

She couldn't get there fast enough to drive the giants off completely. The giants' enormous feet came perilously close to crushing the children.

One stomp, even with Eliska's field in place, would send the children tumbling into the next Layer down. Eliska couldn't let that happen.

She blasted three more giants. The others turned on her in a rage the way she hoped they would.

Some of them tried to punch her or snatch her out of the air. She bombarded their hands, arms, and faces with dozens of shots, but it could never be enough to drive all the giants away. There were too many of them and more grew out of the ground all the time.

She released her field, plummeted the rest of the way down, and landed right in the midst of the children.

She slammed her staff into the ground full force and let off an earth-shaking thump of magic to detonate the Layer.

The ground shattered and the concussion exploded all the giants back to rock. At the same time, Eliska ejected a magical pulse around herself to suck the two adults and all the children against her as they pitched through into the Layer below.

Chapter 44

E liska straightened up and looked around. The children she just saved lay sprawled on a soft, springy bank covered in grass.

Tall, lush trees waved their branches overhead—and then Eliska realized they weren't normal trees. They moved their branches in a deliberate swaying motion that didn't coincide with the breeze rustling the leaves.

She got to her feet and studied the trees. "What is it?" a gruff male voice asked.

"Um...what?" Eliska asked.

"What is it you want? Why are you looking at me like that?"

Eliska froze. "Are you....trees?"

"I am not trees! I am a tree! Can't you see what I am?"

She looked around for some kind of face or eyes or mouth or something, but she didn't see anything but trees.

"I beg your pardon," she stammered. "I....I was just trying to take care of these children. I didn't mean to trespass. We'll leave this forest...."

"You....took care of the children....?" the voice repeated.

The children stood up just then—or some of them did. "Who is that talking?" a young boy asked.

"I think the trees here are alive." Eliska tore herself away from the trees to go check on the adults.

The woman sat a few yards away holding her head and groaning. "My head is killing me!"

Eliska placed her hand an inch above the woman's head. "You have a head injury. You must have gotten hit by some of the rock."

Eliska sent a pulse of magic into the woman's head and reduced the swelling. That was the best Eliska could do right now.

She went over to the man. He lay on his back staring up at the sky with dead, blank eyes.

Some of the children gathered around. "Can you fix him?" a little girl asked.

"I'm sorry, but he's already gone." Eliska shut his eyes. "He was a good man. He died to save you."

"What do we do with him?" a boy asked.

Eliska got to her feet and pointed her staff at the grassy bank. She used her magic to lift out a section of the soil, lowered the man's body into it, and put the dirt back on top of him.

The children stood around staring at the bare mound of dirt. It cast a depressing mood over everyone.

Eliska pointed her staff at the mound and made flowers grow on it. Then she pried a large square rock slab out of the ground and made it stand at the head of the grave.

"There. That's better."

"It needs something else," the boy told her. "We should put his name on it—and maybe some words."

"What was his name?" Eliska asked.

"Athanes," the boy replied.

Eliska took his hand, placed it on her staff, and channeled through him to magically carve the name on the stone. She couldn't read or write, so she used his knowledge to do it and added an inscription just because.

"What does that say?" the littlest girl asked.

"It says, 'He died a hero saving ten children from certain death in the Layers. May he rest in peace.'"

"That's nice," the boy exclaimed. "I like that. I hope someone puts that on my grave when I die."

"What's your name?" the little girl asked.

"I'm Eliska. What are your names?"

"Eloi," the littlest girl piped up.

"I'm Dalana," the oldest girl replied and she pointed out the boy and a younger girl. "This is Anthane and Cheseli."

"This looks like a nice Island. We'll be safe here—much safer than you kids have been lately."

"How do you know?" Anthane asked.

"I saw you in the Layers. I saw you trapped in the chaos when you still had four adults. I tried to come for you then, but things were too dangerous. I came as soon as I could."

"You're a good person, too, if you saved us like that," Anthane pointed out.

Eliska looked away. Some of the children had wandered under the trees to talk to them.

Eliska went over to them. The children stood in different places talking to different trees.

The trees' voices sounded like people. The first one that spoke to Eliska had a deep, gruff, scratchy voice like an old man. Others sounded high and fluty like middle-aged women or even smooth like younger people.

"Come back over here to the group," Eliska told them. "Don't wander off."

"You should stay under our branches," one of the middle-aged female trees told her. "You'll be safe here. We can protect you."

"From what?" Eliska asked. "I don't see any instability here."

"We can protect you nonetheless," the gruff old man-tree told her. "If anything comes, we can use our branches to fight them off."

Just then, the woman entered the trees and started rounding up the children, too. "Come back over here, everyone. Don't wander off."

"We weren't wandering off," an older boy grumbled. "Those trees were really nice."

"I've told you a hundred times, Thaddi," the woman returned. "We need to stay together. It was already hard enough to protect you with four of us. It's going to be even harder by myself."

"Eliska well help us, Aline," Eloi piped up. "She saved us from those giants. She could come with us."

The woman straightened up and confronted Eliska for the first time. Aline didn't acknowledge Eliska earlier when Eliska healed her head injury.

"I'm grateful for what you did," Aline began. "I don't expect you to waste any more of your time...."

"I've been looking for you for days," Eliska fired back. "I saw you in danger in the Layers and I came here to defend you—all of you. I would have come sooner, but circumstances made it impossible. Do you really think I would walk away and leave you alone to defend these children? Don't insult me."

"I wasn't trying to insult you," Aline replied. "I only meant...."

"Can't she stay?" Anthane pleaded. "She buried Athanes."

"Please?" Eloi asked.

Aline looked around at all the children and then cast another critical glance at Eliska.

"You need all the help you can get," Eliska pointed out. "I'm here to help you. I don't want anything in return except to get you and these children to safety."

Aline compressed her lips and sighed. "I don't know if that's possible."

"What are you doing here, anyway?" Eliska asked. "Why are you wandering around in the Coil?"

"Our Island collapsed," Aline explained. "We're on our way to an orphanage in the Lake Country....but the Layers keep shifting so often that we got lost. Now we can't get there." She let herself glance around. "I don't even know where we are."

"The Lake Country is five Layers away from here," Eliska told her. "This Island is safer. We should travel through it until we get closer before we change to another Layer."

Aline narrowed her eyes slightly. "How do you know so much about the Coil?"

Eliska projected her Coil image on her hand and rotated it in front of Aline. "You can see for yourself. We're here. The Lake Country is here."

Eliska pretended not to notice that traveling to the Lake Country would take her in the opposite direction from Tenby.

She came out here to help and protect these children. She didn't want to go back to Tenby until she accomplished that.

She did allow herself to check the position of the margin threatening the town. The margin held a few miles away. Tenby wasn't in any immediate danger—not right now.

She would just have to keep an eye on it. She had no idea what she would do if the margin did threaten Tenby before she got the children to safety.

Who should she choose to save—or at least help? She might leave the children to their deaths, go back to Tenby, and fail to save any of the Watch, either.

She shook those thoughts out of her head and turned back to the image. "Where's the orphanage?"

"I don't see it," Aline replied. "The image is too small."

Eliska pulled Aline's hand forward and placed it under her own. "Add your magic to mine."

Aline did it and they expanded the image. Aline pointed out the orphanage. It nestled in some steep, rugged mountains surrounded by crystal lakes.

"The trees want us to travel under their branches," Eliska went on. "I think we should accept their offer."

"I don't know...." Aline glanced over her shoulder at the trees. "How do we know we can trust them?"

"Do we have another option? We would have to travel all the way around this wood to avoid the trees. That would be rude when they're offering to help us. If something threatens us, you and I might not be able to handle it on our own."

Aline sighed again. "All right. We'll do it your way, but if the trees turn out to be dangerous, we'll go somewhere else."

Eliska nodded. "Of course."

Aline rounded up the children. The trees' activity increased when the party entered the woods.

The children talked a lot on the way. "Where did you come from, Eliska?" Dalana asked.

"I'm just a homeless Coil rat. I was with a group of the Black Watch for a while. Then we saw you in danger in the Layers, so I came out to help you."

Eliska glanced over at Aline. Eliska didn't ask about the other two adults who originally tried to protect these children. The other two adults must have gotten killed in the Layers, too.

"I'm a magic-user, too, Eliska," Anthane chimed in.

She spun around and found herself smiling at him. "Are you? That's wonderful. Maybe you can help me find the orphanage."

"I meant what I said," Aline interrupted. "You don't have to stay with us if you don't want to."

Eliska chose to ignore the remark and concentrated on the children. "So what did you do in your old Island before you left home?"

"We did way too much school," Thaddi grumbled. "We'll probably do way too much school at the new place, too."

"You have to get an education, Thaddi," Aline chided. "You would have no future without it."

"Did you hate school when you were a kid, Eliska?" Anthane asked.

"I never went to school," Eliska replied.

"You're lucky," Thaddi muttered. "I wish I didn't have to go. I hate sitting at a desk all day."

"At least you have somewhere to go," she told him. "I've been alone in the Coil for as long as I can remember. I didn't even have an orphanage to live in."

The children all stopped walking to stare at her. "No way!" Anthane gasped.

"I never learned to read," she told them. "Things might have been different for me if I got an education. In fact, I know they would have."

"You see?" Aline pointed out. "Things could be worse."

"You mean...you never had parents telling you what to do...or anything?" Anthane gasped.

"No," Eliska replied. She almost said something about Yvan, but she changed her mind at the last second.

"How did you learn to use your magic?" Dalana asked. "Did someone teach you?"

"Not really. I spent a day or two with different people here and there. Sometimes they would show me things. Other times I learned by watching strangers. Most of the time I just had to figure it out for myself."

"I want to join the Guardian Templars," Anthane announced. "They'll teach me how to use my magic."

"That's a good idea," Eliska replied. "I know someone who went to them for training."

"We won't be able to send you to the Guardian Templars," Aline told him. "We can't afford it. We're just a poor orphanage. You'll have to satisfy yourself with regular schooling."

"The Guardian Templars are a voluntary order," Eliska explained. "Anyone can join once they come of age. No one has to pay unless a parent sends their child to the Templars for education. Once you join the order, you receive the same training as all the other Templars."

"That's great!" Anthane exclaimed. "I'm going to do it! I could become a great mage!"

Eliska smiled at him. "I'm sure you will."

Aline made a face. "I would appreciate it if you wouldn't fill their heads full of all kinds of fanciful ideas about what's possible for them and what isn't. You aren't doing them any favors at all."

Eliska looked up. "What do you mean? He *could* join the Templars. He would just have to wait until he's old enough—and he can still get an education in the orphanage before then."

"He would be an adult by then. It would be too late for him to perfect his magic. You're giving him false hope for a future he'll never have."

Eliska opened her mouth to argue.

Aline cut her off by stopping in the middle of the path, taking a step toward Eliska, and lowering her voice even though all the children could hear her.

"I'm the one responsible for these children, not you," Aline growled. "I'll still be responsible for them for years after you're gone. I would appreciate it if you didn't say or do anything to try to change that."

Aline turned on her heel and walked off into the trees. She didn't turn around.

The children stood around Eliska gaping at her with their mouths open in stunned shock. Eliska stared after Aline trying to accept that this woman really did just say that.

Eliska went through a frantic scramble in her mind trying to figure out how to deal with this.

Maybe Aline was right. Eliska would deliver the children to the orphanage.....and then what?

Eliska would go back to Tenby—or try to.

Aline would be the one responsible for actually raising these children—her and whatever adults worked at the orphanage.

Eliska found it impossible to believe that Aline or any other adult would actively dissuade Anthane from pursuing a career in magic. Why?

Why would Aline want to hide from Anthane that he really could join the Guardian Templars? It made no sense at all—especially since he wouldn't be able to do that until he outgrew the orphanage in the first place.

Aline and the other adults would have done their jobs. They would give him an education and raise him to adulthood.

Aline was a magic-user. What possible reason could she have to want to stop someone else from perfecting their skills?

Eliska had no parents or any other adults taking responsibility for her upbringing. She would have jumped at the chance to join the Guardian Templars if she'd only found out about it sooner.

Anything was better than learning everything by trial and error.

Aline didn't turn around even to make sure the children followed her. She stormed off into the trees.

By the time Eliska pulled her head out of the clouds, Aline was already a few dozen yards ahead.

Eliska cleared her throat with difficulty, got the children moving again, and followed. None of them had anywhere else to go or anything else to do.

Chapter 45

A line, Eliska, and the children came to the edge of the forest. Developed farming country spread out beyond the trees.

Houses, businesses, and a few nicely constructed municipal buildings lined a paved road leading out of sight. Eliska couldn't see the end of that development. Maybe it went on forever.

Aline breathed a sigh of relief. "We can get supplies here."

Eliska turned to the trees nearest her. "Thank you for protecting us. We really appreciate your help."

"I would appreciate it if you didn't encourage the children to participate in all that fanciful nonsense," Aline snapped a little too harshly. "I have enough trouble keeping them in line without someone like you coming along and giving them ideas."

Eliska's jaw hit the ground. "Ideas....about what? These trees are alive. They talked to us. I was just being polite."

"You know what I mean!" Aline fired back.

"Um...actually, I don't," Eliska replied. "What fanciful nonsense was I participating in just by talking to these trees?"

Aline gasped in exasperation, put her arms around Eloi and Dalana, and steered all the children away. "I would appreciate it if you went back to wherever you came from. You being here is only making my job harder."

Aline pushed the children toward the tree line. Eliska stood rooted to the spot, too stunned to think straight. Did that conversation really just happen?

The children resisted leaving Eliska behind. They kept glancing over their shoulders at her, but Aline didn't even let them say goodbye.

"Don't go out there," a strong, deep, male voice warned from the nearest trees. "Those people shun magic-users. You won't be safe there."

"Why do they shun magic-users?" Eliska asked. "Don't they need Servants and healers to do things for them?"

The same tree raised his voice louder when he saw Aline about to walk out into the open. "There's another town to the north! You should go there! This place is dangerous to magic-users."

Aline grimaced over her shoulder and steered the children toward the road. Anthane hung back, but she only reprimanded him to make him keep up with the others.

Eliska stayed where she was under the branches. "I should go with them."

"The townspeople will kill you if they see you doing magic," the tree told her.

Eliska looked up at the branches. "They actually kill magic-users? Why?"

"They'll try to. Any magic-user would be taking their life in their hands by going in there."

Eliska's scalp prickled watching Aline lead the children closer to the nearest houses. What was Aline's problem?

She was a magic-user and yet she seemed to take issue with everything magical. Eliska didn't get it at all.

The group drew level with the nearest houses and entered the bustle of vendors, businesspeople, and townsfolk going about their work.

The children looked around at everything—and then a man bumped into Anthane.

Eliska didn't see anything remarkable about this man. He carried a bundle of firewood in his arms, so he didn't see the boy standing in his path.

The man spun around, glared at Anthane, and snapped at him much too harshly considering that the collision was the man's fault.

Anthane shrank closer to Aline and the party kept going—deeper into the developed area along both sides of the road.

The incident flipped a switch in Eliska's mind. She didn't come this far to find these children just to abandon them.

She stepped out from under the trees and set off at a fast walk to intercept them. She walked faster than they did. She wouldn't have any trouble catching up with them.

She didn't know how she would deal with Aline once she got there—or afterward.

Eliska supposed she should just follow the group at a distance and not converse with any of them if it really came to that.

If Aline found Eliska's presence so threatening, Eliska could just stay behind the group and only step in if they needed protection.

Eliska couldn't think of any other solution.

Eloi and Thaddi both saw her coming. They burst into huge smiles—relieved smiles—but just then, a different man spat in Aline's face from a nearby doorway. "Curse you, magic-user!" the man barked.

Aline wheeled around to confront him. That one act of spitting on her set off everyone else.

More people turned on the group yelling and shaking their fists. The word passed from mouth to mouth. "Die, magic-user!" a woman shrieked.

"Filthy Coil rats!" an older man roared.

A young girl actually rushed Aline and struck out with her fist. The children cowered closer to Aline for protection as the mob moved in.

Eliska picked up her pace and broke into a run. She wasn't close enough yet for the commotion to put her in danger.

Right then, someone threw half a cabbage across the street and it hit the side of Aline's face. The cabbage came from a doorway. Eliska didn't see who threw it.

More projectiles launched from all sides and rained down on the group. Rotten vegetables hit the children. Eliska picked up speed and charged.

More townspeople surrounded the children raising clubs and household objects. Eliska even saw a few knives in the crowd. The noise coming out of the angry mob escalated to a din.

Some of the children screamed and the mob closed in for the kill. Eliska couldn't wait any longer.

She rotated her staff forward and unloaded on the crowd. She stopped running and stormed the rest of the way up the street blasting people out of her path.

This blatant show of magic ignited the crowd's fury to the breaking point. They all turned on Eliska, but she didn't give a crap about any of that anymore.

She plastered people right and left. She didn't even look to see if she was hitting women, children, old people—anyone.

She sent them flying away to slam against their house walls. Other people flooded in to take the places of the fallen. The townspeople raised pitchforks, shovels, and axes to chop her in half.

She kept bombarding the people in front of her to clear a path to the children. When the townspeople got too close to her from the sides, she took one hand off her staff, planted it on whoever came nearest, and blasted them away.

A cloud of mayhem surrounded the children up ahead. Random stuff rained on them from all sides.

A few magical explosions went off up there. Aline must have been using her magic to defend the children. Maybe Anthane was doing the same thing.

Eliska couldn't even see them through all the bodies standing in her way. This was taking too long.

She nailed her staff down into the pavement, set off a deep thump of magic, and leveled dozens of people in her path.

She cleared the way enough to see Aline on the ground. Anthane and the other children stood over her.

Anthane, Dalana, and another older boy ejected streams of magic at the townspeople. Those three did their best to protect all the other children huddled behind them.

Those three children had obviously never received any training in how to use their abilities. The townspeople threatened to overwhelm the children with dozens of weapons.

Eliska drove her staff down every few seconds and blasted the rest of the way through the crowd to the children.

The three young magic-users made room for her. Eliska turned her staff around and swiped a vicious jet of magic to cut down as many townsfolk as she could, but nothing stopped their enraged stampede.

She slashed her staff the other way. Staying here really would be a death trap.

She made up her mind, spun backward, threw another charm over the whole group, glued all their bodies together, and magicked them out of town in a split second.

She transported everyone to the edge of the trees where she started and knelt over Aline.

Something big and heavy must have hit her in the head again. Blood ran down her temple and stained her hair.

"What do we do now, Eliska?" Dalana asked. "That road is the only way through the area."

"It isn't the only way. We'll have to go north the way the trees told us to."

Eliska raised her hand to touch the wound, but Aline slapped it away. "Don't you dare touch me!"

Eliska gasped out loud. "What is your problem?! You're the one who's supposed to take care of these children. You won't be able to do that if I don't heal you."

"Don't you dare lay a finger on me!" Aline snapped. She tried to sit up and failed. All the children stood around staring at her.

Eliska didn't know what to say. She'd never met anyone who deliberately drove away someone who tried to heal them. Everyone Eliska had ever met did the opposite.

Aline glared up at her in hateful fury. "Get out of here! No one asked you to come here and interfere with our business."

"So I should have left you to the giants?" Eliska asked.

Aline's words hurt worse than they made Eliska mad. She tried to do the right thing. She actually started to believe the Servant's way might offer her some hope.

Now this happened.

If Anríq had been here, Eliska could have asked him if this ever happened to him. Did anyone ever push him away and curse him for trying to heal them? She couldn't believe that.

She couldn't fathom why anyone would turn away someone who genuinely wanted to help, especially when someone like Aline obviously needed it.

Aline rolled onto her side, pushed herself onto her elbow, and grimaced in pain.

Eliska pursed her lips and pressed her hand down on Aline's forehead. Aline tried to fight back and knock Eliska's hand away.

Eliska gritted her teeth and pushed her hand down even harder. She forced her magic into Aline's head and ended up pushing the woman to lie back on the ground.

Aline howled in fury, but Eliska didn't give her the option to fight back.

"Leave me alone!" Aline bellowed.

"If I do that, I'm going to take these children and leave you here to die," Eliska spat. "Is that what you want?"

Aline burst into loud, enraged roars, but Eliska didn't stop until she healed the bleeding and broken bones in Aline's head. Eliska came here to help the children. No one would stop her—least of all Aline.

Eliska took her hand down. Aline collapsed back on the ground.

Eliska stood up and glared down at her. "You better lie still and rest for a minute. If you get up now, you could reinjure yourself and we wouldn't want that."

"Will she be all right, Eliska?" Eloi asked.

Eliska sighed and turned to the children around her. "She'll be fine. I don't know why she has such a problem with magic when she's a magic-user herself."

"The others weren't like this," Anthane murmured. "Athanes tried to teach me things, but she stopped him."

"Do you know why?" Eliska asked.

Anthane shook his head. He wouldn't stop staring down at Aline.

"It doesn't matter," Eliska decided. "We'll go back into the trees and then make our way north like they told us to. Then we can head west until we get somewhere to break through to the Lake Country."

"We won't do anything those stupid trees told us to do!" Aline struggled to get to her feet. She didn't stay down nearly long enough.

She glared at Eliska once and then went through the group of children pulling them all toward her. Aline pulled the children away from Eliska.

"We've spent enough time in these trees," Aline sneered. "We'll go south—then west."

She gave Eliska another dirty look. Eliska didn't understand this woman at all. What possible reason could she have to deliberately take the opposite route that Eliska suggested?

Just then, a wave of noise floated out of the houses and buildings near the road.

Eliska jumped when she saw another mob of hysterical townspeople pouring down the road. They headed straight for the trees where Eliska, Aline, and the children stood.

Eliska spun backward to face the mob. She rooted herself between the townsfolk and the children and raised her staff to defend them no matter what.

Going into the trees would have been the safest place, but Aline got some weird idea about not going in there. She towed the children south—parallel to the tree line.

That left them exposed and the townspeople pivoted to intercept them. Eliska had to adjust her position to keep guarding them.

A few children whimpered behind her. They couldn't fail to see the danger.

The tree branches whipped faster. Eliska didn't dare to turn around to see what the trees were doing.

The mob came in unbelievably fast. The faces in the crowd twisted up in furious masks of murderous hate.

Eliska fired her staff into the crowd and kept shooting. She swiped the beam back and forth to mow them down the way she did before, but they anticipated her.

As soon as she dropped a bunch of people and rotated her staff somewhere else, those behind rushed forward to cover the ground before she had time to wheel back the other way.

They also figured out that she was the more powerful magic-user here. The crowd split, left half their comrades to confront Eliska, and the others veered off to intercept Aline and the children.

Aline moved in front of the children, too. She unleashed her magic on the crowd, but she waited too long and her assault didn't produce any effective defense.

The crowd closed around the children and they screamed. A few townspeople raised their axes and knives to wipe these children out right here under the trees.

The trees responded by slashing their branches at the townspeople nearest them, but the trees couldn't do much while they remained anchored to the ground.

They knocked a few people over, but the townspeople overwhelmed the children and Aline in no time.

Another mob surrounded Eliska. She held them at bay, but she couldn't get past them to save the children. She could only do that by getting them out of here—as far away from the townsfolk as possible.

She only stopped shooting for a fraction of a second, magicked herself over to the children, and surrounded them with both a binding spell to keep them near her and a transporting spell to magick the whole group away.

She included Aline in the spell, but at the last instant, Aline turned on Eliska and shoved her away.

Eliska stumbled trying to catch her balance, but she was already spreading the binding spell around the children to hold them.

She didn't want to make the spell too big. She didn't want to include any townspeople she might accidentally transport along with her.

Aline's sudden move caught Eliska by surprise, and before she even realized what was happening, the binding spell and the transporting spell enveloped the children with Aline outside both spells.

Eliska had half a second to try to change both spells before the townspeople finished off everyone, but it was already too late. One of the townsmen's axes connected with Aline's head and she toppled into the crowd.

Half the townspeople fell on her with their weapons. Eliska didn't have time to change her spells now and she didn't try.

The binding spell seized the children and the transporting spell blinked them all away deeper into the woods where the townspeople would never find them.

Chapter 46

E liska collapsed on the ground, fought to breathe, and buried her face in her hands. "Damn it!"

"Should we go back for her?" Thaddi asked. "She might still be okay. She was okay when we left."

"No, she wasn't," Dalana murmured. "They killed her."

"What do you think, Eliska?" Anthane asked. "Should we go back?"

"We can't go back," Cheseli squeaked. "Those people would kill us."

"They only wanted to kill magic-users," Thaddi pointed out.

"They came after all of us," Dalana countered. "They would have killed all of us. They don't care which of us is a magic-user."

"Eliska?" Anthane quavered. "What's going to happen to us now?"

Eliska dragged her head up. Why oh why did Aline have to push her away like that? Eliska couldn't for the life of her think of one good reason Aline would turn against her.

Eliska could only think of one possible explanation. Aline worked hard to protect the children in the Coil. She lost her other three adults fighting unstoppable forces.

She probably didn't want some stranger moving in and telling her and her children what to do—or pretending to take responsibility for them.

Her attitude got her killed. Now Eliska was all alone with these children.

She shook that off. "Now I'm going to take you to the orphanage. We have a long way to go and we've already wasted enough time with this. We'll head north the way the trees told us to."

Mentioning the trees made her look up at the branches. She still didn't see any faces because the trees didn't have any.

"Thank you for trying to help us," she said to no one in particular. "And thank you for warning us about that town."

"You can travel north under our branches," a woman's voice replied. "We'll protect you as far as the river. That's as far as we can take you."

Eliska sighed. "Thank you so much. I'm really grateful for your help."

"We would do as much as we can to protect the children," an old man's voice replied.

Eliska turned to the children. "Let's go."

She started walking. The children surrounded her all talking at once the way they did before. "Why did Aline dislike you so much?" Dalana asked.

"I was hoping you could tell me. It can't be because I'm a magic-user. She is one—or was one."

"I don't think she likes anyone using magic—not any kids, anyway," Anthane muttered.

"That's so strange." Eliska shut her eyes and shook her head. "Never mind."

Anthane looked up. "You could teach me some magic."

"I guess I could."

"You said people showed you things," he went on. "You could show me things." His eyes flew open and he gasped. "I could help you! I could help you fight the.....whatever-they-ares."

Eliska laughed. "Let's not get ahead of ourselves."

He hurried to catch up with her. He had to push the other children out of the way to get near her. "You saw me back there. I can do a few things."

"Yes, you can."

"So show me. Teach me something."

She found herself smiling at him. "All right. Hold out your hand."

The whole group ground to a halt when Anthane held out his hand. The others watched him square off with Eliska.

"Now send your magic into your hand," she told him.

He frowned. "How do I do that?"

She laughed out loud, turned away, and started walking again. "You have a lot to learn, munchkin. You can practice while we walk. Send your magic into your hand, form a pool, and make it transparent so you can see things in the pool."

"See things like what?"

"Try to see things that are behind you—or anywhere you aren't looking. Work on that and let me know when you're ready for your next lesson."

He frowned at her and then frowned at his hand in deep concentration. She had to stop herself from laughing at the expression on his face. She had to look away.

He kept walking along glancing at his hand every now and then. She didn't see him succeeding in sending his magic into his hand. This could take a while.

"I'm tired," Eloi complained.

Eliska surveyed the area. She didn't want to stop here even though the group was nowhere near the hostile towns.

She considered magicking Eloi to float along behind the party the way the gypsies magicked their trunks.

Eliska discarded that idea and took a hint from Anríq. She picked up the little girl and sat Eloi on her hip while Eliska kept walking.

Holding this child felt completely different from either cooking for the children in Tenby or even fighting the townspeople to defend the group just now.

Eliska couldn't remember ever touching a younger child. Forget about doing anything as intimate as this.

All of these children were much younger than she was—younger than Hani. She practically saw herself as their mother even though she was still so young herself.

She called herself a Servant when she healed that woman's daughter. If that was true, then Eliska would serve all humanity the way Anríq did.

She didn't balk at doing whatever these children needed her to do. That little girl in Tenby wanted him to hold her while he worked. He let her play with the beads in his hair and even did things to make her laugh.

Eliska didn't know how to do any of that, but he was her best example of what a Servant was—if she really was a Servant.

She didn't know if she was or she wasn't, but this path seemed to take hold of her in strange ways. She seemed to be doing this whether she was a Servant or not.

A second later, a different little boy toddled up to her. "Carry me, too!" he pleaded.

Eliska sighed. "I won't be able to carry all of you. You know that, right?" She looked around and handed Anthane her staff. "Carry this—and be ready to give it back to me if I need it."

He studied it. Eliska found herself smiling at that, too. Maybe he thought it would suddenly explode in his hand for no reason.

She hoisted the younger boy onto her back and supported him with one arm while she held onto Eloi with the other. Carrying them both tired Eliska out, but even that somehow made her feel better.

At least she was doing something useful with herself. She wasn't just wasting the days of her life for no reason.

She found herself smiling inwardly at just about everything these children did. They enchanted her more than she ever thought possible.

She didn't understand her own reaction to them because they were nothing special. Not even Anthane had any special gift for magic.

He gave up looking into his hand after just a few minutes. He spent more time studying the surroundings.

He, Thaddi, and a few other boys wandered away from the group to examine some brightly colored mushrooms growing from a fallen log in the woods.

Eliska let them go. She and the other children kept walking, and a minute later, the boys caught up with them.

"Sorry," Anthane mumbled.

"For what?" she asked.

"For wandering off. I shouldn't have done that."

"Why not?" she asked. "Why shouldn't you have? You weren't in any danger. I saw you the whole time."

His head shot up. "You aren't mad at me?"

"Why should I be? You never lost sight of the group, did you?"

"No, but....." He blinked. "You really don't mind?"

"Why would I mind? You boys can go where you want as long as you're sure you can catch up with the rest of us." She studied him. "What are you—about ten?"

"Yeah, but the other adults never let us go anywhere. We always had to stay with the group."

Eliska hid her annoyance by stopping at a stream just then. She lowered Eloi and the other boy to the ground. "We'll stop here and get some water. You can run around if you want to."

The children didn't move. They all stared at her. "Are you serious?" Thaddi asked.

Eliska snorted and climbed down the bank to the stream. "It sounds to me like Aline and the others didn't want you to be children at all. I don't think it has anything to do with magic."

"How can we not be children?" Dalana asked.

"Some people have strange ideas about how children should act—but that isn't me. If you want to wander off, it's fine with me as long as you make sure you catch up with us. Don't make me go looking for you."

They still didn't move. They didn't run around and play. They blinked at her in stunned disbelief.

She tried to distract herself by squatting down by the stream and cupping the water into her mouth.

"You better get some water," she called over her shoulder. "We don't know when we'll find any more."

"The sun will be going down soon," a husky male voice told her from somewhere overhead.

Eliska looked up. "It will? Thank you for telling me. I can't tell from under these branches."

"A family of waterbuck comes down to this stream to drink every evening," a woman's voice told her. "They usually come about an hour from now, but they won't come when you're here."

"Wow! Thank you so much!" Eliska exclaimed.

"What does that mean?" Thaddi asked.

"It means we need to make camp somewhere away from here so we can spend the night. Then I'll come down here and hunt one of the waterbuck so we all get a decent meal tonight."

"You can do that?!" Dalana gasped.

"Of course. How have you all been surviving in the Coil all this time?"

The children exchanged glances. None of them answered.

Eliska did her best to wave that away. "Follow me. We'll go make camp somewhere and then we'll eat some food."

Chapter 47

Yann woke up to the sound of pots and pans banging downstairs. Anríq wasn't in his bed. He must be downstairs making breakfast.

Yann stepped out of his bedroom to go down there, but he stopped in his tracks when he saw his father's bedroom door standing open.

Rien had moved into Niels's and Niyazi's old room. Yvan sat on his bed alone.

Yann took a step forward and immediately saw what was wrong. Yvan's head snapped from one side to the other trying to see all around him at the same time.

He panted each time he did this and his whole body stiffened. He didn't see Yann standing there watching him.

A heavy weight fell into the pit of Yann's stomach. His father had been becoming more and more unstable with every passing day. He had snatches of lucidity followed by these attacks of madness.

Rien held up better, but he still drifted into madness more often than Yann would have liked. He would have liked it if none of them drifted into madness ever again, but that wasn't likely to happen.

Yann made up his mind, crossed the threshold, and pulled his father's blades out of his belt. Yvan didn't notice when Yann stepped away and left his father unarmed.

Yann walked out of the room and pulled the door shut with himself on the outside. He left his father in the room by himself.

Yann could have locked his father in, but Yann wasn't prepared to go that far. Disarming him was bad enough.

Yann returned to his own bedroom and left Yvan's weapons on the bed. Yann continued to the stairs, but he had to pass Rien's room on the way there.

Rien stood in the middle of his room going through the same process of spinning, jerking, and jumping.

He did notice Yann. Rien stopped looking around, sighed, and passed his hand across his eyes. "Maybe I shouldn't go out with you today."

Yann glanced down. Rien didn't have any weapons. He never carried weapons these days. He'd long since handed them over to Yann for safekeeping. Rien didn't trust himself to go anywhere with a weapon.

"I'll leave that up to you. If you feel like coming out, you're more than welcome." Yann jerked his thumb over his shoulder. "Father is staying in, too, so you aren't the only one."

He walked away. Dealing with these two men and their ongoing insanity was becoming a daily project.

Yann went downstairs and pretended not to notice Rien following him.

Marine sat at the kitchen counter while Anríq cooked breakfast. She burst into a massive grin when Yann showed up. He couldn't figure out why. She didn't usually get all excited when any of the others showed up.

"Hail the conquering hero," she teased.

"Shut up," he countered.

She laughed. Then she looked around and saw Rien lurking in the background. "How's your father?" she asked.

Yann forced himself to look away. "He's as good as can be expected. He'll be staying home today. I disarmed him, but make sure you keep clear of him just in case."

She nodded. "Is there anything I can do?"

"Not unless you just now discovered something in O'akim's library that can break this curse."

"I wish I had."

"I don't believe these invisible Darklings are real," he blurted out. "I know Eliska thinks they are, but I'm starting to think they aren't."

"What makes you say that?" Marine asked.

"None of them have attacked us. Maybe there's some other explanation for what hit Vidal—and why haven't you, Anríq, or I gotten infected with this sickness? It's exactly like Eliska says. If this was real, it would have infected all of us and then we would all see these invisible Darklings."

"How do you explain none of us being able to detect any ailment in these men?" Anríq interjected. "If they were out of their minds, we would have found some way to heal them."

"Maybe there's another explanation for that, too," Yann pointed out. "Maybe that curtain of instability is affecting them and making them see things."

"But we started seeing things before we ever came to Tenby or got caught by that curtain," Rien argued.

"Maybe we're in a Layer that affects all of you that way. Maybe it isn't something specific to this Island. Eliska said that, too. Maybe it affects more than one Layer."

Marine shrugged. "You might be right."

"That doesn't help us, does it?" Rien grumbled. "It doesn't help to know that we really are crazy."

"You aren't crazy," Yann countered. "Anríq has told you many times that there's nothing wrong with you. The Coil is going haywire and it's affecting you."

"But not you—or you—or you? Thanks a lot. That doesn't make me feel better at all."

"Does it make you feel better to know that I still need you on the wall?" Yann crushed his shoulder. "Every day you leave the house is a blessing."

Rien looked away and Anríq distracted everyone by serving breakfast. The four friends ate quickly and quietly. No one wanted to hang around looking at each other and talking about their situation.

Marine left for O'akim's library as usual. She spent all her time there, but she still didn't find anything relevant to the Voyant's plans.

Yann, Anríq, and Rien went up to the wall. Americ, Valer, and Rosh gathered from the far corners of Tenby to give Yann their reports.

He passed down the wall reviewing the defenders, their weapons, and their ammunition stores.

For reasons known best to themselves, the people of Tenby still refused to tell Yann anything about their ammunition reserves or even to explain where they got food.

Yann long since gave up even wondering about that. He didn't try to explain how the defenders always managed to replace their rockets and ammunition and how everyone's kitchens magically replaced all the food the townsfolk ate.

It probably really was magic. Maybe this town had as much magic as anywhere else in the Coil, but the townspeople hid it for some reason. Yann wouldn't have been surprised.

He walked all the way down the wall and eventually circled the whole town. He talked to everyone, checked on everything, and surveyed the countryside in all directions.

Anríq and Rien went with him. None of the three stood a post these days. Yann got thrust into taking command of the whole defense. Anríq and Rien acted as his lieutenants.

The Tenby defenders treated Yvan as the Watch Commander on those days when he made an appearance. No one mentioned his absences nor did anyone mention Yann taking charge while his father was out of commission. Everyone acted as if none of this was actually happening.

Yann finally returned to the same spot nearest the gate. "The margin is still holding at the same position," Americ reported. "It never comes any closer."

"Eliska must have done something to it," Rien remarked. "She stabilized it the way she said she would."

"Have the sentries seen any sign of her coming back?" Yann asked. He already knew the answer.

"Nothing," Valer growled. "We haven't seen anyone out there."

"The children are gone, too," Anríq pointed out. "She may have found them and taken them to another Island where they would be safe."

"I sure wish she'd come back," Yann muttered. "I don't like her being gone this long."

"She might have to stay out there to stabilize the margin," Rien suggested. "She might be out there right now holding it away from the town."

"Maybe." Yann started to turn away.

A shout went up from the men on the wall just then. Everyone turned around to look.

The sentries pointed toward the margin and everyone scrambled to man the defenses. Gunners jumped onto the rocket launchers and the Tenby men shouldered their rifles.

Yann raised a pair of field glasses to his eyes, but they didn't help him see through the veil. He could see better without them.

His heart stopped when he saw a line of horsemen in armor riding out of the confusion beyond the curtain.

The man in front carried a red flag with a golden lion embroidered on it. The knights wore purple tunics, each with a strange symbol on his chest.

"I don't believe it!" Rien whispered. "They're actually alive!"

"Do you know these men?" Americ asked.

"We only met them once. They're coming toward the town." Yann yelled down the wall. "Open the gate to let them in!"

"Are you sure about that?" Valer asked.

"They can help us defend this town," Yann replied. "Their mission is to fight the Voyant."

"But the Voyant isn't here," Rosh observed.

They didn't get a chance to discuss it any further before the Chivalric Order of Custodians rode out of the chaos beyond the veil. Their horses walked at a slow plod and bent their heads against the wind.

The knights kept their helms closed to protect their faces. The wind tore at the flags. Most had worn to tatters since the Black Watch met the order in the Layers.

The knights took a long time to cross the distance. They finally broke through the veil and paused there when they saw the gates of Tenby standing open for them.

Chapter 48

Yann gathered a bunch of armed men to go out and meet the knights. He stopped his party halfway between the knights and the gate.

The knights stiffened and then rode forward to a spot fifteen feet away.

Amaury Marais raised his helm and frowned down at the Tenby party. "We belong to the Chivalric Order of Custodians," he announced. "We're here on a mission of importance to the survival of the entire...."

"I know who you are," Yann interrupted. "You're Amaury Marais, Captain of the Guard—and this is your lieutenant, Yves Sylvain. We've already met."

Marais frowned. "You're just a boy. I would have remembered meeting you."

"We belong to the Black Watch. You spoke with my father. Don't you remember my Barbarian friend here?" Yann waved at Anríq.

Marais frowned while he put the puzzle pieces together. "What are you doing out here, boy? We come in peace to negotiate with this town."

"I might be a boy, but I'm Commander of the Watch for this town. I came out here to welcome you inside our walls, but if you'd rather stand out here and negotiate instead, that's fine with me."

"You?!" Sylvain blurted out. "How can *you* be Commander of the Watch?"

"I just am. We're going back inside now. If you want to come, come now. Otherwise, we'll have to shut the gate. We have our own defense to consider."

Yann turned away and waved the Tenby defenders inside. The knights sat in their saddles and watched the other men obey Yann as their Watch Commander.

No one inside Tenby questioned this anymore—if they ever did question it.

Yann led the way inside and heard the telltale clank of armor as the horses started forward to follow.

The knights filed into town and went through the usual routine of frowning at everything when they saw the machines, vehicles, and the townspeople's weaponry.

"What is this?" Sylvain demanded. "What kind of witchcraft are you practicing here?!"

"It isn't witchcraft," Yann told him. "It's just a different Layer of the Coil we haven't seen before. If you men want to dismount and take your armor off, I'll show you a house where you can stay while we fill you in on the strategic situation. We'll need all of you defending the wall the next time something attacks us."

Marais scowled at him for a second, and instead of dismounting, he reined his horse to one side. He rode back and forth through the main street and raised his voice for all the surrounding townsfolk to hear him.

"Listen to me, all you good people!" he called. "We're here on a mission to defeat the Voyant Mendicat—the evil wizard who threatens the Coil with his Dark arts. Our mission is to search for him, find him, and defeat him to restore order to the Coil and bring peace in our time. I call on every able-bodied fighting man to join us! We've tracked the Voyant to this town—which means he's either hiding here or he'll come back here eventually."

"He isn't here," Americ yelled back. "We wouldn't be here if he was."

Marais ignored him. "Take up arms with us and fight the good fight! At the next assault, we'll attack the Voyant and drive him out of the Coil forever. Then we can all live in peace!"

A different voice called out of the crowd of onlookers. "How will you defeat him without magic?"

Everyone turned around to stare at Marine. She stood on a doorstep across the street looking as radiant as ever.

Her satin dark hair ruffled in the morning breeze. Her cheeks shone with light and beauty.

Marais bowed his head in greeting to her. "I'm sure the fighting men of this town know more about defeating the Voyant than you, dear lady," he returned.

"I know he's a wizard more powerful than any other in the Coil," she countered. "I know the Guardian Templars have been trying for years just to find him and learn his plans. How do you hope to do better without using magic? Do you even know where the Voyant is? Do you even know which Layer he's in?"

Marais looked away. "We will find him. Rest assured of that."

"So you don't know where he is, you don't know his plans, you don't know when he'll come after this town or even if he'll come after this town, and you don't have a way to defeat him when he does come."

Marais ignored her, reined his horse aside, and went back to pacing up and down in front of the other townsfolk. "The Voyant came after this town once before. He'll come again, and when he does...."

"What makes you think he'll come again?" Marine interrupted.

Marais lost his cool and turned on her. "He attacked this town! You would do better to keep silent and let those who know better organize a defense for you."

"What makes you think he attacked this town?" she argued. "He showed himself to this town, but it was the Darklings who attacked this town—not him. He stood back and did nothing."

"He's responsible for the instability—and the Darklings," Sylvain interrupted.

Marine cocked her head at him and narrowed her eyes. "How do you know the Voyant came to this town if you didn't use magic? I don't think you're telling us everything. Maybe you want to recruit the men of this town to fight the Voyant to distract him while you pull some magical attack on him unawares. If that's the case...."

"Be silent!" Marais bellowed and immediately realized his mistake. He lowered his voice and went on in the same placid tone as before. "I assure you we have no ill intentions toward this town, my dear lady. Our mission is simply to defeat the Voyant....."

"Which is another way of saying that defeating the Voyant is more important to you than the safety of these townspeople," she returned. "You didn't come here to protect anyone—least of all us."

Yann stepped in. "We aren't discussing that right now. Captain, if you would please dismount and disarm your men, I'll show you a house where you can spend the night. We can discuss the defense later."

Marais gave both Yann and Marine dirty looks, but in a minute, he gave orders to his men to dismount.

Yann had to go through a lengthy hassle of finding a places to stable the knights' horses. Tenby didn't have any stables or even any extra buildings to use as stables.

In the end, he ended up pasturing the horses outside the walls. "That's the best we can do for now," he told Marais. "We won't need horses to defend the town. You'll be able to get your horses back if you need to fight anyone outside the walls."

"I don't like it," Marais grumbled. "The military organization in this town leaves a great deal to be desired."

"That's because we aren't a military organization—and you aren't going to turn us into one. Now take your men back to the house for the night. We'll talk about the defenses tomorrow."

Anríq and Rien flanked Yann and the three friends watched the knights walk away. Americ showed Marais and Sylvain where to quarter their men.

"We shouldn't have let them inside the walls," Rien muttered. "We're going to regret that. They'll cause us nothing but trouble."

"It doesn't look good, does it?" Yann agreed. "Let's go meet up with Rosh and Valer. We'll have a meeting with our own men tonight and decide how to deal with the knights tomorrow after they wake up."

The three friends reentered the town and Yann supervised the Tenby defenders locking the gates before Marine came up to them.

She kept glancing behind her to watch the knights walk away. "You can't let them fight the Voyant, Yann," she insisted. "That would be the worst thing you could do."

"I can't stop them from fighting the Voyant. I can only stop anyone from Tenby getting involved."

"You saw what happened to Wesh when he attacked the Voyant," she went on. "The same thing could happen to them."

"You heard them earlier," Rien interjected. "It doesn't sound like they plan to listen to reason—especially not if it comes from you."

She made a face at him. "I wonder who their magic-user is."

"Do they even have one?" Yann asked. "They didn't sound like they did the first time we met them—and how would they be able to use magic here when no one else can?"

"How else did they find out the Voyant had been here? I don't see how they even made it this far without at least one magic-user."

"If they have one, they're keeping him well hidden," Yann remarked.

"Maybe Marais himself is a magic-user," Anríq suggested.

"Any of them could have magic," Yann pointed out.

"But not enough to fight the Voyant," Rien added. "They wouldn't be going around armored and on horseback if they really planned to fight him with magic. Either these men are grandstanding or else they're....."

He trailed off when Marais came out of the house Americ gave to him and his men. It sat four doors down from the Black Watch's house.

Marais had taken off his helm and some of his more cumbersome chest plates, but he didn't take off all his armor. He clanked when he walked.

His features hardened when he saw Yann and Marine talking to each other.

"Do you know this young lady, Watch Commander?" Marais snarled.

"Her name is Marine and my name is Yann Dilnao. You aren't under my command, so you can call me by my name."

Marais compressed his lips, glared at Marine again, and finally allowed himself to face Yann. "About these defenses...."

"I told you we won't talk about that until tomorrow," Yann interrupted. "And if you plan to fight the Voyant, you'll have to do that outside the walls. We can't let you endanger the town by attacking the Voyant in here."

Now Marais glared outright at Yann. "Our whole mission is to fight the Voyant...."

"So you keep saying," Marine interrupted.

"This might come as a surprise to you, Captain, but my men and I have actually encountered the Voyant before," Yann went on. "So has Marine. Attacking him outright will only end in disaster—for you and anyone who joins you. I can't let you do that inside the walls—and I'll do everything in my power to dissuade everyone else from joining you. I just want you to realize where we stand on this."

Marais narrowed his eyes and smoke billowed out of his ears. "I see. And what is there to stop me from taking command of this town in your place? You're just a boy. You have no experience nor any authority to command anyone."

"Maybe not, but I have risked my life to defend this town more than once—which is more than you can say. I know these people and they know me. I didn't become Commander of the Watch because I wanted to. I became Commander of the Watch because the people of this town asked me to. You might care more about defeating the Voyant than you do about saving these people's lives, but I don't. Feel free to go fight the Voyant anywhere you like and any way you like. You won't do it inside the walls and you won't take anyone with you as long as I have the power to convince them not to go. If that means you have to leave, so be it."

Marais clenched his jaws and snarled through gritted teeth. "I see. Thank you for clarifying your position. I'll consult my lieutenants and we will discuss this further tomorrow."

He clanked away across the street and returned to the same house.

"That obviously wasn't the answer he wanted to hear," Rien murmured after Marais went inside and shut the door.

Marine lunged for Yann, squealed, threw her arms around him, and kissed him on the cheek. "That was awesome! You're my hero, Yann!" She burst out in giggles. "Did you see his face?! Wow! You really told him! That was epic! I couldn't have said it better!"

Yann laughed nervously. He couldn't stop his cheeks from burning. "At least now all the cards are on the table." He turned to Rien. "Go call up the men. We need to talk about this tonight before the knights come out of their house tomorrow morning."

Rien walked away. Marine gushed a few more times about what a hero Yann was. He really wished she would stop doing that.

She finally, mercifully took herself off back to O'akim's library where she belonged.

Anríq waited until she left. Then he chuckled under his breath. "You better shut the hell up," Yann snapped. "Don't even say it, okay? Just don't say anything."

Anríq beamed at him. "I didn't say anything, Yann."

"Keep it that way."

Anríq chuckled again.

Yann cast a brutal scowl over the surrounding town. How did everything turn sour so fast? "I sure wish Eliska would come back. I'm really starting to get a bad feeling about her being gone for so long."

"I could go out and look for her," Anríq suggested. "If Rien is right that she's out there holding back that margin, then she should be close to the town. I should be able to find her easily."

"That's a bad idea. You could get lost out there, too."

"If she's holding back the margin, then she isn't lost. She may need help. I could help her stabilize it and then we could both come back."

Yann looked up. "Do you think so?"

"Only if she is stabilizing the margin—and only if she is close to the town. If she went off to help those children, then she could be anywhere in the entire Coil. I could search for the rest of my life and never find her—and I might not be able to find Tenby again, either."

Yann turned away with another grimace. "It isn't worth it to risk losing you, too."

"Is it worth the risk to get Eliska back? She's a magic-user. If she comes back here, she'll lose her magic the way I have. She can do more good out there."

"Maybe," Yann muttered. "All right. You can go, but if you don't find her right outside of town, I want you to come straight back. Don't get lost."

Anríq nodded. "I will—I mean I won't."

Yann glared at him, but Anríq only smiled at him and clapped him on the shoulder. "I'll see you soon, my friend, and with luck, I'll bring Eliska back, too. I'm sure Tenby is in the best hands."

Anríq turned and walked away. He didn't wait for anyone to open the gate for him. He climbed up to the scaffold, swung his legs over the wall, and dropped out of sight.

Yann had to resist the urge to go up there and watch Anríq walk into the veil. Yann would have liked to feast on the sight of Anríq until he disappeared, but that would only make Yann's job harder. He had enough to worry about already.

Chapter 49

Eliska waved her staff and lowered her skinned, gutted waterbuck over the branch of a tree. She didn't want to put it on the ground where it would get dirty.

"Whoa!" Thaddi exclaimed. "Where did you get that?!"

"You heard me talking to the trees earlier," Eliska replied. "I hid by the stream, and when the waterbuck came down to drink, I shot one with my magic. Then I skinned it and gutted it. It was too heavy to carry, so I used my magic to make it float back here. Now we just have to cook it."

She squatted down in the clearing where she left the children in the care of the living trees.

"Let me help you with that," a gentle male voice told her.

The branches overhead rustled and the trees shed a bunch of different-sized sticks. They all fell on the ground around the clearing.

The children burst out laughing. Some raised their arms trying to catch the sticks before they hit the ground.

Eliska found herself laughing, too. "Thank you. You trees sure are helpful."

"We don't often help travelers," a woman's voice replied. "We don't often see people as kind and caring as you."

Eliska changed the subject. "Gather up all the sticks, bring them here, and we'll light a fire."

The children couldn't help her fast enough. The boys crowded around. "Show me how to start a fire, Eliska," Thaddi insisted.

"I only know how to do it with magic. You should meet my friend Niyazi. He can do all of that stuff without magic. He can hunt and trap animals, light a fire, build a shelter, and do everything—all without magic. He's much better at this stuff than I am."

"Where is he?" Anthane asked.

Eliska pretended to look at what she was doing. "He's in another Layer with the Black Watch." She fired her staff into the sticks and they ignited.

"No way!" Anthane exclaimed. "Teach me to do that!"

"How's your hand window coming along? Master the basics first."

He turned away and sulked, but she caught him looking into his hand off and on for the rest of the evening.

Eliska cut off a section of the meat, built a spit, and cooked the haunch for the children to eat.

She had to smile when they sat around stuffing their faces in contented silence while she cooked the rest of the waterbuck for tomorrow.

They finally licked the juice off their fingers, but they still got it all over themselves.

Eliska used her staff to carve a piece of fallen tree trunk into a bowl and carried water back to the camp to clean everyone up.

"You all really need to take a bath," she mumbled while she wiped the smudges off Eloi's cheeks. "I should dunk you all in the stream."

"No!!" Cheseli exclaimed. "The water would be freezing!"

"I could heat it up for you." Eliska laughed at the thought.

"Tell us more about how it was for you when you were small," Dalana prompted.

Eliska didn't want to talk about that, so she changed the subject again. "I have a better idea. We could play a game."

"We don't know any games," Thaddi told her.

She made an executive decision not to say anything nasty about Aline and the other adults not teaching these children how to play games.

"Look at this." She took some colored pebbles out of her pocket. "We can make up a game with these."

"They're beautiful!" Eloi exclaimed and extended her chubby little hand to play with the stones.

"I found them in the stream and I brought them back for you. See how the light shines on them?"

Eliska held up a bright red stone. The firelight caught it and it cast a million brilliantly colored flashes around the clearing.

The children gasped and pointed. Some of them laughed and even jumped up and down trying to catch the lights.

Eliska held up a clear crystal stone. It turned the firelight into pastel rainbows that delighted the children even more.

She went through the pile of stones creating different colors and patterns around the clearing. Then she handed out the stones to the children and let them do it for a while.

She leaned back on her elbows and enjoyed watching them. Their excited chatter filled the clearing.

Then the trees joined in and commented on the colors and patterns. The children talked back and forth to the trees in rapid-fire exchanges of excited conversation.

Eliska found herself suffering a flood of almost painful affection for these children, but it went beyond that. The thought of something threatening them hurt worse than anything she could ever remember.

Some of them had already died on this journey. She couldn't let anything else happen to the children who survived.

They eventually got tired of the stones, gave them back to her, and gathered around the dying fire.

Eloi sat a little too close and wound up leaning against Eliska. The girl sagged. Forgotten instinct took over and Eliska put her arm around the girl's tiny shoulders, but not even that seemed enough.

Eliska lifted the girl into her lap, wrapped both arms around the little body, and last of all, kissed Eloi on the head.

A white-hot dagger stabbed Eliska in the heart when Eloi rested all her weight against Eliska's chest. Eliska couldn't have let go of this little girl for any money.

Anthane sat down next to Eliska on her other side. "Where are we going to sleep tonight?"

"I'll make a little house for us to stay in." Eliska glanced up at him, and for no reason she could figure out, she raised her hand and ran her fingers through his hair to comb it out of his face. "We'll need to stay warm tonight. It will get cold, so we'll all have to snuggle up together."

He softened at her touch and his eyes widened. "You're so much nicer than Aline, Eliska. I wish you could have been with us all the time."

Tears sprang to her eyes, but she forced herself to blink them away and smile at him instead. "We shouldn't say anything about Aline. I'm sure she did her best to take care of all of you—and like she said, she did a lot longer than I did. She was right. She and the other adults did the hard work. I just showed up at the end."

"What's going to happen to us?" Cheseli quavered.

"I'm going to take you to the orphanage," Eliska told her—and she found herself talking to all of them. "I'll make sure you get there safely—and then all of you are going to grow up and have long, happy lives with people who care about you."

"Will you stay at the orphanage?" Eloi asked. "Please stay, Eliska."

She cringed. "I don't know what will happen after that. The most important thing is to get you kids somewhere safe. There might be other people in the Coil who need my help. You would want me to help them the same way I'm helping you, wouldn't you?"

"Yeah," Thaddi mumbled. "I guess so."

"You're all tired. Come on. It's time to go to sleep."

Eliska got to her feet and picked up her staff, but she just couldn't bring herself to let go of Eloi.

Eliska held the girl in one arm, aimed her staff at the undergrowth on the other side of the clearing, and twisted the branches into a hut like the one the Black Watch built in the snow Island.

The branches twined together with leaves forming the roof. The branches sprouted new leaves to close in the walls. The branches came together at the front to make a small hole to act as a door.

The trees shook down a bunch of dry tinder that she stacked inside to make a soft, insulated mattress. All the children crawled inside.

Eliska thought she would have to go through a complicated nego-tiation process to get everyone to fit together in such a cramped space.

The children must have been much more exhausted than she real-ized. They all bundled up together in a pile and crashed hard.

She laid Eloi near the others. Eliska curled onto her side with her arms still wrapped around the little girl, but Eliska couldn't fall asleep. She stared into the darkness for a long time thinking about everything that happened since she left Tenby.

She never thought she would get into a situation like this. She told herself she only got involved with the Black Watch due to unavoidable circumstances. She couldn't fool herself that the same thing happened here.

She let herself go with these children. She let herself get much closer to them and care about them much more deeply and much more quickly than she ever did with the Watch.

The thought of anything happening to these children made her want to die. She would gladly die to give each of them the life they deserved.

The feelings storming inside her wouldn't rest. Was this what love felt like? She never understood that word until now.

She wouldn't have been able to do any of this if anyone from the Watch had been here to see. She wouldn't have let herself express so much affection and share in the children's innocent joy. She would have kept her guard up.

She envied Anríq his ability to just drop all pretense and give himself to the Tenby children the way he did.

He did it so easily and naturally. He didn't suffer any doubts about it. He just did it as second nature to his silent, reserved Servant ways.

Maybe that affectionate, outgoing behavior was his real self hidden under the rules he thought he had to follow when he became a Servant. Maybe he wasn't really silent and reserved at all. Why did she think he was?

He wasn't here. She was alone, so she could reinvent herself as the person these children needed her to be. That was all part of being a Servant—if she was a Servant.

The thought that she might be one gave her another flood of emotion—powerful, loving emotion for everyone who might need her help.

She felt it for those children she saw begging, but she didn't help them that time. She felt it for the old woman's daughter.

Eliska didn't want to go back to the way she was before. Did that mean she couldn't go back to the Watch?

She wouldn't be able to let her guard down around them. She wouldn't be able to be as outgoing, affectionate, and unguarded with them as Marine was.

Maybe everyone would be better off if she didn't go back. She could just become another wandering Servant helping anyone who asked her.

She shut her eyes and burrowed deeper into the tinder bed with the children. Eloi's little body gave Eliska as much comfort as she gave these children. They were the best thing that ever happened to her.

She shut her eyes, but just then, she heard something—or maybe just felt it. Her eyes snapped open. Yes, she definitely heard footsteps coming closer.

She unpeeled herself from Eloi as softly as possible so she didn't wake up any of the children, grabbed her staff, and crawled out of the hut.

She shot a burst of magic into the fire to make it flare up. Then she aimed her staff out into the darkness. "Who's there?!" she demanded.

"Someone's coming," a young, male tree told her from nearby.

"It's a Barbarian," a female tree added.

"He's a Servant," an older male tree went on. "He won't harm you."

Eliska stiffened and then wilted in relief when Anríq stepped out of the shadows. "What are you doing here?!" she gasped. "You scared the crap out of me!"

"I'm sorry to come so late," he replied. "I only just found you. Yann let me come and look for you. He's worried because you didn't come back to Tenby."

"I can't go back now. I have to take these children to their orphanage in the Lake Country. You can tell him I'll come back to the Watch as soon as I finish. I can navigate through the Coil. I'll be able to find Tenby again—and if you aren't there, I'll catch up with you somewhere else."

He inclined his head to one side and studied her in the firelight. Did she have the word, *Servant,* written all over her face? Could he tell how much she'd changed in just a few days—or was it hours?

His eyes darted to the hut behind her and passed his hand downward in front of himself. A sheet of magic gave him a view of the children inside.

"There are fewer than when we first saw them," he remarked.

"All the adults are dead. I can't leave them. I won't leave them, so don't ask me to."

"I wasn't going to ask you to."

She squatted down by the fire. A mixture of relief and defensive confusion gripped her, now that he was actually here. She didn't know how to deal with him.

"Are you hungry?" she asked. "We have some food here."

He squatted down opposite her. He didn't answer, so she unfolded the waterbuck hide she cured to act as a package for the cooked meat.

She moved around the fire to squat closer to him and handed him a few pieces. He chewed them in silence.

"I'm sorry I threatened you just now," she went on. "I didn't know it was you. We got attacked earlier. I thought it might be those people coming back."

"I'm the one who's sorry for frightening you. I'm glad the children didn't see me. I wouldn't want to frighten them."

"Will you go back to Tenby? Yann probably needs you more than I do."

"I don't know how to get back to Tenby from this Island—and I doubt he needs me more than you do."

She turned bright red and forced herself to look away. "Well, we'd love to have you if you stay."

"I'll stay. I'll help you get the children to safety. Then you can use whatever new method you use to take us both back to Tenby."

"I can send you there now. I just have to combine my magic with another magic-user the way we did in the maze tower. The Coil map shows more detail that way. I can find where things are and where I need to go. That's how I found the children. It makes everything much clearer."

He bit off another piece of meat. "No, I'll stay with you. These children obviously need help. They're lucky to have you."

She colored again, handed him a few more pieces of meat, and folded up the package. "It was very nice of you to come looking for me. No one has ever done that before."

"It would be better if we could send Yann a message to tell him that you're all right. He's worried about you."

She couldn't look up. "You said that."

"The Chivalric Order of Custodians showed up at Tenby."

Eliska's head snapped around and her mouth fell open. "No way! I thought they would be dead."

"We all did. Now they want to take over Tenby and recruit everyone to help them wage war against the Voyant."

She snorted. "Good luck."

"Yann is dealing with them. He's an excellent Watch Commander."

"I'm sure he is." Eliska glanced behind her toward the hut. "I don't think it would be a good idea for you to sleep in there tonight. That really would scare the children."

He burst out in a huge grin and chuckled, but he stopped himself from laughing out loud. He kept it quiet. "I wouldn't do that. I doubt there's enough room in there for me anyway."

"I could make you another hut out here."

"I'll sit up and keep watch. You go ahead. You need to sleep."

She found herself smiling back at him. "Thank you again for coming. I'm really glad you're here."

"I'm glad I'm here, too. Sleep well. I'll see you in the morning."

Chapter 50

E liska crawled out of the forest hut and grinned when she saw Anríq sitting under a tree across the fire.

He had added wood to it during the night to keep it going. Now he rested his head against the trunk behind him. He had his eyes closed.

Eliska got busy setting up a spit over the fire to warm up the leftover meat. She didn't want the children to eat it cold.

She went down to the stream to get water and came back to find Anríq awake. She put the water bowl next to him. "You better take this before the children wake up. They won't leave any for you."

"How will you explain me to them?"

She didn't get a chance to answer before Thaddi, Anthane, and Dalana crawled out of the hut. They stopped there and gawked at Anríq with their eyes hanging out of their sockets.

"Um....what's that?" Thaddi asked.

"This is Anríq," Eliska explained. "He's a Barbarian Servant. He's come to help me take you to the orphanage."

"Look at that axe!" Anthane breathed. "I want one of those when I get older."

"You have some growing to do before then," Eliska told him. "Sit down and eat your breakfast before the little ones wake up."

The three older children sat down on the opposite side of the fire from Anríq. They didn't stop staring at him while he drank the water Eliska gave him and then left for the stream to get some more.

He was just coming back when Eloi and Cheseli came out of the hut with some of the other little ones.

Eloi screamed and then burst into tears when she saw Anríq coming. She wailed with loud sobs that shook the whole forest. Cheseli gaped at him in horror and then dove back into the hut to hide.

Eliska picked up Eloi, petted her hair, and kissed her on the cheeks while she tried to quiet the girl down.

Anríq pretended not to notice and squatted down in the same place by the fire.

"It's all right, Eloi," Eliska told her. "This is Anríq. He's a friend. He's going to help me protect you. Don't worry. He won't hurt you."

It took a long time to quiet the girl down. When she did, Eliska tried to put her on the ground. Eloi screamed, burst out in sobs again, and hung onto Eliska's neck for dear life.

Eloi kept stealing glances at Anríq and then turning her face away so she wouldn't see him.

This whole process repeated more than once before Eliska finally convinced Eloi to let go. When she did, Eliska handed the little girl off to Dalana to hold.

Anríq didn't make eye contact with anyone during the whole ordeal. Eliska hated to think how he felt about this.

She could well imagine what Cheseli was saying to the others inside the hut, so Eliska averted another impending disaster by crawling in there and explaining it to them herself.

She found them all sitting up and too terrified to go outside.

"A friend of mine is outside," she told them. "His name is Anríq and he's here to help us."

"He looks like a monster!" Cheseli croaked.

"He does not look like a monster," Eliska countered. "He's a Barbarian Servant and he came a long way to help all of us. He's one of the kindest people I've ever met and he loves children."

"You mean he loves to eat them," another little boy corrected.

Eliska smacked her lips. "We're lucky he's helping us. Now come outside and don't let me hear you talking about him like that. If you talk to him and get to know him, you'll realize he's a nice person with a very kind heart. Now come on. We need to eat breakfast so we can get moving."

She crawled outside. The children followed more slowly. Then they all stood back against the hut walls and stared at Anríq.

They probably would have kept staring forever, but Eliska made them come over and sit by the fire to eat. They eventually had to get used to Anríq.

He didn't say a word the whole time. He ate the food Eliska gave him and he kept going back and forth to the stream to fill up the water bowl whenever the children emptied it.

The bowl finally made it around to Thaddi. "Thank you," he told Anríq when Anríq handed it to him.

"You're welcome," Anríq replied.

The others all remembered to use their manners after that.

"These trees told us to go north," Eliska told Anríq while they ate. "We ran into a town where they hate magic-users. They attacked us and tried to kill us."

"They did kill Aline," Dalana added.

"Yes, they did." Eliska turned back to Anríq. "Anyway, the trees say the way north is safer, so that's where we're going. Then we'll turn west before we break through to the Lake Country."

He nodded. "Good idea."

"Have you ever visited this Island before?" she asked. "Do you know these trees? They recognized that you were a Servant and warned me that you were coming."

"I don't recognize the Island, but I do know there are Layers where the people hate magic-users. I traveled through an Island once and some other travelers I healed told me to stay away from a certain part of the country to the east because the people there would attack and kill magic-users. It might be the same Island."

"So you might know the terrain west of here? You might know what we can expect there?"

"I would if it was the same Island. If it isn't, then whatever I know about it won't help. There's no way to know if it is the same Island, so I say we just go there and take what comes. I don't see that we can do anything else."

"I suppose you're right."

"What's a Servant, Eliska?" Anthane asked.

She glanced up and discovered all the children staring at her and Anríq. The children listened with rapt attention.

"A Servant is a Barbarian who has forsaken the path of violence and dedicated themselves to healing and helping all of humanity," she explained. "Anríq is a magic-user who goes around the country healing anyone who needs it and protecting people who can't protect themselves—like you kids."

"Wow!" Anthane exclaimed. "He's a magic-user?!"

"So....he isn't a monster?" Cheseli asked.

"No, he isn't. Now finish your breakfast and let's get going. We have a lot of ground to cover."

She used her staff to put out the fire. Anríq stood off to one side and waited. Eliska had to go through the whole group, clean all the juice and fat off everyone's faces, and make sure they relieved themselves before the party moved out.

Eliska led the way. The children crowded around her the way they did yesterday. Anríq stayed in the back.

The younger ones spent the first few minutes casting glances at him over their shoulders. After a while, they got used to him and forgot he was even there.

Eloi caught up with Eliska and asked to be carried again. Then the same little boy wound up getting a piggyback ride from Eliska while Anthane carried her staff.

The party fell into the same routine all the way to the northern edge of the forest.

"Thank you for all your help," Eliska told the trees before the party went out into the open. "I hope we meet again."

"You children behave yourselves and help Eliska," a deep male voice told them.

"We will!" all the children chorused.

Eliska blushed when she caught Anríq grinning in the background, but he didn't say anything.

The party set off across country heading farther north. Eliska started to get tired from carrying the two children.

She held out until they made it to a road leading down to a river. "Can we stop and get some water?" Anthane asked.

Eliska stopped walking and put the two children down in the open. She narrowed her eyes at the horizon. "Something's wrong."

"What is it?" Anthane asked.

"I'm not sure yet." Eliska took her staff back from him. "Something's out there—something Dark."

Anríq came forward to join her. "What is it?"

"I'm not sure, but it's surrounded by the Dark." She opened her hand window and surveyed the terrain ahead. "It's down by the river—in a gulley."

Anríq passed his hand downward in front of his face. "I'm not picking up any intent toward us."

"I'm going out there to see what it is. I don't want to go that way if it's something that could put us in danger—and going around it would take too long. You stay here and guard the children."

"You shouldn't go alone," he countered.

"We can't leave the children unguarded," she pointed out.

Anríq's hard blue eyes swept the countryside. "This is a bad idea. If a Darkling attacked you, it could neutralize you and then we would all be in trouble. I'm going with you."

She opened her mouth to point out that neither of them could leave the children unattended, especially not with Dark forces abroad.

Gratitude for Anríq stopped her from arguing with him. She made up her mind. "I'll magick them so they're invisible. You children follow us. I'm going to put a spell on you to keep you together and also to keep you silent. You won't be able to talk or move around freely, but you'll be hidden. No one will be able to see you or hear you. Understand?"

All the children nodded. She aimed her staff at them, cast a binding spell around them, and also silenced them. They couldn't open their mouths.

She erected a shield over them and made it invisible. Then she nodded to Anríq.

He took down his axe, unhooked his club, and they advanced step by step toward the river.

Eliska kept her hand window open and her staff pointed in front of her. Her hand window showed a mass of Dark energy tucked down in a hollow by the river.

"It looks like it's trapped there," she whispered to Anríq on the side. "It looks like it can't get out."

"I don't recognize it. It isn't a Darkling. It's too small."

They made it to the top of the riverbank. Eliska didn't see anything dangerous anywhere around. The river looked peaceful and harmless.

A few fishermen cast their nets at the next bend downstream. They didn't notice anything out of the ordinary.

Eliska told the children to stay here while she and Anríq climbed down into the hollow. She shut her hand window so she could hold her staff with both hands.

A charge of tension went through both her and Anríq when they turned the corner and saw the Dark mass wedged between two ridges.

Millions of Dark fibers twisted and roiled in a ball of hideous motion around a central mass. Eliska couldn't see anything inside the ball.

She and Anríq exchanged glances. She checked the hilltop behind her. The children were still there and still safe.

She took a deep breath and fired her staff at the ball. Her magic stripped away the Dark to reveal a man lying sprawled on the ground between the two ridges.

"Vidal!" she exclaimed and took a step forward, but she stopped herself from going near him.

He wasn't wearing his uniform anymore. He still had his pants on, but he'd lost his shirt, jacket, boots, and weapons.

Cuts and scratches covered his face, arms, chest, stomach, shoulders, back, neck, hands, and feet. Bruises darkened every part of him that Eliska could see.

He splayed his arms out to both sides and dug his fingertips into the two ridges on either side of him. He kept grasping at the two edges like he had to stop some unseen force from ripping him out of position.

His eyes darted from place to place without seeing anything. He kept gasping with every breath.

Anríq lowered his axe and club. "At least he isn't armed."

Eliska took a step closer to Vidal. He definitely saw her that time. His eyes snapped to her face and he gasped again. "Eliska......Eliska......you have to help me......they're coming after me.....they know who I am....they won't stop.....until they find me...."

He grimaced in an excruciating mixture of misery and terror. His eyes darted away, came back, and then looked off in the other direction.

"What happened to you, Vidal?" she exclaimed. "Why are you....why were you surrounded by the Dark?"

"They found me!" he choked. "They found me....and now they're coming for me.....They won't stop....I thought I got away from them......"

"Is he seeing invisible Darklings again?" she asked Anríq.

He advanced to her side and raised his hand to touch Vidal's forehead.

Anríq yanked his hand away and scraped his palm down his thigh. "The Dark is inside him. This isn't the same sickness that got the Watchmen. He's gone over to the Dark."

"You mean the Dark took him," she corrected. "Listen to him. He's scared out of his mind—and look at all these cuts. The Dark attacked him—or it looks that way."

Anríq curled his lip and turned away. "I can't heal him. He's too Dark. Those cuts are Dark magic. He may be too far gone."

"We can't just leave him here."

"Bind him, then," Anríq growled over his shoulder. "Make sure he can't escape or attack anyone."

She turned back to Vidal. He stayed where he was. He didn't try to get up. He plastered himself back between those two ridges like he might be trying to back away from something.

"Come with us, Vidal," Eliska told him. "We're taking you back to the Watch."

"They're coming....." he whimpered. "They're coming after me... .."

"Who is?"

"He means the Dark," Anríq interrupted.

"You don't know that," she countered. "Someone really could be coming after him. They may have already gotten to him."

"Then we would put the children in danger by bringing him near them."

She thought it over. Anríq might be right about that, but she couldn't turn her back on Vidal—not after losing so many other Watchmen.

She made up her mind, cast a different binding spell around Vidal to immobilize him, and then magicked him to float behind her.

Anríq shot Vidal a hard glare. "How will you heal him without poisoning yourself?"

"I don't know, but I can't turn my back on him. He might be infected with the Dark, but he isn't so far gone that he can't ask for help. Would you be able to walk away from him if he asked you for help?"

"He didn't ask me for help. He didn't even see me."

"I know. He asked me."

"Exactly. The Dark recognizes the Dark. Maybe this is his way of luring you in."

She didn't answer that.

Becoming a Servant or whatever she had been doing these last few days—she didn't know much, but she did know one thing.

Giving service to other people was the only thing that could counteract this poison inside her. Service was the only cure. Caring about people and helping them was the only cure.

Vidal wasn't trying to lure her to the Dark. She didn't believe that for a second.

She and Anríq returned to the hilltop where she released the children. "Who's that?" Dalana asked.

"It's a long story," Eliska replied. "He's someone who needs help, but he's sick. He won't bother us. Now come on. We have to go."

The group set off across country heading north again. Eliska got Anríq to help her check the Coil projection in midafternoon.

"We've gone far enough north," she decided. "Let's find a place to camp and spend the night."

Chapter 51

The party headed west and found another river. Eliska had to stop herself from trying to talk to the trees.

She used her staff to steer Vidal to a clump of vegetation to one side. She put him down behind some bushes where the children wouldn't see him.

She tried to talk to him, but he just kept repeating over and over that someone was after him and that they wouldn't stop until they got him.

She left him there while she and Anríq made camp. The children all gathered around her the way they did last night.

She served everyone the last of the waterbuck and set some aside for Vidal, but he didn't respond when she tried to give it to him.

"Let's play another game," Thaddi suggested after they all finished eating.

"What do you have in mind?" Eliska asked.

"You're the one who is so good with games," he countered.

"Okay, I know one. I mean….I saw some kids playing this. I've never played it before, so I'll be learning right along with you."

"What is it?" Dalana asked.

"Everybody sit in a circle." She waited for them to get into position and then handed each person one of her brightly colored stones. She also gave one to Anríq.

"When I say go, you'll use your left hand to pass your stone to the person on your left. At the same time, you have to hold out your right hand to the person on your right so that person can put their stone into your hand. Then you have to take that stone, pass it to your left hand, give it to the person on your left, and hold out your right hand to get the next stone. The first person to drop your stone is out and the circle gets smaller until we get a winner."

The children frowned at each other. She had to explain it twice more before they understood well enough to play.

When they all decided they were ready, she said, "Go!" and everyone started passing their stones.

They only lasted a few seconds before Cheseli missed her pass and dropped her stone instead of putting it in Anthane's hand.

"That's no fair!" he exclaimed. "She made the mistake! I can't be out!"

"You're out, Anthane," Eliska decided. "Step out of the circle."

He complained a lot and finally backed off. Cheseli missed her stone on the very next round, so it all evened out in the end.

The children laughed hard enough to mess themselves up. Anríq stayed in the circle almost until the very end. Thaddi sat on Anríq's right. The boy couldn't miss Anríq's big hands.

Eliska caught him grinning as the tension mounted. The circle dwindled to just Eliska, Anríq, Dalana, and Thaddi.

They had to move away from the fire to sit close enough to each other.

"Come on, Thaddi!" Anthane cheered from the sidelines. "You can beat them!"

"Don't drop it, Eliska!" Cheseli chimed in. "You have to win!"

All four competitors laughed through the next round and Dalana eliminated Anríq. He laughed when he joined the children watching from outside.

"Who are you for now?" Anthane asked him.

"Eliska, of course," Anríq replied.

Her cheeks burned and she turned back to the contest in front of her, but in the next round, she missed. That left Thaddi and Dalana as the two finalists.

They passed well for a couple of minutes before Thaddi dropped his stone. Dalana shot to her feet and raised her fists in triumph.

The children mobbed her laughing, yelling, and congratulating her.

Then everyone gathered around the fire. They tried to make the same colored patterns with the stones in the firelight, but it didn't work. The surrounding trees didn't offer a dense enough backdrop.

Eloi climbed into Eliska's lap much sooner than last night. Eliska combed the girl's hair back, kissed her, and adjusted Eloi's position to make herself more comfortable.

Eliska accidentally jostled the girl on her knee and Eloi burst into giggles. Eliska followed up by bouncing her knee faster and harder. Eloi galloped up and down and shrieked with laughter.

The other children laughed, too, but pretty soon, their exhaustion started to catch up with them.

Two other children scooted close to Eliska and leaned against her from the side. She put her arm around one of them and Eloi started to droop against Eliska's chest.

The other children's energy drained away in a matter of minutes. They stared into the flames and their eyelids started to droop.

Eliska became aware of Anríq sitting across the fire from her. He watched her intently and didn't look away.

His gaze made her uncomfortable. She got the distinct impression again that he could see exactly what she was doing and why. He might even have figured out that she was trying to make herself into a Servant.

She would never dare to call herself that—especially not to him. She wasn't a Servant. She never would be or could be. She wasn't a Barbarian and she never took a vow of silence.

She didn't know what she was, but whatever this was—whatever path she was on—it seemed to take hold of her. She couldn't get off it now even if she wanted to.

She didn't want to. She started to dread the moment when she got the children to their orphanage. Did she really plan to walk away from them and leave them with a bunch of strangers?

If this Servant's path was real—if she really belonged to it the way she was starting to suspect she did—then everyone else in the world would need her as much as the children did.

They wouldn't need her anymore because they would be safe with people who would take care of them. The world would need her more—and she would be obligated to serve all of humanity, not just those children.

She couldn't sit here with Anríq staring at her, so she pried herself out from between the children, put Eloi down, and used her staff to construct another hut.

She had to use dirt and tree roots this time, but the structure turned out to be much sturdier and warmer than the hut of branches in the forest of living trees.

She carried the little ones inside and they all curled up together. "Sleep tight, my precious little ones," she whispered. "I'm going to check on Vidal. Then I'll come back to you."

The feeling in her chest threatened to explode when she stroked their hair and kissed each glowing, angelic cheek in the darkness.

She tore herself away. Anríq sat alone by the fire. "I'm going to check on Vidal," she told him. "Then you should get some sleep. Don't stay up again tonight."

"I won't," he replied. "I couldn't."

She smiled at him. She was starting to feel the same kind of dedication and affection for him that she felt for those children—and for everyone. He was a member of the human race, wasn't he?

She'd been keeping an eye on him and making sure he was okay since they first met. She made sure he had enough to eat and that the Watchmen knew what a prize he was.

He followed her into the shadows. He unhooked his club and sent a stream of magic into it to make it glow so he and Eliska could see where they were going.

Vidal lay on the ground where she left him. She still hadn't freed him from the immobilization spell.

He didn't gasp and jerk around because he couldn't move his body, but his eyes still raced everywhere in the darkness.

Eliska squatted down in front of him and held out the bowl. "I brought you something to eat, Vidal. Do you think you feel like sitting up and eating it?"

He looked away. "You shouldn't have come for me."

"I didn't. We thought you were a Darkling. The Dark took you, didn't it?"

He made a pathetic, terrified little mewling noise in his throat, twisted his features in a grimace of hysterical misery, and craned his head all the way to one side so he wouldn't look at them and they wouldn't look at him. "It's me, Eliska," he whimpered. "It's me."

"What's you? Who's after you?"

"I.....I messed up...." He choked and started to sob, but no tears came. He searched the darkness off to one side while his whole body contracted in agony. "I......I tried to get away from it.....I tried to make it go away....but it came back....."

Eliska glanced up at Anríq, but he only shrugged and shook his head.

"What happened, Vidal?" she asked. "How did the Dark take you?"

"The Dark...." he croaked. "They communed with the Dark.....they infected me with it...."

Eliska's blood ran cold. She didn't want to hear this, but it was too late. She already asked. "Who? Who did this to you?"

He turned around and his crazed eyes locked on her with terrifying power. He really did burst out in sobs mixed with hysterical, horrific laughter. Tears streamed down his face while he forced out the words.

"My parents! They belonged to a coven that communed with the Dark. They used their rituals to bring me into the Dark.....and then they.....committed horrific acts......and I....I did it, too.....I didn't know.....and then.....I did know.....I....." He broke off without saying what he did.

Eliska swallowed hard. She didn't want to hear this, but the dam broke and it all came pouring out.

"I grew up with it.....They used my blood in their rituals....and made me carry out their sacrifices.....I didn't realize what was happening until I got older.....and then I tried to end myself, but the Dark took me over and stopped me......I tried a dozen times to get away, but they always brought me back.....I didn't know what to do....." His voice spiked off the charts.

Every nerve told Eliska to run as far away from Vidal as she could, but she couldn't move. None of this was his fault. His parents raised him with it.

He raked his cheek across his shoulder, straightened his features, and fought his voice under control.

When he spoke again, the words tumbled out of his mouth in an unnaturally calm voice. "I didn't know what to do, so I used my magic to eliminate my own magic. I became an imp so they couldn't track me down. I ran away and joined the Black Watch." His wild eyes skimmed out into the night one last time and his voice cracked with buried misery. "I can't go back! I'll die before I go back!"

"Back to the Watch?" she asked.

"Back to the Dark!" he bellowed. "I fought them off a hundred times! I ran away from the Watch to protect my brother Watchmen from myself! I would never put them in danger....."

He broke off and crumpled in another pathetic mass of terrified despair.

"I can't become what I was!" he whimpered. "I can't let myself. I have to fight them no matter what they do to me."

He spun around and tried to sit up to lean closer to her. "You can't take me back to the Watch, Eliska! Promise me you won't take me back to the Watch—not like this! Don't put them in danger."

"What about you? What will you do?"

He looked away and his whole face spasmed in cruel terror. "I have to keep fighting them. I have to hold the Dark at bay.....just a little longer.....until they come for me....."

"Isn't there anything anyone can do?" she asked.

She opened her mouth to ask if there was anything *she* could do, but she already knew the answer.

There was something she could do. She could take his Darkness the way she took Barsali's. She could poison herself even more than she already was.

He read her mind and broke down sobbing again. He kept crashing back and forth from one emotion to another.

He buckled over into the dirt and his shoulders shook with all the wretched misery fighting to get out of him.

"You don't know!" he croaked. "You don't know the things I've seen and done. You don't want to see. I'm the one who did it. I'll never be able to get rid of that....and I don't want to. Just leave me here. I'll hold them off as long as I can. Just.....just don't tell the other Watchmen. Don't let them find out what I am."

He broke down completely. He kept his head turned away so she couldn't see his face.

Her throat tightened listening to him sob. She couldn't even imagine the memories he must be carrying. She didn't want to know, but she would have done it to heal him. She would have taken even that, but he didn't want her to.

Maybe this was his version of service. He turned his back on all of that—on his parents' way of life—and dedicated himself to the Black Watch.

No one in the Watch ever found out what he was. She didn't have to wonder about that.

Yann, Yvan, Omer, Barsali, Neils, Niyazi, and Rien all respected Vidal. They all thought he was a good man—because he was.

He never gave them any reason to question him. He turned his life around and became the exact opposite of everything his parents raised him to be.

She couldn't listen to him sobbing like this—not without doing something. She couldn't heal him.

He gave everything to hold back the Dark. When he couldn't do that anymore, he separated himself to protect his brother Watchmen. She couldn't take that away from him.

She raised her hand to touch him and hesitated. Touching him meant feeling the vast depth of Darkness eating away at his soul. He carried as much poison as she did if not more.

Her hand hovered over his shoulder marked with dozens of scratches. The Dark forces already attacked him more than once. They wanted him back, but he fought them. He would keep fighting until they killed him.

She let her hand fall on his shoulder. The Dark seethed just below the surface. He had to marshal every scrap of his remaining sanity to keep fighting, but he did it.

He completely fell apart when she touched him, but she didn't pull away. She left her hand there for a long time. She would have stayed with him all night, but he eventually pulled himself together and rotated onto his back.

He sniffed and rubbed his face across his shoulder again. He couldn't move his arms with the immobilization spell around him.

"You go back to those children," he husked. "They need you more than I do."

"Are you sure? What should we do with you?"

"Leave me here. I'll be all right."

"I can't do that, Vidal," she told him. "I can't just dump you and walk away—not when you're in danger."

He tried to smile at her and failed. "Don't worry about me. I'll take care of myself. You take care of those children." He jerked his head toward the camp. "Go. Go now."

She didn't know what to do, so she stood up and backed away. Anríq accompanied her back to the camp where he made his club stop glowing and hung it back on his belt.

She sat down by the fire. Too many thoughts raced through her mind.

Anríq sat down next to her. "What are you going to do?" he asked.

"I don't know," she murmured. "I don't know what I can do."

"He sounds pretty certain about you leaving him here."

She didn't answer. She owed it to the children to get them to safety. She'd already committed herself to that course.

Keeping them safe meant keeping them away from Vidal. She'd already taken a massive risk by bringing him this far.

It would be even more dangerous to keep him around the children than it would be to take him back to the Watch.

She thought it over for a long time. She got lost in her own thoughts, especially about how his story affected her.

If he worked that hard to hold the Dark at bay, what did that say about her future? Would she eventually fail to contain her poison? Would it take her over and turn her completely to the Dark?

She would need to make sure she got far away from people before that happened. She might even have to eliminate herself—but how?

Anríq broke in on her thoughts. "You should go to sleep."

She looked up at him. He gazed down at her from inches away. He sat right next to her.

Thank Heaven he was here. He got her through this even if he couldn't help her make any decisions. She sure as hell wouldn't want to go through this alone.

At least one other person knew Vidal's secret history. She didn't have to carry that secret alone, either. She wouldn't have been able to.

She didn't blame him for keeping it from the Watchmen—or for begging her not to tell them.

They should think he died as a loyal Watchman. He was a loyal Watchman. He still fought the good fight even now.

"Do you want to go inside or do you want to sleep out here?" Anríq asked. "I'll keep watch if you want to sleep in there."

"I don't want to go inside." She didn't have to tell him why. She didn't want her Darkness or anyone's Darkness near those children.

Vidal's story carried enough Darkness on its own to poison anyone who went near it. She wanted to keep the story away from them, too.

"Lie down," Anríq told her.

She tipped over and realized on her way down to the ground how exhausted she was. She couldn't stay upright a second longer.

She curled up by the fire, and out of nowhere, he rested his hand on her shoulder exactly the way she rested hers on Vidal's shoulder.

The weight of Anríq's arm flooded her with relief. He was here. He knew the worst and it was still okay.

She shut her eyes and disappeared into oblivion.

Chapter 52

Eliska stopped in the undergrowth and looked down at the spot where Vidal had been lying last night. He wasn't there anymore—not the way she remembered him.

A tangled ball of Dark fibers rolled, twisted, tangled, and seethed in front of her. No binding spell held it in place.

She stood still holding the bowl of food she brought for him. She could have used her staff to strip away the fibers and expose the man underneath.

His warning came back to her. He wanted her to protect everyone by leaving him behind. She took one last look at the ball and walked back to the camp.

She didn't make eye contact with Anríq when she got there. She sat down with the children and talked to them instead. She didn't want them to know about Vidal.

Anríq stood up a second later, walked off in the same direction, and came back. She kept her head turned so she wouldn't see his reaction.

She got the children up and moving and she didn't look back when the party headed west again. She didn't even check to see if Vidal was still there.

"We should make it to the orphanage tomorrow," she told them. "Just hold out a little longer."

Her encouragement rallied them all. They dropped into a zone of grim determination and pushed through every difficulty to keep going no matter what.

Eliska sank into the same dimension of mindless persistent determination. The obstacles didn't matter anymore. She would get there one way or another. She just had to keep going.

She carried Eloi in her arms and the little boy on her back. Fatigue didn't touch her anymore. It meant nothing compared to making sure the children made it to their destination alive and unhurt.

Two other little children started crying by mid-morning. Eliska checked to find out what was wrong and discovered blisters on their feet.

Anríq healed them and carried both children after that. He probably could have carried more, but no one asked.

The party had to climb some steep cliffs to a high plateau. As soon as they crossed it, they would come to a part of the landscape where they could break through to the Lake Country.

She slowed when she got near the other side and spotted a light in the distance. She dreaded what she would see and the sight didn't disappoint her.

A glowing halo of golden light shone over a countryside rolling, erupting, and disintegrating all over the map.

The landscape heaved out of position, swallowed whole towns, and then exploded into mountains that dissolved in explosions a second later.

Anríq materialized at her side. They both stared out at the Voyant laying waste to the countryside. The whole fabric of reality swelled, ruptured, and undulated to the farthest horizon.

"Is he insane?" she half-whispered.

"We should break through now. We can't go any farther without risking the children's lives."

She nodded and turned away with an effort. She couldn't watch this.

She steered the children back to the middle of the plateau. "I'm going to bind us all together and then we're going to break through the Layers," she explained. "We'll end up in the Lake Country in a few minutes."

"What is that light out there?" Anthane asked.

"I don't have time to explain it to you right now. Everybody gather around."

She herded the children into a group. Anríq took his place on the other side of them where he would be able to defend them if the party ran into any Darklings in the Layers.

Eliska cast a binding spell over the children, but she left herself and Anríq outside it. They would be free to move around and fight when they needed to.

She raised her staff, but at that moment, the upheaval tearing this Island apart erupted out of all proportion.

The Voyant disappeared and the valley floor beyond the plateau blasted out of place.

Bedrock split the surface, tilted into steep cliffs, and toppled sideways. Those slabs smashed into the ground with withering force and sent tremors through the ground.

Cracks forked across the landscape and widened into fissures plunging to crevasses. The plateau detonated and threw the whole party into the air.

Eliska fired a spell at the children and magnetized herself to them. Anríq wheeled off into the confusion. She didn't have time to catch him before she lost sight of him.

The Island shattered with unbelievable ferocity. Eliska couldn't remember any Layer shattering like this before.

Countless boulders and even whole mountains hurtled through the confusion. Deafening booms drowned out the children's petrified screams, but they couldn't do anything.

Eliska pinwheeled away and flying clouds of debris slammed her from the side.

She became aware of Dark forces whipping and slashing through the chaos. She couldn't see any part of the Island still intact. Did it shatter and send the party into the Layers?

She spun around trying to see any Darklings coming after the children. She didn't see any, but she did see a solid wall of black rushing her from the side.

This direction had been facing south when the party stood on top of the plateau, but the plateau wasn't there anymore. Nothing was there anymore, not even any floor or sky or horizon or anything.

The Dark rushed her at mind-blowing speed. She turned to face it. Would she lose herself in there? Would it call on the Darkness inside her to finally take her over? Would she turn against the children in her madness?

She braced herself to fire on the Dark. She didn't know what she would be able to do, but she would go down fighting either way.

Right at that moment, a tumbling ball of Dark fibers rocketed out of nowhere. It came from behind her and streaked past her at high speed.

It collided with the Dark Layer moving in to catch her.

The impact smashed the ball into a million tiny fragments of Darkness scattered in the confusion, but the blow also shattered the Dark Layer.

The Layer imploded and an almighty sucking force ripped Eliska and the children through the breach.

She barely had time to see Anríq getting pulled through along with them.

The next instant, the whole party blasted into another Layer beyond—a Layer full of more disembodied mouths not attached to any kind of creature.

Fangs studded every mouth and they all turned on the travelers. Eliska yanked herself from one side to the other shooting everything in sight.

Anríq pounded the mouths with his club, exploded them with magical blasts, and fought his way closer to the children to protect them.

He and Eliska took positions on opposite sides of the cluster, but the momentum that threw them into this Layer kept pulling them sideways at the same speed.

Gravity seemed to work sideways instead of down—or maybe the Layers got twisted around the wrong way.

Eliska didn't see where the party was going. She had to fight her hardest just to keep the mouths away from herself and the children. She couldn't get near enough to Anríq to help him.

Anthane got her attention by throwing out his arm and pointing. "Look, Eliska! There's another one!"

She glanced over her shoulder and almost forgot to keep fighting when she saw another Dark Layer moving in from the same direction. Vidal wasn't here to save her this time.

She spun around to face it. "Anríq!" she roared over her shoulder. "Anríq—help me!"

"I'm coming!" he yelled back.

She didn't dare to turn around to see what he was doing. Explosive booms kept thumping from his club. The mouths roared and screeched back there.

Without warning, another mouth whizzed past Eliska heading for the Dark Layer. It collided with a bunch of other mouths as though some unstoppable force threw it in that direction.

Anríq held onto one of the mouth's fangs and let go just as the thing passed Eliska. He twisted into position next to her.

"I'll strike it with my club as hard as I can!" he yelled over the noise. "You hit it with everything you got! Understand?"

She didn't really, but she nodded anyway. At least someone had a plan to get them out of this.

He whirled away and attacked another mouth coming at him from behind. He hammered his club into the mouth only to get caught by another one rushing him from behind the children.

The mouth slammed into him before he had a chance to hit it—or maybe he didn't want to hit it.

He grabbed one of the fangs and let the mouth carry him within striking range of the Dark Layer.

The mouth veered away just in time to avoid plunging into the Dark.

He let go, spun away, and raised his club. "NOW, ELISKA!!"

She fired at the same instant he struck out with his club. He smashed it into the Layer and she concentrated all her firepower on hitting the same spot.

A catastrophic explosion went off and the Layer blasted inward with brutal force. The eruption slammed Eliska backward. She couldn't let herself, Anríq, and the children get sucked back into the chaos.

She swept her staff in a circle, caught all of them together, and transported all of them straight into the Darkness in front of her.

She had to fight through hurricane winds. Stinging vapors slashed her face and body. She heard screaming behind her and Anríq roaring.

She stretched her magic as far as it would go in all directions to surround anyone close enough to fall under her protection.

She shut her eyes and dug deep to get through the next few seconds. Nothing else mattered. She just had to get Anríq and the children to the Lake Country. He would take them the rest of the way.

Another bone-crushing smash hit her from somewhere. She didn't take the time to see what she was bumping into.

She jammed the end of her staff into it and unloaded every particle of the magic she still had left.

The whole world blasted in her face and then the party crashed down into a deep body of freezing cold water.

Chapter 53

Eliska broke the water's surface and paddled there trying to figure out where she was and what happened.

Eloi spluttered a few feet from her, submerged, and started to sink. The girl flailed her tiny arms, but she couldn't hold herself up.

Eliska grabbed her and lifted Eloi back up to the surface, but the rest of the children floundered all around her. She couldn't get to them all in time.

Anríq stroked from one child to the next grabbing them. They clung to his big body, but he couldn't save them all, either.

Eliska fired her staff under the water and created a shelf for them all to stand on. She lifted the shelf to the surface until they could all stand up with their heads out of the water.

The children gasped, sobbed, and retched water out of their lungs. The sun shone on a crystal blue lake surrounded by towering mountains.

"That's it!" Anthane gasped and pointed up at the highest mountain. "That's the orphanage! We made it! We're in the Lake Country!"

Some of the other children laughed. Others started crying.

Eliska pulled them against her. "It's all right. We're going to be all right now. Come on. Let's get out of the water and dry all of you off."

She raised the shelf a little higher. The water dropped to everyone's ankles.

Eliska and Anríq didn't put the children down. Those who could walk accompanied them in a group across the shelf to dry land. Eliska made the shelf move with them so they could all walk on it all the way there.

The children collapsed on the grass while Eliska and Anríq built a fire. She took off the children's clothes and hung them on sticks over the fire to dry.

She would have wrapped them in her cloak to keep them warm, but it wasn't big enough for all of them.

In the end, she constructed another mud hut around them and over the fire with all of them inside it.

She made it big enough for Anríq to join them this time. None of the children shrank away from him or treated him as anything other than one of them.

She took off as many of her own clothes as she could appropriately get away with and hung them up, too.

"I'm hungry," Cheseli complained.

"I'll go." Anríq stood up.

Eliska opened her mouth to protest, but in the end, she only wound up saying, "Thank you."

He left her alone with the children. "He's nice," Cheseli remarked after he left. "He isn't a monster at all."

"I told you so," Eliska countered. "That was very rude of you to say. I'm sure you hurt his feelings by treating him that way and saying he would eat you."

"He didn't hear me," the girl pointed out. "He was outside."

"He's a magic-user. He heard you. Believe me."

"Should we do something about that?" Thaddi asked. "Should we apologize?"

"Don't say anything. Just be nice to him—as nice as he's being to you."

"I didn't think a Barbarian could be that nice," Dalana murmured.

"He isn't like other Barbarians."

"Definitely not," Dalana exclaimed.

"What game should we play tonight?" Anthane asked.

"Show us how well you've mastered your hand window," Eliska told him.

He turned bright red. "I haven't had time to practice."

"You've had all day and I've seen you looking at it. Show me what you can do."

He stuck out his hand, but he refused to look at her.

A flow of magic sparkled into his hand and started to form a watery surface. It wavered and turned into a glassy, crystal film.

Without warning, a rocket of fireworks spurted out of the pool. They shot around the hut and exploded in sparklers, fizzing pinwheels, and starbursts.

The children screamed in terror and cowered from the sparks. Then it was all over.

Anthane bowed his head in shame and buried his closed fist in his lap. Dead silence fell over the hut.....and then Thaddi started laughing.

His laughter spread through the group and the whole group busted up laughing. Eliska found herself joining in.

Anthane looked up. She smirked at him.

A grin slowly split across his face and then he dissolved in relieved laughter, too. The children fell over themselves rolling on the floor.

"Do it again, Anthane!" Dalana yelled over the noise. "Do it again!"

Anthane glanced at Eliska and she nodded. She was laughing too hard to speak.

He hesitated, extended his hand, and slowly uncurled his fingers. A hush fell over the children...and then another geyser of sparks shot around the hut.

The children all laughed louder and longer this time. The little ones tried to grab the starbursts.

Anthane kept it up for a long time before everyone collapsed from exhaustion. The children fell over each other panting and flushed with pleasure.

Eliska beamed at him. "That was great—much better than the hand window. You're going to be a great magic-user."

He burst into a huge grin of pride. "What can I learn next?"

She nodded at a pile of sticks next to the fire. "Let me see you set fire to those."

He frowned at them....and kept frowning at them.

He was still sitting there glaring at the sticks when Anríq came back with a skinned long-tailed gar. "I don't think this country has any waterbuck."

"It doesn't matter because we'll be going to the orphanage in the morning."

"What game should we play tonight, Eliska?" Cheseli asked.

She cast a heartfelt gaze around the hut. "I don't think I want to play a game tonight. I just want to stay with you all and talk."

They talked, but she didn't talk much unless one of the children asked her something.

The truth started to sink in, now that she finally got them here. Tomorrow morning, she and Anríq would take the children up to the orphanage. Then she would have to say goodbye.

She still didn't see how she would ever be able to walk away from them, but she would have to. She knew that now.

Whatever happened to her on this trip, it wouldn't be denied anymore. The rest of the world needed her help and service. She couldn't turn her back on that.

So many people needed her help. She wouldn't be able to help them all. She just had to help the person standing in front of her.

She wouldn't be able to stay anywhere for long. She would be able to stay and connect with people even less than she did when she lived only for herself.

The world would always call her away to continue her journey and to do what she could wherever she could do it. She no longer had a choice about that.

She always had a choice, but this overwhelming drive to do something—to make things better—it wouldn't leave her alone. She couldn't live any other way, now that she tasted what it really felt like.

She and Anríq fell into a comfortable rhythm of cooking the food, fetching water from the lake, adjusting the children's clothes to dry evenly, and then bedding them down for the night.

The hut stayed warm enough that they didn't need to get dressed. They dropped off one after another and left Anríq and Eliska sitting up alone.

"You don't play with the children the way you did in Tenby," she observed.

"You're doing it perfectly well on your own. They don't need me to do it and they don't want me to do it. They want you."

She flushed and looked away. "It wasn't deliberate."

"It wasn't deliberate. It was natural. The way you behave around them comes naturally to you—and to them. They have every right to feel attached to you."

She couldn't answer.

He didn't ask what she would do tomorrow when the group made it to the orphanage.

She never told him about her decision to become a Servant—or whatever the hell this was that she was becoming.

She didn't tell him what happened to her on this trip.

"What will you do after this?" she asked.

"I already told you. I'll go back to Tenby." He looked up. "You said you would go back. Did you change your mind?"

"I just thought...." She opened her mouth and faltered. Should she tell him?

He stared at her waiting for her to finish. "Why wouldn't you go back?"

"Because.....if I went back.....I would lose my magic again....and so would you."

"And?" he prompted.

"And don't you think you could do more good for people out here with your magic? What could you really do in Tenby?"

"I would fight the Darklings—or whatever comes after the town." He bent over the fire again. "I would go back because the Watch needs me. Yann needs me."

"What about everyone else in the world who needs you?"

"Everyone else in the world will always need me. I don't know who they are or where they are or what they need me to do, but I do know who the Watchmen are and where they are and what they need me to do. I know their mission is a good one and I know I'll be helping everyone in the whole Coil by helping them. That's why I would go back."

"But I wouldn't be able to help them. I can't fight Darklings on the wall the way you can."

"You did help them. You did fight Darklings on the wall. None of the Watch would have survived that last battle without you and Marine defending them. I wouldn't have survived, either. We're all alive because you were there."

She looked away. She couldn't accept that.

He didn't break the silence and she fell back into her own thoughts.

His assurance didn't answer any of her questions. She already knew she had to leave the children at the orphanage. Her new path demanded it.

Did that mean turning her back on the Watch, too? Didn't her new path demand that, too? How could she forsake the whole world for three men?

That was all the Watch had left—three men.

If Yann, Yvan, and Rien were worth it to Anríq, why shouldn't they be worth it to her?

Didn't she hold up Anríq as the example of what a Servant should be? If he thought losing his magic by going back to Tenby was a good idea, who was she to argue with that?

She wasn't even a Servant—not really. She was just a wannabe pretending to be a Servant—so how did she really know what the right answer was?

He always seemed to know the answer, but he didn't outright tell her she should go back. He said he was going back.

He didn't answer any of her questions. Of course he didn't. Only she could do that.

Chapter 54

E liska took a deep breath, hoisted the two children into her arms and onto her back, and started the last treacherous climb to the orphanage.

It clung to the rocks high on the mountainside. She used her hand window to locate a tiny, crooked path up the cliffs. No one could see it from the ground.

The party fell silent on the way up there. Did the children realize they were about to say goodbye to Anríq and Eliska—probably forever?

She rehearsed exactly what she would say to them to explain why she had to leave, but she already knew it didn't matter. Whatever she planned to say would go right out the window when the time came.

She cherished these last precious moments of carrying Eloi in her arms. Eliska's own fatigue felt like the greatest blessing of her life.

She kept dropping kisses on the little girl's head. Did Eloi even understand why?

Eliska could have kept carrying these children forever if she had to. She could have carried all ten of them at the same time. Anything would have been better than coming to the end of this journey where she had to put them down.

She didn't look up to see how close the group was getting to the orphanage. She didn't want to know.

She disappeared into a timeless state. There was no orphanage. There was no destination. There would be no parting at the end of this.

She would just keep walking for the rest of eternity. Every moment would pass exactly like this one.

The children were still with her. They would always be with her. They would never leave. She never had to say goodbye—not ever.

The sun slipped behind the mountains before the group made it to the entrance doors. The sunset cast the mountains in colors and then shadow.

She stopped in front of the doors and everyone else stopped. They made it.

A magnificent panorama of mountains and clear blue lakes spread out to the distant horizon. It was one of the most stunningly beautiful Islands she'd ever seen in her life.

She lowered Eloi to the ground and the little boy climbed down. The children all gathered around to stare at the orphanage entrance. Were they really going in there? Were they really going to do this?

No one moved to break the spell. That left Eliska to do it.

She climbed the steps, turned the giant wrought-iron doorknob, pushed the door open, and the children followed her into a tall, tiled hall that echoed with their footsteps.

Anríq inched through the door behind them and left it standing open.

Eliska and the children stood in the entrance hall looking around at everything. The orphanage might once have been a castle that had fallen into disrepair.

Carved marble cornices surrounded every doorway and window frame, but they all showed plenty of chips and other signs of age. Paint peeled from the vaulted carved ceilings.

An enormous chandelier hung from the ceiling directly over the entrance hall, but dust and cobwebs hung from its many crystal prisms.

A giant sweeping staircase rose from one side of the entrance hall to a broad landing overlooking the hall from the second story.

While Eliska and the children stood there taking it all in, a woman stepped out of a side room and saw them.

The woman kept her hair pulled back in a strict knot behind her head. She wore a full-length black dress with no decoration and the collar buttoned tightly around her throat.

She raised her eyebrows at the party. "Can I help you?"

"Um....yes," Eliska blurted out. "These are the children Aline, Athanes, and the others were bringing to stay here. All the other adults died on the journey, so my friend and I brought the children the rest of the way. Aline said you were expecting them."

The woman shot a critical glance at Anríq, but she cast an even more critical glance at Eliska. "Who are you?" the woman demanded. "How do you come to take responsibility for someone else's children?"

"We're just travelers," Eliska mumbled. "We're no one. We just saw the children in danger and stepped in to help. That's the only reason. We wouldn't have if the other adults had been around to do it."

"How did they die?" the woman demanded. "You better not have had anything to do with it."

Eliska narrowed her eyes and got ready to launch into a full-scale assault on this woman. How dare she accuse Eliska of having anything to do with the adults' deaths?

Dalana cut in a lot more harshly than Eliska would have. "Eliska didn't have anything to do with their deaths," Dalana snapped. "They were all dead by the time Eliska found us except for Aline—and she died right after that. Eliska saved us—more than once."

"Yeah," Thaddi added. "We wouldn't be here now if not for Eliska."

"She played games with us," Eloi piped up. "Aline and the others never did that." The little girl cocked her head and gave the woman an extra piercing glare. "Do you play games?"

The woman clamped her mouth shut in a big hurry. "You children come inside. You're only four months late. We thought you were all dead in the Coil."

"You wished we were, you mean," Anthane snarled.

Eliska saw the situation about to fall apart around her ears. "That's enough, all of you. We're here now. You'll all be safe."

"Do you really have to leave, Eliska?" Cheseli asked. "Can't you stay a little longer?"

"I don't think our hosts would appreciate that—and our friends in the Black Watch need us to come back and help them defend their town."

She dropped all effort to keep herself together. She put her arms around Dalana and then Anthane.

"I'm going to miss you all." Her throat constricted and she let the words fall out of her mouth without even trying. "I love you. I love you all."

"You're the best, Eliska," Anthane mumbled into her shirt. "I'll never forget you."

"Will we ever see you again, Eliska?" Cheseli quavered and then burst into tears.

Eliska pivoted over to her and put her arms around the girl. Eliska couldn't hug all of them fast enough or long enough. "I sure hope so, precious angel. I really hope so."

She felt herself starting to lose it, so she tore herself away.

"Look. I want each of you to have these." She pulled out the colored stone and placed each one in some child's hand.

She should have taken more time to individualize each gift and make sure that the right stone went to the right child.

She couldn't stand to drag this out any longer than she absolutely had to. She rushed through it and handed out the stones in a blur.

"Take these and remember me when you look at them. Remember what I told you about becoming a great magic-user, Anthane. Don't any of you let anyone tell you that you can't become something great. Do you understand? I'll always be with you. I promise you that."

She kissed each of them as fast as she could and turned away before she broke down right in front of them. She didn't want them to see her crumble. This would be hard enough for them as it was.

Anríq didn't get involved. He just stood back out of the way and waited for her to be ready to leave.

She finally forced herself to step back. "You children be good and do your best in school. Don't be like me. Get an education and make something of yourselves."

"We will," Thaddi replied.

"Bye, Eliska," Dalana murmured.

Cheseli was crying too hard to say anything.

"Bye, Eliska," Anthane choked.

The woman moved in and steered the children toward a room behind the staircase. She didn't even bother to introduce herself to Eliska.

Eliska blocked the woman out of her mind. She inched backward toward the door and watched the children get farther away. Anthane raised his hand to wave goodbye to her.

She raised hers to wave back and the children blurred in her tears.

She clamped her eyes shut and turned away. She didn't want to be here anymore.

She considered magicking Anríq down the mountain. She could find the route back to Tenby from there. She wanted to put the Lake Country behind her forever.

A distant rumble snapped her eyes open. She found herself looking straight through the open entrance door at the beautiful landscape dotted with lakes.

The mountains surged out of position and blasted upward to stratospheric heights. A wave of destruction whipped down the mountain range impossibly fast, overtook the orphanage, and all those mountains erupted into giants.

They reared out of the bedrock, bellowed to the skies, and then morphed into enormous creatures rampaging across the landscape.

Their massive feet thundered through the floor and then a brutal explosion hit the orphanage.

Eliska spun around and dove for the door leading to the room where the woman took the children.

Eliska's one thought was to get to the children before those giant creatures brought down the whole mountain on top of the children's heads.

Anríq lunged for her to grab her and pull her back, but neither of them made it more than a few feet.

The floor flipped up in a breaking wave. The tiles shattered apart and then a brutal smash collapsed the roof over Eliska's head.

The avalanche pounded down on top of her and Anríq. She barely fired her staff in time to create a sphere of protection around both of them, but not even that could protect them from this.

The cave-in flattened Eliska and Anríq onto their stomachs on the floor. Her field compressed and almost snapped.

Just as fast, an almighty sucking wind from some Layer ripped all the rubble away from the destroyed building. The roof and all the rock and debris stripped upward and tore Anríq and Eliska with it.

She caught one glimpse of the scene of destruction tearing the mountains apart. The orphanage wasn't there anymore. The mountains weren't there anymore.

They disintegrated as one giant after another rocketed out of the surface, changed into some hideous creature, and then stormed off to pulverize whatever was left of the Island.

Eliska's sphere soared farther and farther away through the Layers. Vapor and shadow closed in front of her to block her view of the Lake Country, but the Island no longer existed.

An answering undulation of chaos and mayhem spread across the countryside and obliterated everything in its path.

Chapter 55

E liska flung herself down next to one of the living trees, buried her face in her arms, and burst into tears. She didn't care anymore that Anríq was standing right there watching her.

She poured out all her despair over this and everything else that happened. She couldn't take this. She couldn't give everything she had to these children only to lose them on the very threshold of the orphanage they all worked so hard to find.

She could just imagine what Anríq was thinking about her right now. He probably wanted to hurry up and get back to Tenby before some other disaster struck.

Without warning, he sat down next to her and put his arm around her. She lost it completely when he touched her. She couldn't take this.

He didn't say anything. His silence somehow made this so much worse. How could she survive this? She didn't want to survive this.

The sensation of the children hugging her still imprinted on her skin through her clothes. Her body would never be the same, now that she'd felt that. She couldn't unfeel it.

She would always remember the feeling of Cheseli shaking with sobs because Eliska was about to leave. She would always remember Anthane's broken undertone and his breath puffing through her shirt when he said he would never forget her.

She didn't know what to think when Anríq shifted his arm and started running his fingers through her hair. It was nothing more than what she'd been doing to those children all these nights. Jesus, what was she going to do now?

She couldn't follow this path if she started to care about everyone this much. She never cared about anyone this much—not ever.

Now she knew why she held everyone at a distance for so long. She didn't want to feel this. She didn't want to care about people she could never have.

The pain building inside her became unbearable. It burst out of her in rage. She grabbed the first thing that came to her hand, which turned out to be her staff.

She hurled it away and it struck another tree, bounced off, and landed on the ground.

She glared at it still sobbing her guts out. She hated her staff. She hated her magic. She hated everything about her life if something like this could happen.

As soon as it landed, she buckled under an oppressive weight of anguish. She covered her face and dissolved in tears. She couldn't remember ever crying this hard in her life, not even when she was little and alone in the Coil.

She couldn't cry then. She didn't even understand then what she'd lost. She didn't lose anything because, by the time she realized, it was all already gone.

Why did she have to find out? Why did she finally have to learn what love was—only to have it snatched away at the last minute?

She could have lived with knowing the children were alive and safe at the orphanage. She could have walked away and never seen them again.

Why did the Island have to collapse while she was still in it? Why couldn't it wait just a few more minutes until she and Anríq returned to Tenby?

Then she never would have known. She would have lived her whole life thinking she did her job by getting the children to safety.

Anríq took his arm down, but he didn't go away. He stayed there sitting at her side no matter what.

He would never leave. She knew that now. He would sit there forever until she said she was ready to go.

How could she? How could she go on after such a colossal failure? How could she face the Watch again—or anyone who wanted her help?

This path offered her one hope to redeem herself and she botched that in the worst possible way.

She never should have taken the children to the orphanage. She should have kept them in the wilderness and protected them for the rest of her life. Then they would be alive right now.

Vidal gave his life to help her get the children to the orphanage. That went to waste, too. Christ, what was she thinking even imagining she could be a Servant?

That outburst of tears eventually came to an end, but the pain didn't go away. She straightened up, but her raw, puffy face only bore testimony to the agony in her heart.

It would never go away. It would add its poison to the growing well of Darkness that was her innermost being.

She stared at the ground in front of her. The trees no longer talked to her. They probably realized by now that the children died on her watch.

That woman had been right to question Eliska's right to take responsibility for those children. Eliska was rot and corruption to anyone who came near her.

How could she go back to the Watch like this? Vidal knew better. He knew to separate himself from the Watch to protect them. He never wanted them to know the truth and he was right.

Anríq sat in silence for what might have been hours. After a while, he got up and walked off into the trees. That would be just perfect if he left her, too. She deserved it after today.

He didn't leave. He came back a few minutes later with the wooden bowl they'd been using to fetch water for the children.

He sat down next to her and held the bowl out to her. "Drink this."

She took it and drank it, but as soon as she put it down, she started crying again. The children just held this bowl a few hours ago.

"They're all gone, Anríq!" she wailed. "They're all gone!"

"I know," he murmured back.

"Wesh—Barsali—Omer—They're all gone!" She broke down in wretched sobs thinking about all of them. "What's the point of caring about people if they're all going to die?!"

"The point is to care about them," he murmured back. "What else is there but to care about people?"

She couldn't stand that. She folded under the weight of unbearable grief. She couldn't care about people. She couldn't survive the pain, but she did care about them. That was the real problem.

The more she cared about them, the more it hurt, but she couldn't stop herself. Overpowering love cracked her heart in half when she thought about each of those children. Their memories burned a hole in her mind.

She loved them more now than she did before. How could she survive that?

The same unstoppable love overflowed her being when she thought about all of them. Wesh. Barsali. Omer. Neils. Niyazi.

She even felt that for Yann, Yvan, Rien, Marine.....and Anríq. She couldn't stop the torrent once it started.

It poured out through this crack in her heart and through her eyes. She'd never felt any pain as bad as this.

She really hoped she never felt it ever again, but she already knew she would. It would torment her forever. She would never be able to stop it.

She went through a confused tempest of emotions all competing against each other and trying to destroy each other.

What was her life worth without this? What was the point of wandering through the Coil with no one?

Now she had someone. She had a whole bunch of people.

Wesh, Barsali, and all the others cared about her. They cared about her as much as she cared about them.

Yann and everyone in Tenby cared about her. They wanted her back with or without magic.

They all needed her—and not for her magic. They needed her as much as she needed them. She would never be able to turn her back on that.

Anríq left again after a while. He walked away while she remained sitting under the trees.

They rustled their branches. She hated to think of them finding out that the children were dead.

Her eyes welled up when she thought of all the care and attention the trees gave the children. They went so far out of their way to help the children and protect them. She couldn't bear to tell the trees the truth.

Anríq came back a little while later with another gar. He lit a fire and set the skinned gar over the flames to cook.

She saw him going through all the motions of service. He was taking care of her the way she needed him to.

He wasn't capable of doing anything else. The children's deaths didn't change anything for him. He just kept helping the person in front of him at any given moment.

She kicked herself for not talking to him more. She was really terrible company right now, but he didn't care about that. He never cared about anything like that.

He just went on fulfilling his mission. He would always fulfill his mission no matter where he went. He wouldn't stop just because some of the people he helped died in a random disaster.

He cut cooked meat off the gar carcass and handed it to her before he served himself. The two of them had been going through the same routine since they first met.

She took the food out of his hand and ate it. She owed him that much. She owed the world that much and a hell of a lot more.

The gar was too big for the two of them. He took the leftovers off the spit, stripped all the extra meat off the bones, and wrapped it in a piece of hide in one of his bags.

She finally broke the silence by croaking, "I'm sorry I don't know any games."

He glanced up at her. The look in his eyes made her tears well up again.

She wouldn't fall asleep holding Eloi tonight. Eliska's arms felt so empty without the little girl sitting on her lap and curling up to go to sleep.

Anríq broke eye contact to turn away and rummage in his bags. She didn't think anything of it until he turned back in her direction and held out something.

She took it and looked down at one of the green colored stones from the stream. It was exactly the same kind she'd used to entertain the children.

It flickered and glinted in the firelight, but she didn't hold it up to make prisms and patterns. She couldn't stand that.

She revolted at first that she gave all her stones to the children. She didn't even keep one for herself to remember them by.

Now he gave her one. He was the only person alive who knew what it meant.

A bright green prism forked across her vision when the light struck her tears. The stone blurred, but the memory didn't.

Chapter 56

Yann strode down the wall checking everything. He stopped next to one of the rocket launchers.

Rosh and two other men lay on their backs under the pedestal. "How's it coming along?" Yann asked.

"Almost there." Rosh gasped and handed his tools to the man next to him. "Five minutes—tops."

"As soon as you finish, send Nestor to bring up some more rockets," Yann ordered and continued down the line.

The Tenby defenders worked all over the wall to load their rifles, bring up fresh crates of ammunition, and fortify the scaffold.

Yann made it back to the gate and met up with Rien. Yann inspected Rien extra closely. He'd been down for the count with nightmares since last night.

Yann didn't expect him to come back, but here he was.

"What's the story?" Yann asked.

"Your father is coming up," Rien murmured.

Yann stiffened. His father had been going back and forth between functioning on the wall and getting locked in his bedroom to stop him from attacking anyone. He and Rien had become increasingly unpredictable these last few days.

Yann couldn't change his plans at the eleventh hour, so he went back to checking the defenders.

He surveyed the landscape beyond the wall, but only for a second. He already knew what was going on out there.

The veil of chaos that threatened the town kept moving off. It didn't come back, but that didn't help anyone.

The landscape all around Tenby kept disintegrating in random eruptions. The veil didn't make any difference anymore.

Blasts kept ejecting out of the ground all around the town and shot hails of dirt clods and rock shards flying through the air.

Fire, torrential rain, blizzards, tornadoes, and more curtains of wild magic swept back and forth across the landscape. Some of these hit the town, but just as many came within feet, miles, or even inches of missing.

The tension and confusion kept everyone jumping at the slightest sound—and the disintegrating situation offered plenty of sounds for everyone to jump at.

Booms, blasts, explosions, and crackles of lightning echoed across the countryside. Everyone's nerves inside Tenby were nearing the breaking point.

Yann didn't know when the hammer would fall on Tenby. No one could possibly know when it would happen or what form it would take when the Coil finally wiped this town out of existence.

It would happen soon, though. Everyone knew that and raced to prepare as much as possible.

All these disruptions and landscape changes didn't seem to indicate Darklings attacking. When it happened, Yann didn't think Darklings would be the ones to do it, but anything was possible.

He armed the defenders just the same. Better to be armed and not need it than to be unarmed when they needed it.

The landscape outside the walls had gotten too chaotic for anyone to go outside without risking their lives. It wasn't safe to pasture the Chivalric Order of Custodians' horses out there anymore, either.

Yann arranged to move the horses to some of the larger gardens in the center of town. The gardens had lawns and woods big enough for the horses to graze in safety.

Rosh and his companion finished working on the rocket launcher. They stood up to give it one final check.

Yann turned away to climb down the scaffold to the ground. He had a dozen more stations to check before nightfall.

He spotted Marine crossing the town on her way home from O'akim's library. She saw him at the same time, smiled up at him, and waved.

He waved back and smiled—and then his smile evaporated when he saw his father come out of the Black Watch's house.

Yvan paused on the doorstep and looked up at Yann, too. Yann didn't know what to expect from his father. Yvan must be feeling better if he came outside.

Yvan no longer tried to assert his authority with Yann or anyone else. Everyone in Tenby just accepted now that Yann was Commander of the Watch.

Someone had to do it and no one could count on Yvan to function one hundred percent of the time. Only Yann could do that.

Yann started down the stairs to the ground. He had to assess his father's mental state before Yann did anything else.

He really wished he didn't have to constantly check on both his father and Rien just to find out if they were fit to go on duty—or even to leave the house.

Yann put his foot on the steps when Rosh called out, "Sir! Look! We got company!"

Yann sprang up to the top of the wall again. Every man around him straightened up to stare across the countryside.

The veil hovered a few miles away. All the explosions, earthquakes, and wild weather patterns in between posed a much bigger threat.

Yann caught a glimpse of two people coming through the veil in the distance. He couldn't see them clearly.

"Get on that rocket launcher!" he snapped to his side. "Arm all defenders and prepare to fire!"

Two dozen men flattened themselves behind the wall and rested their loaded rifles across it. Rosh sprang onto the rocket launcher and swiveled the tubes toward the veil.

Word traveled fast down the wall and more men brought up their weapons to defend Tenby. Yann still didn't see more than two small figures coming out of the mayhem, but he didn't want to take any chances.

Rien pulled up behind him and then Yvan climbed up the scaffold. No one moved or breathed for a second.

The strangers stepped through the veil into the confused jumble of rock geysers and whipping clouds of vapor, sleet, and flying particles caught in the wind.

The two figures burst into a run heading straight for Tenby. They crossed a hundred yards before Yann recognized Anríq and Eliska coming in fast.

"Hold your fire!!" he bellowed down the wall. "Lower your rifles and hold your fire!"

The word went down, but no one backed off. Rosh stayed where he was and so did everyone else.

Yann whirled away. No one better shoot Anríq and Eliska—not after Yann had been counting down the hours until they came back.

He shoved past his father and Rien, but neither of them tried to stop him. They followed him down the scaffold on his way to open the gate.

Right at that moment, at the worst possible time, Amaury Marais came out of his house and hustled over to intercept Yann.

"Our augury indicates the Voyant will attack this town tomorrow at dawn," Marais began.

"Not now," Yann snapped out the side of his mouth.

"We have to organize now," Marais insisted. "We have to be ready to meet him when he comes."

Yann lost control for a second, turned his head, and barked, "I said not now!" before he thought to stop himself.

Marais opened his mouth to say something—and saw Yvan and Rien both following Yann to the gate.

Marais knew by now who was the real Commander of the Black Watch in this town. Marais had gotten in Yann's face more than once to insist on consulting Yvan when he was indisposed.

Yann turned his back on Marais and hauled open the gate, but Anríq and Eliska took a long time to get across the open country between the veil and Tenby.

The landscape exploded all around them. Eliska fired magical blasts from her staff, but those died away within a few yards of the veil. Her magic and Anríq's vanished as soon as they set foot across the margin.

After that, they just had to run for it. A brutal eruption of rock jutted out of the ground right in front of Eliska. The land tilted up and nearly knocked her over.

She teetered for a second and Anríq turned back to help her, but she recovered and sprinted over the rock to the other side.

Both of them kept getting caught in wild weather and magical whirlwinds. He stumbled and she dodged aside to intercept him.

She grabbed his arm to help him just as a whipping sheet of Dark energy bore down on both of them.

She turned her back to it, took the lash across her shoulders, and roared out in pain, but she didn't move until it passed.

She dragged Anríq to his feet and pulled him forward until they both ran full speed again.

Yann grabbed his glaive in both hands and stormed through the gate with a group of armed men around him. They pivoted in all directions trying to see any Darklings coming out of the confusion, but none came.

Anríq and Eliska charged into their group panting hard.

"Come inside!" Yann yelled over the noise. "Get out of the wind!"

He pushed them behind him, scanned the surroundings one more time, and he and the defenders backed through the gate before Yvan slammed it shut.

The wind died once they got inside, but the whirling clouds of vapor and debris came right up to the walls before they drifted farther away.

Eliska looked up into the colored swirls racing across the sky. "This is bad!" she murmured. "This is so much worse than when I left."

"It only keeps getting worse," Yann told her. "We won't last more than another day at the most before the whole thing blows up."

"Is the Voyant doing it?" she asked. "Does he keep attacking?"

"He never attacks," Rien replied. "He always just stands out there glowing like he usually does. He sends the landscape to do his attacking for him."

"And he's shown up while you've been away," Yann added. "Which proves he's after something other than you."

"It makes no sense," she exclaimed. "No one in Tenby is after him or threatening him or even thinking about taking his power."

"The Chivalric Order is trying to threaten him," Yvan pointed out.

"They aren't succeeding, though, are they?" Rien countered. "I don't see them threatening anyone.....except Yann."

"They aren't threatening me, either," Yann replied over his shoulder and turned back to Anríq and Eliska. He couldn't help but grin when he looked at her. "I'm so glad you made it back. I was really worried."

Her cheeks colored and she smiled back up at him. "It's really good to be back. I missed you guys."

"What took you so long? Did you stabilize the margin like you said you would? Anríq said he would bring you straight back, but he wound up staying gone a lot longer than we expected."

She opened her mouth to say something, but right then, Amaury Marais came back over to them. "I'm afraid I really must insist, Watch Commander. If our augury is right and the Voyant will attack tomorrow morning, then we have to prepare the defenses now. If not now, then when?"

Yann compressed his lips. He couldn't lose his patience with this man again.

Yann got Anríq and Eliska back. He could finally take the time to deal with Marais.

Yann turned around to face him. "All right. I'm available now. What would you like to talk about the defenses? How would you like to prepare them in ways we aren't already preparing them? As you can see, we're already doing everything possible to defend the town."

"You haven't recruited anyone to launch an assault on the Voyant."

"I already told you I wouldn't let anyone from Tenby participate in any assault against the Voyant. If you want to assault the Voyant, you can take your men and go do that outside the walls."

Marine's voice broke in on their conversation as she caught up with the group. "It's worse than that. If you assault the Voyant—even outside the walls—the instability could backfire on us and destroy the town even if we don't take part in the assault."

Yann waved at her. "You see? I'm afraid I'm the one who really must insist. I can't let you endanger the whole town by assaulting the Voyant."

"Then what are you going to do to defeat him?" Marais demanded. "I don't have to stand here and listen to the judgment of children on matters that affect millions of people."

"I don't see how we can defeat him," Yann replied. "I don't see how anyone can, but I know no one can defeat him by attacking him head-on. I don't know what augury you're using to divine his plans, but it obviously isn't powerful enough to defeat him or you would have done it already. He's the most powerful magic-user in the Coil. He controls the whole Coil. For all we know, he *is* the Coil and defeating him would destroy the Coil."

"That's impossible!" Marais fired back.

"Is it? What information do you have that disproves it? What information do you have on the Voyant at all? If the Guardian Templars don't have that information, I don't see how you can have it instead."

Marais glared at him and then spun around to confront Yvan. "Are you just going to stand there and let him talk to me like that? Aren't you going to do anything about this?"

"I would be doing exactly the same thing in his place," Yvan replied. "I've seen everything he's doing, all the preparations he's making, and heard all the orders he's giving. I wouldn't be able to do it better."

Marais jerked back to get in Yann's face and pointed at him inches away from Yann's eyes. "I won't allow an untrained boy to stop me from carrying out this mission. The fate of worlds hangs in the balance. This could be our one chance to defeat the Voyant and you want to piss and whine behind the walls. Fine. You do that. You don't have the backbone to save the Coil, but you won't stop me from doing it. My men and I will go out to battle against the Voyant tomorrow. If you or anyone else tries to get in our way, you'll pay the consequences."

Chapter 57

E liska cringed while she, Anríq, and the rest of their party
watched Amaury Marais storm off back to his house.

His threat against Yann quivered in the air, but when he turned
around and saw Eliska and Anríq standing there, Yann only grinned
again. "Now, where were we when we were so rudely interrupted?"

"Aren't you going to do anything about that?" Eliska asked. "How
are you going to stop him?"

"I'm not going to stop him. I'm going to let him leave."

"You can't let him assault the Voyant!" Marine insisted. "This Layer is already breaking down around our ears. Assaulting the Voyant
would destroy it completely."

"The Layer is going to collapse one way or the other," Yann replied.
"We can't stop that even if I could find a way to keep the knights
inside—which I can't. If they leave, at least we won't have to deal with
them anymore."

Rien sighed. "I suppose it's asking too much to hope the Voyant is
coming after Tenby because of them."

"He can't be," Yvan pointed out. "He was coming after us before
they ever showed up here."

"Forget all that!" Yann clapped Eliska on the shoulder and pulled
her away. "You two come back to the house. I want to hear everything

you've been doing since you left. This calls for celebration and tonight might be our last night. Come on."

He steered her back to their own house. Yvan, Rien, and Marine came with them.

Yann shut the door and blocked out the noise and commotion outside. She took a second before she let herself relax in the familiar living room.

The tension and anxiety keeping Tenby on a hair trigger threatened to snap at any moment. The whole town shivered with pressure ready to explode if anyone made one wrong move.

Yann barely seemed to notice it at all. He went into the kitchen and started taking pots, pans, and food out of the cupboards to make something.

He talked over his shoulder while he worked and then Marine went in there to help him.

"From what I can tell, these people have unlimited supplies of everything," he began. "They never talk about conserving rockets or ammunition or supplies. Don't ask me where they store the stuff. I've searched the whole town."

"We all have," Rien added. "I think they are using magic to do it."

"O'akim would have told me if they were," Marine interjected. "Don't you think they would be using magic to heal their sick people if they could do it that way? They wouldn't have to use these archaic methods of healing."

"Maybe they're keeping that hidden, too," Yvan suggested. "Maybe they have some rules about sharing their secrets with outsiders."

"You would think they would at least share information about the defenses," Yann added. "You would think defending the town would be important enough to at least tell us how many extra rockets we have."

"Maybe they think it isn't important because they have unlimited rockets," Marine chimed in. "Maybe they don't think they need to tell you."

"It can't be that. I've asked a dozen different people a dozen different times. They always manage to change the subject or something happens where they pretend they didn't hear me. They're giving us the runaround."

"Are you really just going to let the knights ride out of here without trying to stop them?" Eliska asked.

He made a face at her across the counter, but he grinned when he did it. He really looked genuinely happy to see her and Anríq back.

"I don't see any profit in trying to stop them from doing anything," he returned. "Trying to get them to do anything would only get us into a fight against the knights and we can't afford that. They've been a thorn in our sides since the day they showed up here. I say let them leave and assault the Voyant or whatever they're going to do. Then they won't be Tenby's problem anymore."

"Tenby won't have any problems anymore because Tenby won't exist anymore," Ricn pointed out.

"Tenby would be on the way out even if the knights never came here." Yann switched off the stove and took a stack of plates out of the cupboard. "All of you better sit down and eat your last meals."

The group dissolved in talk. Yvan took the plates from Yann and set the table while Yann and Marine served.

Everyone sat down, but somehow or other, the subject always steered back to the Tenby situation.

Yann said he wanted to know everything about what happened to Eliska and Anríq on the outside, but neither he nor anyone else ever seemed to get around to asking.

Eliska ate in silence unless someone asked her a specific question. Anríq fell back into his silent ways, too.

Eliska didn't want to talk about what happened in the Layers. She really hoped she lived her entire life without explaining it to anyone.

Anríq knew. He would always know. He became the repository of all her Darkest secrets. He knew about Vidal. He knew about the children.

He probably even knew about her becoming a Servant—or trying to become a Servant. She didn't see how he could watch the way she acted around the children without figuring it out.

He would never tell anyone. She didn't worry about that.

Sharing these secrets with him brought her closer to him somehow, but it also created another level of strain between them that wasn't there before.

She found it difficult to make eye contact with him even when he sat directly across the table from her. She didn't want to see in his eyes that he'd been there for the Darkest moments of her life.

She cared as much about everyone at this table as she ever did, but they didn't really know her—not the way he did.

They would never know the real truth—not unless they somehow found out about what happened to her on that trip.

He carried that secret for her. He alone knew who she really was. He was the one who saw her playing with the children and holding Eloi and carrying them in her arms. He was there when she said goodbye to them. He heard her tell them that she loved them.

She stared down into her plate and suffered another brutal wave of despair thinking about them, but a second later, Marine distracted her by laughing.

"And then O'akim tripped over and the whole tray splattered all over the nurse." Marine dissolved in giggles. "You should have heard her yelling at him. I'm surprised the whole town didn't hear."

Eliska came back to her senses. Anríq wasn't looking at her—not in any serious way. He shoveled his food into his mouth and looked up at each person as they spoke.

"Why do you spend so much time in that library if O'akim doesn't have any information on the Voyant?" Rien asked.

She rolled her eyes to heaven. "There is more to life than the Voyant, Rien. O'akim has books in his library with information not even the Guardian Templars have. I don't think any other town in the entire Coil knows what these people know."

"What about those cities?" Eliska blurted out before she thought to stop herself. "You said they had all the information they needed on their computers."

"What's a computer?" Yann asked.

Marine tried to wave it away. "It's one of those machines. It processes huge stores of information and allows people to communicate over long distances."

"The machines in Tenby look too similar to the machines in that city," Eliska went on. "They have to be related to each other."

Marine shrugged. "You might be right."

"Then it follows that the cities could have all the information in O'akim's library. You were the one who said the people in the cities would be able to find out what the Voyant was up to. If the cities and Tenby are connected, then maybe there's a way to access their knowledge from here."

"How would we do that when Tenby doesn't have computers?" Marine asked.

Now it was Eliska's turn to try to shrug that away. "I don't know. I don't know anything about this stuff. You do."

Marine smirked at her. That was the moment when Eliska realized that everyone at the table was sitting in silence listening to her.

She glanced around and went back to pushing her food around her plate.

"Are you feeling okay?" Yann asked. "You aren't eating."

"I'm just really tired from the journey. I think I'll go get some sleep. Thank you for the food. It was really delicious."

She pushed back her chair and hustled upstairs to the room she once shared with Marine. It looked exactly the same. Of course it did. Eliska and Anríq had only been gone a few days. Marine wouldn't have changed anything.

Eliska stayed upright just long enough to prop her staff next to the bed where she used to keep it. Then she flopped down on the pillow.

It felt good to lie down in a bed instead of on the ground or on a bed of tinder in a leaf hut in the forest, but she couldn't enjoy it.

She buried her face in the pillow and all the memories came rushing back. She would give anything in the world to be slogging over the countryside carrying Eloi in her arms right now.

She must have been more exhausted than she realized. She fell asleep and woke up a few hours later when Marine came in.

The light coming through the window flickered with Dark colors and shadows moving through the vapors outside of town. Night must have fallen.

Marine slipped into the room without turning on the light. "Sorry I woke you up," she whispered.

"That's okay," Eliska replied. "I'm sorry I'm not very good company tonight."

"Don't worry about it!" Marine chirped. "You're tired. You should go back to sleep."

"I guess it will all blow up in our faces again tomorrow."

Marine sighed as she settled down in bed. "I sure wish I could do something for O'akim."

Eliska raised her head. "What do you mean? He obviously loves you."

Marine didn't turn that into a joke. She lowered her voice and it trembled when she murmured in the darkness. "It's the same thing that happened with Brother Matherus and the Temple. It's so hard to get attached to these people knowing something terrible is about to happen to them."

Eliska looked away even though Marine couldn't see her in the dark. "I know."

"I know Yann feels the same way," Marine murmured. "All the Watchmen went through this in Middleborough. Now it's happening again. It will probably keep happening everywhere we go."

"It's amazing how Yann has taken over as Watch Commander," Eliska remarked. "I hardly recognize him."

Marine snickered in the darkness. "He was born for this. He just moved into it so naturally. No one questions him anymore, not even his father. I've never seen Rien so dedicated to anyone."

"It's incredible how confident Yann is. I couldn't believe the way he talked to Marais earlier. I don't think even Yvan could do that."

"It isn't the first time. Yann talks to everyone like that now. He practically runs the whole town."

"I don't know why I thought it would be otherwise. I don't know why I always think of him as a kid when he obviously isn't one."

"Maybe he was one when you first met him, but he changed."

"I can see that. I guess it's been coming for a while now." Eliska glanced over at Marine in the next bed. "I'm sorry about O'akim. I wish there was something we could do."

"We're doing everything we can by giving these people just a few more days of the life they love." She sighed, turned onto her side facing Eliska, and folded her arm under her head. "What about you? How was your trip?"

Eliska shrugged. Thank the stars it was too dark in here for Marine to see Eliska's expression. "There's nothing to tell. We took the children to safety and then we came back."

Marine gave a huge yawn and then sighed. Her voice faded as she drifted off. "That's nice. I'm so glad you made it back."

Eliska didn't answer. She listened to Marine breathing more deeply and she didn't move again. That left Eliska lying awake staring at the ceiling.

That would be her default answer from now on. She got the children to safety. Then she came back to Tenby. It wasn't a lie. No one needed to know the details.

Chapter 58

Yann sat down on the couch in the living room. Anríq sat on the floor across from him, rested his battle axe on his lap, and ran his sharpening stone down the edge of one blade.

"How did the trip go?" Yann asked. "Did something happen to Eliska?"

Anríq didn't look up. "Nothing happened to her. You can see she's fine."

"She isn't fine. She acts like something's bothering her."

"We took the children to safety. It wasn't easy and now we'll be facing another battle in the morning. You can understand all that. She has a lot on her mind, but that's normal for her. She always does."

Yann frowned. "Are *you* okay?"

Anríq looked up for a split second before he went back to work. "I'm fine, Yann. You can see that I am."

"So what happened out there? Why didn't you come back right away?"

"I went out to the margin like you told me to, but Eliska wasn't there. I saw her through the Layers. She was taking care of the children, so I went to see if she needed help. They weren't that far away from Tenby, so I didn't think I would have a problem getting back. Their Layer turned out to be farther away than I thought it was, and once I got there, I couldn't get back on my own. Eliska said she could send me back right away, but she didn't want to leave the children until she got them to safety. All the other adults were already dead, so I decided to stay and help her. That's all that happened. We took the children to an orphanage in the Lake Country and then we came back to Tenby. You know the rest."

Yann frowned at his friend and then let it go. Yann leaned back on the cushions and let himself relax. "I'm really glad you made it back. I was worried."

"I know and I'm sorry I stayed out longer than we planned. I came back as soon as I could—and Eliska never planned to stay out longer than she had to. We wouldn't leave you high and dry."

"Did you see anything out there that might help us? Did you see anything that could help us against the Voyant?"

"We didn't see anything that could help us, but we did see the Voyant. We saw him attacking the countryside—or at least causing the instability."

"What did you see? What was he doing?"

"He was floating in the air the way we've seen him doing before. He was looking out over the countryside while the whole Layer disintegrated. He took out cities, towns—whole landscapes laid to ruin."

He opened his mouth to say something else, stopped himself, and went back to sharpening his axe.

"But if that's true, then he would have been doing that at the same time that we saw him here," Yann pointed out. "He couldn't have been in both places at once."

"He's magical," Anríq reminded him. "I'm sure he wasn't here the whole time and I don't doubt the Voyant could attack two Layers at the same time if he really wanted to. He wasn't here the whole time, was he? I know he wasn't because he wasn't here when Eliska and I came through the veil."

"No, you're right. He wasn't here the whole time." Yann frowned and rubbed his chin. "I wonder what it means."

"It means the Coil is becoming more unstable—and it also means he's getting more involved in causing it to become unstable. He's going after individual Islands. He must want to destroy them specifically for some reason."

"I sure wish he'd make up his mind what he wants to do about us. If he wants to kill us, why doesn't he just strike and try to kill us? If he wants to capture us, I wish he'd hurry up and do it. I don't understand why he keeps fooling around with us—and everyone else."

"I don't understand it, either. I don't think anyone can understand it. Wesh seemed to think these cycles can sometimes take centuries. If that's the case, then all of this will be going on long after we're dead and no one will ever understand it. Even if we could understand it, we can't stop it—certainly not by killing the Voyant—or defeating him or whichever it turns out to be. He's part of the natural cycle. He might be the one causing it, but it will keep happening no matter what we do."

"You don't paint a very hopeful picture of our prospects," Yann countered.

"It's a very hopeful picture of our prospects. It means we aren't responsible for saving or potentially losing millions of lives."

"Then why are you doing all of this? Why are you going through with this if you think there's nothing we can do to change the outcome?"

"What else would I be doing—turning my back on what could be the most important fight in hundreds of years? Eliska asked me to help you and I don't see anyone else even coming close to finding out what the Voyant is doing—much less stopping him. This is the best way I can serve humanity as far as I can tell—regardless of the outcome."

"I guess you're right. I wish I could be as certain as you are."

"The Servant's path is simple. The rest of you have it much harder than we do."

Yann opened his mouth to say something else, but he broke off when he heard footsteps on the stairs.

He got to his feet when his father entered the room. "I heard voices." Yvan frowned at Anríq. Anríq never talked this much around anyone but Yann. "Is everything all right?"

"Everything's fine," Yann replied. "We were just talking about what Anríq and Eliska saw out in the Layers. There's nothing to worry about. You can go back to sleep."

"You boys don't stay up too late, okay?" Yvan turned back to the stairs. "We have a big day tomorrow."

"We won't," Yann called after him.

Yann remained standing until he heard his father go upstairs and shut his bedroom door. Then Yann sat down again.

"You haven't asked him yet, have you?" Anríq asked. "You haven't talked to him about why he joined the Watch and whether he wants you to follow in his footsteps."

Now it was Yann's turn to look away. "No, I haven't. He's been going back and forth with nightmares since you left. He's been confined to his room completely out of his mind more often than he's been outside. I don't want to bring it up—not now."

"Don't you think now is the most important time to bring it up?" Anríq asked. "You said before that you wouldn't get another chance and now you have it. You don't know how much longer you have with him. You better ask him soon."

"I know," Yann mumbled.

"I would ask him tonight if I was in your place."

"I couldn't do that," Yann countered. "It's the middle of the night."

"If the knights are right and the Voyant comes after us tomorrow—or the Island collapses and we have to go on the run again—you might not get another chance."

Yann couldn't look at his friend.

"Why do you hesitate?" Anríq demanded. "Talking to him could give you the clarity you need to make your decision. You wouldn't have to live with the question hanging over your head."

Yann didn't answer. He already knew everything Anríq was saying.

Anríq let his sharpening stone fall in his lap and arched an eyebrow at Yann. "What is wrong with you?"

Yann tried to shrug and wound up squirming. "Maybe it doesn't matter."

"What doesn't?"

"Maybe it doesn't matter why he joined the Watch. Maybe it doesn't matter how he came to have a child before he took his oath. Maybe what he did and what he thinks about it doesn't make any difference. I just have to make my own choice and live my own life."

Anríq laid his axe aside. "That's one way of looking at it, but if you did that, you wouldn't be able to use his opinion and approval to make the decision for you. You couldn't decide to join the Watch because you were worried about letting him and the other Watchmen down."

"There are no other Watchmen," Yann mumbled. "There's just him and Rien."

Now Anríq was the one who didn't answer. That silence weighed Yann down with the oppressive finality of worlds ending.

If Yvan and Rien died, Yann wouldn't have to worry anymore about whether they agreed with his decision to leave the Watch—if he decided to leave the Watch.

He wouldn't have to decide to leave the Watch. He would be out of the Watch one way or the other. He would be alone to do whatever he was going to do.

He had no idea what he would do even if they did survive, but in a way, it didn't matter anymore. His life lay before him for the first time a completely blank canvas for him to write something on it. He just had to figure out what that was.

Chapter 59

Yann stepped outside the house and squinted through sunshine streaming into Tenby. The mass of vapors, Dark Layers, and debris still spiraled in the atmosphere, but this one ray of light shone right inside the town.

He stopped on the doorstep and watched the Chivalric Order of Custodians saddle up their horses. All the knights wore their armor, but they hadn't put on their helms yet.

Townspeople gathered from all over to watch. Yvan, Rien, Anríq, Eliska, and Marine came out of the house behind Yann.

The noise coming from outside the walls built to a thunderous roar. A whirlwind of vapor and flying shrapnel shrieked past the walls, but it still held off for some reason.

The men on the wall all turned around to watch the knights, too. The situation outside Tenby couldn't possibly get any worse.

Marias and his men kept shooting death glares at the Watch, the men guarding the wall, and the gathering townsfolk. The knights didn't try to hide their blatant hostility toward everyone.

Marais went through his men checking their equipment. They gathered their weapons, put on their helms, and mounted up.

Marais left his helm open so everyone could see his face.

He steered his horse into the street and reined the animal to pace up and down in front of the townspeople. "Good people!" he called out. "The Voyant Mendicat plans to demolish the entire Coil and not just you but a lot of other good people along with it. He's out there razing Islands at will, submerging them in chaos, and he'll come for Tenby, too. He already has! Do you really want to stand by and let him get away with that?! Are you so cowardly that you would lie down and die before you raise arms to stop him? My men and I are bound by a sacred oath to fight him, defeat him, and save the Coil—including you! Which one of you has the stomach to join us and become the hero your families and neighbors need you to be?"

No one answered. Yann spotted a few people glancing in his direction.

"You've all been misled about the Voyant's intentions," Marias went on. "He won't spare anyone in this town. He'll slaughter women, children, the elderly—he doesn't care! Our only chance is to defeat him outright and bring order to the Coil."

Yann couldn't listen to this. Marine's warning came back to him.

He stepped out into the street and walked halfway across it so everyone could see him. He didn't get in the way of Marais's horse, but Marais reined the animal to a halt when Yann stopped in front of him.

"Well, Watch Commander?" Marais sneered and dipped his eyes once to Yann's uniform. "Why don't you tell these people the truth about the Voyant's intentions? Why do you let these poor people continue to believe they have a hope of survival as long as the Voyant is still alive?"

Yann surveyed the town. Everyone looked at him now. They all waited for him to say something.

He took a deep breath. "I don't know the Voyant's intentions and neither do you. No one does, and if you want anyone to believe you understand his intentions, you're lying for your own gain. I do know one thing, though." Yann turned to the townspeople, raised his voice, and waved at the knights. "These men don't care about you. These men are going out to fight the Voyant no matter what, even if doing so puts you in danger. Why do you think the Voyant hasn't destroyed Tenby already? He could have. He could have flattened us days ago, but he doesn't do that—not even when shows himself to us. Why? Don't ask these men. They don't know the answer, either—but we do know that anyone who attacks him gets destroyed a hundred times more violently than they attacked him. That's what these men plan to do to Tenby. They plan to go out, attack the Voyant, and Tenby be damned. Anyone who goes out with them will die—and we'll probably all die, too, thanks to their recklessness."

Yann broke off. He could have said a lot more, but he decided to leave it there.

He'd already said as much to most of the defenders on the wall. Now everyone heard him.

Marais laughed extra loudly in Yann's face and then rolled his eyes at the townsfolk.

"Look at this boy—sniveling behind his mother's skirts!" Marais roared. "He's the biggest coward of them all—and he wants all of you to be as cowardly as he is. Would you follow him into your cellars to hide—or follow me to glory and victory out there?"

Yann stayed where he was. He didn't worry too much about anyone calling him a coward.

Just then, one of the men yelled from the top of the wall. "There's a Dark Layer moving in on us! It doesn't look like it's holding off!"

Yann turned away. He didn't have any more time to deal with the knights.

He scrambled up the scaffold with the rest of the Watch right behind him.

The Dark Layer merged with the chaos. What had been shadows of mayhem now deepened to a solid mass of impenetrable black.

Tangled fibers squirmed and writhed on the surface, crawled forward to chew their way into the lighted spaces, and reformed into a dense mat of Dark that no light could penetrate.

Debris and flying particles along with rubble, slabs, and dirt clods from explosions all over the landscape got sucked into that Dark void. Whatever went in didn't come out.

"We have to go out there," Eliska murmured. "We have to hold it off. We can't do that from here. Your weapons won't work. Anríq, Marine, and I will go back out there. We'll get our magic back. We can hold it off better from out there."

"You'll die out there," Yann countered.

"We'll die in here and so will everyone else. Come on, Yann! You can't fight everything with rockets. We have to use magic. Keeping the three of us in here is only leaving the town vulnerable."

He clamped his mouth shut. He didn't want to let them go—not after he just got them back.

She was right, though. He could only fight magic with magic.

"All right," he muttered. "You can go. Just…" He didn't say it. If Anríq, Eliska, and Marine went out there, they would get lost in the storm. Yann would never see them again.

Eliska's eyes told him the same thing. She knew exactly what she was saying, but she did it anyway.

She didn't wait for him to finish. She sat down on the edge of the wall, pushed off, and jumped.

Anríq jumped off and landed next to her. So did Marine.

Yann got a sick feeling in his stomach watching the three of them walk off into the confusion. The wind caught their hair and whipped Marine's dress and Eliska's cloak in all directions.

Anríq unhooked his club and took down his axe. Eliska raised her staff.

A clang of metal distracted Yann. "Open the gate!" Marais bellowed. "Open it!"

One of his men who happened to still be on the ground rushed forward, unlocked the gate, and heaved it open for the knights to pass through.

Marais snapped his helm shut and led the way carrying his lion flag. The other knights followed him and headed out into the fields beyond the wall.

Yann watched them without a word. He didn't jump up and down and yell and scream for them not to go. He said his piece. The time for talking was over.

The man on the ground left the gate standing open like the back-stabbing traitor that he was. If that didn't prove Yann's point, nothing would. These knights didn't care if they left the gate standing open for the Dark forces to come in and annihilate the town.

That one man hustled back to his horse, mounted up, and rode out through the gate to join the others. Two men from the wall climbed down to shut the gate instead.

"Arm all the defenses," Yann ordered and turned around to yell to the townspeople. "Get under cover and take shelter the way we planned! Get everyone off the streets!"

He barely got the words out when Rien whispered, "Look."

Yann glanced behind him and froze when the Voyant materialized over the landscape. He didn't appear until right that moment. The knights of the Chivalric Order of Custodians couldn't have known until right then that the Voyant would even show up.

Anríq, Eliska, and Marine stood far out across the fields. The deep black of the Dark Layer framed their silhouettes.

Yann couldn't see anything else through all the magical explosions pounding against the Layer. Those explosions clustered in three different places to show where the friends fought the Layer to hold the Dark away from the town.

The knights filed out onto the field and lined up in front of Voyant. "Get ready!" Yann called down the wall. "Here it comes!"

The men took their places. The gunners mounted the rocket launchers. The Tenby defenders leveled their rifles out at the tempest rising to a hurricane.

The Voyant still didn't attack—not like that. The chaos didn't close around Tenby—not yet.

Marais raised his banner on high and bellowed something, but his voice got lost in the wind.

The Voyant never moved. He stayed exactly where he was as the knights spurred their horses into a punishing charge. Their hooves pounded through the ground, up the wall, and into Yann's legs.

Yann opened his mouth to call out to his men, but at that moment, Marais and the forwardmost knights plunged into the Voyant's halo with all their weapons raised.

An almighty explosion plastered Yann in the face as the shockwave hit the town. The wall pulverized underneath him. The gunners never got off a single shot.

The next thing Yann knew, the full force of the Coil's churning Layers hit Tenby and tore the town apart. All the tension and explosive anticipation that kept the town on the edge of annihilation erupted in one catastrophic rupture.

The town evaporated in a cloud of spinning rubble, torn boards, shattered glass, bodies ripped apart, horses ejected into the mayhem, vehicles hurled into space, and everything solid in the town exploded to smithereens.

Yann wheeled his glaive all around him trying to see any Darklings—or anything else. He lost sight of his father and Rien, but plenty of Tenby people got thrown into the confusion along with Yann.

Deafening concussions boomed and thumped all over the place. Yann ducked to avoid getting pulverized by a flying wall section that looked like it might once have been part of the hospital.

People tumbled past him screaming and trying to grab each other, but Yann still didn't see any Darklings.

He floundered trying to orient himself and find a way out of this madness. He couldn't see anything solid—no floor, no ceiling, no walls. Everything whirled and hurtled and spun in a mass of chaos.

Vapors, magical mist, Dark shadows, and random curtains of different kinds of weather and elemental forces slashed across the Layer.

They hit Yann, pummeled him head over heel, burned him, froze him, soaked him, and battered him. He could only take it and try against all odds to keep a hold on his glaive just in case something did attack him.

He squinted into the mayhem trying to see anything when, without warning, another body slammed into him from the side. Arms strapped around him.

"I got you, boy!" Rien yelled in Yann's ear. "I got you! Hold on to me!"

Yann grabbed him and held on. "Where are we?!" Yann called back.

"How the hell should I know?!" Rien bellowed. "Just hold on!"

Yann didn't plan to let go, but right then, another brutal impact hit both men and sent them flying. Yann didn't see it coming and couldn't figure out how Rien did.

This Layer felt like solid stone slammed into them from the side, but the two men must have been the ones to slam into it.

They smashed through the surface and rocketed into a completely different Layer. Water droplets sprinkled on Yann's skin.

He started to open his eyes to see where he and Rien were, but right at that moment, a long beam of some kind of metal wheeled out of nowhere and impaled Rien through the back. His body saved Yann's life.

Rien gasped out loud, his eyes snapped wide open to stare into Yann's, and Rien's arms clamped around Yann in a death grip.

"NO!!" Yann roared, but it was too late.

Rien went rigid and then all his muscles went limp. The beam's weight tore Rien's body out of Yann's arms.

He tried to hold on, but right then, another implosion went off a dozen yards in front of him.

What looked like a wall of glass erupted inward and then sucked everyone and everything through it, including Rien.

Yann pitched into a springy net of some kind of energy fibers, snapped them, and started falling at high speed toward a rocky, barren mountain range thousands of feet below.

Rien's body pinwheeled off into nowhere. Yann couldn't get to it in time and Rien was already dead.

Yann relaxed in the knowledge that he would be dead in a few minutes, too. He didn't want to live in a world where everyone he loved and cared about kept dropping dead all around him.

He only cared about how sad his father would be when Yann splatted on those mountains over there.

Yann didn't see his father anywhere, so maybe Yvan would never find out. Maybe he would live a long time believing that Yann was still alive out in the Coil somewhere.

Just then, a magical field caught him in midair. He started to slow down until he floated gently toward the ground.

He spotted Anríq, Eliska, Marine, and Yvan standing off to one side on a mountainside.

Eliska aimed her staff at Yann, surrounded him with a ball of magic, and guided him down to the ground. He didn't splat, but surviving felt a thousand times worse. Now he had to be the one to tell the others that Rien was gone.

<u>End of Book 2.</u>

Keep Reading

Corrupted Coil Series: Book 3: Dark Poison

With the last surviving Watchmen from Middleborough gone, Yann, Eliska, Anríq, and Marine are alone in a world falling down around their ears. Safety comes more rarely and might have to be bought with a price too high for the friends to pay.

When circumstances separate Yann and Marine in one Layer of the Coil and Eliska and Anríq in another, these lost souls are going to find out more than they ever wanted to know about each other. Dark secrets and nightmares come out of the past to haunt the friends and they'll have to rely on each other in ways they never thought possible.

Forming new bonds and relationships might save their lives in a landscape of destruction—or it could be the last straw that brings them all down in the end.

You can find it at your favorite book retailer.

Sign Up Once--Get all Theo Mann's free books including brand new releases

S ign Up Once--Get all Theo Mann's free books including brand new releases

With the Corrupted Coil becoming increasingly unstable and the human world torn apart by war, the Barbarians expects their Chieftain's sons to become his greatest warriors and take over his power after him.

When twelve-year-old Anríq's dormant magic comes to the surface, it will destroy everything he knows about his life, his family, and his future.

When those he most cares about turn against him, he'll have to find a new source of strength within himself and the allies to help him do what must be done before it's too late.

Sign up at www.theomann.com to read it for free

About Theo
Mann

I write 70 books per year—and yes, before you ask, all these books are my original creative work. Nothing written under my name is AI-generated or ghostwritten because I write better than AI and any ghostwriter out there.

People don't read fiction for entertainment or to escape from reality. People read fiction to see their humanity reflected in another person's character and story.

This is my promise to you. When you read my books, you'll see your own humanity reflected in the characters and stories. I take this commitment to my readers very seriously. My books are an intimate form of communication between us. I would never disrespect my readers by turning that over to a machine or another writer. This is my bond between me and you as my reader.

I write 20,000 words per day as my daily work output. If anyone with a public platform would like to challenge me to prove this in a controlled environment, feel free to contact me on this website's contact page.

I worked as a professional ghostwriter for fifteen years. Now I'm on a mission to set a Guinness World Record by writing 700 books over the next ten years and 1400 books over the next twenty years, all originally written by me. See my website for the full book list.

I'm also the author of *Proof for the Existence of God* and the *Crimes Against Fiction* blog. You can find all my nonfiction work at www.crimes-against-fiction.com.

If you have a story idea, or if you would like me to explore a series in more depth, or if you'd like me to explore a character by writing a spinoff series about that character or world, leave me a message on my website's contact page. I answer all reader emails, so ask me anything, tell me what you liked and didn't like, and let me know where you'd like your favorite series to go. I would love to hear your ideas and find out what you'd like to read next.

Find out more at www.theomann.com.

Also by Theo Mann (so far)

www.ingramcontent.com/pod-product-compliance
Lightning Source LLC
Chambersburg PA
CBHW070540030726
47505CB00001B/105